motherland

motherland

Maria Hummel

COUNTERPOINT
BERKELEY

Library of Congress Cataloging-in-Publication Data

Hummel, Maria.
Motherland : A Novel / Maria Hummel.
ISBN 978-1-61902-237-9
1. Families—Germany—Fiction. 2. World War, 1939–1945—Germany—Fiction.
3. Family secrets—Fiction. 4. Historical fiction. I. Title.

PS3608.U46M68 2014
813'.6—dc23

2013026157

ISBN 978-1-61902-237-9

Cover design by Ann Weinstock
Interior design by Neuwirth & Associates

COUNTERPOINT
1919 Fifth Street
Berkeley, CA 94710
www.counterpointpress.com

Printed in the United States of America
Distributed by Publishers Group West

10 9 8 7 6 5 4 3 2

For Manfred Karl Hummel

mutterland

Mein Vaterland ist tot
sie haben es begraben
im Feuer

Ich lebe
in meinem Mutterland—
Wort

—Rose Ausländer

motherland

My Fatherland is dead
They buried it
in fire

I live
in my Motherland—
Word

—translation by Eavan Boland

Hannesburg

December 1944

When Liesl heard the noise from the cellar, her hand shook and the coffee spilled. The liquid spread in claws across the counter, its color neither brown nor red nor black, but some combination of all three, earthen and old. A hopeless feeling rose in her chest. She had discovered the grounds deep in the pantry yesterday, tucked behind a post, in a tiny tin next to a tiny pot of jam, both labeled in the first wife's hand. It was surely the last real coffee in all of Hannesburg, boiled with the last of the morning coal, the sharp selfish heaven of its scent rising toward her face. Then it splashed everywhere.

She heard the noise again, a grating, chinking sound, and then the murmur of the boys. What were they doing down there? Everything made her startle this morning. She had sent the package to Frank two weeks ago, confidently inking the address of the Weimar hospital where he was stationed as a reconstructive surgeon. *Nothing suspicious in here,* she hoped her bright, erect letters would imply. Yet she hadn't heard back from him. Two weeks, and two more letters had passed. She told herself that with disrupted railway schedules and parcel searches, the package could take much longer to arrive. If the officials found what she'd hidden inside, if, if—she pressed her hands to her temples.

The baby stirred in the cradle by her feet. He refused to sleep in his crib by day, preferring the small portable nest of wood that moved from room to room. He refused stillness, too. Whenever the house went too quiet or his cradle stopped swaying, he woke and cried.

She used her shin to shift the cradle side-to-side, side-to-side, as she tried to scoop the coffee back into her cup. She wanted it. She wanted it for herself, and because Susi must have wanted it once, to have gone through the effort of preserving such a miniscule portion. Then again, Susi had saved everything: thread too short to sew with, buttons to lost shirts, the heel of a shoe, the page of a missing book. In the kitchen, relics from the former cook still lingered, too: the hourglass, a cast-iron cauldron for cooking on a hearth. Because the former Frau Kappus had thrown out none of them, neither would her replacement. This made the rooms impossible to keep clean. There were so many objects and they each demanded the particular attention of a household used to servants, and not the friendless new mother of three boys.

Downstairs, a dull thud. Ani said something in his exuberant voice.

Liesl didn't want to see what they were doing. She had potatoes to peel and Hans's hems to let out and a quick trip to the butcher to make, all the while darting glances above the treetops for Allied planes. She had to finish knitting six pairs of socks for the Frauenschaft collection to send to soldiers in the Ardennes. She had to grit her teeth through the radio program that Hans liked switching on, that always started with the "Horst Wessel Song," its notes marching through her head like a line of ants, eating up everything. She wasn't sure what bothered her more— that motherhood was so much more unnerving than she'd expected, or that the Party's speeches now sickened her. Every day, panic and mistrust pooled like black water in her gut.

She reached for her cup, then a soup pan, pouring the coffee back. It was silly to warm it again, but all morning she'd longed for one hot sip, almost burning. For the heat and the sour bitterness to fill her mouth. To taste the quiet, simple mornings before her marriage, when she'd sat by the window of her room at the spa, lonely, but full of hope and purpose.

Another thud below. It sounded like meat falling. Liesl rushed for the stairs.

The boys stood before a crack in the cellar's west wall, their faces silvered by weak window light. A giant chunk of wall lay on the floor. Hans stood closer to it. He looked much older than ten; in a few years he would have the height and shoulders of a man. His face resembled his father's more than ever: the same craggy mouth and jaw, same blue eyes under a thunder of brows. In contrast, Ani's features were still fluid and childlike, shifting with every thought. Right now, they rippled with surprise as the crack quivered and widened.

"What's going on here?" Liesl demanded.

Neither of them answered. Hans had his arms down, his palms open and aimed back, as if he were shielding his brother from an attack. He winced when the crack split and a metal spade poked through, but Ani ran forward, saying, "Look, look!" The spade retreated. Pale worms shoved the grit aside, wiggled for space. It took Liesl a moment to realize that the five tiny heads all belonged to one hand. Filth crusted the fingernails and knuckles, but the flat palm shone. The hand's twisting made something go cold inside her, and she backed up a step, bashing into one of the shelves Hans had carefully organized for their air raid shelter. The boys ignored her.

"You're through," said Ani, and he reached out formally and shook the hand. It engulfed his fist up to the wrist. "Welcome to our cellar, Herr Geiss."

"Thank you, young man," said a gruff, muffled voice, and the hand retreated.

"It's Herr Geiss," Ani said, finally acknowledging Liesl's presence. "He's connecting us."

"Connecting who?" said Liesl.

"Us. Cellar to cellar," said Ani.

Metal glinted in the hole again. "Good morning, Frau Kappus," said the voice.

"I don't know what your father will say about this," said Liesl.

"It's for our safety," interrupted Hans. "People can get trapped. It happened in Kassel and Darmstadt. If we neighbors adjoin our cellars, then we have a better chance of survival. Everyone knows that."

"But a hole might weaken the wall." Liesl put her hands on Ani's shoulders and pulled him back. "Herr Geiss, I must ask you to cease this until I correspond with my husband—"

She heard her voice falter as the spade continued to work, as Ani shook free and hurried to the crack again, breathing into it. Two weeks ago, Liesl had woken to the thumps of Herr Geiss sandbagging both their roofs, clambering from red tile to red tile on his thick old legs. She knew he called her the "young wife," as if Susi were still alive and Frank had somehow acquired an auxiliary spouse. She knew that Herr Geiss was the reason Hans never got caught for poaching kindling from the willows in the Kurpark. Herr Geiss had ties high up in the Nazi Party, and people feared him. He had been Frank's neighbor since Frank's boyhood. He had helped delay the surgeon's deployment after Frank's first wife had died. Every week, he gave Liesl extra ration cards, ones meant for his widowed daughter-in-law, his only living relation, who refused to leave Berlin.

Yet Liesl also knew that Herr Geiss didn't trust her. Herr Geiss had told Frank that if his "young wife" did not watch his boys well, he'd see them safely away from her, to a farm in the country. All over Germany, families were splitting up in order to protect their children, but Liesl couldn't bear the idea, and had told Frank so.

"He won't send anyone away," Frank had scoffed. "He likes you."

One afternoon following a thunderstorm, she'd opened the gray living room blinds to see Herr Geiss looming over their house from his second floor. At the sight of her, he'd flinched, then frowned. She'd blushed, suddenly aware of her narrow hips, her red springy hair, and their contrast to Susi's blond, groomed curves. The young wife. Or maybe the wrong wife.

"It'll weaken the wall," she said again, over the scraping.

There was a grunt. "I'll brick it up after I make the hole," Herr Geiss said. "You'll hardly know it's there."

The basement light stripped the flush from the boys' skin and accentuated their skulls. Even plump-cheeked Ani looked like a statue poured from molten metal, his rosy lips darkened to brass. She realized that she'd never heard the boys laugh down here.

A thin cry came from upstairs.

"All right," Liesl said, not moving. "But I'm writing to Herr Kappus about this."

The cry lengthened to a scream.

The scraping paused. "Where's that child?" said the voice from behind the wall. "I hear a child crying."

She did not answer Herr Geiss, but she turned and mounted the first step. "Ani, Hans, time to go upstairs."

"I want to stay here," said Hans.

"I want to stay here," said Ani.

"It's time to go upstairs," she said, louder.

The baby wailed. The boys did not move. They stared at the hole, transfixed.

"If you don't come, there will be no dinner for either of you," she snapped.

The mention of food made the boys wilt back from the wall.

"We were just looking," Ani said, his eyes wide. He was such a beautiful boy—it struck her every day like a splash of water to the face.

She cleared her throat, sure Herr Geiss was still listening, thinking, *Cruel stepmother, depriving these growing boys.*

Or was he thinking that she ought to have a firmer hand with them?

"I found some elderberry jam," she said.

Ani started toward her, but Hans hooked his fingers over his brother's shoulder, holding him back.

"Fine, then. Two minutes," she said, hastening up the stairs. Slap-slap-slap, a pathetic retreat in house slippers.

Later, when the older boys were washing up, she carried Jürgen carefully back down the steps and listened to the silence until she was sure Herr Geiss had gone.

A thin veil of light fell through the cellar's low window. Blinking, she felt her way along the crumbly wall. After five paces, she sensed a shift in the air, a cold draft stinging her ankles where her tights had ripped. She stopped, peered. The gap was the size of a man's shoulders. Through it, blackness poured, the same coal-soaked air as their own cellar's, but somehow richer, deeper. She looked closer. At least a meter of packed dirt and stones separated the houses' two walls. It must have taken days to dig, and probably the help of other men. Herr Geiss could have asked her first. But why would he? Herr Geiss knew best. He was a member of the local air raid committee, and he had studied everything there was to know about protecting their houses from bombs.

"What do you think of this?" she murmured to the baby, holding him up to the crumbling edge. Jürgen stretched out a fat paw and batted the dirt and stones. "Do you think your *Vati* will approve?"

A few stones tumbled. The baby swatted at the wall again and more dirt fell. He began to giggle, and reached out with both hands, grabbing the rim with open fingers.

"Stop," she cried. She pulled the baby back to her chest with her left hand and lurched back toward the steps.

Her knee thudded against something heavy and cold. It was the vat that had held the family's sauerkraut every winter. This year, the sauerkraut had rotted in the weeks after Liesl had arrived, after the housekeeper had abandoned the family. Liesl hadn't known that pushing down the cabbage was part of the housekeeper's daily duties until the morning she looked out from the second story and saw Frank dumping the moldy brew out onto the grass. She couldn't get the image out of her mind: Frank's back quaking uncontrollably as he upended the earthenware tub and scrubbed it clean. But he'd never said anything to her—no accusation, no explanation.

For his last package, she'd made a stollen dough from Susi's handwritten recipe, kneaded and shaped it carefully around a film canister stuffed with reichsmark and a map of Germany, and paid a local bakery more than the loaf was worth to bake it hard and golden. In every step of the stollen's production, Liesl was conscious of her inevitable failure. It would never taste like Susi's. It would never get past the censors. Nevertheless she'd wrapped the loaf carefully in butcher paper so it wouldn't grow stale and wrote a note warning Frank about the "fig" she'd baked whole inside. She wondered if he'd understand. She could tell by the soft way Frank looked at her that he didn't think she was capable of deceit. He'd ironed her old life flat with his desire, then molded her into what he needed. The young wife. She leaned her cheek into Jürgen's warm skull. The new mother.

Ani held the badge in one hand, rubbing it clean with his other cuff. Then he raised the eight-pointed star to a place above his heart and addressed her solemnly, "Could you please sew this on for me, please?"

The white metal glowed. "What is it?"

"The badge of the Reichsluftschutzbund," said Hans, hovering behind. "Herr Geiss has asked us to be members."

"I see," said Liesl. They were all in the kitchen, Jürgen awake and fiddling with a cup, Hans and Ani dusty and triumphant and hungry. The blood had returned to their faces. They no longer looked like statues but poorly tended children, their hair shaggy and clothes mended past politeness. Hans climbed into the chair at the head of the table and picked at his nose.

"Hans," she said.

He withdrew his hand and rubbed it on his leg.

"Are you sure he meant to give you that?" she said. "It looks official."

"It is official." Hans hunched over his plate and picked up his knife and fork. "What's for dinner?"

Liesl showed him her saucepan. Hans scowled but said nothing. Ani continued to grin, adjusting the placement of the star. "Herr Geiss says we need to paint our beams with limes so they don't burn," he said.

"Limes!" exclaimed Liesl.

"He means quicklime," said Hans.

Ani adjusted the star again and gave a quick, one-armed salute. "And our neighbors', too."

Liesl winced. "The two of you are—" She could just imagine Frank's face if he saw a military badge on his six-year-old's chest. "Your father will say you are too young for this."

"I'm almost old enough to join the Jungvolk. That makes me old enough for duty," said Hans. The word "duty" sounded dark and cold coming from his young throat. He met her eyes. "But I want Ani to have it."

As their gazes locked, Liesl felt an understanding flash between them: The unhappiness they both shared should not be spread to Ani, radiant Ani, fingering his eight-pointed star and imagining that green limes could be found in a winter so barren that all Liesl could drum up for dinner that night was boiled potatoes, applesauce, and a quarter of wurst for each of them. Ani could eat sawdust and sleep on nails as long as his faith in one thing was not broken—that his father would come home. He had a skinny body and a handsome head, and his grin split his face like a knife did a melon, pure and true. In school other boys teased him for his innocence, for his big questions—"Why are our ears shaped like bathtubs?" he asked her one day—and Hans defended him. Hans wrote his father careful, stern letters, and he always reported about Ani's safety, his contentment, in an overly mature tone, as if Ani were an inside joke they shared. *Anselm is learning his letters*, he wrote. *You can guess that he has his own way of holding the pen.*

She began to serve out the potatoes, their buttery aroma filling the kitchen. "You can carry the star in your pocket for now," she said.

"It's not the same," Ani protested.

"I know," said Liesl. She had drunk the coffee cold, in one gulp, after coming back upstairs, and tasted none of it.

It took Liesl a long time to cut up the rabbit she had bought from Herr Unter, a neighbor who raised them in hutches behind his house. The white animal had looked plumper alive. Now it was as flat as a sock, and the small sinews kept slipping in her hands as she tried to separate skin and flesh. When she finished, she had only a handful of meat. She dumped it in boiling water, adding chopped carrot, onion, barley, and a pinch of brittle, graying rosemary.

It was a small meal, but she still felt obligated to be grateful for it. She had grown up with her aunt's and uncle's stories of starvation after the last war. Her aunt claimed that she'd chewed yarn dipped in grease to make her stomach feel full. Her uncle said he'd eaten a soup made from boiled crickets. They told, and sometimes shouted, these stories to their six children and Liesl, to remind them all to appreciate their laden table. Liesl had excelled at gratitude. She ate it for supper, always the last to be served. She wore it on her back, always clothed in her aunt's stained, cast-off jumpers. She listened to it all night, positioned as nurse outside each incoming baby's room, ordered to wake if he cried. She would be in Franconia still, head bowed and dutiful, if her friend Uta had not rescued her with the chance to work at the spa in Hannesburg.

She set a lid ajar on the pot and crept upstairs to find Ani swooping his wooden plane through the air, Jürgen sleeping under an afghan by his brother's hip. Hans was out gathering sticks for kindling.

"He wakes up if I move," Ani whispered, and then made a crashing sound through his teeth as his plane dove down. The view beyond the half-fogged window was gray-white and peaceful. It had been an entire week since the last air raid, and Liesl had a strange slack feeling whenever she looked at the sky, as if a rope once pulled taut was suddenly ripped free and falling.

"You're a good brother," Liesl said.

Ani put his nose to the window, avoiding her tender gaze. "How come you don't have any brothers or sisters?"

His frank question made her flush. "My parents just had me," Liesl said.

Ani drew a circle in the fog on the glass. "But how come they don't visit?"

Liesl sighed. She had been wanting to tell the boys that her mother had died when she was six. That she knew and understood their loneliness. But another part of her resisted. She did not like Hans and Ani thinking this was how the world worked: that mothers died and fathers disappeared, as hers had, soon after the pneumonia had taken her mother. War-addled brains, her uncle had said. Shiftless, said her aunt. They'd received one postcard from him from Chicago, USA, and never heard from him again. Liesl did not want Ani to know that once both parents vanished, a child became a burden to be passed around until some practical use was found for her. If she had favored her bonny, buxom *Mutti*, it might have been easier. But Liesl had resembled her father—thin and serious, with brown-red hair that frizzed loose from its braids. She wasn't good at mending or strong enough for mucking stalls. She thrived at enduring the pummeling devotion of small children, however, and finally found her place as the caregiver for her sturdy, wild cousins, teaching them each to read and write and swim in the Badensee, as her mother had begun to teach her before she died. It wasn't until Liesl had abandoned them for a position at the spa that she'd realized what she wanted: her own life, and one day, her own family.

"They passed away," she said finally. "But maybe you can meet my cousins sometime," she added, though she knew her relatives would never leave their farm and village, much less Franconia.

Jürgen stirred and woke, lifting his head, staring at them with wide, uncomprehending eyes.

"How did your parents die?" Ani asked.

"In the war. Your brother's hungry," she said, and carried Jürgen down to the kitchen to heat his milk.

Someone knocked loudly on the front door. A hard, official sound.

The fist dug into the wood and made it ring.

Liesl felt her body moving across the kitchen with Jürgen, heard her voice call to Ani to stay upstairs.

Her hand circled the doorknob but did not twist it open. The brass went from cool to warm, as she waited through another round of knocking. Jürgen slumped against her shoulder, sucking at his fingers. She sorted through the worst scenarios. Officials had opened her package to Frank. Officials had lifted the loaf of Christmas stollen, surprised at its weight, and broken it open to find the canister at its center, filled with the money and map he'd requested. They'd arrested Frank and sent him to a prison camp. Worse, someone had shot him on the spot for attempted desertion.

Bile rose up her throat. She couldn't speak. She couldn't open the door panicked like this.

She gripped the handle and imagined lesser problems. Someone had caught Hans cutting willow sticks for kindling. Someone—many someones—didn't approve of her marrying the handsome doctor two months after his beloved wife had died in childbirth. "We've done nothing wrong," she would tell whomever it was, but that wasn't really the point, was it? The point was to be liked, or if you couldn't be liked, to be overlooked.

The baby twisted his face into her neck. She turned the knob and opened the door.

"*Heil* Hitler." Herr Geiss's arm flashed.

Liesl adjusted Jürgen on her shoulder and raised her right hand. "It's you," she mumbled, flooded with relief and irritation. His physique reminded her of a pig's—compact, strong, and small. She could see bare skin peeping out above his house slippers, the sliver of neck-flesh that his coat did not cover.

"He's getting big," her neighbor said, nodding at Jürgen. The baby gurgled, revealing his six teeth.

"Almost nine kilos now," Liesl said. "Are you coming about your badge? I'll get Ani to fetch it."

Herr Geiss's slippers whispered on the snow. They were so old that his big toes cracked out the bottom edges. He blew out a gray cloud. "No, not about the badge," he said.

Did he know something about Frank? The thought chilled her. "Would you like to come in?" She stepped back, but Herr Geiss did not follow.

"My daughter-in-law is arriving," he said. "In a week's time. She's finally decided to leave Berlin and move in with me." He huffed another cloud. "She has no other kin now. Her mother died in an air raid."

"That's—that's sad news," Liesl said, unable to stop herself mentally calculating. An old widower and an unrelated young woman sharing a roof. An unseemly combination. And one that would use up all her neighbor's extra ration coupons.

Herr Geiss continued to stand there. He pulled a pair of black gloves from his pocket but did not put them on. The dark fingers hung from his pale hand. "My house . . ." He paused and cleared his throat. "I have an acceptable house, of course, but it needs some improvement."

"It's a lovely home," Liesl said, puzzled, as Jürgen snuggled into her neck. "You should really come in," she told her neighbor. "The baby's getting cold."

Herr Geiss shook his head. In the street behind him, a car bumped slowly through the dusk, stirring up slush.

"I have good brooms and mops," he said. "My Hilda used the best wax. I still have four good cans of it."

The first flakes of snow began to fall, brushing the brick garden wall and melting. Liesl blinked hard. "You want me to clean your house," she said slowly. "Don't you have a *Putzfrau* who comes?"

A white fleck landed on Herr Geiss's bald skull and vanished. "She's expecting any day. I don't know anyone else I trust—"

So that's how he saw her in his dismal hierarchy of human beings: not fit to mother, but fit to polish his floors. Yet she couldn't refuse. Liesl tried to smile. "Then of course you can count on me."

He looked relieved. His heavy chin wagged as he thanked her. Suddenly he seemed to her like an aging caricature of the Aryan face she'd once admired: his fair hair melted away, his eyes too blue, his jaw too strong, his thick soldier's body grown squat as a headstone.

"I'll set things straight in no time," she said with false lightness.

The snow fell harder, faster. It frosted the black gate and the heap of frozen dog turds that a fat dachshund deposited there every morning, led on its leash by Frau Hefter, a woman made invincible to neighborly criticism by the silver Mother's Cross pinned to her coat for bearing six healthy German children.

Her neighbor flashed his own tobacco-stained dentures. "Good night, then," he said cheerily and reached out to squeeze Jürgen's foot. The baby chuckled and pawed at the air. "Such a nice boy," he said, turning away. "He has his mother's smile."

Herr Geiss trudged down the walk, pausing when he reached the gate. "Tomorrow would be best," he said, glancing back over his shoulder.

"Tomorrow," she repeated.

Liesl was on the edge of the bed, her head pitched toward Jürgen's cradle, when she woke to the sirens. Without opening her eyes, she threw off the eiderdown and grabbed the coat she kept hanging by the bed. She shoved her feet in Frank's old Wandervögel boots. They gapped around her ankles even when she yanked the laces. She lit the lantern with a clumsy match. Her hands fumbled around Jürgen's ribs as she lifted him, and he looked around dopily and sank against her arm.

She clomped to the hallway, calling for Hans and Ani.

Ani burst alone from their bedroom in his pajamas, his eyes melted black by the lantern.

"Where's Hans?" she said.

The boy pointed behind him. Liesl hurried into the bedroom where Hans was kneeling over a long row of white Juno cigarettes, each of them fat as a finger. He plucked them up one by one. He had "found" them by the railroad tracks that morning.

A plane droned in the distance. Jürgen cried and writhed, his pelvis grinding into her hip.

"What are you doing?" she shouted at Hans.

"Here." He held a Juno up to Jürgen.

The baby grabbed it before Liesl could stop him. The cigarette poked from his fist.

"He can't play with that," Liesl said, prying at the baby's fingers. "Now get down to the cellar with your brother."

"It's not a real attack," said Hans.

Jürgen ripped the cigarette free from her, shoved it in his mouth. He chortled, his six teeth crawling with hairs of tobacco. The siren groaned again.

"That's going to make him sick," Liesl exclaimed as she forked the tobacco from the baby's mouth and flicked it on the floor. Jürgen licked his lips and stared down at the mess.

"I could have traded that," Hans muttered.

"Why would you want to make your brother sick?" she demanded.

"I'm scared," Ani said from the pitch-black hallway. "I don't wanna go down there."

"Don't be a baby," said Hans. "You're not the baby."

As if on cue, Jürgen began to cry.

"Both of you. Downstairs. Now," Liesl shouted. Her hand closed on Hans's collar. He recoiled as if stabbed. The siren cut off in midmoan. They stared at each other, waiting, the silence huge and terrifying. The sky rumbled but the siren did not respond. Although Hannesburg had not been hit directly, the Allies had decimated neighboring Frankfurt last spring. A waiter at the spa had gone there and taken pictures of the destruction: buildings burned to hollow ruins, littered streets, and lines of women, standing on the rubble, passing buckets from an unseen reservoir while the city fixed its busted pipes. Liesl had been more troubled by the women's hard, stiff faces than the fires—they looked as if someone had fixed their dread in stone.

"See. It's over," said Hans. He held up his bouquet of cigarettes. "I knew it was far away."

"They haven't sounded the all clear," said Liesl.

"But you know it's over," said Hans. "We can't even hear any planes."

Liesl listened, waiting for the drone, the crash.

Ani whimpered into her waist. His head was a warm soft ball. "It's so cold," he said in a muffled voice.

"Grow up." Hans raised his free hand and whacked Ani across the back of his knees.

Ani moaned.

"Stop," Liesl said, suddenly beyond exhaustion. She took a breath to shout at Hans again but her voice didn't come. She couldn't even look at him, this stubborn, angry, miniature Frank, so she held Ani and Jürgen closer. "It's safe to go back to bed now," she said gently.

"I want to be with you," Ani said. "Please, Mutti?"

At the word "Mutti," her heart stuttered. She saw Hans dart a look at her. It was the first time either of them had called her any name but "her" and "you."

"You can all sleep in my room," she heard herself say in a buoyant voice. "In our room. You can have Vati's bed."

Ani clapped his hands. Hans's eyes narrowed, his lips shriveling as if he tasted something bad.

She couldn't stop herself. "Or we can push them together and make one big bed," she added. Heat filled her face as she stared defiantly down at the boy. His expression did not change but it hardened and pulsed.

"Hurrah!" Ani cried and grabbed his eiderdown. "I want my own blanket."

"Moving the beds will mark the floor," said Hans. "Vati will see the scratches."

"Nonsense," said Liesl. "We'll be careful." She touched his shoulder. He flinched.

"We'll be warm! I want to keep Mutti warmy-warm," said Ani.

"You're not the baby." Hans twisted away from her, pushing ahead of Ani to get into the bedroom first, his bouquet of cigarettes still held high.

Air raids unsettled Liesl's stomach, so she set Jürgen in his cradle and left the boys alone to go to the bathroom. Frank jokingly called it "the Icebox" because its temperature was always several degrees colder than the lined metal cupboard where they kept their milk and butter. She felt her way to the frigid toilet and sat down.

Frost caked the lone window in the Icebox. The pane was small and Frank had covered it poorly with blackout drape, so she could see out a crack to the closed shutters of Herr Geiss's house. Liesl wondered what she would find there tomorrow. Herr Geiss had lost his only son to friendly fire more than a year ago. His wife had died years before. He lived in the villa alone, three floors all to himself, and rarely entertained any guests. Even Frank told her that he had not entered the Geiss house since Frau Geiss had passed. What would the rooms be like? How would she possibly finish cleaning them?

A loud continuous moan broke her reverie: the all clear. As she clumped back down the darkened hallway to the bedroom, she resolved to tell the boys the plan was off. They could sleep in their own beds now.

"We made a bad scratch," Hans said from inside.

Hans stood at the foot of the beds, holding the sputtering lantern. Ani had already claimed his spot in the center of the two mattresses, his eiderdown pulled up to his chin. Jürgen dozed in his cradle. Liesl hesitated, her order dying on her lips.

"We made a baaaaad scratch," Hans said again.

Liesl couldn't see anything on the boards but dust and some long, fine, golden strands. Susi's hair. She fought the urge to wipe them up.

"Save the kerosene. We'll attend to it in the morning," she told Hans, and tucked Jürgen's blanket tighter around him. Then she climbed in next to Ani. Bone-tired. She slumped back on the pillow and shut her eyes. Her lids blinked when the room went black.

"I'm warmy-warm next to Mutti," Ani announced.

"Sorry, Ani," said Hans. From the placement of his voice, Liesl could tell that he was still standing at the edge of the bed. "You've got the crack."

"I'm next to Mutti," Ani said again, and she felt one of his small fists push into her eiderdown and softly brush her shoulder. She kept her eyes closed.

"It's still the crack," said Hans. "In the middle of the night, you'll fall through."

"Hans," said Liesl.

But the older boy's voice went on. "You'll fall down through the floor and the cellar and all the way to the center of the earth where there is a big-nosed, hairy dwarf who will cook you in his stew."

"Will not," said Ani, but his voice was uncertain.

"Enough," Liesl said wearily. "That's an awful story."

"And then he'll take your skin and wear it," Hans said, his voice sly.

"Enough!" Liesl sat up and glared in his direction. She could barely make out the slump of his shoulders.

Instead of complying, Hans crawled onto the bed, over his brother's body, leaning close to his ear. "When you wake up, we'll think your body is you, but inside you'll be a big-nosed, hairy dwarf," he said rapidly. "The real Anselm will be dead."

"GO TO YOUR ROOM," Liesl shouted, surprised by the force and volume of her voice. Hans scrambled off the bed. Ani whimpered under his blanket. Jürgen began to cry. With a curse, she threw herself out of bed and fumbled toward the baby, to rock him.

The room filled with the baby's aggravated sobs. Ignoring the other two boys, Liesl sang and danced with him until her shin slammed the bed. Pain jolted up her leg and she yelped. The baby cried on as if he'd been hit.

She heard Hans grab something on the bedside. A match hissed, struck, the flame making his face flower in the darkness. He glowered, motionless.

"You ought to be ashamed of yourself," she said to him. "Don't they have enough to give them nightmares?"

Hans didn't answer.

Liesl turned away from him, stroking the baby's sturdy, muscled spine. She walked to the shuttered window where she always looked down on the garden, and paced back again, bouncing and shushing. "Please go back to your room," she said to Hans.

He cast his eyes downward at the cigarettes on the table. His long lashes brushed his cheeks. Then he gave a tough little laugh and scooped up the white handful.

"I'll sell these for you," he said in Frank's jocular, teasing voice. "What do you want, a new dress?"

Later, alone again, Liesl tossed on her bed. She'd shared the room with Frank for only thirty-six nights before he was ordered to serve in Weimar. For thirty-one of those nights they'd slept across the room from each other, her breath whispering, Frank's soft snores rising. Thirty-one nights before she'd woken to him sitting at the edge of her bed, like a father watching his sleeping child. She'd opened her blankets and taken him in. *Is it all right?* he'd whispered when she'd shuddered at his touch. *Yes. It's all right. Yes.* Five nights with their bodies moving against each other, awkward at first, then falling into pattern, into sleep afterward, legs twined like roots below soil. Had she disappointed him in comparison to Susi? Frank had always returned to his own bed by morning.

They'd never spoken about it. They'd rarely spoken aloud about anything but the house and the children and the war. Of Frank's childhood, she knew little. Of hers, he knew only the name of a town, a pleasant description of a farm. They hadn't reminisced about their brief courtship at the Hartwald Spa, where she'd run the *Kinderhaus* and he'd treated the minor ailments of Nazi officers and their wives. She supposed Frank didn't think about the past or the present because they were too mixed up. He was grieving, and then he was married, and then he was drafted. And then he was gone, and still grieving, and still married. When he went to sleep at night in Weimar, which wife did he miss?

Liesl lay on her stomach, eyes open. In the dark she couldn't see the wardrobe that still hung some of Susi's dresses, or the dresser that held Susi's jewels, or the mirror above the vanity that had once reflected back a blond woman with round cheeks. But she felt the objects watching her with their sharp corners, their creaks. And beyond them she felt the great open space around her, space enough for two beds, a man and wife, and a baby, too. How different this room seemed compared to her tiny alcove at the spa, where there was nowhere to sit but one chair and the narrow cot, and whenever her best friend Uta came, Uta took the cot, messing up Liesl's neat coverlet while she chatted and smoked. That room had reeked of girlhood, of their long, gossipy talks, of ash, of the herbs Liesl gathered and made into fragrant sachets, of wool stockings hung up to dry. She wished Uta would write. But Uta never wrote letters, except once, to announce she'd made it to Berlin and liked her job at the private officers' club.

Liesl curled her fingers in her blanket and pulled it tight over her shoulders, around her chin, tighter and tighter, the way she'd done as a girl when she was scared of the dark. *Miss me*, she thought, first to Frank, and then to her oldest friend, and then to the dim, loving face that had become her memory of her mother. She pulled again until the wool strained over her back and she couldn't move for holding herself.

Liesl tried not to suck in her breath when she saw the Geiss pantry: the ham hanging from a hook, a substantial wheel of Emmental, the tins of coffee and sugar, seven bottles of Riesling (she hadn't meant to count, but her eyes did it for her), jars of sauerkraut and pickles, the red fingers of *Würstchen*, chocolate in purple wrappers. No wonder Herr Geiss had ration cards to spare.

"I don't cook," Herr Geiss said in an embarrassed voice. "So I have to make do with the ready-made."

"Yes," Liesl said, the musky scent of the ham almost choking her. Half of her wanted to throw it out the window and half wanted to tear into it with her bare teeth. She took a deep breath and jiggled Jürgen, who was looking around with dazed eyes. "Well. We all make do."

They stood awkwardly in the Geiss kitchen, a bucket of mops and brooms and cloths between them. It was clear by the shininess of the brooms that Herr Geiss had gone out and procured some new cleaning gear. She reached out and touched a blue-painted handle. "Very nice," she said.

"It's enough, then?" he said. "You don't have to do the stove. I clean that myself."

Not the stove. Just the rest of a three-story house. She nodded.

"What do you hear from Frank? Saving lives, is he?"

"He's busy," Liesl said quickly. "His surgeries are very complicated." She carried Jürgen back out to the stairs and called for Ani.

"I asked Frau Hefter to watch the infant," Herr Geiss said from behind her. "She's magic with children."

Liesl froze. She'd had two awkward *Kaffees* with Frau Hefter, in which the other woman had asked her maiden name and pointedly stared at her beaky nose.

"She's happy to help," said Herr Geiss. "She loved Susi and her children, you know."

Liesl waited for Ani to appear, and still it took a long time to hand Jürgen over. Or maybe it took only moments, but it seemed as if thousands of them were needed to wrap the baby just so, to pull his wool cap down against the winter wind, to kiss his brow and kiss it again, to watch his arms wave as Herr Geiss took him and positioned him the way Frank did, higher than a woman would, so that Jürgen's head hung slightly over his broad shoulder.

And then it was done. Her arms were empty. They fell to her sides. "It sounds funny, but he sleeps best in a busy room," she said.

The baby cooed and Herr Geiss giggled. "Ah, you are so light. So light," he said as he carried Jürgen down the stairs. "What is she feeding you?"

Liesl lined up the mop, the broom, the cans of polish. She couldn't even look around yet; she was trying to unfasten her mind from the baby, now being marched away from her. She hadn't spoken with Frau Hefter since the October day she had rushed out of the house to catch Marta, Frank's longtime housekeeper, in the ration lines. Liesl had found some extra coupons and wanted to bestow the prize on the housekeeper, who had taken Jürgen shopping and given her the morning off. From meters away, Liesl recognized the graceful matronly figure of Frau Hefter standing beside Marta, making kissy noises at the baby in the pram. Jürgen dimpled and beamed. She was almost upon them when she heard what they were saying.

"Remember the time Susi visited the spa?" Frau Hefter said. "She wanted to stay a whole month, but he made her come home early. Now I wonder why."

"*She* loved company," said Marta. "She would come down and talk to me during the children's naps. She was never too proud."

Their voices dropped out of earshot again, and then Marta said sourly, "*Unkraut vergeht nicht.*" *Weeds do not perish.*

It could have been her aunt's voice speaking that dismissive phrase. For the Gypsies who came through Franconia with their begging children. For the town drunk. For the ugly black cat who dragged herself around, pregnant, every spring and fall, and left behind kittens no one wanted. *Unkraut vergeht nicht.*

Liesl spun around and hurried home. The houses beside her blurred into a broken line of brown and white, but she didn't cry.

She managed to remain stone-faced around Marta all day. When night came, she sobbed into her pillow. The noise woke Frank, who was across the room on his own bed, having not yet touched her as a husband. He sat up in the dark and demanded to know why she was weeping. The story came out, muddled by sobs. Frau Hefter and Marta. They hated her. They had called her a weed.

"A weed?" He sounded amused. His derision angered her. His distance bothered her even more. Why wouldn't he touch her?

"You know what I mean," she said, and then pulled the eiderdown over her head, refusing to say anything else. In the morning, before Liesl fully understood what was happening, Frank had accused Marta of calling Liesl a *Mischling*, a half Jew, and endangering the family with her lies. Marta had quit. Liesl wept and railed at Frank for misunderstanding her and scaring off the only household help she had. He had groused that she shouldn't involve him in the overemotional affairs of women. Eventually their fighting had led to kissing, and kissing to Frank finally climbing into her bed at night. The children somehow noticed the change in both parents and became more agreeable. There was a blissful week when it seemed the broken, grieving Kappus family might begin to mend together. And then Frank had to leave for Weimar. And then the employment office said there might be a six-month delay in finding a new housekeeper. All available workers were needed in munitions factories.

Weeds do not perish, Liesl thought angrily whenever Frau Hefter passed with her constantly pissing dachshund. *Yes, I am here to stay.*

And here she was, elevated to a *Putzfrau* herself now. She allotted herself five hours. Jürgen would enjoy the superior mothering of Frau Hefter, Herr Geiss would go to his *Stammtisch* at the local pub, Hans would stand in line for milk, and she and Ani would work together to whip the cobwebby Geiss house into proper order. Rags in hand, they began together in the kitchen, washing cabinets, but then he drifted away.

"What are you doing, Ani?" she called after a few minutes.

His voice was small and distant. "Cleaning."

"What are you doing, Ani?" she called again, a quarter of an hour later.

"I'm cleaning . . . Mutti," he said from the exact same spot.

His use of the endearing name didn't thrill her now. It sounded like a bribe. She wrung out her rag, draped it over her wrist, and went to find him. The air was stale and musty, the furniture heavy, but not especially dirty. And yet something was strange about the Geiss house, something she couldn't put her finger on.

Ani stood in the hallway. He was holding a waxen statue of the Führer, his hands curling around the knee-high boots. "Does the Führer know about the dwarf?"

"Oh, *Bübchen,* the dwarf's not real."

He stroked the boots with his thumb.

"Your brother just wanted to scare you."

"Why?" His voice was very small.

"Because he doesn't want you to be a baby anymore."

She said it carelessly, focusing on her feather duster. Ani placed the statue back on the shelf and grabbed the next object, a porcelain figurine of a shepherdess, flowers crowning her hair and spilling from a basket.

He held up the simpering face to Liesl. "Can I take this home?"

"No, you may not." Liesl grabbed the figure from him, setting it back on the grimy wood beside the Führer. "Why don't you go explore for a while?"

Ani looked injured. "I was helping."

"I know you were." She bent and touched his cheek. "You're a fine help." She took the rag from Ani's hand and tucked it in her apron pocket. "You were such a good boy, you deserve a break. Go scout for me, all right?"

Ani gave a gusty sigh and wandered off down the hall. His shoulder strap slid down. He had lost some weight, she decided, with a rush of worry.

"Come back and tell me what you find," she called after him. "Just don't touch anything."

The Geisses and the Kappuses had been neighbors for fifty years, since before Frank was born, and the two villas angled toward each other, as if they were meant to be a pair. *Now we're the Siamese twins*, Liesl said to herself, thinking of the tunnel. Through one of the living room windows, Herr Geiss had a perfect view of the Kappuses' front door. Liesl paused at it, watching her new home from the outside: the heap of dachshund turds beside the rusting gate, the stoop marked by the small footprints of the boys. The deep brambles of the garden. An air

of waiting hung over everything. It must have been brighter and more
orderly when both Frank and Susi lived there. It must have looked like
a house full of life, instead of one half empty.

Yet now that Liesl stood in Herr Geiss's house, she could feel the
weight of his own loneliness, and it was far heavier. The air was almost
wet with it, soaking the dark arms of the couches, the bare walls.

She looked up, startled by her revelation. That was it: All the walls
were bare. Not a single painting or mirror hung anywhere.

Liesl called for Ani three times before setting off to look for him.
Her heels clacked through the silent hall. Dust was already beginning
to settle again, fuzzing the face of the Führer, the pretty shepherdess.

"Ani," she said again. "Where do you always go?"

Finally she heard his muffled voice from a bedroom down the hall.
"In here."

"It's almost time to get the baby and go home," she said.

No response.

"You better not be making any messes," she warned as she stepped
through the doorway.

Tilted canvases filled the room beyond, some in frames, some loose,
their brass staples showing. Some were of laden tables of fruit and
game, and others were of women, and one or two looked very old and
dusty. An easel stood empty by the window. Light flowed into the room,
thick and gold with dust. It clung to the tubes of paints collected in a
basket, and the stiff, color-spattered coat that Frau Geiss must have
worn as a smock. Ani was sitting in the opposite corner, his legs crossed,
looking at an unframed canvas. His small hands clutched it from either
side. Liesl saw the smears of grime on his fingers.

"Ani, that's not yours," she said as she strode in. "Put that down, or
you'll get it dirty."

He released the painting slowly. It showed a young blond mother in
a white dress, holding her baby in a white-walled garden. The woman's

large pale arms circled the child, who was sitting upright, playing with a wooden boat, its sail striped with red. Tenderness suffused the mother's face. It was easy to see her resemblance in his upturned nose, his soft square jaw, even the way he touched the sail, with a gentle, pondering finger.

The child was Ani. Around him and his mother, violets bloomed, their centers black. On the mother's left hand was the ring that Liesl now wore.

Weimar

December 1944

For Hans, he had a book. For baby Jürgen, he had a rattle that he'd carved from a pine branch with one of the hospital scalpels. For Ani, he had a pair of shoes. They were good leather shoes, not the wooden clogs that most kids wore, not the shabby paper sandals of the poorest families, but shoes that smelled of hide, of the days before the war when schoolboys kicked real footballs into real nets. What a sound— that gasp of rope, that swish of victory. Frank had not heard it in years.

The shoes' former owner had cracked a few wrinkles in the leather uppers. They jagged and branched like lightning. Brightness scuffed the soles. But shoes this well made could last Ani for years, the toes stuffed with newsprint, and then with his growing feet. Ani could run in them. He could balance atop a stone wall and hop from one garden to another.

Frank had hidden his sons' gifts alongside an amber pendant the color of Liesl's eyes. He had bought it off a nurse. He had paid too much, but he'd wanted something special for her. Together, all his presents nestled under a loose plank, next to the cans of lard and bouillon cubes that Liesl had sent him, ten packs of Junos, a bundle of reichsmark, and a needle and thread to darn the socks he would rip to shreds covering the two hundred fifty kilometers back to his hometown. The gifts and supplies gathered dust in the darkness. Frank sat a few feet above them on the bed, his cramped hands curled on top of an empty rucksack. In his mind, he packed it. He stuffed the shoes in the rucksack first, then the necklace, the rattle, and the book.

He felt bad about the book. It wasn't a good gift like the shoes. He could already sense his eldest son's somber eyes on him, interpreting the gesture. New shoes for Ani. A book about horses for Hans. Hans didn't like horses. He liked tanks. He would be ten by the time Frank returned, and Ani halfway to seven. They would be taller and thinner, and they wouldn't run to him the way they once had, blond heads cupped under his chin.

Frank imagined their future shyness, even their anger. He recalled his words to Hans, *I was six years old when my own father left to serve our country*, his voice brimming until it broke. His emotion had embarrassed him and he'd gripped Hans by his thin shoulders until the boy's eyes popped. *I had to be the man around here, understand?*

It was not what he'd meant to say.

Frank slumped lower, jarring his arms. Jolts of pain shot up his wrists. After spending six hours trying to reconstruct a young Rhinelander's severed nose, Frank's fingers had curled into a clutch. He tried to stretch them flat, but they ached and stabbed.

To shake off the pain, he tried to imagine standing now and sliding the rucksack onto his back. It didn't feel right. The corner of the book would jab his spine.

A siren whined. Out the window, Frank saw a string of ambulances bumping into the rutted hospital yard from the east. To the west lay the road to Weimar, the cultural capital, where the country's greatest poet had lived and died.

It was the third influx that day. They had radioed ahead and Frank had been ordered to rest through it.

"You couldn't cut a straight line through a loaf of bread," the scrub nurse had said, herding him out.

Frank averted his eyes from the pane. He tried not to listen to the sound of doors opening, the orderlies calling out directions toward the delousing chambers. He kept mentally shoving things into the rucksack. It was a nightly habit, indulging in a dark fantasy of the Russians closing in from the east, Warsaw, Poznan, then his escape and flight. He had been plotting it since the October day he'd arrived, a rusty reconstructive surgeon expected to repair the limbs and faces of men blown apart in battle. And while the soldiers' skin healed until they were ready for the surgeries he wasn't sure he could accomplish, he'd found the rucksack and added the cigarettes, wishing guiltily for the war to end before he had to cut into men.

Boots clacked down the hall outside his room. Frank hid the rucksack under the coverlet.

The steps grew louder. Then a whistle. It was Captain Schnell tweedling a popular song. The lyrics bubbled through Frank's mind: *"Es ist so schön Soldat zu sein, Rosemarie . . . Nicht jeder Tag bringt Sonnenschein, Rosemarie." It's so nice to be a soldier, Rosemarie. Not every day brings sunshine, Rosemarie.* Susi had always hated it (*Don't make me Rosemarie!*), and so sometimes he'd sung it to tease her. Frank felt his face go heavy, remembering.

Schnell's head poked through the doorway. "Taking a break?" he said. "They'll be delousing for quite a while."

Frank raised his hands, wrists parallel, like a prisoner. "Linden sent me away. To rest."

Dr. Linden, Frank's anesthesiologist, had nicknamed the captain *der Schnellwachsener* for the hair that continually grew from his ears and nose. But hair wasn't really Schnell's main feature. It wasn't weight, either, though Schnell had the same barrel figure as Göring. It was the color of his cheeks: so pink they were almost garish. It looked as if he rubbed his face in beet juice every morning.

Schnell was a Party fanatic, the sort Frank had spent most of his spa years avoiding, infuriating Susi. *You could be a* Gauleiter *by now, if you'd just try to fit in.* Fitting in didn't mean Frank had to agree with all the rhetoric and flag-waving. It just meant being pleasant at the right times. If pleasantness had had a Party, Susi would have been its *Führerin*. No one had ever been able to refuse her warm smile, and she didn't care who succumbed to her, as long as they increased her social power. Susi could butter up the most rabid of Frank's patients, a Dachau colonel known for publically beating an insolent waiter, and remain completely apolitical. It was a fact that still fascinated and troubled Frank.

"Won't help, though. I can't sleep," Frank added.

The captain's eyes flickered over Frank's fingers, as if he suspected the surgeon was exaggerating the pain. "Yes," he said. "Well. A delivery came for you today."

Frank forced himself not to wince. In Liesl's last letter, she'd hinted at sending a package containing money and a map. As Schnell clacked across the threshold, the room tightened and shrank to a tiny cell. Frank focused on the rusty joints of his cot.

The captain held out a thin slip of paper. A telegram. The swastika had been wrinkled by someone's thumb.

"Take it," said Schnell. "You're a lucky man."

The paper slid into Frank's shaking palm.

"The OKW has summoned you to Berlin," said Schnell. He was pink all the way up to his ears.

Frank kept his face blank as he read the orders: Report to the Schwester Theresa Krankenhaus in Berlin by February 10. He had never heard of the Schwester Theresa Krankenhaus, but the deployment was a ticket to hell. Berlin was under constant bombardment: the Americans by day, the British at night. If the Russians crossed the Oder (*when* they crossed the Oder), they would join the party with their howitzers.

Frank stared at the paper, trying to compose himself. February 10 was six weeks away. The stiff straps of the rucksack bulged into the back of his thigh.

"From what I hear from Dr. Braun, they're consolidating several reconstructive teams to Berlin," said Schnell. "The whole hospital will be devoted to patients like yours."

Dr. Braun had hastily trained Frank when he'd first arrived in October and then moved on. Frank hadn't thought he'd made much of an impression on the brusque, gray-headed surgeon—but he must have been following Frank's cases, which, Frank had to admit, had been mostly successful. A whole hospital! To work with more skilled surgeons, to finally have the right equipment, to teach each other as the British had done at Sidcup in the last war. His mind began to swim at the possibilities—the collegial atmosphere, the medical breakthroughs.

It had to be a mistake.

"Am I the only one?" he said, thinking of his team, Linden and Frau Reiner.

"So far," Schnell said, and held out his hand. After a moment's hesitation, Frank gave the telegram back to him.

"You seem surprised," said Schnell, and then after a pause, "I wasn't."

The generosity in his tone sounded genuine. Frank rubbed his throbbing hands.

"Ever modest!" said Schnell. "We'll have an armed escort for you," he added. "Are you a good shot?"

Frank shifted on the bed. "I trained," he said, and his eyes fell on Schnell's shining boots. "But I'm not—"

"I learned to shoot when I was seven years old," Schnell said, and described holding the giant gun while his father walked him through the steps of loading, aiming, firing, and swearing on his life to protect his mother and sisters.

"Once I had to stop a thief," Schnell said. "I blasted out his knee in the dark." He touched the Celtic cross pinned exactly halfway up his torso. "So I blast him with a bullet and he starts screaming," he said. "I drop the gun and light the lamp."

Frank shook his head. What would he tell Liesl?

"And what do you know, it was our neighbor," Schnell said in a wondering voice. "Our next-door neighbor."

"It's been a long day," Frank said, and pressed his fists to his eyes, but Schnell went on, describing how his mother burst in and started weeping, and the neighbor screamed in pain as the police came and took him away.

With his eyes closed, Frank's mind spun, imagining what would happen if he wrote home about the news. *A summons to Berlin.* He imagined Liesl's frown as she scanned the letter. *Someone must have noticed the work I've done here.* But Berlin! The last stronghold of the Reich. Escaping Weimar would be far easier when the Red Army came.

Schnell's cough snapped Frank back into the room with the peeling yellow paint.

"Strange thing was, I knew it was him before I saw his face in the firelight," the captain said. His cheeks were so bright they pulsed.

Frank had to look away. He grunted. "Smart kid."

The siren sounded again outside and the captain glanced out the window.

"We had to become soldiers so young, didn't we?" Schnell murmured, and again he appeared to be waiting for some acknowledgment: *Yes, on the thousand nights when my father did not come home, I lay in my bed and imagined I was him in France. And yes, I shot those bastards, shot them all dead. Now my own sons are aiming into the same dark and firing.*

"We did what we had to do," Frank said finally.

"That's exactly so." Schnell sounded pleased. He slapped the doorjamb. "Have a good sleep."

Frank said good-bye and listened to the boots receding. Yet instead of lying back, he raised his eyes to the glass, the crowded yard. More boys from the Volkssturm. The only thing the hospital had not run out of in the past month was razor blades. The patients were all too young to need them. They came from the front full of heady, agonized optimism, their chatter filling the white-painted rooms. They came with fever, frostbite, and festering wounds but were everlastingly grateful to be hauled out of reach of the Russians. Better to die among their own than to have their balls ripped off, their eyes gouged out with spoons.

Germany was retreating, drawing all its resources back to the capital. And he was a resource. *He* was a resource. But he was also a husband and father.

Frank pulled the rucksack back out, tipping open its dark mouth.

Another ambulance drove into the yard, carving black tracks in the snow and mud. An orderly threw its doors open. Frank watched as the wounded unloaded, some hopping down, some easing to the bumper and sliding off. Others were carried.

The last came out on a stretcher, his body limp, his face engulfed in bandages. It was impossible to see if his eyes were open, and yet his chest swelled when the orderlies lifted him down.

The deep breath seemed to say *I made it*. Frank's eyelids hurt.

By the time the last patients reached the door to the hospital, he heard a quick patter in the hall and someone calling his name.

He shook his fingers hard, the knuckles knocking together until they straightened. Ignoring the pain, he stood.

The rucksack slapped the floor, the leather sighing as it fell against itself. He pushed it under his mattress.

On the way from his barracks to the hospital's main building, Frank passed into the freezing night. A cloudy night, safe from raids. Into the bluing air he walked, feeling its color and sharpness grip him. His lashes hardened and stuck. He passed in sight of the guard station and the hospital's incinerator, both in the distance, on opposite sides of the field outside Weimar where the military encampment rose. He passed the humps of summer grass, buried under trampled snow, and the ribbons of moonlight that showed the wheel ruts. He passed the old Frank, who would not have noticed such things, the man before Susi's death, who had not felt beaten by time. He passed the darkness of the pines beyond the fields, and the thought of Liesl, clutching him like a life preserver in her sleep the night before he'd left Hannesburg. He passed the end of the war and kept walking back to the war's beginning, when the job at the spa was just a stopping place on the way to his surgical career, just a temporary title so he could spend time with his young sons and give his wife the luxuries she longed for. He passed his father's death of a sudden stroke, and the move into his father's villa so that his sons could run and sleep in the same childhood rooms, and bounce a ball against the same garden wall. He passed the beginning of the war and walked back to the day he assisted in his first surgery, fixing the cleft palate of a teenage girl, and heard the chief surgeon's approving silence at his incisions, his capacity to focus. The names of great medical men had still burned in his mind then: Antonio Branca, Heinrich von Pfolsprundt, Sir Harold Delf Gillies. They rose like flares into the sky of his future and faded slowly, year by year, first as he realized that he would never be a great man and, later, that he might never be anyone at all. But the weight of a scalpel in his hand had never changed. And his hands were stronger and surer than ever, as if they had been waiting to do this work.

He passed the sunken spot in the snow where Frau Reiner, his scrub nurse, had thrown up after their first solo surgery—on nineteen-year-old Helmut Alliner—extending a local flap over the boy's shattered cheek. He passed his own sleepless nights before Alliner's surgery, and every surgery after, knowing he was finally learning his craft, but on live men, while his sons grieved alone with their new mother. He passed the day he married Liesl, and the weeks after their wedding, when he'd slept on a separate bed, afraid to make her pregnant, afraid she would want to be. He passed the night they'd first made love. Liesl had shuddered at first, then clung to him, wrapping her legs around him and biting his shoulder so her moans wouldn't wake the baby.

He passed a stick poking up from the snow, where a German shepherd used to be tied. It had been a hospital mascot until one night in November when an ambulance had run it over. Garren Linden had loved the dog, and he begged Frank to try to save it, so they tried, gassing the beast's muzzle until it calmed, and stitching up the great big wound in its head. It died anyway, and they got drunk together and took the dog to Bundt, the Pole who ran the incinerator, and watched its fur catch fire.

Clutching his coat close around him, Frank went the long way, around the back of the main ward. He entered a side door by the storage room, where supplies were running out. The loss wasn't drastic yet. Replacement medicines, equipment, and bandages still arrived weekly, checklisted and accounted for, but each month the crates were fewer. Rumors reached them that all the country's factories were being converted to munitions-making, that deep in the mountains near Weimar, the army was building a giant weapon that could reach London and Moscow and New York. The missiles would fly, enemies across the oceans and plains would die, and the German people could go home. And home would be the whole world.

No one believed the rumors, but no one spoke up against them, either. All night, planes roared overhead. When it was cloudy, it was impossible to tell which countries had sent them into the sky.

Frank worried most about the dropping stores of morphine. Nothing else relieved the suffering of burn victims, and he had two patients who would die from pain without it. He cracked the door and peered in the storage room. Light fell over the shelves, and bottles glimmered. He heard a muffled giggle, and shut the door. His stomach twisted as he took the hall toward the examining room where Frau Reiner usually triaged his patients. He breathed into the feeling, wondering why, why be jealous of a couple of people sneaking some fun in these bitter nights? But it wasn't jealousy exactly. It was the feeling you got after a funeral, when you saw a woman laughing, and she looked ridiculous with her mouth hanging open like that and her breath chuffing out, and you wished you could remember how to do it, let go of yourself so lightly, so easily.

A flood of new patients entered the hall, led by an orderly, and Frank winced at the beaten faces of the German army. A few noticed the stripes on his coat and fumbled for their caps as he passed, but others just stared at the floor, struggling to put one foot in front of the other. How long before the surrender? If there could be time enough to go to Berlin—

A soldier swayed into him. He reached out and propped up the kid, the weight like a wet sandbag in Frank's palm, until the kid's comrades grabbed him and pulled him along. It all happened without a word.

Frank halted for a moment, ashamed of his wish. Then he passed his own name, whispered by the orderly. *Doktor Kappus, one of our best surgeons.* And then he was at the examining room door.

The patient's face was still covered when Frank arrived. Gauze encircled the face from the nose down to the chin, smoothing the man's profile to an egg. A thatch of thin, mud-colored hair poked from his head. On his upper cheeks, a sickly beard was growing. He appeared to be asleep.

Frank approached him silently. The man's chest rose and fell with a steady breath, and from underneath the gauze came a light wheezing, like the last gasp of air in a bellows. Bones protruded in his exposed wrists. There was a natural heft to the patient's frame, but hunger had carved out every hollow.

Frank heard the scrub nurse come in behind him, and he twisted to glimpse Frau Reiner's black hair, pouty red lips. The widow from Wuppertal. Linden was in love with her.

"Cause of injury?" said Frank.

The nurse read from a letter in the patient's pocket: A large piece of shell had entered the patient's mouth and come out the other side. Considerable damage to the skin and muscles, though the jaw was mostly intact. "Four weeks ago," she said. "He's been in a field hospital."

Frank eyed the dirty bandages. "They should have brought him here sooner," he said. He nodded at her to peel them away, watching the tension in the skin beneath. What once had been a jaw and chin now looked like a shallow basin of flesh with a drain in the middle. The vertical, outward slopes of a healthy cheek caved inward, and the healing skin was thin and blue, the pulp of muscle still visible under it. However poor and useless the dressing, though, there was no sign of infection. A relief. Another few weeks of healing, and the man might be operable. He gently set the bandages back in place. They weren't necessary, but he didn't want to shock the patient if he was used to wearing them.

"Officer or enlisted?" Frank said as he checked the man's neck. It was completely intact. Linden would have no trouble with tracheal anesthesia. He gestured to the nurse to open the patient's shirt, and the man's eyelids fluttered. Frank bent next to her and fitted his stethoscope to his ears. He could smell Frau Reiner's hair. It had a clean, earthy odor, like warm hay.

"Officer, I believe," said Frau Reiner. She straightened and returned to the papers again.

The heartbeat was strong but rapid. A milky sheen suffused the skin of the chest.

"Might need a transfusion," said Frank.

"Lieutenant," read Frau Reiner. "Heinrich Hartmann."

Frank jerked. His stethoscope whacked the table and woke the patient, who looked up with startled gray-blue eyes.

"Lieutenant Hartmann," said Frank, forcing a smile. "I'm Doktor Kappus."

He waited, but the eyes blinked, unrecognizing. Could it be another man with the same name? Both were common enough.

"You've been brought here for surgery," Frank said, and explained how they let the face heal before they reshaped it. "The more skin we have to work with, the better," he said.

"Heinrich Hartmann, birthplace Hannesburg," said Frau Reiner. "Your hometown."

The patient stared blankly. He and Frank hadn't seen each other since they were children, but surely Hartmann would remember the name. If not the son's, then the father's.

"He's deaf," said Frau Reiner, still reading. "It says here that you can communicate with him in writing, that he can read and respond."

"I think I might know him," said Frank, already scribbling on a pad. "I think we went to school together." He was surprised how happy and agitated he was to meet an old schoolfellow again, someone from the days when his own father had gone off to fight. Someone who remembered the clatter of horse hooves down Elizabethenstrasse, the egg man and milkman making their rounds. But Hartmann, of all people! His mind whirred back: Hartmann's father had never come home from France. Hartmann's mother had reared him alone, nurturing his brilliance and scorn until they shone like the beams of searchlights.

Frank inked his full name, and *Do you remember me?* He held the paper up for the bandaged man to read.

The eyes scanned the words. Frank waited for them to flare with recognition. Instead they moved to Frank's face and the head slowly shook.

You were my father's student. Herr Otto Kappus.

A hesitation and then another shake.

Frank's stomach began to knot. *Heinrich Hartmann from Hannesburg, yes?*

This time the man's hand rose and wagged for the pen. Frank put the pen in it and held the pad vertical while the hand scratched.

Yes.

And then the fist fell to the table and the eyes closed. Just like that. Interview over, leaving Frank standing there, his next question ready, his fingers curling to write it. The whitewashed room gaped around him, and his coat felt thin and stiff.

"Christ, he's exhausted," said Frau Reiner. "How are we going to feed him enough?"

Frank didn't answer, breathing into the uneasy feeling that spread through him whenever he was reminded of his father's death. The room blurred. Beyond the double doors, he heard the clatter of wounded men being herded to the delousing chambers. There, they would strip and hang their clothes to be gassed and sterilized while they showered in another room. It had to be done, but the practice bothered Frank. The hospital welcomed its patients like criminals.

"Once you start talking about old times, he'll know who you are," said Frau Reiner. She stood close to him.

"I don't think he talks much," muttered Frank.

"Best kind of man."

He switched on his headlamp and peered into the hole that had been Hartmann's mouth. The light flashed over the glistening maw, the exposed roots of teeth. Every bite the man took had to be an agony. "We'll be able to reconstruct the mouth, but it will probably take more than one procedure," he said to her, pointing. "He's fortunate, though. The mandible isn't fractured. He hasn't lost bone, just tissue."

"I heard you're leaving," Frau Reiner whispered.

He pretended not to hear her, straightening, snapping off the lamp. He eased it from his sweaty temples and handed it to her, avoiding her eyes. "Let's have a full set of X-rays, and get the dentist to look at him," he said with brusque cheer. "Was there anyone else I should see?"

At the front of every classroom in Frank's childhood perched the same figure, thick and bunchy in the hips, erect in the spine and cowlick. Hartmann's voice always issued forth as an amused whine, even as a child. His peers had loathed him, and some of his teachers, too. Frank could still remember crabby, graying Herr Nuss, standing in the dusty schoolroom light, telling a story:

When the king built a castle near the mill, he hated the noise of it, the wheat grinding in the stones. So the king took his case before the judge. Make him move the mill, *he demanded.* I am king. *The judge ruled for the miller. The king had to move his castle or put up with the racket. And the king obeyed.*

"This is law in Germany," said Herr Nuss. "This is *Rechtsstaat*. Even our rulers have to bow to it."

Hartmann's big head shot up. "Then how come you don't have to wash your desk every day, and we do?" he wanted to know, and most of the kids watched approvingly as Hartmann got the switch.

But Frank's father had adored Hartmann. Herr Kappus had never had a student like him, in all his days as a Latin teacher. What he admired most was Hartmann's fluency. For Herr Kappus, son of a janitor, conquering every cognate had required superior strength and resolve. He excelled at instructing the average student, but how much more thrilling to bask in the light of a star! He followed the young critic and poet's progress as he left gymnasium and entered university, as Hartmann published tracts on Heine and Goethe, always informing Frank of the latest achievement.

Frank was glad his father couldn't see his favorite now. He circled Hartmann's bedside the next day, not stopping but watching all the same as the patient sat up and began playing skat with his neighbors, as the afternoon light whitened the ward's windows. Hartmann's bandages were off, per Frank's orders, but he wore a green scarf to hide his face. Beside him, the other patients looked suddenly exposed. Brimges's nose had a fat, tubular pedicle feeding it from his temple, and Alliner's destroyed cheek was purple with healing scars. They were patients who'd come to Frank as monsters, and now their fearsome visages were finally giving way to mere ugliness. He knew that they hated their new faces, but at least they could grow used to them. They could walk down a street without terrifying women and children. What had Alliner said? *At least I don't look like a creature no more.*

Frank rubbed his sleepless eyes. Around midnight, he had begun speculating that the new patient wasn't Hartmann at all but someone posing as him. He recalled the boy's big brow, his pale eyes. Had they developed into this elegant, destroyed skull? It was possible, but weren't the ears all wrong? Hadn't Hartmann's ears stuck out from his head? This man's lay flat.

When a nurse brought Hartmann some soup, Frank watched the scarf come off and the mouth attempt to eat. He sat down silently beside the patient, regarding the lipless hole flexing at the pressure of the spoon. Hiss, suck. The muscles had knit together to make a flap that worked like a second, outer tongue. Its motion made the thinnest skin bleed along the cheekbone. Hiss, suck. A dry noise, a wet noise, machine-like, inhuman. Hartmann's neighbors glanced at him and then away.

Frank leaned forward and dabbed at Hartmann's blood with some gauze. He felt the gray-blue eyes fall on him, then back to the soup.

Hartmann took three more spoonfuls. Hiss, suck. Then he offered Frank the bowl.

"You should eat it all," Frank said before he remembered the patient was deaf. He took the bowl and gestured at Hartmann to finish, but the flap sucked inward against the teeth and the man pulled his scarf back over his face.

Frank set the soup on the window ledge, found a pen and paper. *You need more nourishment in order to heal.*

The eyes read it. The shoulders shrugged slightly, as if to say, *What else is new?*

Are you in pain? How intense?

The response came quickly: *How intense is drowning?*

Do you want morphine? Frank wrote, grateful he did not have to utter the word aloud, in earshot of other patients. Not everyone was offered relief.

Not yet, wrote Hartmann.

You don't have to suffer.

Hartmann read the sentence and leaned back, looping his hands over his knees. He seemed to be studying some spot in the air above the other patients' beds. He shook his head slightly, as if amused by the statement, as if he now owned pain the way he'd once owned knowledge.

Frank took a breath and scrawled. *How is your mother? Would you like me to write to her?*

There was a hesitation, and then the hand took the pen. *I really don't remember you.*

Hartmann's blue eyes were hard and cold, but the corners glistened. Frank held the message for a moment. The scarf rippled with the patient's breath. Frank wondered if Hartmann's nerves still sent pure signals up his skull about the pain of his stretched lips. Or was their communication as broken and fragmented as the flesh? Could the neural paths be restored by surgery; could the wounded man feel whole again? He'd pondered this question with every patient, but less so each time.

Alliner had told him, *It feels like a sharp mask is inside my skin. Like I got two faces. Only one is made of glass and it doesn't move,* and that night Frank had dreamed he was on stage, his own face heavy and split by a second face. He'd woken gurgling and pulling at his throat, and decided not to ask again. In a few short months, he'd learned to force his mind away from whatever he could not accomplish. Contemplation led to horror, and horror made it impossible to see the small gains of his incisions and grafts.

But Hartmann. He couldn't look at Hartmann without seeing memory itself. Every day at their elementary school's end, all the boys had burst up from their desks except the star, who'd stared at his cloudy, sponged-off slate. No one had ever walked home with him but the occasional brainy girl.

Excuse me again, Frank wrote. *Mistaken identity.* He picked up the soup bowl and spoon. "Let's have some more, shall we?" he said aloud, scooping some broth.

Hartmann gestured for the pen again and put the pad by his side as he wrote another message.

Nothing wrong with my hands. I can feed myself.

Writing letters home was a strain. Frank didn't know how to explain about the glassy-eyed patients who arrived with centimeter-deep pools of lice on their sunken bellies. Or how the wards sounded at night, full of groans and foul, rattling coughs. He didn't want to pain Liesl, so he mostly stuck to comments about the weather and responses to news of his sons. He didn't know how to tell Liesl that he loved her, either. Some nights he just held the pendant he'd bought for her until it warmed in his palm. Other nights, he looked at her picture, trying to memorize her features. She wasn't classically pretty like Susi. Her nose was too large, her thick red hair didn't obey hats or combs, but the snapshot had caught the catlike arch of her brows, her winsome, radiant smile.

Yet the night after Frank met Hartmann, he wrote to Liesl about the transfer to Berlin, and this time the letter emerged easily. It almost sounded like another man writing, someone confident with words, a father who knew he was making the best choice for his family, a good German who did not believe the war would end. He also mentioned his old classmate, changing the details to make it seem as if he and Hartmann had mutually recognized each other. He'd sworn he would operate on Hartmann somehow, before he left. *I owe it to him.* The two stories wound together: a surgeon describing his devotion to injured men. *I owe it to them*. When ink covered the whole paper, Frank folded it without reading it and dropped it in the hospital's outbox.

All day he tried to imagine Liesl reading it, but couldn't. What would she think? How would she know that he still had the rucksack packed and hidden beneath his bed? That if ever she called to him, he would come? He could never say such things with the censors.

The package from her appeared in his room the following afternoon, as if summoned. He opened it gingerly, but the box had clearly been raided long ago, its paper ripped and retaped, the tape dirty from transport. If there had been money or a map, it was gone now, stolen before the package even reached the hospital. All that was left was an innocent, golden, Christmas stollen, wrapped in butcher paper, and a brief letter.

Frank looked out the window toward Schnell's office, relieved and astonished at his earlier foolhardiness, the dangerous game he'd asked Liesl to play. Someone's greed had saved them somewhere along the way. He scanned the letter.

I had no nuts or fruit, Liesl had written. *Just a few raisins and one big fig. Enjoy! Your loving wife.*

Frank turned the loaf over in his hands. He'd never heard of figs in stollen, but Liesl had her own country ways of cooking: big, salty, hearty slices of things, lots of butter, meats baked wet and soft. It had taken some getting used to, but he missed it now. It pained him to think of her receiving his letter in return, announcing his departure for Berlin. He would write her another note tonight.

Since it was hospital tradition to share the bounty of care packages, Frank brought the loaf to the small annex where the medical staff ate its meals together. He didn't like most of them. The other doctors were young, ambitious, and talked about the patients as if they were conquests and not people. The technicians were too quiet and deferential. He really wanted only to offer the holiday bread to his friends by the window:

the anesthesiologist, Garren Linden, his comforting hulk leaned against the sill, and Anna Reiner, the only nurse who dared to infiltrate the men's conversations. She looked tiny beside her bearded admirer. She kept smoothing her black hair behind her ear while Linden talked about Beethoven.

"Eight nice, proper slices," Frank announced, making small marks on the floury top with his scalpel.

The other staff members were chattering about Ardennes. One of the younger doctors had a cousin who was part of a secret operation to go behind Allied lines. The doctor had a way of talking loudly and then softly so the whole room ended up listening to him. His hair sat on his head like a shellacked sponge. "He speaks perfect English because he spent a year in Minnesota," the doctor said. "He's supposed to pretend to be a lost American, and then sabotage their plans."

"It seems like the Amis would jump on any reason to go home," Frau Reiner said politely.

"*Ja* and they've already got two," blurted Linden. "French beer and French whores."

Everyone laughed except the doctor, who said, "Please, not in front of the lady."

Frank watched Frau Reiner grin and chuck Linden on the arm. "That's right, you oaf."

"My apologies, Madame," Linden mumbled, but he looked pleased.

"Apology accepted," the doctor said without a trace of humor. "At any rate, we Germans talk with our throats. Americans talk with their noses." He described how his cousin mastered the American English accents by ladling a teaspoon of water into his mouth and trying not to spill a drop as he spoke a sentence.

"Good. Day," said Frau Reiner in English.

"No, no," said the doctor. "They'd shoot at you for that. The words to greet people are 'How Dee.'"

"How Dee," Frau Reiner mimicked with great seriousness, her eyebrows rising. "How Dee, sir?"

Her voice sounded so pinched everyone laughed again. Only Bundt, the Pole who operated the hospital incinerator, shook his head and stared at the stollen. A sickly smell emanated from him. The incinerator was a poorly built brick oven out in the field behind the hospital. Its engineer had been called away for duty elsewhere before he'd finished it. The incinerator leaked smoke and took too much fuel, but Bundt stuffed it daily with infected linens, trash, amputated limbs, and sometimes the unidentified dead. Then he dumped the ash into a nearby cistern, an open, concrete-lined pit that had been the barracks' latrine before indoor plumbing. The cistern's frozen sluice would smell unbearable in the summer, but no one expected the hospital to last that long.

Frank began to cut.

"The surgeon begins his delicate work," said Frau Reiner.

"Who wants an end piece?" Frank said. To his surprise, it felt pleasant to be slicing bread in the cold, barely heated room, surrounded by his countrymen. Christmas had hardly happened at the hospital and Frank missed the year-end traditions. A spicy fragrance rose from the sweet loaf. His mouth watered.

"I'll take the end," growled Linden.

He handed the crust to Linden and kept cutting. Crumbs fell onto the wooden table, on the graffiti carved by the soldiers who had once trained here. The golden bits dribbled across a deeply gouged swastika, a scrap of lyrics from the "Horst Wessel Song," *Der Tag für Freiheit und für Brot bumsen bricht an! The day for freedom and bread fucking is coming!*

A crumb of the stollen made its way to Frank's mouth and he paused for a moment, letting its sweetness spread over his tongue. It was then that he looked down and saw what Bundt was looking at.

It could have been a fig, but the color and texture were wrong. It was black and shiny and it protruded from the open bread ever so slightly in the bottom right corner. Liesl had baked a film canister into the stollen. No doubt it held the money and map. The sight of the smooth, dark case made his ribs tighten. There it was, a little black egg, ready to hatch: the promise he'd made to her to run. As soon as the time was right.

Linden was biting into his slice, his jaw working. "Excellent," he pronounced with a full mouth. A crumb fell on Frau Reiner's sleeve. She stared at it a moment before brushing it away.

"I'll take a middle piece," said Bundt. He had not moved a muscle, but it felt to Frank as if the Pole had taken three steps closer, was looming right over the table. His eyes were the color of a wet pelt.

Frank frowned at the stollen and sliced hard at the end, making the bread vault off the table and into his lap, then put on a show of trying to catch it, and let it tumble to the floor. It hit the dirty boards with a thud. His companions cried out.

"No matter," Frank called and dove down, quickly breaking off the hunk with the film canister and stuffing it into his sock. The floor smelled like mud. Bundt's tiny feet did not move, and Frank noticed how his shoes were nothing more than strips of leather sewn to socks and bits of blackened board. He had to look close to see their counterfeit nature, to guess how cold it must be to walk outside every day and shovel trash into an oven, to perform this thankless task and know there was no reward but not being sent to a prison camp.

Frank rose with the bread held high. Lint and dust smeared the white flour. He whacked it off. "Good as new," he said, slicing furiously. He felt the others exchanging glances; they had all been in surgery with him, had seen the quick precision of his movements. He heard their thoughts, *Is this one cracking up, too?*

"Clean as new," Frank said again, handing around the pieces. The doctors and technicians took them reluctantly, examining the bread for dirt. Only Bundt ate his without even looking at it. His brown eyes bored into Frank's as he chewed.

"You haven't even tasted yours—are you trying to poison us?" said Frau Reiner, smiling.

The film canister dug into Frank's shin. He used his other boot to try to shove it deeper into the sock as he took a bite of the bread. He chewed the dry sweet slice, then swallowed. "I'm trying to make it last," he said.

One afternoon, Frank's rounds ended with a gastrointestinal mystery case in the smaller ward where they housed the patients with infectious diseases. He didn't like visiting this ward because his own cases were so vulnerable to contagion, but another doctor wanted him to examine the open sores on the patient's face. The patient had worked as a guard at the criminal camp on the west side of Weimar. The doctors there had given up on him.

Frank wound his way through the beds. The patient was easy to find. He did not look like the others. He did not look like a soldier at all: His cheeks were too pale and soft, and he did not shift his legs restlessly like the men who had foot trouble from marching. He hunched away from them, his blanket drawn high. Around his mouth, ulcers spread away like a trail of thick red ants.

Frank sat down on a stool beside the bed, pressing a knuckle into his tired back. He'd already read the notes, but he introduced himself and asked the man the same questions again. The soldier insisted he hadn't swallowed anything strange, and he ate little more than bread and soup, but he couldn't keep anything in, and what came out was bloody. His malaise increased daily. "I don't need surgery," the man said, fluttering his fingertips over the sores. "If that's what you're here for."

"No, you don't," said Frank. He pressed the man's belly. It felt firm and springy. The man's heartbeat was normal. His breath was even, his green eyes clear.

"No pain?" said Frank.

The man stared at him as if he didn't understand the question.

"Are you feeling any pain? In your stomach, or . . . ?"

"Some," the soldier said. "When I go."

"Have you ever bled like this before?"

The soldier shook his shaved head.

"How about the sores?"

Another shake.

Gastrointestinal hemorrhaging was not uncommon among the infantry, but its causes were hard to pinpoint. Since it was the soldier's first experience with the condition, Frank suspected a parasite, but he couldn't figure how the bug had not infected the rest of the POW camp. Pathology wasn't his specialty, but he decided to ask anyway: "Are the prisoners sick?"

The soldier shrugged. "If doctors get to them," he added with a harsh little laugh.

"What do you mean?"

The soldier mumbled that he'd heard that the doctors at the camp were injecting live subjects with infected typhus blood. To perfect a vaccine.

Frank's tongue felt heavy as he asked the soldier to speak up. His own hospital's typhus patients were kept in a private, darkened room, a row of mumbling bodies splitting with fevers and bloody rashes. A third of them would die.

Just then a black uniform drifted by. One of Schnell's underlings. The patient turned his head to the side and pursed his lips. Frank waited. The patient blinked, his lashes thick as a child's.

"Anything else you want to tell me?" Frank said.

"I'm weak," said the man. "I can't walk thirty meters."

Frank reiterated the other doctor's prescription: Atebrin, rest, and broth. "If you're still passing blood in a week, they'll reevaluate."

As he left the soldier's bedside, a strange sensation crept over Frank. It was a wet dirty feeling, not an itch exactly, and not a chill. Frank had felt it several times since arriving in Weimar, and at first he suspected lice, but he was careful with his clothes and no amount of hygiene made it go away. It crawled down his shoulders and up to his temples, and down to his gut and up to his brow, and in the cracks of skin around his knees and groin. Sitting down, lying down did nothing to help it. It coated his whole exhausted torso, shifting its clammy grip.

He didn't know anything about the prison camp, except that its prisoners mostly worked in local munitions factories. A different set of doctors staffed KZs. Until October, until he'd left Hannesburg, such places seemed very far away. The problem of the enemy's captured soldiers an abstraction. The problem of dangerous native foreigners, Jews, Gypsies, also an abstraction. Frank didn't know any "foreigners" except the two Jews who had been his medical school professors. He doubted they were communists, but one had left the country; the other moved to the ghetto with his family and had subsequently fallen out of contact.

In Hannesburg, Frank had assuaged his regret over doing nothing to resist the crackdown on non-Germans by reminding himself that he didn't "fit in," as Susi had wanted. He had never voted for the Nazi Party. He'd hung no pictures of Hitler. He spent minimal time at the spa, hurrying home to his wife and sons. He kept his father's book collection intact, knowing dozens of banned volumes were scattered throughout it, and neglected to inform Susi of a conversation with his father, a month before his death, hinting that the elder Herr Kappus had given money to help an old colleague's family after the synagogue had burned. They'd managed to get visas out of Germany. *I'm an old man. I have nothing to lose,* his father had said, waving away Frank's offer to assist him. But his face had looked gaunt, as if something had frightened him. Weeks later, he was dead of a stroke.

Frank took a breath, but the disgusting sensation only deepened. An orderly pushed a giant tub past him on a cart. Frank put his hand on his shoulder.

"Give me that," he said.

"But Herr Doktor," protested the orderly. Frank brushed past him and began emptying bedpans, pouring the sluice of piss and excrement into the tub on top of the soiled bandages. His skin shuddered inside his clothes. He gripped the cart handle harder, shoved it out the door.

A soft gust of paraffin followed him, and then cold air smacked him in the face. The edges of his eyelids tightened. Sweat on the back of his neck froze into tiny icicles. He blinked, pushing toward the incinerator, the cistern beyond. A squat brick oven and a concrete hole—they were the only structures in the flat field before the pine woods. They inhabited the desolate space like a pair of unlikely friends. Smoke rose from the incinerator. It took in flesh and bandages and gave out cinders and ash. The cistern received, a rapidly filling pit behind a low lip of gray wall.

The cart lodged in the snow. Frank shoved. The liquid sloshed again, a drop slapping Frank under the eye and freezing there. He wiped it away with a curse.

Bundt stepped out from the other side of the oven and watched him, unmoving. His stolid form balanced between the ruts, his hand trailing a cart behind him. Frank's eyes fell to Bundt's dainty feet, tiny parcels wrapped in wool and strapped to wood.

Ani's shoes would fit Bundt.

Frank wiped his brow and pushed again at the cart.

There was a crunching sound as the Pole began to walk toward Frank, a smirk creeping across his flat, moon face. "Pull," he said.

"Pull what?" said Frank.

"Pull," repeated Bundt, advancing until the stench of his coat and hair clogged Frank's nose. His forehead and cheeks wore tiny freckles of ash. "Can't push in snow," he said softly. "Pull."

"Look, I have something—" Frank started to say about the shoes, but Bundt reached past him and yanked the cart up, freeing its wheels.

"See?" he said.

Frank nodded, breathing through his teeth. He and Bundt were so close now he could count the individual hairs in Bundt's eyebrows.

"If you run," Bundt gestured at the soldiers patrolling the hospital yard to stop deserters, the snow-punched fields beyond. "How far you must go?"

The warmth in his voice caught Frank by surprise. "I don't know what you're talking about," he said.

Bundt hung his head, smiling blandly.

Frank wiped his mouth with the back of his wrist. *Shoes*, he thought, but he couldn't say it.

Bundt continued to smile. "You are just waiting for the real time."

"The what?"

"The real time," Bundt repeated. "For to see your family again, right? You have sons? I have sons."

Blood pounded in Frank's ears. He grabbed the tub of piss.

"Threaten me, and I'll report you," he heard himself say. Then he staggered away from Bundt and hauled it to the edge of the concrete pit, pouring the contents onto the yellowish-red crust below. Six meters square and almost three meters deep, the walls of the cistern were dark with stains, but it never seemed to fill. A meter down jutted a ledge where the last war's soldiers must have rested their feet. The last war. His father's war, lost, lost badly, plunging Germany into a shame so deep Frank remembered the odor of it, like rotten potatoes, permeating his childhood.

He threw the tub down and filled it with an ashy, white armload, then dumped the contents in the cistern. Something flickered across the broken crust. A gray animal, furtive and delicate. He watched until it vanished. When he looked up again, Bundt was already halfway toward the ward, towing his bloodstained cart behind him.

Just before Christmas the year before, Susi had announced she was pregnant again. They were sitting beside their tree, beside the creamy candles that had not yet been lit, after the two boys had gone to bed.

"You need another son," she'd said, smiling. "It's the right time."

"The right time," Frank had repeated, shaking his head.

"It *is*," she'd assured him. In the dim light, her eyes looked lustrous. He'd known her all his life. In kindergarten she and Frank had built a house together with blocks, and in the *Leisestunde*, when the children were supposed to be absolutely silent and listen to the birds outside, he'd made faces to get her to laugh. She was the girl he'd followed home one day, without understanding why, and had hung on her gate until she came out to speak with him.

But she was different now, too, a mother, a commander of boys. And their precious domestic life was a small fire in a world of shadows.

Unable to put words to the mix of pleasure and dread he'd felt, Frank had kissed her. Their lips locked and pulled apart with habitual efficiency. He wished he'd kissed her harder.

"I'm happy," said Susi.

Frank reached out and righted a candle that had tipped. He and Susi had both been so careful since Ani's birth, when she'd lost so much blood she'd fainted. He'd almost stopped making love to her altogether, although sometimes in his sleep he would wake with them already entwined, his body tense with lust.

The pregnancy had indeed made Susi happy, and the boys, too. It hadn't occurred to Frank until he saw Hans and Ani that spring cuddled around their mother's growing belly that they had all wanted something to look forward to, and the boys and their mother were already pulling together for when he'd be called away. Part of him wanted to be called. The fall of Stalingrad, the grim reports from France made it certain. All the fathers were gone or going, and it was time to join them. To do his duty instead of rotting in a safe corner of the Fatherland.

And yet still he drove to his office in the spa's grove of yellow buildings, and checked the throat of a man who choked on a fish bone, and the prostate of an aging diplomat, and drove home. Occasionally, sitting alone with his charts and instruments, Frank imagined himself in uniform, boarding a train, as his father had decades before. He pictured Susi's round eyes filled with tears as he said good-bye. The stoic, shadowed faces of his sons. The vision made his palms sweat, but he returned to it often, wondering, until the day his youngest son was born.

He had not been in the room when Susi had died. They'd cleaned it up before they'd called him. They'd swabbed the blood from her body and his living son's, and they'd covered her and wrapped the boy. The room smelled like carbolic acid when Frank was finally invited in. The sharpness stung. Nothing moved in the whole scene—not the nurses, not the machines, not the still body of his wife. Nothing moved, except his son, blinking with his ancient eyes.

He gazed without feeling on the stillness and the child, and backed out of the room. The obstetrician followed on his heels explaining about the hemorrhage, Susi's dropping heart rate, everything happening so fast. Frank had the impression he was being told this a second time, that he had already been informed of his wife's death on the way to the room, but he hadn't listened. Outside, in the courtyard he smoked and stared at the ground until the obstetrician left him. Then he was alone, but he didn't feel alone, because the wind was blowing, and his skin felt raw as a sunburn.

Within an hour, the other *Frauen* came, Frau Hefter leading the pack. He spoke finally and they heard his babble. They saw his dry hard gaze. They shushed and tutted, and organized the funeral and burial. They fed Susi's family, her parents and brothers, who came to mourn from their new home in the Ruhr. They bought cans of formula and kept the infant's small needy body away from Frank for days. He tried to play with his other sons. He sat on the floor with them but he couldn't follow their simple games, and after a while, they circumnavigated him like a piece of furniture. He did his best to thank his friends and neighbors at the funeral, but his words sounded like nonsense. He sat in his father's study, holding the baby, staring at the books, until Marta told him to go back to work.

Only when he was treating patients again did he feel anything other than panic, and most often it was a shuddering sense of compassion for the physical pains they experienced. Once, after Frau Wilhelm left the examining room, coughing with her cancerous lungs, he'd locked himself in the custodian's closet and sobbed for a quarter of an hour, without tears. He could never tell when the grief would overtake him. It even emerged with a case of lice in a spa waiter's head. Just seeing the man's pink scalp crawling with bodies—life feeding on life—made Frank reel back and excuse himself, gagging.

By the time the draft notice finally came, he was thinking about quitting clinical practice for good and applying for an administrative job. It wasn't as if he had many real patients anyway. He could crawl up inside a numbing heap of paperwork for the rest of the war, maybe even the rest of thirty years, and after that it wouldn't hurt anymore.

By the light of a lamp, he'd read his draft letter over and again— reconstructive surgery unit, Weimar—while pushing Jürgen's cradle with his foot. Army hospital. Two weeks' training. Surgery unit. Three grieving boys. And everything he'd given up for Susi—his career, his freedom—handed to him again. The baby gazed up at him. Jürgen had not yet learned to smile, but his eyes were fathomless. *My son*, thought Frank, flooded with remorse and love. Back and forth he pushed, letting the curved wood swing.

At night, Frank buried his anxiety about going to Berlin by worrying instead over how to fix Hartmann's face in just one operation. He paged through his books on reconstructive surgery, frowning at how little the medicine had advanced since the last war. There were his notes, written in his big, exuberant twenty-year-old hand. How new it had all seemed when he'd been a student! He remembered his reverence for the pedicle: strips of skin cut from arms, necks, and abdomens, and fashioned into living tubes to nourish destroyed faces. The pedicles slithered over the neck, hugging a missing nose, a ravaged cheek. For weeks, one could bring healing blood and tissue to the open flesh, but it wasn't pretty. The men looked as if they were being devoured by snakes made of their own skin.

The use of the pedicle required multiple procedures. Distant flaps had to be moved up the body. A surgeon would connect a strip from the abdomen to an arm. After a few weeks, when the bridge of skin was secure, the surgeon disconnected the strip from the abdomen and reattached it to the head. The belly fed the arm, and then the arm fed the face.

The pedicle was a more effective procedure than a skin graft, because it almost always ensured a healing flow of blood and nutrients. Yet it had slowly fallen out of favor. The pedicle took too long. It looked ghastly. There was a risk of infection in each transfer. The metaphor of the pedicle was unnerving, too: A man had to be attached to himself in order to heal, and the attachment was so fragile and tender it could be ruptured with the tiniest of movements. The patients complained of its sensation on the face; the extra pudge of skin made them feel as if they were being muffled. On the arm, they felt shackled.

Hartmann might not need a pedicle, but he had a pedicle problem. He would need to be cut, and heal, and be cut again. After the first cut, he would look worse. He would feel worse, too. The stitches would be itchy and painful. They would make the flesh bubble and crimp. They might even rip out. A second operation wouldn't be possible in four or five weeks. If Frank left his work undone, there was no guarantee that someone would continue it.

He ought to talk to Hartmann, to see if he could pull any strings to get himself transferred to Berlin. He rose and passed the door to the infectious disease ward. The typhus rumor gnawed at him. Linden had shrugged at it. *Why poison your free labor?* Frau Reiner agreed. *How would they contain the disease?* But the crawling sensation began again. Frank tried to shake it off by coughing and rubbing the hair on his arms.

Hartmann was sitting upright, writing in a small notebook. His hair looked clean, his clothes crisp. The nurses must be taking good care of him. Frank had seen to that, telling them that they were caring for a poet, who might celebrate them in verse one day.

As Frank approached, Hartmann set down his pen and slowly closed the notebook. His posture caught Frank's eye—that slight bowing of the shoulders, the hips thrust forward—he was a man caving into himself. The vision contrasted sharply to the boy with the stick up his spine at the head of the classroom. Frank felt a sting at the sides of his mouth, a bitter grimace. *You and me,* he thought. *We finally understand suffering.*

Yet when he sat down to write to Hartmann about the transfer, he found he couldn't do it. The pencil sat heavy in his hand. When it moved, it shaped different letters.

Do you remember Susi Waller?

Hartmann's eyes blinked. *Yes. I do.*

I married her.

A hesitation, and then, *She was a lovely girl.*

We had three sons. She passed this year, with the birth of my youngest.

Hartmann scratched an immediate reply: *I'm sorry.*

Did you ever marry?

No. Then a pause. *Moved around too much.*

I never figured you for the army.

You didn't know me.

Do you still write poems?

Hartmann shrugged.

My father admired your poems.

One of the few.

Modest!

Truly. Hartmann shifted on the bed. His legs extended in front of him, the trousers bagging around his calves and thighs. *I wish I remembered him.*

Frank's throat closed, and he sat there stiffly, gripping the pen. He remembered his father. He remembered mostly that he disappointed him, by being rash and loud, a carouser, an uneven student. By loving Karl May more than Thomas Mann. By pursuing Susi, whose "iron will," his father said dismissively, made up "for what she lacked in imagination." His father hadn't lived long enough to see Frank complete medical school, to meet his sons. He imagined they would be closer now.

You say he was a teacher? wrote Hartmann.

Latin.

Hartmann looked up, out the window near his bed where frost climbed in intricate webs. Then he bent to the paper. *Can I trust you?*

Of course. I'm your doctor.

Need more assurance than that.

Frank wondered what game Hartmann was playing now. He wished they could just talk instead of write.

My father admired you, he wrote finally. *I wouldn't betray his memory.*

Hartmann took the paper and stared at it for a long time. Frank thought he had fallen asleep. But then the pencil began to move.

There are—Hartmann's hand paused—*gaps. Things I can't recall. Voices I hear. Buzzing and ringing. I didn't want to admit this. Because I want the surgery. I don't want to be sent somewhere else. "Unwertes Leben."*

One by one, Hartmann's confessions rolled into hard pebbles, knocking inside Frank's skull. Hearing voices. Buzzing and ringing. *Unwertes Leben,* the term for the mentally unstable and infirm. The government obliged doctors to register patients with mental illness or serious brain damage and then transfer them to state institutions. Frank had never been to one such institution, but he heard they were purposely underfunded. *Unwertes Leben.* Life unworthy of life. Frank watched Hartmann cross out each word he'd just written, making a black tangle of the page. He wished he still believed that the German law would protect Hartmann, a German soldier, the way it had protected the miller in the case against the king. He took the pad.

There's a hospital in Berlin, he wrote. *I may be transferred there.*

Hartmann shook his head vigorously. *Fix me here.*

It will take multiple procedures. Berlin would be the safest place.

Berlin will be pulverized.

Frank opened his palms, his sympathy ebbing again. That was Hartmann all right. That imperial manner even when he had a monster's face.

They sat in silence. Outside the window, a few flakes of snow drifted over the darkened field, the hunkered black shape of the incinerator.

Hartmann started scribbling again. *For now you could help me remember.* Frank felt the slate eyes on his, searching. *Were we really friends?*

He took the pencil. *Yes.*

News of the OKW's orders and Frank's imminent transfer to Berlin must have spread, as the incoming ambulances brought fewer and fewer patients in need of reconstruction. Frank spent half his days doing rounds, checking on his healing soldiers, listening to their complaints. They seemed to appreciate him less the more available he was (*I can't sleep in this place. How long till you can cut my legs apart again? The itch, can't you do anything for it?*), so in the afternoons he hid in the supply room and read his books again, looking for the best way to fix Hartmann. He didn't receive any more packages from Liesl. Instead, she'd written him a long letter about the boys, concluding with a few lines that casually congratulated him on the promotion. *We're all proud of you. The boys want to visit you in the capital,* she wrote, as if it were as easy as taking a holiday. Maybe she thought it was. There was no way to know how much news was making it west. The national broadcasts were full of lies.

As soon as I get settled there, I'll apply for a furlough. I know it's time I came home, he wrote back, hoping she would understand that he did not intend to get caught by the Red Army, no matter where he was stationed.

Schnell surprised him washing up one afternoon after a routine leg graft surgery. "I heard more news about your hospital," he said. "It's almost ready. Seventy beds in total." He beamed at Frank, pink and pleased.

"Room enough for my current patients?" said Frank.

Schnell nodded distantly. He was watching Frank's hands rubbing themselves together in the cold stream. "The beds may be already spoken for."

"Lieutenant Hartmann is an old classmate of mine," Frank said.

"Is he?" Schnell sounded curious.

"Could you tell Braun I'd appreciate the favor?" said Frank.

"Lieutenant Hartmann," Schnell said over the falling water. "One of his men had accused him of writing treasonous messages before the explosion."

Frank kept scrubbing, trying to hide his surprise. "He's a poet," he said. "He writes a lot of gobbledygook. Maybe the fellow misinterpreted."

"There will be an investigation," said Schnell. He coughed. "Meanwhile I was quite sorry to hear about your patient from Buchenwald."

Frank frowned at the name. "Where?"

"The soldier from the prison camp," said Schnell. "His infection killed him."

The man had been ill, but not fatally so.

"What infection?" Frank said. He turned off the faucet and faced the officer.

Schnell's eyes shifted, as if somehow he were looking through Frank instead of at him. "I know your time is valuable," he said. "I won't let our staff bother you with any other nonsurgical cases."

Although his voice was mild and unthreatening, it didn't matter how he spoke.

Frank's gaze fell to his hands. *What infection?* he wanted to ask again, but the words did not come. He watched the water drip off his fingers. Wet and cold, his hands seemed like separate creatures, small animals that moved and grasped and sewed flesh without him. They had no voice but the voice of repair. They would go to Berlin to do their work.

"Thank you," he muttered finally. He kept his head bowed until he felt the other man turn away.

He went to Hartmann that evening. He wrote down every memory he had of the other boy, from the miller and the king story to his father's tales of Hartmann's prowess in school. Then he told his own.

You know the Schloss *in the center of town,* he wrote. *One year, we were allowed to go inside, and a bunch of us boys sneaked away and tried to find the wine cellar.*

Tell me the colors.

Frank looked up, puzzled.

Hartmann's hand moved again. *Of what you saw.*

He thought a minute, and then the pencil began to shape letters.

The walls were white. When we found the stairs down, yellow. Under the earth, gray-black. I had trouble breathing down there. Thick dust and so much glass.

His hand tired, even more than it did in surgery, but he shook it and kept writing. He was starting to like the silence of sitting with the other man and taking a long time to say a few words. And strangely, he was starting to like the words, too, how they hurt a little when he thought of them, how they were like tiny pins fixing his memory in place.

We got lost. You helped us find the way out. You read the labels and you knew the wines were organized by year.

He finished with a flourish and tap of the pencil, and showed it to Hartmann. The man was silent, but water filled the corners of his eyes again.

You got tight with a girl named Astrid. She stayed with her aunt and uncle for a while. He did not write that the other girls laughed secretly at Astrid for liking Hartmann, the undesirable one.

I don't remember her.

She was pretty and plump, wrote Frank.

Sounds like you're talking about poultry.

Frank shrugged and grinned. He heard a sucking sound under the scarf and wondered if Hartmann was laughing. He didn't know what to say about Schnell's warning. Hartmann's failed transfer to Berlin. The skin under the scarf was healing, the scabs thickening and loosening. Soon they would fall off and leave purple-pink scars. The distorted mouth would be able to flex and open, and eventually it might even learn to speak.

You were accused of treason. Do you remember?

Something flinched behind the scarf. *Yes. All that writing burned up.*

There's supposed to be an investigation.

Hartmann's eyelids drooped.

I'm tired, he wrote.

But Frank's hand kept moving. *Do you remember when the fair came to town?* He went on, doing the best he could to conjure his memory of the clown and the bearded lady and the tattooed man.

That I remember, wrote Hartmann. *And the Gypsy who ran a booth, he stole the candlesticks from the church.*

Frank didn't recall this, but he nodded.

He ran away but he left his dog, some little mutt, wrote Hartmann. *Some of the kids wanted to drown it. They dragged it to the Kurpark.* Frank watched Hartmann's hand stop and go completely still. Hartmann made a sucking noise, as if impatient at his hand's immobility, but he did not write any more. His fingers curled into a fist. Fine blond hair covered his whole wrist, fanning toward his knuckles.

The silence was different than silence in speech. In speech, when a man stopped talking he used his eyes or his mouth to say what he didn't want to say aloud, but the hand held no expression. The sentence trailed off like footsteps in a blizzard.

Frank wished he felt sorry for Hartmann, but the poet's wordlessness suddenly left him cold. He couldn't feel anything for the little mutt, although he could easily imagine its death, the children's hands pushing the muzzle under the surface of the pond, paws kicking and splashing. A froth of breath. The furry body gone still. He could see it perfectly, although the memory was not his own, and he felt only the ice of recognition.

He patted Hartmann on the shoulder and rose and left the ward.

Back in his room, he did not bother to turn on a lamp. Keeping his hat and coat on, he eased the rucksack from under his bed and took out Ani's shoes. He carried them in the crook of his arm, out the door to the empty black and silver yard. His feet found the tramped path to the incinerator. His breath hung in ghosts as he slipped and stomped on the frozen crust, his ears already stinging. He set the shoes on the snow beside the dark, squat oven. They looked too small and supple, too alive, to belong there. He swallowed hard. After a moment, he prodded them into the shadows with his foot. Then he turned away before he could grab them back. He began whistling a tune as he walked inside, his boots cracking the ice. He stopped when he realized the song was "Rosemarie."

Hannesburg

January 1945

Liesl wanted to like Berte Geiss. She needed a friend, her own friend, especially after receiving Frank's letter about his transfer to Berlin. It would just be a wartime post, a real opportunity, he assured her, the underline swift and light.

Frank wasn't coming home. He wasn't preparing to slip away from the surrender that they both knew was imminent. He was stepping deeper into the hornet's nest and pretending he didn't hear the buzzing all around him.

Although she wrote back a simple note of congratulations, Liesl kept the letter in her apron pocket, squeezing it from time to time so that it lost its creases and crumpled. Whenever she took it out, his words looked more and more garbled. The writings of a madman. She and Frank had never fought before, but now she was angry with him. It made her wish that she liked the taste of cigarettes, so she could puff out gusts of smoke.

She didn't want Frank to think that she didn't believe in him, or worse, that she couldn't continue to care for the children on her own, so she held her tongue. But Berlin was a trap. It didn't hold real opportunity at all, unless you counted being captured and starved by the Red Army.

Liesl was sure the poor, fleeing Berte Geiss would agree. She fantasized often about Berte's impending arrival, which had been mysteriously delayed twice. Her mind filled with hazy dreams of the two of them cooking and sewing together, laughing over the boys' antics, of linking their arms as they marched out into the cold gaze of the neighborhood. She had anticipated a homely young woman with a sad, sincere smile, someone she felt she could trust. Her fantasy Berte wore a plain bob and tucked her brown hair back behind her ear. Berte would profess an affinity for Chopin and a private longing to travel to Greece one day and see the Acropolis. She wouldn't have any friends here, either.

When the real Berte finally arrived, Liesl was standing in the window, trying to dress Jürgen, a daily task that required vigilance and muscle, as the boy hated clothes. "Sit still," she told him with gritted teeth. She heard a loud noise outside and automatically checked the sky, but it was a dark car pulling up in front of the Geiss house. Herr Geiss emerged first, then strode around the puffing tail pipe and opened the other door. No one appeared. He waited, his heavy face darkening.

Jürgen squirmed free of her hands and rolled on his belly, cutting off access to his shirt buttons. "Come here, you," she said as he giggled.

Below, Herr Geiss extended an arm and yanked. A female form tumbled out, her blond hair spilling in her face. She staggered right, then left, then stood, swaying, gazing up at the enormous house. She was clutching a handkerchief in one hand. She pressed it hard to her mouth, then buckled and threw up all over the snow. Herr Geiss looped both arms around her and muscled her into the house. He did not introduce Berte to Liesl until two days later, when Liesl and the children were coming back from the post office.

"These are your neighbors," he said to Berte, and introduced Liesl as the "new" Frau Kappus. "I leave you women to get acquainted." He bowed his head and hustled away.

Berte extended a limp, cool hand. At first glance she seemed pretty, but then it became clear that something almost imperceptible was wrong with her face—her chin was too small, her eyebrows too plucked and sparse. She looked like the smudged painting of a doll.

"Would you like to come in for some tea?" Liesl asked.

The girl shook her head. "I'm still exhausted."

Beside them, Ani and Hans began to swordfight with sticks they'd picked up along the way home. Jürgen struggled up in his pram and stared over at them.

"Their father must be handsome," Berte commented. "For you to put up with three little boys."

Liesl didn't know what to say. "They're good boys."

"You're dead," Ani cried, stabbing his stick at his brother's heart. "I'm not little," he said to Berte.

"Don't shout, Ani," Hans muttered with a glance at the girl.

"You're dead," Ani whispered triumphantly. Hans knocked away his stick and they started fighting again.

Liesl proposed that Berte go with her to Elizabethenstrasse the next day. "I could show you the shelters in case you get stuck shopping during a raid. And the best butcher and baker."

"Oh, thanks, but I like to find things on my own," Berte said. "It makes me feel like I've accomplished something." And then she turned around and walked back into the Geiss house, the boys' sticks still whacking.

A few days later, Liesl tried again as she and Berte crossed paths near the Kurpark. She offered to share their wash kitchen on laundry day. "I wouldn't mind the company," she said, smiling into Berte's blank face. The girl's nostrils were red from rubbing.

"I've already hired a laundress," Berte said. She pointed down a path. "Is that the way to the sulfur fountains? Do they taste really awful? Actually, don't tell me. I'm going to try them anyway."

A few days later, on the way home from the market, Liesl spotted a blond-haired woman strutting down the street ahead of her. The woman's boots were red saffian, laced halfway up her shapely calves. Her coat was Persian lamb, designed in an hourglass shape, though it was a couple of sizes too big, making it hard to see the outline of her body.

Could it be Berte Geiss? Maybe. Berte Geiss was liable to wear something too showy and expensive for their small town, but she wouldn't strut. Berte would scurry with her head down, as if late for an appointment. Nevertheless something about the woman was familiar.

To her surprise the woman stopped at the Kappuses' gate. Her head tilted back to take in the whole villa and her blond hair spilled back, revealing her high cheekbones and rosebud mouth. Liesl frowned. It couldn't be.

The woman turned and looked back, and Liesl felt her knees go to jelly.

It was her. It was Uta.

Liesl reached down and tucked Jürgen's blanket around him, suddenly unsure how to respond. *It's Uta,* she told herself. *Why aren't you glad to see her?*

Because something had to be wrong. Uta would never show up unannounced unless something was wrong.

"Liesl! There you are!" Uta's hand shot up into a wave. Her furs rippled around her as she hurried toward them.

Liesl waved back. Then her eyes dropped to the gray potatoes, the chicken hanging its dead feet out of the edge of the basket under the pram. Seeing Uta's gloves, she was suddenly aware of her broken nails, her thick knuckles, scarred from cooking and cleaning. She reached down and lifted Jürgen so the baby was between them as Uta leaned in for a kiss, smacking both cheeks.

"What a surprise to see you," Liesl said. "All the way from Berlin?"

Uta nodded, her eyes fastened on the graceful upper balcony of the house. "I can't believe you're all alone here. You must have some good friends in the housing office."

Liesl gestured at the Geiss home. "Our neighbor keeps us off the list."

"Good neighbor," Uta said in an appraising tone. "How old is he?"

"Too old," Liesl said, not smiling. "This is Jürgen."

As she lifted the baby toward Uta, he gurgled and scrunched up his face.

"Goodness, you'd think he would have gotten bigger than that. It's been months since I saw you last," Uta said, her expression mirroring the baby's skepticism.

"They don't grow that fast," Liesl said with a forced laugh. "But he can already sit up on his own now."

"Marvelous," Uta said without enthusiasm. A silence fell between them. Liesl knew Uta was taking stock of her, of the pram and the potatoes, the limp dead fowl, of the house and the absent husband, wondering if Liesl should be pitied or envied.

And wasn't she trying to figure out the same thing? Uta's fur coat gave off a lush, feathery smell. Her red boots were the brightest thing on the whole street, except her lips, smudged lightly with forbidden scarlet lipstick. You could see her from a kilometer away and know the kind of woman she was. Yet up close, looking into that warm open face, Liesl felt a rush of affection for her oldest friend, whom she'd met at nine at the Badensee, teaming up to watch all their young charges—her nieces and nephews, Uta's grubby little brothers. How much they had been through together: the endless BDM meetings where they'd giggled through the patriotic songs, Uta's trouble with the local burgher's son, then leaving Franconia for jobs at the spa. Uta seemed shorter and rounder, as if something in Berlin had punched her down. Her blue eyes had new cracks at the corners.

Liesl threaded her free arm through Uta's and pulled her toward the door. "Come meet the older boys. You'll like them better," she said. "They talk and take orders."

"Mm. Will they fetch me a hot steamy bath and some steak tartare?" Uta replied in her mellow voice.

Liesl laughed. "More like a pile of snowballs and a dead spider they found in the cellar."

As they crossed through the gate they stumbled into each other, and Liesl smelled her friend's cologne. The scent was pungent, baptismal; it drowned her nose and left an aftertaste of limes and sugar.

Liesl sighed. "I'm glad to see you," she said, meaning it.

"I heard your pram squeaking behind me the whole way down the street," Uta said softly. "You didn't seem that glad."

"It isn't like that——" Liesl said, but Uta kissed her again on the cheek.

"I won't stay long, all right?" she said. "I just need to make some arrangements."

Hans crept away from the window as the strange woman entered the house. He padded softly down the hall to his grandfather's study. He liked to sit at the desk and draw airplanes. Sometimes he drew Messerschmitts and other planes he had seen, but more often he drew imaginary planes, equipped with special weapons: red and white flame-shooters, dragon-toothed torpedoes, and blaster bombs that could blow up whole cities. Because paper was scarce, he made his drawings in the margins of his grandfather's books, and whenever his stepmother came by, he dropped the pencil and pretended to be reading. "What book is that?" she would ask, and if it wasn't a title she recognized, she would smile and let it go.

His father wouldn't have let it go. Vati didn't like the boys touching Grossvater's books. He treated them like statues, rare and precious, insisting on dusting them himself. "Get out of there. Let them be," he said whenever he saw Hans in the room.

"But I'm supposed to read," Hans objected once. "Or I won't grow up."

"You don't need books to grow up," his father said. "Follow your heart."

Hans didn't understand what to make of that advice. How could he know if his heart was right? For example, he wanted to love his real mother forever, but her face was fading in his mind. The other day he had spent a good hour trying to remember if she had ears like his, with the lobe connected, or like Ani's, with the lobe detached. Also, was it wrong that his ribs no longer ached every time he thought of her? Was it bad to decide his stepmother was kind, even though she did everything the wrong way? He wished she wouldn't let Ani be such a baby. He wished she would grow her hair long and braid it. He wished she would give him Vati's letters, but she folded them all up and hid them somewhere.

He drew the nose of a plane, a sharp thin tail. He added wings, four engines, and a cockpit window. A B-17. It should be silver-blue. It should float like a ship. His hand paused. Then he hastily sketched in a face, *X*'s for eyes, a body slumped against the glass. This plane had a dead pilot. It was falling from the sky.

He was drawing in a book of poetry and the next poem was called "The Plum Tree." Normally he didn't read the words in his grandfather's books, but the first line ended with the word *"Mirabellen."* After his mother's death, the house had filled with the yellow plums. *Mirabellen* were in season, so everyone brought some. The scabby orbs piled high in the kitchen and attracted flies. Hans had tried to eat his way through them. First they were delicious, and then they tasted rancid. The words in the poem were like the plums, too many, heaped and dense, and he shoved his way through them, fumbling to understand what the poet was saying about the branch and the fruit. Yet when he reached the last line, something loosened inside his skull and broke free. *Das Ende finde ich.*

The hairs on the back of his neck began to rise the way they did when he was afraid in the dark cellar.

He heard a smacking noise and saw his brother standing in the doorway, chewing. Hans shut the book. "What are you eating?"

"Mutti wants you to come down and meet Fräulein Müller," Ani said.

The casual use of "Mutti" rankled Hans. "I'm busy," he said.

Ani took a black licorice from his pocket and popped it in his mouth.

"Where did you get that?" Hans said.

"Fräulein Müller."

Hans frowned at the book's cover. The title read *Im Osten. In the East.*

"She's got chocolate, too."

Hans sighed and climbed down from his father's chair, suddenly aware of how hungry he was, how his stomach had retreated from the waistline of his trousers. He licked his hand and smoothed his hair back. He caught his reflection in the glass cabinets and took a deep breath, stretching out his chest.

"Why do you look at yourself so much?" said Ani.

Hans ignored him, speeding up his pace and tripping on a fringe of carpet, tumbling to his knees and hands. His brother stood over him, still chewing, as if he had expected the fall. Hans felt a flare of anger at the attentive look on Ani's face. Ani was always scrutinizing people as if they were books to be read. He asked so many questions at school that both the teachers and the other students disliked him, and Hans had to fight more than once to keep older boys from taunting his brother. His mother used to scold Hans for it, but his stepmother looked as though she wanted to cry every time she saw his bruises.

Hans brushed off his stinging hands and was about to stand when his eye caught on the thing that had tripped him. Not the carpet, but a loose wedge of wood sticking up. A loose plank. It might have treasure beneath it: gold coins or jewelry they could trade for more food and firewood. Or it might be something secret that Ani shouldn't see, like the account book that his stepmother showed him once when his brothers were asleep, a disappointing tally of the household's large expenses and small income.

Suddenly he heard her, calling their names. Hans clambered to his feet and clapped his brother on the shoulder.

"I was watching *you*, silly," he said. "If you can see me in the reflection, then I can see you, too."

Within two short hours, Hans discovered many horrible things about Fräulein Müller: She talked too much, she made his stepmother forget important things like the fact that he did not like mustard anywhere near his potatoes, and she smoked and waved her hand in the air after every puff, shooing the stinking clouds to other people's heads. The way she dressed also filled him with misgivings; her skin peeked out in places he was used to seeing cloth and he wished it were not so visible.

During their midday meal she complained to Hans about his habit of scraping his fork against his teeth when he ate.

"It makes the most hideous sound, darling," she said, patting his arm.

During dinner, she made his stepmother blush by complaining that stale bread gave her a toothache.

Worst of all, Fräulein Müller was to sleep on the sofa in Hans's grandfather's study. His stepmother did not indicate how long the woman would stay, nor did she make any accommodation for the disruption in the boy's daily routine.

"We never use it," his stepmother told Fräulein Müller. "Except Hans. He likes to read books in there sometimes. But he can find somewhere else."

A strange expression had come over his stepmother since her friend's arrival. It was a lot like Ani's just before Christmas this year. December 1944 had been the first year Ani had talked reverently about the stollen his mother baked for them, or the tree and its lighted candles. His gaze kept rolling back in his head, as if he were trying to see it again in his mind. Every time Fräulein Müller laughed, their stepmother laughed, too, and she did the same thing with her eyes.

Hans waited until they were washing the dishes. He told his brother to come with him. With a last glance over his shoulder, he saw their stepmother cuddle baby Jürgen in her lap and hold a bottle of milk to his lips. Fräulein Müller's hand trembled as she dunked a dish in the water.

"Emmy says Göring waited too long to marry her, or she might have had more children," Fräulein Müller said. "She says he's never gotten over Carin."

His stepmother looked puzzled, and then that Christmas look stole over her face.

"Go on," Hans whispered to Ani, and the younger boy obediently began to climb the steps.

"I don't know what it's like for you," Fräulein Müller said. "But Emmy says if she had to do it all over, she'd never marry a widower. Always playing second fiddle to a ghost."

His stepmother bent to the baby, her red hair curtaining her expression. "She shouldn't talk that way about her husband," she said softly. Her shoulders started to shake.

Hans swallowed. He had never seen her cry, and the sight troubled him.

"*Ach, Liebling.* You miss him, don't you," Fräulein Müller said after a moment. She swished the sink with her hand, dredging up silverware. The forks and spoons streamed, glinting. "You'd miss him less if you had a housekeeper."

Hans shouldered his coat and tiptoed up the steps to the unheated second floor. He always sensed his father's presence in the silent rooms on the second story, maybe because his stepmother had overtaken the first floor with her cooking, sewing, and baby-tending. Without Marta, the bedrooms and study didn't get cleaned much, and the dust that layered over the books and unused medical equipment could have touched his father's skin the last time he was here.

He hurried into the study and told Ani to wait in the hall.

"Why?"

"To keep watch," Hans said. "Give the Indian signal if you hear anyone coming."

He waited until his brother left before kneeling. The plank was stuck hard. His grandfather's letter opener grated at the wood, the cold metal warming in his hands.

Always playing second fiddle to a ghost.

His mother wasn't a ghost. She was real. She had left them all at the hospital's entrance, kissing the top of Hans's head, telling him to watch after Ani. The next time he'd seen her, she'd been boxed in oak.

Sometimes he imagined going through the hospital doors to find her still in there, waiting for the family to bring her home. Her hair would fan out over the pillow, and her covers would be pulled up high, over her stomach and chest. A nurse would be sitting with her, because his *Mutti* always made friends, wherever she went.

The plank sprang loose with a squeal. Dust rose from the hole. The grit caught on his eyelids and in the back of his throat. He tried not to cough.

Inside lay a single sheet of paper, facedown.

Frowning, he lifted it, turned it over, and sat back on his heels in the dim light of the lamp.

It was a charcoal outline of a man, naked, his body splayed over a couch. One leg was propped on the cushions and one dangled off; the man's penis slumped against his lower thigh. He was not large or muscled, but narrow in the chest. His face was turned away.

A tiny word was written in the corner: *Bloss. Bare.* Though there were no clothes on the man, he looked as if he was still hiding himself, as if he had just averted his eyes before the artist could see too much. Hans recognized him. It was his grandfather.

He dropped the picture and pushed the plank back into place. A dirty taste filled his mouth. He stood quickly. He kicked the carpet back over the plank, shrugged on his coat, and walked down the stairs, passing Ani's small, thin silhouette.

"Nothing," he said without looking at his brother. "Now I have to check on our supplies in the cellar."

"Nothing?"

"Would I lie? Get your coat and you can come with me."

While his brother jogged off to the closet, Hans skirted the kitchen where the women were talking and slipped down the dark steps. His stepmother's voice followed him, and he heard snatches of her words: "so hard to . . . they all need new clothes . . ." He kept the lamp hooded until he was halfway down and then let the smoky yellow light spring over the dirt walls. The lower he went, the more his breath began to slow. Everything in their shelter was his construction. He had made it practical and comfortable for them. He had made it a second home, their real home if the one upstairs was bombed.

Just before he passed out of earshot, Hans heard Fräulein Müller say, "That older one, he's in love with you."

An invisible hammer slammed into both of Hans's knees. He froze, listening for his stepmother's answer, but Jürgen made a fussy cry and a chair scraped as she rose and creaked back and forth across the floor with him.

Stumbling on clumsy legs, Hans thundered down the last steps and into the damp, carpeted room lined with shelves holding their food, gas masks, water, fuel. Just last week, he had hung some old green curtains on the wall, where windows might ordinarily go. He angled the light over the room, the curtains, breathing hard gusts of hate at Fräulein Müller and her oozing voice. If they had an air raid tonight, he would tell her there wasn't space. There wasn't really, not if their two neighbors ever needed to squeeze in. She could go back to Berlin and find somebody else to insult.

"You breathe like a horse," said a young woman's voice.

He spun to see a dark shape on Herr Geiss's side of the hole.

"What's it to you?" Hans retorted.

The dark shape didn't reply.

"What are you doing down here?" he said.

"I was looking for a tool to help me open a suitcase," she said. "The lock's stuck."

"Herr Geiss can help you," Hans said.

"Herr Geiss isn't home." The figure shifted and poured through the hole, Berte Geiss's mouth and cheeks suddenly snagged by the light of the lamp. Her round eyes blinked at Hans.

"What are you doing down here?" she asked.

"Checking on supplies." Hans moved off with his lantern, adjusting the canned sardines on the shelf.

"You do that a lot."

He didn't answer. He didn't talk to girls at school. He didn't know why anyone would think he liked any female at all.

"Would some of your supplies include a pair of pliers?" said Berte.

He shrugged.

"A screwdriver? I'm down to my last pair of hose." When she pleaded, her voice sounded younger. He went to the tool shelf and slid his hand around two handles.

Footsteps thudded down from above. "What are you doing?" said Ani, his skinny legs pausing on the steps.

Hans shoved the tools in his front pocket, suddenly aware of the metal digging into his right thigh. "I'm helping Frau Geiss with her suitcase," he said, watching the girl disappear through the hole like a drop of ink sliding off a desk. As he followed her into the wall, the earth scraped his skull. A damp crumb kissed his neck. He paused.

"You can come if you want," he said, without looking behind him.

In the second-floor hallway, the girl vanished through a threshold. He knew it was her bedroom even without stepping through the doorway because it gave off a vague flowery scent, and though it was as dark as the rest of the house it seemed warmer. It was also mysteriously and intensely cluttered. From the hallway, he could see heaps of dresses and shoes, spilled jewelry, open drawers, an empty sleeve trailing across the wooden floorboards, as if inviting another two-dimensional guest to dance. He backed up and called his brother's name.

"In here," Ani said from somewhere on the same floor.

"Hurry up," hissed Berte.

Hans took the tools from his pocket and held them out before him. He breathed in deep before entering the room, closing his lips around the air.

She sat on the bed, a lamp lit beside her, her skinny legs slightly parted, the suitcase on her lap.

"Totally *kaputt*," she said. "I told him not to be cheap."

"Who?"

Her eyes flashed over him. "You need a haircut. Doesn't she ever cut your hair?"

Still holding his breath, Hans stretched out his hand to take the suitcase, but the girl's knuckles whitened. "I'll hold it, silly," she said. Her voice was cross.

He bent down and inserted his screwdriver into the lock, aware of his heavy head angled toward her chest, aware of its rise and curve. His hands jiggled above the gap between her thighs.

"Who's the woman visiting your stepmother?" she asked.

"I don't know," said Hans.

"She looks rich."

He hesitated. He had heard Fräulein Müller drop the name of the *Reichsmarschall* and his wife, but he didn't believe a person like her could know someone like that. She was probably puffing herself up.

"I don't think she's rich. She only had one suitcase."

The lock did not budge. Hans fumbled for the pliers, dropping the screwdriver on the ground with a clonk. "Ani, where are you?" he said testily, as if his brother was responsible for the noise.

"In here," said the voice again.

He knocked at the lock with the pliers.

"Hurry up," Berte said again, but now her voice was curious and he felt her eyes on him.

"I'm trying."

"I got married when I was sixteen," she said. Her breath blew a small warm wind against the crown of his head.

He drew back. "May I break it? If I break it, I can probably open it."

Her thin shoulders rose, making her unbuttoned collar fall open.

He closed the pliers on the lock and twisted, ripping into the brass. His hands ached. The metal groaned but did not give. "It's really stuck," he said, hysteria in his voice.

"You're a little *Kohlenklau*," she said. "I saw you snitching wood from the park."

Coal snatcher. Hans blinked. His eyeballs felt hot and dry. His lids scraped over them. He kept twisting the pliers.

"Will you steal something for me sometime?" She leaned in, her cheek radiating heat into his. He wanted to pull away. He wanted to calmly stroll from the room and get his brother and walk down the stairs and out through the cellar hole into his own house. But instead his hands kept cranking at the metal until it shrieked and broke and her cheek was touching his. Her softness startled him. He jerked back, and then the suitcase sprang open to reveal snakes of hose, all heaped and coiled on top of one another, in the pale, variegated shades of flesh. The girl gave a cry. She pulled the suitcase away, her knees closing, her hands fluttering down to the stockings.

Hans stared at her. He dimly remembered drawing a Lancaster that morning. He recalled listening to their little black radio for any reports from Weimar. He remembered Ani and his infernal licorice. But he couldn't remember how to say good-bye to the girl and leave. It was completely beyond his comprehension, that simple casual courtesy, *Gute Nacht.*

"I didn't mean to break it," he said.

Then loud planes passed overhead and they both flinched, waiting for a siren. In the pause, Berte sank her hand deeper into her stockings and a tremor of genuine fear crossed her face. She looked as if she was going to be sick.

The siren did not sound. The girl withdrew her hand from the suitcase. "Why are you still here?" she said in a tight voice.

Once Hans started moving, he did not stop, not to drag Ani from the adjacent room, not to ask what he was doing, not to pause in the cellar, or wish his stepmother good night. He went straight to bed with the screwdriver and pliers still in his hand, holding them under his pillow, their hard edges grinding, clanking every time he turned over. *Kohlenklau*, the double *k*'s like a door slamming twice. *Will you steal something for me sometime?* For the first night since his father had left, Hans did not dream of him.

In the silence after the planes passed over, Uta sagged onto the couch in Otto Kappus's study and looked up at the ceiling. "I'll never forget my first sight of you," she said. "A little daisy from the fields, and now look at you: the very picture of *Bürgertum*."

Liesl pulled an eiderdown from the wardrobe and handed it to her friend, listening with one ear for Jürgen, sleeping in the other room.

"Remember how I used to visit you on Sunday nights and tell you all the spa gossip?" said Uta. "I always loved your room. It was so peaceful, so sweet, so positively Liesl." Her blue eyes glistened. "But this is yours, too. I'm happy for you."

Liesl sat down on the edge of the couch. "Thank you," she said.

"What did you use to make that room smell so good? Something with orange slices."

Her room. It had been so small, any scent had filled it. And high up. She'd been able to look out, down to the courtyard where clients walked in robes to the sulfur baths and massage rooms, but no one could ever see back in.

"I stuffed an orange with cloves," said Liesl. "When we could get oranges." She thought she heard a muffled cry, and wanted to rise, but felt her friend's eyes on her and stayed still.

"That's right," said Uta. "You were always handy with herbs. You used to make me marigold water for my hair." She smiled. "Did I tell you what Göring said to Emmy about her hair the other day?"

Liesl hesitated, silent. She didn't want to hear about Emmy Göring's hair, though she missed her talks with Uta. Sunday gossip nights had been a tradition, and in the loneliness of her life at the spa Liesl had looked forward to news, any news, especially Uta's chatter about this or that officer or his mistress's or wife's scandalous behavior. An unspoken contract between the two friends dictated that they would always find fault with the other women for wanting a man too much. You didn't let men stake their claims. You didn't believe in *Kinder, Kirche, Küche*, like the girls they'd grown up with, now farmer's and baker's wives, orbiting their children, their church, their kitchen.

You stayed free.

Stay free—it had been both their prayer and their battle hymn. *Stay free* when two adjutants fought over Uta in the courtyard, their knuckles thudding like hammers into meat. *Stay free* when a peach-faced Bavarian officer started leaving poems for Liesl at the *Kinderhaus*. No love, and certainly no marriage. Uta put her singing first, and Liesl pledged her heart to the state. Instead of loving flesh-and-blood men, she loved the voice of the Führer, and instead of loving her own children, she fell for the pitiful orphans in paper clothes in *The Soviet Paradise*, and sat through speech after speech against the horrors of Jewish Bolshevism.

But her fervor had died long before Frank proposed, and now it all seemed like such a long time ago. Another life.

"No, what did Göring say?" Liesl forced herself to say. "To Emmy?"

"Never mind. You don't care," said Uta, propping herself on one arm. "I'm here because I want to find Dr. Schein."

The name sent a jolt down Liesl's spine. She tiptoed to the hall and peered into the darkness, toward the boys' room. No noise. She pulled the door shut and sat down at Frank's father's desk, the only other chair in the room.

Again? She wanted to say, but instead she asked if Dr. Schein had moved from the city where they had gone together seven years ago, first by train, then two kilometers on foot, their cheeks burning as the neighborhoods got shabbier and shabbier.

"Maybe," said Uta. "They said he relocated his practice."

"Did you ask at the registration office?" Liesl said.

"Still listed in Franconia. But he's not there."

"It was a long time ago," Liesl said. "He could be anywhere by now."

"I know," Uta said. "But you could go to your husband's old office and find out where Dr. Schein moved his practice. Say your husband needs to reach him. They'll be able to make some calls. I've got money if you need to grease the wheels."

Liesl walked to the wall where there hung a watercolor of the town's famous lone white tower. It was a drenched picture, the tower smudged by fog and rain. She stared into its dreariness, trying to pull herself back to the conversation.

"There wasn't anyone in Berlin?" she said finally.

"If this child's father found out about its existence, he would make me deliver it and take it away from me," said Uta. "He knows I'm not cut out to be a mother."

Liesl touched the wall that connected the study to the bedroom where she and Jürgen slept. She remembered how they both stumbled on the broken cobblestone near Dr. Schein's, how Uta had clutched her arm and asked, *What am I doing?* and she had said, *You're doing the right thing*, because they were both so young. They needed to stay free. But now the thought of walking that walk again turned Liesl's stomach. "We can raise the baby here," she said quietly. "Frank and I will do it."

Uta made a noise. "You would, wouldn't you?" she murmured. "That's why you're my one true friend." Then she sighed. "I can't bring a monster into the world."

"Your child would never be a monster," protested Liesl.

"Maybe not mine. But his might," Uta said, and then uttered a name Liesl didn't recognize. She smiled grimly. "He likes his work, and he works at Plötzensee Prison."

Plötzensee Prison, where Nazi resistors went to die, by guillotine or hanging. Liesl could not meet her friend's gaze. "Does he know you're gone?"

Uta didn't reply right away. "He's paying for my singing lessons," she said. "He's terribly critical of everyone, even Piaf and Dietrich, but he thinks I have real talent." Her pupils were so huge the irises had vanished.

Liesl folded her arms. "I didn't know you still wanted to sing," she said.

"I want to be free," said Uta. "When the war's over, there'll be Amis and Tommies crawling all over the country, wanting to be entertained. I'm learning English songs on my own."

"You can't plan for that," Liesl said sharply. "You can't just plan for that."

"Why not?" said Uta. "Your life has changed. Why can't mine?" She pulled up her right sleeve, revealing a familiar flash of gold: the thick modern bracelet that her first love, Hans-Paul Jost, had given her years ago. Uta had never sold or traded it, despite his betrayal. She unsnapped its amethyst clasp and set it on the desk.

A thin, urgent cry rose from the other room. "I'll do what I can for you tomorrow," Liesl said. "I need to turn out the light now." Without waiting for a reply, she flicked the switch. Darkness bloomed over the room, erasing every shape: the desk, the bracelet, Uta lying on the sofa with her black-soaked eyes.

Liesl climbed in bed but couldn't sleep. She stared at the outlines of the cradle, trying not to resent her friend. It was good to see Uta again, and Uta was in trouble again, serious trouble. Liesl couldn't have one condition without the other. And now Liesl had three innocent children to care for, and not once had her friend considered them. Arriving with her red boots and her pride. *I've got money.* Well, why couldn't she spend it finding a doctor herself?

Liesl punched her pillow. She turned her mind to the book she was reading, but it was just an old tome of fairy tales. The characters never changed. Good girls stayed good, and the bad ones were witches. She turned her mind to Frank. Not Frank now, not Frank-heading-to-Berlin-and-abandoning-them-all, but Frank-who'd-wooed-her. It was girlish and naïve, she knew, but it comforted her to sort through their brief courtship, and the years of chance meetings at the spa before that, wondering when the romance had begun.

Frank had never shown any interest in her, not until after he was widowed. No. He had been too faithful to Susi for that. That first day by the pond, Liesl was sure she'd seemed like a silly, stupid teenager to him, all soaked and dripping over the Steitz boy she'd rescued. "Not stupid," Frank had confirmed later. "Maybe silly. You looked like a drowned cat."

That didn't sound particularly enamored. Well, all right. A husband shouldn't notice young girls. And yet if he hadn't defended Liesl that day, and she him, would she trust him now? Was love just made up of simple incidents in which you brought out the best in another?

The day had begun ordinarily enough, with Frau Steitz, the wife of a high-ranking S.S. officer, arriving at the *Kinderhaus* flustered, pushing her twin nine-year-old boys ahead of her.

"I have an appointment. With Dr. Kappus," she said, retreating out the door. "I'll be back in an hour or two. Be good, Ernst. Be good, Max."

After five minutes of watching the boys pretend they were panzer units and smash the toys in the one-story cottage, Liesl took them to the pond and accidentally dozed off. She woke to a wet thud and the sound of someone screaming, "Max, Max!" One of the boys was floundering in the water, the other gripping a floating log. Liesl leapt up, dazed, and threw herself into the pond.

A few thrashing minutes later, one twin ran for help while Liesl helped the other twin hobble onto the grass and sank down beside him, spreading out her robe, propping the boy's skull.

"Ernst pushed me," he said.

"It was an accident," she said in a firm but consoling tone. Inside, she panicked. She would be fired for this, and then what? Back to the farm where no one wanted her? Her wet suit wilted against her belly with each exhale.

"Can you sit up?" said a male voice.

Liesl leapt up to face him, tall, blond, a spa co-worker she knew by name only. Unlike most of the staff, he wore no uniform, just a rumpled white shirt and wool trousers, and he carried a large leather bag loosely in his fingers, the way a tennis player might hold his racket after a game.

"Oh," she said. "Is his mother coming?"

Something about the man's expression made her aware of her wet hair, plastered to her forehead and ears. She lifted the rank locks and pushed them back.

"I heard the shouts." The man set his leather bag on the grass, kneeling down beside the boy. He spoke quietly to him, first putting pressure on the head wound, then asking Max to squeeze his fingertips and toes, and touching each joint as he did. Without even looking at Liesl, he opened the bag, tossed her a white lab coat, and told her to put it on before she got hypothermia. Chills slid up her arms as she shoved them through the cotton.

"Am I going to bleed to death?" said Max.

"You'll have a headache, that's all." The doctor looked Liesl in the eyes. The frankness in his gaze unnerved her. "Keep a good watch on him," he said to her. "Wake him up once or twice tonight—"

"I'm not—" Liesl said, puzzled. She attacked her wet hair again, trying to sweep it behind her ear. "Do you know where his mother went?"

The doctor looked puzzled. "No."

An awkward silence fell. The doctor pulled out a silver pocket watch, staring at the face. Max sniffed and leaked more tears. Liesl hugged the white coat closer, peering up the hill to the circle of yellow-painted buildings where officers soaked and relaxed.

"You have another appointment?" she said.

"Just bedtime." The doctor gave a comic frown. "I have my own children to get home to."

"That's wonderful. How many?"

His cheeks flushed. "Well, just one," he said. "And one on the way."

Liesl's congratulations faded as Ernst and his father appeared on the crest of the hill and barreled down the grass toward Max. Colonel Steitz wore his S.S. uniform buttoned to the top, his robust body puffing out of the tight black cuffs and collar. Earlier that summer, he had ordered two of his officers to beat up a waiter behind the kitchen. The waiter had made a snide comment about the Führer's height. The beating had left him half deaf.

"What happened here?" the colonel snarled when he reached them.

Liesl felt the corners of her mouth quirking into a stupid grin, but she couldn't speak.

"Your son was just being a good German boy," the doctor said. "He has to risk his life at least once a day."

The colonel laughed and sank down to his knees beside Max. "Twice a day for my boys."

"Ernst pushed me off the log," said Max.

"*Ach*, Max." His father cuffed him lightly on the chest.

"He did. She didn't believe me."

Liesl shrank back, but the colonel didn't even look at her. "No one likes a tattle," he said gruffly to his son as the doctor told the colonel to watch Max carefully that night.

"I want some hot chocolate," Max said.

"I'll be back on Friday," Dr. Kappus said. "I'd like to see him again then, Colonel Schultz."

"Steitz," said the colonel. He gathered Max up in his arms and lifted him like a bride. "You're all right, Maxling," he murmured into his son's wet hair. Ernst stepped closer. Suddenly both boys seemed much younger, and their father larger, like the statue of a man.

"Good day, then," the doctor said, turning away.

The colonel reached out and grabbed his sleeve. "And my wife? Where is she anyway?"

The doctor gazed at the hand twisted in the cloth.

"Frau Steitz," the colonel bellowed. "Where is she?"

"I have no idea." The doctor didn't move, but his neck grew hard cords.

"She had an appointment with you at two," Steitz growled. "Surely you saw her?"

As the doctor shook his head slowly, Max shifted to better regard the scene.

The colonel's eyes began to bulge. "She had an appointment—"

"Oh, that's right," Liesl heard herself say. "She told me she was going for a walk instead." She ignored Max's sudden stare.

The colonel snorted. "Well, they didn't hire you for your brains, did they?" he said, and resumed climbing the hill with his sons.

Liesl bowed her head and waited for the doctor to leave, but he remained beside her, watching the family retreat. Wind shifted over the pond. Near the far shore, a duck paddled alone, its brown feathers ruffled white.

When the family was almost out of sight, Liesl straightened. "Good day, then," she said.

The doctor bent wordlessly and picked up his leather bag. A wadded blue napkin rolled out across the grass to reveal a slice of almond pastry. Whipped cream squeezed out the sides. He made a soft, embarrassed noise, half chuckle, half sigh. Liesl plucked up the cake, rewrapping the napkin.

"For your son," she said, holding it out. The cake was heavy, flesh-weight.

The doctor's fingers grazed hers as he accepted it. "My wife, actually," he said, with a rueful smile. "It's a bribe."

Liesl picked up her bloody robe and folded it under her arm.

"She wants to know why I won't bring her here," he said. "Our little Hans could run around and she could relax. She deserves to relax."

"It's a good place for that," Liesl said.

Water trickled down her scalp.

"Pardon me," he said, and grabbed his bag. "Who are you here with anyway?"

Liesl blinked. On her index finger was a tiny tuft of whipped cream. She rubbed it away with her thumb, spreading the grease. She felt him watching her. She forced her voice to be light. "I run the *Kinderhaus*." She pulled off one sleeve of the coat, but there was a sudden motion beside her, like a bird flying past her waist. When she looked down, she saw his broad hand encircling her wrist.

"Please keep it. You're still cold," he said, and showed her the prickled skin on her arms.

She'd refused, of course, blushing. Frank had shrugged, checked his watch, and rushed away, patting the cake in his pocket.

The hospital where Frank used to work was an old castle of a building. Its plumbing and lighting dated from the days before electricity and running water, and it had adapted uneasily to modernization. Iron hooks for oil lamps still remained, curving like torture instruments from the walls. The new lighting gave the old plaster a damp, cheesy hue and drove the spiders to the darkest corners, where they spun deep furs and dotted them with egg sacs. The engineers had not been able to submerge all the new pipes, so cords of metal ran everywhere, catching Liesl's reflection and warping it as she hurried down the corridor to the medical records office.

The pram rattled before her. Jürgen's hat slid off just as she reached the door. She stretched down to straighten it. When her fingers grazed his bare skin, she halted. She cupped her palm over his forehead. Hot. He rolled his face away and whimpered. She touched her own brow for reference. It didn't feel much warmer than her hand. The baby blinked, but his eyes seemed unfocused. She ought to turn around. She ought to turn around right now, but she had promised to help Uta.

Inside a man sat before a large collection of ledgers. They rose in neat towers all over his desk and lined the shelves behind him from floor to ceiling. A few gaped open on the desk, exposing long columns of numbers and letters. The air had the stifled quality of a room that contains too much paper. The man did not look happy to see her. His hands drifted fitfully over his columns as she explained that her husband needed to get in touch with an old colleague.

"He has a special case just like one Dr. Schein had," Liesl said, hoping the excuse would be enough.

The man checked his stacks with his eyes. He seemed afraid that she would make some sudden move and knock them down. He softened slightly when he heard Frank's name but insisted it was not part of his job to handle the addresses of outside doctors. His job was handling *patient* records at *this* hospital.

Well, then who might be in charge of the addresses of doctors?

The man shrugged. Had she tried the registration office in the *Reichsbüro*?

"He's not listed," Liesl said. Jürgen began to cry and she picked him up, patting his back.

"I don't have time for this," the man snapped. He glanced side to side, as if he suspected someone else was hiding in the room with them.

Jürgen moaned. Liesl set him clumsily back down in the pram. She pulled his blanket over him, then pulled it off again. The baby twisted. Suddenly he no longer resembled a miniature human, but some other life-form, something trapped.

"I really can't help you," the man added, yet at the same time he slid across the desk a directory. It was a big book, with tiny handwritten corrections. Liesl swayed there a moment, hovering over Jürgen. The baby grabbed for a ribbon she'd tied to the pram handle. She gave it to him and he began to suck on the satin.

The man cleared his throat.

Liesl grabbed the heavy book and sat down. It was organized by type of practice, and then by city or town. She didn't find Schein among gynecologists, so she began looking in every category, scanning for his name, secretly hoping not to find it. The man at the desk looked at her from time to time, and then back to his stacks.

She had been in the room with Uta that day. Uta had insisted on her presence, groping for Liesl's hand but clamping her wrist instead. *I won't do it without her.*

Liesl had watched Uta, gassed and half asleep, while the doctor did his work. She had kept her eyes on her friend's slack, quiet face, but she had heard the clatter of instruments, the slurry noise of flesh coming out of Uta's body, then slapping the basin. Uta had been spared that. Uta had woken up in pain, but freed. She hadn't witnessed a murder. Liesl had.

Jürgen began to kick his feet against the side of the pram. She towed it back and forth with her free hand. The baby spat out the ribbon. Soon he would wail. She was only halfway through the listings. The old man glared at her and clacked his dentures. His skin was the same color as the walls. But she didn't have time to return his scorn—a cry erupted from Jürgen's mouth, a full-fledged scream, as if someone had just stuck him with a knife. She leaned over him and the book slid from her lap and crashed to the floor. The man at the desk glared. She leapt up and shoved the pram out, bashing the threshold.

Outside, she pressed Jürgen to her chest. She carried him all the way home, the boy sobbing, then lying hot and quiet in one aching arm. Her other hand pushed the empty pram, its pale insides shaking over the cobblestone.

Uta was sitting with her feet dunked in steaming water when Liesl burst in and set Jürgen down on the table, stripping him.

"Where are the boys?" Liesl said.

"They've been playing in the cellar," Uta said. "I can't stand it down there but I've been listening."

Jürgen began to cry again as she exhumed him from his clothes, but even beneath the noise, she thought the cellar was too quiet. She wedged the half-naked baby against her shoulder and walked to the head of the stairs, calling the boys' names.

"That child's going to catch a cold," Uta observed.

"He has a fever," Liesl snapped. "And I didn't get the address."

Uta was silent. Her bare feet stirred in the water.

"The boys might have liked a hot bath, you know," Liesl said. "Did you ask?"

"I should have gone," said Uta. "Was it a man in charge? I'll go tomorrow." She pulled her feet out of the tub and wrapped them in a towel.

Liesl took the naked child in one arm and filled a bottle of cool water with the other. She pressed the nipple to his lips.

"Hans, Ani!" Liesl called, and tickled the baby under the chin. His mouth remained closed. "I left you in charge of them. It's cold down there," she said.

"They won't have anything to do with me," said Uta. "They know you don't want me here."

Finally Jürgen's lips opened and the water went in, just a few drops. He squirmed and made a tiny sad sound.

"Of course I want you here." Liesl tried the nipple again.

Uta tilted her head. "*You* aren't pregnant, are you?" she asked softly.

"No." Her monthly bleeding had come, regular as clockwork, two days after Frank had gone.

"Maybe I should go today," Uta said, reaching for Liesl's boots. "Is it far?"

Before Liesl could answer, shoes pounded up the steps from the cellar. Ani fell into the kitchen. Hans stumbled and toppled over him.

"What are you doing?" Hans shouted, rolling and scrambling to his feet, his eyes traveling to Uta holding his stepmother's boot. Red spots bloomed on his cheeks. "Where is she going? I can stand in the ration lines. Herr Berger likes me. He gives me the best bones."

Liesl turned her back on them and curved herself around the baby, shushing him although he hadn't made a sound. His eyeballs bulged in his hot head. She held the cold bottle to his cheek, then belly.

"Why's my baby brother naked?" she heard Hans say.

"I don't feel good, Mutti," came Ani's voice.

She pivoted and touched his brow. Cool. His eyes were muddy, lost, but not burning. "You don't have a fever," she said. "Lift your shirt."

Ani's ribcage showed as he flashed his abdomen. No spots.

"Does your throat hurt?"

Ani shook his head. Jürgen cried weakly, tears squeezing from his eyes.

"Shh, shh," Liesl whispered, wiping them with the corner of his blanket.

"You'll be all right, Ani," Uta said. "Your brother needs her now." She shooed them away, back to the cellar, telling them to play a little longer while their mother got Jürgen to sleep, to be big boys and she would give them each a special treat from Berlin. Liesl heard Ani protest and Hans tell him not to act like a baby, and she was relieved when the footsteps descended again. It was too damp and chilly downstairs for two growing boys, but they would be safe there, no matter what.

For three days, Hubertstrasse 6 fell into an uneasy routine. Liesl nursed Jürgen around the clock, monitoring his fever as it spiked. Uta watched the boys in the morning and then went outside with Hans in the afternoon to get food. The man at the records office promised to write his contact in Franconia, but it could take weeks for a reply. Meanwhile Uta cooked, Uta washed dishes, Uta swept floors. Her blond hair fell everywhere, snagging on the sofa pillows and curling in the sink, clinging to the kitchen broom. Her humming filled the air. She was bossy and abrupt with the boys and they did not like her. Hans faded into the farthest parts of the house, and Ani stayed close by Liesl's side. He slept and read beside his younger brother, acting like a second, bigger baby. When he woke, he always complained about his stomach. Liesl was sure it had something to do with Uta's oddball cooking, but she told him they should be grateful. Without Uta, they wouldn't be eating at all.

"I don't know what we'd do without her," she said to Ani. "You'll get used to her food."

"I don't want to." Ani frowned. Were his cheeks unusually pale? She stared at their curves and hollows. For a moment, he looked like an unearthly creature, and then he was Ani again, complaining. "She's the worst cook in the whole world."

Jürgen's eyes opened and he began to wail. He reached for her. She scooped him up and pulled him to her chest. The wails diminished to sobs.

"The worst cook in the whole world," she said over the mewling. "Are you sure?"

Ani nodded.

She checked the baby's temperature with her palm. Cooler than yesterday, but still too warm. "Then you haven't heard of the cook in Clever Lina's house," Liesl said, thinking of her fairy tale book. "Now, he was awful."

Ani's eyes grew bigger.

"I don't suppose you know about Clever Lina," Liesl said with mock disappointment. She set the baby down on a blanket. "She had a little brother that she found in the nest of a tree. She called him Birdie. She loved Birdie, but her father's cook hated him." She paused, realizing how awful the next part would sound.

"Why did he hate him?" asked Ani.

"He was an extra mouth to feed. So Clever Lina took Birdie and ran away."

Jürgen's bottom lurched up and he heaved himself forward on his arms. It was the first time he'd ever propelled himself anywhere.

"Look at him," Liesl crowed. He had to be feeling better. She cheered, and Ani clapped his hands. They watched Jürgen lurch again. He grinned and gurgled.

"What was the story?" Ani said in a funny voice. "What was the story you were just saying?"

She met his troubled eyes and frowned. He didn't usually forget plots.

"The one about Clever Lina?" she said.

"Yeah, the bird. What were you saying?"

"Does your stomach still hurt, Ani?" she said.

"But what is it . . . the story you were telling?" He sounded frustrated. "What's the story you were telling?"

"I'll tell you at bedtime. Don't worry. Clever Lina saves her brother. Does your stomach still hurt?"

He moved his palm over his ribs. "A little."

"I'll cook tonight," she promised. "And I'll tell you the whole story later."

"All right," said Ani, and when their eyes met she saw his hopefulness.

"Come here," she said and hugged his thin shoulders. "We're going to fatten you up," she said into his hair. His head smelled sour and plastery, like the basement walls. This poor winter-war child. He was like the parsnips her aunt used to send her to dig from the root cellar in January, damp and pliant, all the sun gone from them.

At bedtime, Ani asked to hear the cook story.

"About Clever Lina?" Liesl said.

Ani nodded. "You remember that one you told?" he said. "It's really good, Hans."

"I probably already know it," said Hans. But he was the one who listened to her while Ani dozed off.

Clever Lina and her brother ran away together. Soon they heard the cook's messengers coming after them.

"Never forsake me, and I will never forsake you," she said, and the boy promised. And she changed him into a rosebush, and herself, the rose, and the messengers went home, baffled.

"You fools," cried the cook. "Cut down the rosebush and fetch me the rose."

But the next time, Lina made the boy promise again. Again, she changed him, this time into a church, and herself, into a bell, and again the messengers went home.

"The cook was so mad that he went himself the last time," Liesl said. Ani's breaths were deep and easy. She fell silent.

"And that's it?" said Hans from the depths of his blanket.

"No," said Liesl, and she described how Lina made Birdie promise a third time, and changed him into a pond and herself into a duck. She told how the cook tried to drink up the pond, and the duck drowned him, and Lina and Birdie went home safe. But she couldn't help feeling the story was already over long before.

The true end was the vow that brother and sister had made to each other.

Never forsake me, and I will never forsake you.

They could change into anything—they could survive it all—as long as they promised that.

The next afternoon, Ani cuddled with his baby brother again and slept in the window. Liesl left them and went to Frank's files and found the name of the doctors he'd recommended. She dialed one number and found it was disconnected. She dialed another and was told the doctor had been drafted. "Do you know anyone who makes house calls?" she asked the sharp female who answered, and got the number of a certain Dr. Becker. On the phone, Dr. Becker sounded brusque but he agreed to come the next day.

Just after she hung up, there was a light rap on the door. Liesl peeked from the second-floor window: A uniformed teenager stood on the stoop, his black boots grinding into the snow. Clouds of breath gusted from his mouth. It was bad news. It had to be. But Frank was playing the model German now. No more packages, he'd instructed. No more fantasies of escape. It was Uta's lover, then. He had tracked her down.

"*Heil* Hitler." Liesl clumsily bashed her hand on the knob when she raised it.

Without a word, the boy saluted, held out a letter, and spun around, marching down the walk. Liesl ripped the envelope open with stinging fingertips.

The notice was from the housing office. Two refugee families would be moving in next week. Their names were Dillman (five persons), and Winter (six persons), all women and children. Each family would require its own rooms, its own stove for cooking, and access to the bathrooms and the wash kitchen in the cellar. An official would come to start refitting the rooms tomorrow, so they needed to clear all their possessions out now.

She clomped to the gate in her boots, hoping to catch the messenger. Surely he would know more—couldn't he at least tell her where these Dillmans and Winters were from? What sort of occupations they had?

But the messenger was gone, vanished around the corner. As Liesl folded the telegram, she felt someone's eyes on her and looked up to see a movement in the window on the second floor of Herr Geiss's house.

What did we do to you? she wanted to ask. Her boot prints covered the walk to the front gate, making soft tracks in the fresh snow although she hadn't been outside in days. But she had never walked with such a long free step. She never ground her footsoles as she took a corner, allowing her hips to swivel and sway. And what had Uta shouted yesterday, "I'm off to get some Goebbels meat—one pound of bones, and two pounds of snout!" She told Frau Hefter when she walked by with her dachshund, "Your dog is quite the bureaucrat. He wags his tail for you, but he gives everyone else his crap."

Uta still had not found Dr. Schein, but she said she was getting close. The man at the records office had turned up information that Schein had applied for a visa, but found no paperwork about his departure. Uta was sure he was concealing himself somewhere.

"How will that help you?" Liesl said. "If he's not even practicing anymore?"

But Uta stirred a stew of stringy rooster meat on the stove and didn't answer. Twice Liesl thought she saw her friend's hand steal over her flat belly. The gesture filled Liesl with sadness and hope.

"He's awake," she heard a voice behind her say, and saw Ani in the doorway, holding Jürgen. Then the older boy's bright face contracted suddenly and he staggered. Liesl scooped the baby from his arm.

"Careful, Ani," she scolded. "I'll make you some nice tea and tomorrow the doctor will come, all right? We have a lot to do tonight," she added. "We're going to have people moving in. Refugees."

The boy gave her a puzzled frown.

"Refugees are people running away from the Russians. From places where it's not safe for Germans anymore."

When she read him the telegram, she watched Ani swallow and stand straighter.

"Was somebody shooting at them?" he asked.

"Probably," she said.

"And burning their houses?"

She could see the fear in his face. "I don't know, Ani. Is Hans filling your head with this stuff?"

"Will they be hungry?"

"If they are, we'll share what we have," Liesl snapped, hitching Jürgen higher on her hip. "Now stop worrying. I'm sure they'll have children, and you can play with them."

He gave a little nod. She put her free arm around his shoulders and squeezed. "Stop worrying," she said again.

"Can I go find Hans and tell him?" Ani asked.

Liesl looked at the sky, empty of planes. It would be nice to have an hour home alone with Jürgen, to feed him and dress him without rushing with the buttons and bottles and pins. It would be good for Ani to get some fresh air.

"No," she said. "There could be a raid."

"There won't be," Ani pleaded. "I promise I'll be careful. You never let me go out, just Hans."

"No," Liesl said again, locking the front door, locking out the chill and brightness and constant eyes of their street. Eleven people. It would never be quiet in the house again. It would never be hers again.

"Why don't you get out a *Max und Moritz* and I can read it to you," she added a moment later, but heard Ani's footsteps already thumping down the stairs to the cellar.

Liesl was shocked by her instant dislike of Dr. Becker. She had dressed carefully for the visit, in one of Susi's blue wool dresses, which was loose everywhere but had no fading or stains. She let Jürgen whine on the floor outside the Icebox while she raced to comb her hair and fix it back with pins. She had sent him downstairs with Uta and Hans so Dr. Becker could examine Ani in peace.

Her own deliberations made her nervous and irritated. She didn't know precisely what she wanted the doctor to confirm—that nothing was wrong with Ani? Something *was* wrong with Ani: his stumbling, his stomach pain, the absent way he talked.

Her anxiety skyrocketed when the doorbell rang, and she had to ball her hands in Susi's pockets to hide their shaking. Dr. Becker was right on time; he was professional and polite, with a clean soap smell. She could imagine Frank inviting a fellow like him over for dinner, and he would be a tidy eater, and, after the meal, sing folk songs with them in his clear tenor. She told herself there was nothing the matter with Dr. Becker, but she still found herself staring with disgust at the little curling hairs at the back of his head as he walked up the stairs before her.

"His baby brother just got over a fever," she said.

"But Anselm's temperature is normal?" He glanced back at her.

She flushed at his scrutiny. "Mostly normal."

His eyelids dipped slightly.

"I haven't taken it today," she said, and they proceeded in silence down the cluttered hall to Ani's room.

Dr. Becker had the same headlamp as Frank, and before he even sat down to examine Ani, he pulled it dramatically from his bag and let the boy switch it on and off. When Ani stuck it on his own head and peered up, Dr. Becker gave a tiny smile, though he must have seen hundreds of children do the same trick. Liesl smiled, too.

"Ani," she said. "Tell the doctor what's bothering you."

"My stomach hurts sometimes," said the boy, handing back the headlamp.

"He took a dislike to my friend's cooking," she said.

"Anything else?" the doctor said to Ani.

"No," said Ani. Then he added in a smaller voice, "I just keep falling down, but most of the time it's when I'm sleeping."

"You keep falling down," the doctor repeated, his voice rising slightly.

The boy was sitting in a square of light from the window. It made his hair shine, but his skin looked bruised and pale. "I have bad dreams all the time," said Ani. "I fall on people who are falling on other people in a big hole, and no one can get out because the soldiers have guns and the houses are burning behind us."

"You didn't tell me that," said Liesl. Was he dreaming about the refugees?

He raised his face to her, his brow pinched. "Hans says I'm a baby if I cry about bad dreams."

Her collar felt tight on her throat. "*Ach*, Ani, don't listen to your brother. You come to me if you're scared."

Something went dark in Ani's eyes.

"And sometimes when you're awake, you also fall?" persisted Dr. Becker.

The boy shrugged.

"What else is wrong, Anselm?" said the doctor.

The boy shrugged again, his gaze on his knees. He wouldn't say anything more, so Liesl had to supply the answers to Dr. Becker's questions about food and bowel movements and how many hours Ani slept, but the boy's bowed head made it seem as if she had silenced him. That there was another truth lurking, waiting to be found. She ground her fingernails into her palms while the doctor's stethoscope roved Ani's chest and back, as he checked the boy's eyes and ears. One part of her was certain the man would find nothing, and another expected the worst: some terrible cancer or blood problem that would devastate them all.

The room was bare except for the boys' beds, the deceased Frau Geiss's paintings of the sailing boys on the wall. The floor looked scratched and dull, and she wondered when she'd find the time to polish it smooth. Tomorrow it would become their living room.

Finally the doctor nodded and packed his tools back in his black leather bag. He motioned for Liesl to follow him into the hall and closed the door. He was going to tell her something awful. She could see it in his shoulders, the way they humped in his gray coat.

"His brother's fever only lasted a few days," she said to his back. "But he didn't have any appetite, either."

Dr. Becker halted. "You keep mentioning the baby. Do you need me to examine him, too?"

"No. No, he's better now."

The doctor regarded her with his keen brown eyes.

"Truthfully," she said. "You can see him if you want."

Dr. Becker did not let his gaze falter. "Anselm looks malnourished," he said.

Heat surged up Liesl's neck. "I feed them good, hearty meals," she retorted.

"Maybe he's not eating them."

"He eats! They all eat! They'd eat the plates and silver if I let them," she snapped. The doctor didn't respond. She put her hand to her eyes, pressing her tear ducts with her forefinger and thumb. "I'm sorry," she muttered. "I don't sleep well."

From upstairs came a clang, then a grating sound. The man from the housing office was trying to install a stove in her and Frank's old bedroom. She opened her eyes and tried to smile. "You can see how difficult it is," she said. Clang, grate, clang. Her skull rang with the sound. "Sometimes it's too much," she added, and her voice sounded frightened.

Dr. Becker's eyes narrowed. "Of course."

"But then I always tell myself, tomorrow will be better!" she said.

"Sometimes children . . ." he paused. "I see all kinds of things these days. Have you ever caught him eating something other than food?"

"Of course not." She tried to joke, "Unless you count my friend's cooking."

"How long has your friend been cooking?"

"Just a week."

Jürgen's cry echoed from downstairs. He was in their old living room with Uta and Hans and eleven pieces of furniture. They couldn't move it all upstairs, but she couldn't decide what to keep.

"Anselm has been hungry longer than a week, by looks of it," said Dr. Becker. She staggered as he pulled her by the shoulder away from the bedroom door. "I'd have a good look around." His voice wormed into her ear. "See if you find anything in the house that's open. Soaps or paints. If you find something, let me know immediately. I think he's hiding something."

She stepped away, her mouth twisting into a smile. Imagine Ani hiding something!

"But couldn't he have what the baby had?" she said. "Just worse because he's older?"

"Their symptoms don't match," Dr. Becker said. He reached for his black bag.

Clang, clang, and then something heavy grinding in the grit of the floor.

"Maybe it's another illness," she said, faltering at his gaze.

He shook his head. "I find that a doctor's visit is quite a curative in situations like this," he added cheerfully. "Visit me again Friday if he doesn't improve." He began walking toward the stairs.

"But—" she said.

Wood scraped the landing below. It was Hans, pushing a cherry nightstand. "What are you doing?" she said.

"I'm taking it to the cellar."

"The damp will rot it," she said.

"Where else am I supposed to put it?" said Hans, blinking his too-long hair from his eyes.

Bang, thump.

"Good day, then," said Dr. Becker, reaching the stairs.

She heard her high voice expressing how grateful she was that he'd made a house visit. She rushed to the banister and held on to his coat, with just her thumb and fingertip, the way staff guided guests at the spa who got too drunk and rowdy. It was the kind of touch that signalled deference and respect, and she wished he would respond to it, would understand that he'd gotten it all wrong, the hunger was not *in* the house, the hunger had come from outside, from the plane-filled skies, from the burning *Rathäuser*, from the widows and orphans crawling all over Germany with their carts and rags.

"Ani wouldn't lie to me," she said over the banging.

Dr. Becker looked at her hand and gently shook it off. "I'm afraid we don't know that," he said.

Ani was sitting in the pool of light, holding one of his planes. She sat down next to him, suddenly terrified of the crook in his spine, of the bones that popped from his wrists.

"I'm not sick, am I?" he said.

She drew him to her, her skin shrinking the slightest bit when they touched.

"Not really sick," she said. "But the doctor asked you some important questions."

He nodded into her elbow.

"Did you tell him the truth?"

There was a pause and he nodded again.

"You haven't put anything funny in your mouth?"

"No."

"Have you been hungry?" Her voice shook.

He was silent.

"Ani."

"I'm not hungry." He sounded patient, as though he was spelling out a word for her.

She ran her hands over his shoulders. His warm breath gusted through her sleeve.

"Soap doesn't taste very good, does it?" she said in a light voice. "It looks good sometimes, but it doesn't taste good at all."

Ani pulled away from her. "I don't eat soap."

"What about anything... different? Something you picked up outside?"

He shook his head.

"Are you having bad dreams about the refugees?"

"I'm tired of questions," Ani said.

There was a loud crash upstairs. Liesl ducked. Ani covered his ears.

"They're coming," he whispered, his eyes focused on empty space. "Watch out. *Hide.*"

"Ani," she said.

"*Hide,*" he said again, and made the noise of an explosion.

She pried his right hand from the side of his head.

"Ani. I want you to wake me if you have any more bad dreams."

He rolled away from her, his palms cupped back to his skull. "Shhh. Stop crying. They'll hear us," he pleaded in a desolate voice.

Above his head, the children in the paintings sailed on blue water. She smoothed her skirt over her knees and stood, her joints groaning. She felt suddenly old, older than the sleepless night of her first air raid, older than the night Frank left for Weimar. She would have to tell Frank, but how? How could she explain what was happening to Ani? The tendons in her fingers throbbed as she turned the doorknob and let herself silently out.

The next day Liesl sent Hans to the spa to beg one of her old friends on the kitchen staff for some special treats for Ani. Hans came back with a package wrapped in newsprint and a cake box.

"What's in here?" Liesl asked, taking the box from Hans. It felt light, as if there was hardly more than a single slice of cake inside.

"That's *Rouladen*," Hans said, thunking the package on the table. The juice from the beef and bacon rolls had leaked through the newspaper onto his fingers and he licked them slowly, attentive as a cat, as Liesl cut the string on the cake box. The rising scents of the meat made her woozy. Malnourished! Ani would soon be eating the richest meal in Hannesburg.

She lifted the box lid and cried aloud. Inside sat a golden ring, dusted with sugar: a miniature *Gugelhopf* cake. It looked almost too perfect to eat, and it was so small, barely enough for each of them to have a couple bites.

Uta leaned in, inhaling. "It's positively 1939," she said. "Remember how we lived on cake and cream that summer?"

Liesl blushed as the boys' eyes turned on her. She had spent most of that summer alternating between homesickness and euphoria, grateful for her job at the *Kinderhaus* and certain she would mess it up.

"All those cherry tortes?" said Uta. "The almond fingers?"

Liesl shook her head, perplexed by her friend's nostalgia. That morning, Uta had wanted to go to the spa with Hans, to visit her old friends.

I though you were hiding, Liesl had said.

Uta had frowned. *No, you're right. You're right.* But the decision had put her in a blue mood all day, as if Liesl had imprisoned her. Lately Uta had stopped talking altogether about staying or going.

"I don't remember," Liesl said aloud.

"I suppose you were too busy knitting scarves for soldiers," Uta said now. She turned to the boys. "Your stepmother must have saved the frostbitten chins of an entire panzer regiment."

"Let's cut some slices," Liesl said, and doled out the tiny pieces.

She watched Ani's long-lashed lids tremble at the surprising richness. He set his fork down after half a bite. His slice had a curved gouge in its middle.

"Look, a smile," he said, showing it to Liesl.

"Eat the smile, too," she said, watching the sugar glisten in the light.

He frowned. "If I eat it, it will be gone."

"Actually, it will be inside you," said Liesl, her voice falsely bright. "Please eat it."

Hans shoved his last bite in his mouth and chewed.

"Just eat it, Ani," he said, spewing crumbs.

"I can't," Ani said. He pushed the plate away. His chin dropped to his chest, and his shoulders pinched inward, as if he were trying to make himself smaller. "I'm full."

"I'm not." Hans reached across the table, fork lifted. Ani kept his head bowed.

"Not quite 1939, but close," Uta said, pushing her own plate away. "It used to be sweeter."

The older boy's fork kept descending.

"Hans," Liesl said in a warning tone. "That's your brother's slice. You had yours."

"But I'm not full!" Hans said, his face crumpling. "I'm not full!"

That night Liesl made Hans stand before her in his underclothes to make sure he hadn't lost weight, too. He hadn't. In fact he had grown a centimeter, according to the last mark on the closet doorjamb. Liesl leaned over him and made a new mark with a pencil. "You're getting to be such a big boy," she exclaimed, and was surprised when Hans blushed and bit his lip. "I mean, what else could I expect from 'the man' of the house?" she added, quailing at her clumsiness when he shoved past her and leapt into bed, pulling the covers over his head.

Despite the evidence that Hans had grown, she watched both him and Ani at mealtime now, intent that every spoonful she cooked made it into their mouths. She gave Jürgen milk with egg stirred in it, putting the bottle to his lips whenever she could. He twisted his head from side to side, as if to say, "Enough, enough." No traces of his fever remained, and his color was good. He rolled about the floor, bashing chair legs.

"Watch out! He'll get drafted soon," said Uta. "He could take on a Russian tank."

Ani regained some of his old energy. The day before the new tenants' arrival, he joined Hans running upstairs and downstairs, clearing any last valuables from the first and third floors. Liesl delighted in watching him. *See?* she told Dr. Becker in her mind. *Does that look malnourished to you?*

"Why are we scurrying about like serfs?" Uta complained at the constant racket. "They should be grateful to have a roof over their heads."

Liesl ignored her. Labor was a way of dissolving her days into an attainable perfection. A wardrobe could be tidied and polished. A window could be washed of fly specks and dust. As long as she was moving, cleaning, sweeping, she would not become paralyzed by worry. Besides, she wanted to have everything ready for the strangers who were going to take over her home. To have a week's worth of coal piled beside their stoves, a bucket of water for coffee and washing, the sills clean of dirt. To give them washed walls and polished floors, rooms that felt *prewar*, like the golden *Gugelhopf* cake.

Every morning, Liesl woke ready to attack a specific room, a box of unwanted things, to finally clear Susi's clutter from the villa. The man from the housing office came one day with his teenage sons, a horse, and a blue sleigh with paint so cracked and faded that it must have dated to the last century. He and his sons piled the sleigh high with the villa's stained tablecloths, the broken gateleg table, the ugly paintings of grapes and apples.

Their horse was tall and gray, with a lock of black mane that fell in his eyes. A gelding. He was old enough to work hard, but he looked like a handful, the way he tossed his head around at every little noise outside.

Liesl was watching him when she heard Uta come into the boys' old bedroom—soon to be their living room. "I'm glad to have all that junk out," Liesl said. "But it makes me miss her."

"Who?"

"Susi."

"You didn't know her."

"But I do. I can't explain it," Liesl said. Deep in a bedroom corner, behind a box of moth-eaten towels, she had found one of Susi's sanitary pads, faintly stained. She'd stood there, holding the thick cotton a long time, before finally shoving it deep in the linen closet.

"I should go back to Berlin," said Uta.

Liesl licked the corner of her apron and wiped at Jürgen's sooty face. "I thought you were staying to find Dr. Schein."

"I came to find him," Uta said. "But I stayed . . . I don't know why I stayed."

Outside, the mover's sons gestured for Hans and Ani to come closer and they did, cautiously, their hands in their pockets.

"I don't want you to go," Liesl said.

"I know." Uta tucked her blond hair back behind her ear. She no longer set it in curls each night. It was longer and bushier and made her face look round and out of place, like a clock wearing a wig. Yet she still stubbornly wore her gold bracelet, the one Hans-Paul Jost had given her on the day of their elopement. They'd gone into a jeweler's to pick out rings but emerged with the bracelet instead. Uta had thought she'd have the next day to buy a ring. She didn't know that the marriage would be consummated but never officialized, the elder Mr. Jost would intercept them, and Hans-Paul Jost would disappear from her life, leaving her the one shining token of his affection. *My lucky shackle*, Uta called it. A thick, smooth band of French design, it was part of Uta's mystique at the spa, but now it clashed with the apron and the unfixed hair.

"You'll never take that off, will you?" Liesl said, gesturing.

"I had it appraised. Apparently the designer died young and it's worth a fortune now," said Uta, holding up her arm. "But no. It reminds me of where I came from." There was an edge in her voice.

They regarded the boys together. Ani seemed much smaller than his brother.

"He's doing better," Liesl said hopefully. "Don't you think?"

"Maybe," Uta said.

"I think he probably just got what Jürgen had," said Liesl. She sat down on the sofa, picked up the baby, and let him play with her shirt buttons. "I don't think we need to see that doctor again, but I do need to build Ani's strength back up. I wish there was some way to get some lamb. My aunt used to make a wonderful lamb in sour cream."

Uta turned away from the window, her mouth compressed to a line.

"Even a little liver, instead of all this gristle and bone," Liesl said lightly. "Frau Hefter, how does she feed six children?"

When Uta didn't answer a second time, Liesl set Jürgen down on the floor with some metal spoons. "I'm trying, you know," she half shouted. To hide her tears, she thundered downstairs and all the way outside. She passed Hans and Ani, both watching the horse with wary, worshipful faces.

She walked right up to the gelding and reached out to comb his nose with her fingers. The velvet nostrils flared. She ran a hand along his neck. His fur tickled her palm with delicious spikiness, but when his musty, salty scent washed over her, the tears began to spill. Her mind flooded with images of the farm where she'd grown up: the steam of the barn in winter, the draft horses looming, giant as trees. She had always been lonely there, even caring for her nieces and nephews, but life hadn't hurt so much. She wished she could see the animals again: their dusty, caked coats, the way their eyes did not look straight out of their faces, but sideways, watching everything coming and going.

The horse snorted. He nudged toward her pockets. "You be a good boy," she croaked, smiling into the tears. "You be a good boy, now." Then she brushed her wrist against her face and hurried back inside, ignoring the dumbfounded gazes of Hans and Ani.

"You always liked horses, didn't you," Uta said as Liesl thumped into the room again. "I was always jealous of how much they liked you."

Liesl slid into slippers, picked up Jürgen, and sat him on the couch. He squirmed and made a noise of protest, craning for the floor. She put his fingers on one of her buttons.

"And I know you're trying," said Uta. "There isn't a woman on earth who tries harder than you."

Liesl snorted. "I can think of a few."

The child's fingers pushed her button in and out, in and out.

"It's just—what will you do if Frank never comes home again?" said Uta.

Liesl shrugged. She felt the tears coming again.

"What will you do if this house gets destroyed?" said Uta. Her usual sardonic tone was gone.

Jürgen chuckled and grabbed her hair. He twisted it around his finger.

Liesl's chin shot up. "What would you do?"

"I don't know," Uta said. "I don't know anymore. That's why I'm asking you."

In the window's light it was clear Uta was pregnant now. A sickle of flesh was growing at her waist, under her jawbone.

"I don't know, either," Liesl said. "I have them. Frank. The boys." Jürgen yanked and her scalp stung. "Stop," she murmured. "I have this life."

Uta wiped her face with her hand. She tried to smirk, but her lips wobbled. "I don't want this life," she said. "That's why I should go back. They must miss me like crazy. And I can look out for your husband when he gets there."

"But you're safe *here*," Liesl whispered. "And the baby."

Uta dotted the edges of her eyes with a handkerchief. "*Ja, ja*," she said in the singsong, detached voice that women of their village had used when a crop failed or a barn burned down.

"Is my life really so awful?" Liesl demanded.

Outside, the man slapped the reins and the sled budged so slowly it seemed as if the landscape was shifting around it. Uta fisted her handkerchief and tucked it back in her pocket. She sniffed. "No," she said. "It's not awful at all."

After her disappointment with Berte Geiss, Liesl tried to rein in her expectations for the new neighbors. Still, she felt predisposed to prefer the Dillmans. A humble family of miners from Silesia. They were already clear in her mind. According to the papers from the housing office, the wife was young and her children had simple names like Otto and Gertrude. Their clothes would be threadbare, their teeth crooked and gapped, but their cheeks ruddy, full of health. They would go to bed early, like good country people, and rise with the dawn.

The Winters, by contrast, hailed from a city in East Prussia that had a squalid reputation, and the children had grand, unpronounceable names like Giselher and Dankwart. Furthermore, they appeared to be almost all teenage boys, and capable, Liesl thought, of supporting their mother so she shouldn't have to rely on strangers to take them in. The Winter family business was cleaning and repairing typewriters, which meant they would stink up the house with ink and solvent. And the noise! Clattering keys, dings, rattles, clunks—how would Jürgen ever nap?

Liesl worked to set her prejudices aside as eleven o'clock passed. The families were supposed to arrive at noon with the man from the housing office. Ani and Hans were already stuffed into starched shirts, and Jürgen wrapped in his best jumper. They played miserably under her vigilant watch. Even Uta had risen to the occasion and curled her hair, but it was still too long and hung around her neck instead of her cheeks. She wore a look of amused disdain as Liesl bustled upstairs and downstairs, checking the rooms one last time. They sparkled, speckless and fragrant with the leathery smell of polish that Liesl had applied herself until long after midnight.

Finally the doorbell rang. The two families flooded through the threshold in no particular order, so it was hard to tell a Winter from a Dillman or a Dillman from a Winter, though one family seemed, as a rule, to have darker hair. Preceding them up the railing was a combined odor: wood smoke and urine and sour milk. How long had it been since they'd had a proper bath or sleep? Their clothes appeared pasted onto their bodies; the girls looked like baby dolls stuffed into the wrong outfits. The boys' pants were short as knickers.

They didn't stop still for proper introductions, either. The two mothers craned past Liesl to see the rooms beyond, and the kids burst through to take the stairs and check things out for themselves. Their steps made a thunder and their hands smudged clouds onto the polished rail. Within moments, all shine was gone.

"Dillmans upstairs, Winters downstairs," a new man from the housing office said. He stood behind the families, holding a sheaf of papers. He had a crisp uniform and clean, trimmed fingernails, as if he, too, had dressed up for the occasion. "Dillmans upstairs, Winters downstairs."

But the kids didn't listen. They ran pell-mell into every empty room, and Hans leapt after them, calling out, "Wait, wait."

Ani followed his brother, clinging to the rail. The jerky, weak way he moved caught one mother's eyes.

"Children," the mother said, reaching for the boys who were already too far away.

"He's not contagious," Liesl said loudly, her cheeks burning. "He's not contagious at all."

And then they all were looking at Ani, the kids and the mothers and the government official, and she saw how different he seemed from the other children. Their limbs were made of muscle and sinew, their dirt-smudged faces mobile and full of curiosity. Ani gave them a smile, his usual innocent, hopeful smile, upper teeth poking over his lip, but the blue pallor of his skin distorted it and made it look sad and hungry. "This is my house," he said, his head flicking once, twice, three times to the right, his eyes blinking rapidly. For a moment, the entire stairwell fell silent as the boy twitched and jerked.

Weimar

January 1945

In the cafeteria, Linden, Frank, and Frau Reiner ate the way they operated on patients: together, not looking at one another, making jibes
from the corners of their mouths. There was nothing to savor about
the meals. The cook's chief ingredient appeared to be exertion; he made
his stews with so much noise that people joked that his hands must be
made of the same iron as his pots. Crash. Clank. The pungent, greased-
up flavors always stuck in Frank's throat.

One day Frau Reiner launched into an extended complaint about
the nurse's undersupplied accommodations. "Frau Hupper has two
pillows and she won't share either of them with the new girls," she said.
"Everybody knows, but she pretends she doesn't notice."

"Maybe she's saving her pillows for Herr Hupper," said Linden. "Mail,"
he added, pointing at the delivery boy. Mail. The high point or low point
of a day. They all stopped talking until the boy came to their table.

Frank was expecting a letter from the chief surgeon at the new
hospital in Berlin. He'd written about Hartmann's case, hoping the
surgeon would be intrigued enough to accept the patient. Instead, the
boy handed him a letter from Liesl, and something with an OKW seal
for Frau Reiner.

"It's a transfer," Linden said to the nurse. "They're sending you
away, too."

Frau Reiner ran her finger over the seal and did not open it.

Frank ripped into his letter, scanning the loopy, cheerful handwriting of his second wife. After a few sentences, the words began to blur. He caught a phrase here and there, *housing office* and *they sound like clean families* and *bed in your father's study*, but his mind balked at picturing what Liesl was describing: his childhood home invaded, his sons crushed into a closet bedroom, his wife and baby sleeping on the study's dusty floor.

He let the papers fall next to his soup bowl and attacked the stew. It tasted like a rat's backwash. After a few bites, he set his spoon down.

"Bad news?" said Frau Reiner. She had pushed up her striped sleeves and taken off her white cap, and she looked like a farmwife sitting down for supper.

He forced himself to shrug as he explained the refugees moving into his house, squashing his family into a single floor, while the neighbor's house gaped empty, housing one man and his daughter-in-law. What had happened to Herr Geiss's promise? He'd told Frank that the house would stay off the refugee list. "Just eleven women and children tramping all over my home," he said.

"Bad luck," said Linden. He turned to Frau Reiner. "Why don't you open it?"

Frau Reiner placed her thumb under the envelope flap and tore. Linden tried to scan it over her shoulder, but she pulled away. "I'm going to Berlin, too," she said, her tone unreadable.

"I knew it," said Linden. "And now they'll send me to Bavaria to put the cows to sleep."

"Different hospital," said Frau Reiner, still reading. "But it's in the center of town."

"How romantic," said Linden. "You and Frank can meet by the light of the incendiary bombs."

Frank shifted in his chair. Linden's banter suddenly irritated him. He kept seeing filthy kids climbing on his parents' wedding furniture, sleeping in his beds. One family might have been tolerable, but two? How did such things happen?

Out the window, Bundt pushed his cart to the incinerator, still wearing the same rags for shoes.

"Stupid Polack," he heard himself say. "He thinks I'm going to run. He accused me of it the other day."

His friends looked at him, their mouths slightly open. In all their conversations, none of them had ever mentioned desertion.

"Crazy, isn't it?" Frank took a sip of bitter ersatz coffee. "I'm about to be promoted."

"Bundt?" Linden's brown eyes widened with disbelief. "He can't even speak German. Were you reading his mind?"

"He was reading his smoke signals," said Frau Reiner.

Linden smirked and swabbed at the crumbs in his beard.

Frank felt a rush of aggravation again, this time at himself, for playing along with the endless, pointless joking, for drawing Bundt into it. He folded Liesl's letter. He creased the sentences about the new hordes filling his house, and stuffed them away. He scraped up the last of his stew. The din of the room filled his ears.

After dark, he went to find Bundt. He wanted to buy the shoes back. The least he could do now was to send all his gifts home, to give his family some pleasure.

The Pole had his own small quarters off the main ward. Frank knocked. After a silence, he opened the door and looked in. The room was unheated, no light but dim moonrays leaking through one small window. Frank shivered in his coat. A blanket rested on the floor, folded into an exact rectangle, like a flag on a coffin. A photograph hung from a nail. It showed Bundt and a young woman, practically a girl, with a baby in her arms. That was all. The room had no closet and no shelves. If Bundt had found the shoes, they weren't here. Or maybe they were hidden under the floor. Frank prodded the planks with his toes, looking for a loose one. He heard a voice on the other side of the wall and jumped back a step. Then he realized Bundt's room bordered one of the wards. At night Bundt must have slept on the floor, beneath the level of the patient's beds.

Frank slipped out the door and was halfway down the hall when he ran into the Pole.

"Evening," Frank said.

Bundt nodded and slowed his gait, and Frank slowed, too, but they didn't stop; they kept passing each other. Bundt's ashy smell filled the narrow space.

"Did you find them?" Frank blurted when he was almost beyond the Pole.

Bundt halted. He was holding thick fireplace gloves in one hand and he looked down at them. "These?" he said. "I get these because my hands was burning. From one of nurses." He smiled up. "Pretty one, too."

"I gave you some shoes," Frank said.

Bundt cocked his head. "You gave me shoes," he repeated in a puzzled tone.

"I was saving them for my son," said Frank.

"You gave me boy shoes. For my son?" Bundt's grin widened.

"No. For you." Frank found himself grinning, too, a big, sloppy clown grin. "They're not in your room. I know you hid them somewhere," he said. "Name your price. I'll pay you for them."

Bundt's body went utterly still. His round cheeks fell sharply from their bones. "You search my room," he said slowly. "What I have in there? I have nothing."

"But I'm offering to pay you," said Frank. "How much do you want?"

Bundt's eyes were cold.

"You pay me all your money for a thousand years, and it not be enough," he said finally.

"Never mind," Frank muttered, and started off down the hall.

"Ten thousand years," Bundt called after him.

It was sleeting outside when Frank read the chief surgeon's letter twice, three times, and then scribbled Hartmann's name into the operating log. All the way to the wards, the roof rattled with the sound of the frozen rain, and his mind ran over the confident but respectful tone of his future colleague. The surgeon hinted that if Frank's remote skin graft on Hartmann was a success, then Frank might be able to put together a clinical trial in Berlin. Such scientific study wouldn't end with the end of the war. The promises made Frank heady, but he steeled himself to stay calm. Hartmann's surgery would be a test, he told himself. If he succeeded, if he proved himself, perhaps he could bargain for a furlough to go home before Berlin.

You can't be transferred, he wrote to Hartmann, perched on the edge of his bed. *But he thinks I can try a remote skin graft. If it takes, you may only need a minor second operation.*

How soon?

Frank grinned. *We can start prepping you tomorrow.*

Hartmann seized his hand. Its dry, claw-like texture surprised Frank. It felt like the hand of an old man. He spoke aloud, without realizing it, "It's all right, don't thank me yet," but then he felt the hard thing Hartmann had shoved from his cuff into Frank's. A white wedge. Frank pulled away, and for a moment they just stared at each other;

Frank was conscious that some new kind of transaction had passed between them, not just the sympathy of doctor and patient, or of old childhood friends, but something more demanding and dangerous. His stomach twisted. *I have a career now*, he whispered internally. *I have a wife and sons.*

He rose without speaking and left Hartmann's bedside. He didn't dare glance to see if anyone had noticed, but he shoved his hands into his coat, pushing the wedge of paper deep.

The sleet stopped abruptly and a silence spread over the wards. He heard his own footsteps passing by the foot of the patient's beds, and their broken conversations resuming. He heard one fellow complaining about his frostbitten feet, and another relating the exact recipe for his father's *Spätzle*, and others bargaining for cigarettes and magazines. The patients had an extensive black market, trading goods and services. Once Schnell had cracked down on a patient offering sexual favors, but for the most part the bartering ebbed and flowed undisturbed.

He passed through the far door and entered the storage room, relieved to be alone among the silent crates and bottles. What if the paper was simply a message for Hartmann's mother? Or something humble like a recipe or a list of possessions? Or a will? What if it was intended for someone else? He fingered the smooth wedge. If he opened it, he would be taking responsibility for what was inside. He could be implicated. He could be arrested.

A movement outside the window caught Frank's eye. He peered out.

There had to be at least thirty people walking down the road. They wore dresses and suits several layers thick against the cold, making their figures puffy and oversize. They were all women and children, except for one elderly man. They surrounded a single wagon pulled by a horse. Out of it jutted a tarp-covered rectangle, moored on every side by ropes. A small rip in the tarp showed a golden wood beneath, and the round knob of a chest of drawers. The chest appeared to be the only furniture they were transporting. But the roads to the east were broken ruts of mud and snow—how had they gotten it this far?

Schnell and his guards walked out to the group with their guns drawn, shouting and gesturing. A woman produced papers from inside her coat, and the captain paged through them. Then he shoved them back at her and barked another command. After a moment, she climbed into the wagon and with stiff hands began unknotting the ropes holding down the tarp. Schnell's shoulders twitched as she struggled with the twine. A kid jumped up beside her. The guns rose perceptibly. She ordered the boy down with an anguished look.

Finally the ropes came free and the woman peeled back the tarp, then pulled at the top drawers. Whatever was inside was so heavy, her arms wagged as she propped it up. She said something to Schnell, and he yelled again, his face pink.

With a look of pain she pulled the drawer fully out, and a few black insects rose up. They were smaller than buttons. They circled lazily, drifting down. The soldiers danced back, guns higher. She tipped the drawer. Inside, golden-brown ledges, the sleepy motions of tiny bodies. Honeycomb. They were beekeepers.

Schnell waved them on. Frank turned away, impressed with the woman's calm. Her fearlessness pricked at him. He slowly opened Hartmann's papers.

The first page, in tiny, crabbed handwriting, was an inscription. *Man without a Face—These poems are to be published in the event of my death. They are dedicated to Frank and Otto Kappus.—Heinrich Hartmann*

The second page had only ten words on it. The third, barely fifteen. Frank read and flipped, and read and flipped, puzzled. The poems didn't make any sense at all, their language warped and knotted, their images tortured. There were no rhymes, no rhythmic lines, no sentiments at all except the most twisted kind. What did *black hands / swamp and clutch* mean? *Flog spark cuttle?* Here and there phrases stood out that made

Frank think of that winter, its bleakness and fear and lonely hours. *Only the strong / have fallen*, Hartmann wrote. *When every tree / wears / the shadow / of white.*

Maybe it was brilliance. Or maybe these were the writings of a madman. They certainly didn't contribute to Hartmann's case for sanity.

Frank folded the packet and stuffed it under a ledge. His mind spun back to the surgeon's explanation of successful remote grafts, how some doctors in Strasbourg had mapped vascular tissue and found the greatest concentration in the groin skin, making it most reliable for a remote graft. Of course all this was new, very new, the surgeon warned. Two or three separate surgeries using local flaps would be safer, but that option could take six months. If Frank felt the risk was worth it, then he could try a combination of techniques, remote and local. The chief surgeon seemed to be suggesting that experimentation was the order of the day—who knew how many patients lay ahead of them, and how quickly they would have to learn and adapt to the ravages of war?

Hartmann was running out of time. The graft could be done. It could be done.

Two shots rang out, and Frank peered out the window again. The refugees and their wagon had hustled nearly beyond the hospital grounds. The mothers looked back in fear, but the soldiers weren't aiming at them. They were firing at the ground, leaping back, a strange, menacing glee on their faces.

It took Frank another moment to realize: They were shooting the bees.

Hartmann's body looked shrunken and flat on the operating table. His ankles and feet protruded from the sheet, bony and gnarled, like roots exposed by storms. Linden loomed over his head, showing the patient the silver hook of his tracheal speculum, the machine that would pump ether and oxygen through it.

Linden was a lavish explainer. He claimed that patients were more comfortable if they knew what his machine was doing, as if in two minutes they might digest his several years of training, not to mention the sight of the metal and tubes, and the clinical clip of his words (*intra-tracheal, stop-cocks*). Today Linden was especially dramatic, overcompensating for the patient's deafness with wild gestures and expressions. His hands flung outward. His eyebrows rose and waggled.

Hartmann's gaze wandered from the machine to Frank, and then to Frau Reiner, arranging the tray of surgical instruments. She was clattering, too—her usual lithe, swift movements clumsy and disturbed.

Frank closed his eyes, mapping his stage of the procedure: Remove the scar tissue, make an oblique excision on the right cheek and rotate the fat flap, suture, add opposing sutures, excise remote graft . . . and there he stalled, wondering how fast his hands could work. It would take hours.

"Do you think he understands?" Linden asked from the head of the bed.

"Well enough," said Frank. His arms and fingers were tense, ready. In Berlin, the surgeons would work in teams, learning from each other. He couldn't fathom the luxury of that. He moved next to Linden.

"Ready." He nodded at Hartmann, then slowly peeled away his scarf.

Frank studied the man's destroyed face for the last time. He took in the broad forehead, the straight, even brows and nose, the blasted drain of Hartmann's mouth. He'd grown used to focusing on each half of Hartmann's face separately. Either he looked Hartmann in the eyes above his scarf, friend to friend, or he looked at the wound, doctor to patient, examining the healing tissues, the remains of the upper lip. He tilted the head back to see into the mouth, mapping the mucosal membranes. He noted the tiny hairs growing on the cleft of skin under Hartmann's nose.

"We'll begin then," he said to Hartmann aloud.

The patient made a sucking sound, and his drain-lip flexed. Was he trying to say something? "Get him some paper," Frank said to Frau Reiner. But when she produced it, Hartmann waved it away.

Frank and his assistants retired to the sinks outside to scrub in. They soaped in uncharacteristic silence. Above them planes rumbled, and they all stopped for a moment. No siren. They scrubbed again: knuckles, palms, wrists. The soap was slick, hard, and greaseless, and no matter how Frank rubbed it, it wouldn't lather.

"Might as well wash with a stone," offered Frank, waiting for Linden to twist the observation into a joke. But Linden didn't say anything.

"This stuff would make better ammunition," Frank added.

More silence.

"What's with you two?"

He saw his friends exchange a glance.

"Just concerned about the surgery," Frau Reiner said after a moment.

Frank looked at Linden, who simply shrugged.

But their usual animated expressions were missing. They let him walk first back into the room and took their positions as somberly as pallbearers. *So be it*, thought Frank, irritated. *No time to get cold feet now.*

He waited for Linden to thread the patient's throat with gas. A chill crept over his damp, waiting hands.

They did it in seven hours. Frank's legs grew weary after three and he rested on a stool, but his fingers cramped only in the last ninety minutes: suturing and suturing, first the subcutaneous netting holding the skin together, and then the apposing sutures that would be cut in a few days.

One line ran up the right side of Hartmann's mouth, where Frank had turned the skin inward to repair the damage to the mucosal cavities. There, hair would likely grow soon, furring the inside of Hartmann's cheek. Hartmann's mouth wouldn't be able to move until both sides healed, and then he would have to learn to use his newly made lips, if he chose to try to talk again. Deafness sometimes made it difficult to recover speech.

A thin veil of new skin covered the left side of Hartmann's mouth, concealing more scar excisions. High on his right thigh, blood leaked into fresh bandages. Never had Frank worked so long or so intensely, but he hadn't slipped once, not once in the whole delicate procedure. The stitches would have made a king's tailor proud.

If Hartmann healed without edema or infection, his scars would slowly fade. Within a year, Hartmann's face might look crooked and punched in, but it would have a real mouth, a jawline.

As Frank held Linden's heavy Agfa and took pictures of the finished surgery, he felt a rush of gratitude for his colleagues. They were still working. Frau Reiner was readying hot saline packs for Hartmann's face and the patch on Hartmann's inner thigh, where they'd taken the graft. Linden was cleaning his catheter and machine. He'd given Hartmann enough gas to sleep through his first dressing.

"Thank you," Frank said. He didn't know how to talk to them seriously, to say how much he'd miss them, how proud he was of them all. To keep them from seeing the tears in his eyes, he rushed from the room, saying he would call for an orderly to return Hartmann to his bed. "He needs hourly monitoring," he called back. "I want to see him as soon as he wakes."

The moment Frank passed through the operating room doors, disappointment washed through him. His eyes roved the antechamber with its utilitarian shelves and sinks, adjusting to the lesser light. His murky reflection wobbled over the steel basin as he washed his hands again and blearily shoved his arms into his coat and buttoned it. He realized he'd expected the surgery to foil him in some way, to find himself fumbling with an excision or a suture, and he hadn't fumbled, not once.

Through the doors, he heard Frau Reiner murmur something to Linden, something about "relief," and Linden's hoarse reply, mostly inaudible except for the words "not professional."

Maybe they thought he'd gone too far with this surgery.

Or maybe they had never trusted his skill.

His mouth filled with a bitter taste. Well, it was done. Everything was done here.

It was dark when Hartmann finally started to stir. Frank was already sitting by his bed, massaging his cramping fingers in the dimness. The lights had been turned out in the ward to conserve electricity, but several of the patients had procured their own kerosene lanterns. Shadows flickered on the walls as Frank held up a note.

The surgery went well. Are you in pain?

The patient's dressings quaked and a soft hiss escaped him. Frank couldn't tell if it was a yes or no.

I'll call for some morphine, he wrote.

Hartmann's shoulders convulsed and he began to throw up a green-black liquid. Frank had anticipated nausea after so many hours under anesthesia, but he had to move fast, or the man might choke or tear his sutures. He yelled for a nurse and lifted Hartmann's bony skull in his hand, propping him up, using the pillow to catch the vomit. Hartmann shook again. The vomit smelled metallic. The sutures strained.

Frank heard footsteps and called out an order for morphine, fresh dressings; he heard his voice clear and direct, but it sounded as if it were a long way off, that he and Hartmann were in another room, another ward, away from the rest of them. The skull he was holding was not a head, but a life, and it was unraveling into a sour, stinking spit. Hartmann's convulsions were so violent he would tear out the stitches. Frank gripped him by the ears, forcing Hartmann's head straight. "I don't know if you can hear me, but you have to relax and keep still. You have to keep your mouth still," he said. He heard a wordless, anguished groan in return, and he wrapped himself more tightly around the head, knowing his touch was causing agony.

The retching slowed and ceased. Frank let go. The nurse came. Hartmann's lids fluttered as she reached for his dressings.

"Give him the morphine first," said Frank, shaking with exhaustion. "Make sure he can sleep through the night."

He waited for the shot to kick in but still felt Hartmann flinch as he checked the bloodied sutures. The stitching had held. Frank's relief made him so tired that his eyes stopped focusing. With clumsy fingers, he wrote a note to Hartmann promising that he'd return in the morning to discuss the surgery, and then he stumbled his way back through the rows of beds.

The next morning Frank brought Hartmann's poems in one pocket, and a mirror in the other, touching it from time to time. The mirror felt like a giant coin. Hartmann was awake but immobile, slumped toward his feet. He looked at Frank with dull eyes, then looked away.

Good morning, Frank wrote, sitting down on the edge of the bed. *You're looking well.*

Hartmann didn't respond, and Frank bowed his head for a moment, uncertain how to proceed. The morning after surgery was often the hardest for patients—the after-effects of the nausea combined badly with the patients' disappointment that they would never be their old selves again. Until the moment a man went under the knife, he believed the knife would restore the past, instead of shaping a new future. Frank remembered Alliner weeping silently for hours.

As the silence between them deepened, Frank busied himself with examination: heart, lungs, palpation of the abdomen, the old ritual of touch and listening that joined doctor and patient. Even in the worst cases, it comforted him to go through these tasks. Hartmann's respiratory rate was low, but other vital signs were normal.

With a mounting dread, Frank checked the sutures. Miraculously all but two remained unbroken, and they could be restitched with a local anesthetic. By the light of day, it was clear that the graft skin was a different shade than the rest of Hartmann's face, and pocked with a few hairs that would eventually fall out. The swelling had worsened overnight, which was to be expected, but it made the graft look as if it were straining to break free. He felt Hartmann's eyes on him and he forced his expression to remain neutral. The work was good, the stitches clean and even.

He switched on his headlamp and shone it into Hartmann's eyes. He read the chart. The nurse had given Hartmann another shot of morphine at dawn. He had taken some water and had not thrown up again.

Frank fumbled with his pad, writing an apology, then crossing it out. *Would you like to see yourself?*

Hartmann took the silver oval. He faced his reflection, but his eyes didn't focus.

It's a beginning, Frank wrote. *The mouth will heal the fastest. You should be able to eat solid food in a week or two.* He explained about how hot saline packs promoted circulation, and stressed the importance of avoiding tension on the sutures. *No smiling. You must be a serious man,* he added, wondering if he should joke.

Hartmann handed the mirror back to Frank. He took the pad and scribbled. *You'll be going soon then.*

Before Frank could respond, Frau Reiner gestured from a few beds away, asking him to sign an order.

"How's he doing?" she asked in a low voice as Frank wrote his signature.

"He'll get used to it," Frank said.

When he got back to Hartmann's bedside, he felt for the sheaf of poems. He pulled them from his pocket and held them out, his hand shaking at their barely discernible weight. Hartmann didn't move. He had fallen asleep. His half-shuttered eyes took on a trusting, boyhood softness.

Frank tucked the poems back in his pocket again, suddenly unable to part with them.

Hannesburg

February 1945

Dillman. The nameplate appeared above the Kappuses' within two days of the tenants' arrival. The little wooden slat, inked in a neat childish hand, was the only thing small and neat about the clan, which spilled out of its third-floor rooms and into the wash kitchen at all hours. The four girls (the lone boy, Otto, was serving in the Ukraine) scattered their ribbons and shrill giggles everywhere. They had somehow managed to procure a record player and played their two albums at all hours, dancing their big, clomping feet across the floor. Of all of them, only the second oldest, Frieda, seemed genuinely kind—in a downcast sort of way. She was also the prettiest, having escaped the freckles and frizzy brown heads of the rest of the Dillmans. For this, her sisters treated her with a mix of reverence and scorn.

Frau Dillman trotted about, elaborately, almost joyously polite the first week of their habitation on Hubertstrasse 6. She sang out her praises for the rooms, the view, the neighborhood. But when Liesl confronted her regarding the nightly wail of the record player, Frau Dillman's shoulders grew as rigid as a cornered cat's. After Liesl stopped her a second time to confer over the soggy underthings left strewn about the wash kitchen, Frau Dillman's eyes began to blink hard whenever they crossed paths.

"Overrun and overplucked," was Uta's comment when Liesl complained about their new neighbor's touchiness. "She's too tired to get along."

This was the new Uta, glazed and contented by her pregnancy.

"Can't you side with me for once?" Liesl retorted.

"I am siding with you. You can't change her, so just let her alone."

So Liesl tried to leave Frau Dillman alone, even when the woman complained, in a voice laced with resentment, about the broken heaters in their rooms. "Perhaps someone from the housing office can come," Liesl had said, and made the request, but no one came. Likewise the employment office had never come through with a new housekeeper, and the local Wehrmacht office could not get any more packages to Frank.

It was as if the country were slowly becoming paralyzed. Soon, they would all stop moving, one by one, until Hans and Ani froze in their Luftwaffe games and the Dillman girls in their last dance step.

But not Frau Winter.

Frau Winter was up at all hours, ready to talk. She burst from her apartment at the slightest creak of the steps, her black, old-fashioned widow's weeds swirling about her. Her fierce face looked as if it had been molded by glaciers, a terrain of deep crevices with two frigid pools for eyes. Frau Winter never smiled. Her laugh was a throttled rasp. But there was something intangibly confident and pleased about her, as if she had been waiting all her days for life to turn so brutal, and now that it had, she had the satisfaction of being prepared.

Her teenage sons were never home, so she cornered Liesl. Each of her stories was a swinging fist: When they evacuated East Prussia, her eldest daughter was carrying her infant on a pillow, covered in a blanket. They had to muscle and shove to get on a train. They had to jam in with hundreds of others, so tight it was as if they were hanging by their shoulders. "Like we were the clothes in the wardrobe," Frau Winter said in her sonorous, imperfect German. It wasn't until the next station that the daughter realized that the pillow was empty. Her baby had fallen somewhere.

"And then my Hilde took herself," Frau Winter said, lunging forward, as if tackling someone invisible in front of her. It took Liesl a minute to realize the girl had thrown herself in front of a train or out of the train, she wasn't sure which. She didn't want to know.

"And then Friedrich, *ach.*" Frau Winter had shaken her head. "We had to get off the train to look for Hilde and we could not get another one. So we walked for days and he just collapsed. There was no doctor. Your husband is a doctor, yes? So maybe he would know what happened when a man just collapses like that and says his chest is tight to breathe. Maybe heart attack. But what could we do but keep walking?"

When Liesl blinked, her eyelids felt too dry. She handed Frau Winter the bucket of meager cleaning supplies she'd scrounged for her—a box of soap flakes, a brush, a pile of rags—and fled.

Frau Winter's glittering grief undid her. It made her fear the worst. Frank trapped in a besieged Berlin, and Ani . . . Liesl had taken him to Dr. Becker, who sent him to the hospital clinic to have his blood tested, and now they were waiting through four teeth-gritting days for the results. Ani was gaining weight again, but the Dillmans and their constant ruckus woke him at night, crying out from nightmares. *They keep falling on me, Mutti.* He clutched his belly in pain. Sometimes he staggered as if someone invisible had whacked him from behind. She had the same conversation with him over and over.

Did you eat something funny? Something you ate made you sick.

Nothing.

You must have eaten something.

I didn't eat anything.

Ani. Tell the truth to me.

It was Fräulein Müller's cooking, Mutti, and he grimaced and blinked. *Anyway, I'm getting better now.*

After the boys were in bed, Liesl posited various theories aloud to Uta. Ani had worms. Ani had eaten some poisonous mushroom in the cellar.

"Write to the boy's father," said Uta. "He knows him best."

But Liesl still hadn't. She couldn't, at least not until the blood test results. Frank had just finished a miracle surgery on his old classmate. He needed to go to Berlin now, to become the surgeon he was meant to be. And besides, she didn't want Frank to think she couldn't care for the children. To send them away to his sister, to one of Herr Geiss's contacts in the country. The baby was learning to walk—but not to anyone, just to her. Jürgen slammed his chest into her and hugged her with all his trembling strength. If she left the house without him, he cried. He was too big for his cradle, so she made a pallet on the study floor for them both, and all night he pressed his warm body into her spine and clutched her hair. He was the only reason she could sleep at all.

"Did Anselm admit to eating anything?" Dr. Becker said after he closed his office door, leaving Ani alone in the examining room. They had been inside together for nearly half an hour without her, their murmuring too indistinct to catch any words.

"No. Did he tell *you*?" She didn't mean to sound so defensive.

He regarded her for a moment, then nodded. "He didn't tell me, but his blood showed a high concentration of lead," he said.

"Lead," Liesl repeated faintly. The word conjured images of pipes. Lead pipes. But the pipes at Frank's house were made of copper.

"Enough to cause motor and cognitive damage," said the doctor. "Too soon to say if it's irreversible." Then he lit a cigarette, took a few puffs, and stubbed it out while she summoned a response.

"Could the test be wrong?" Liesl said, her mind sorting through all the possible objects in their house. Hans's toy soldiers? Was he eating *them*?

"Unlikely." The doctor shoved his hands in his coat pockets. "I haven't seen these exact symptoms before, but they're not atypical for lead poisoning. It would also explain the fatigue, the loss of appetite."

Poisoning. The word didn't belong to Ani. Not dear Ani who'd fed his baby brother his bottle that morning, and asked, *Why doesn't milk taste like grass?*

A sudden patience descended over Liesl. "But I don't understand why he would eat something like that," she said slowly. "He's not a baby. He knows what he's putting in his mouth."

Dr. Becker lit another cigarette. "Exactly why this is so troubling," he said. "Very troubling."

All through Dr. Becker's house call, she'd resented him, even though he had been kind. Here in the office, it was opposite. His clean soapy smell had the acid tang of lye, and his brown eyes looked cold. With a shock, she recognized the expression in them. He wasn't sympathizing with her anymore. He blamed her.

"Can't we give him anything? A medicine?"

"There is a chelating agent that would bind to the lead and help him excrete the metal," the doctor said, "but it's risky to use with children." He explained that the agent could cause fever, abdominal pain, even a coma if Ani took too much. A proper diet, and no more exposure to lead, would be safer, and then if—

Liesl cut him off. "I give him a proper diet."

The doctor cleared his throat. "This is a serious case. He's worse than I saw him last. In addition, his recurrent nightmares appear to be infringing now on his conscious mind. He hears voices that aren't there and experiences false sensations. He may need further examination." He pulled out a form, scribbling in it.

"He's a good boy," Liesl said. She heard a soft thump in the other room, and wondered if Ani could hear them.

The doctor kept scribbling. He did not look up as he spoke. "Best-case scenario—he stops consuming lead now, and the symptoms subside.

Worst case—the effects are permanent. The cognitive damage can be irreversible." He set the pen down.

"What are you writing?" Liesl asked.

"If his lead levels don't go down in two weeks, I am filling out a form that requires you to take him to an institution for psychiatric evaluation and potential admission."

She gaped at him. She couldn't fasten on his meaning.

"It's my legal obligation, Frau Kappus. Such cases are best handled by professionals." His fingers stroked the form. "I had some clinical training ten years ago at a very fine asylum in Kiedrich, where the patients are well cared for. And if Anselm's case gets more serious, he can go on to Hadamar."

Hadamar. She knew that name. Liesl reached for the form. Dr. Becker tucked the paper in a folder, out of reach. He leaned back in his chair, regarding her, with all the weight of his medical degrees pulling down at the walls, heavy and glassy. She rubbed her cheeks with her hands, trying to find the right response.

"For the safety of our fellow citizens—" he said.

"Why would you do this to him? What do you have to gain?" she interrupted, her voice finally coming to her.

The doctor looked surprised by her question. "As I said, this is simply standard medical procedure, Frau Kappus. Our system places the decision about a patient's illness in the hands of those most qualified to make it."

"My husband's a doctor," she protested. "My husband is qualified."

"Ah, your husband," he said, his eyes holding hers. "I'd like to hear his opinion. I'll write to him promptly." He picked up his pen again. "What's the address?"

"I'll write to him, and he'll contact you. Good day, Herr Doktor," she said. As she rose, she saw the street below. For a moment the pedestrians all looked alike, all stalled in their places, gray coat, gray coat, gray coat, as if someone had planted them there. By the time her mouth opened to call for Ani, the people were moving again, but she couldn't dislodge the image from her mind.

Liesl held Ani's hand tight as they crossed the street. His fingers had lost their softness. They were just sinew and bone now, and she hated the cold feel of them. She wanted to stop right where she was and breathe on them until they warmed, until the boy plumped to his old healthy self again. Terms from the doctor visit snagged in her mind. *Lead poisoning.* It dredged up memories of reading about lead-poisoned Romans slaughtering their own families. *Chelating agent.* It sounded like something cold and final—surely there was some other medicine they could give to children. Ani was a scared, grieving little boy. She'd seen children with all sorts of silly tics and imaginary friends—could Ani really be irreversibly ill? *Hadamar.*

"Where are we going?" Ani stumbled after her, and for a brief flash, she pictured him in institutional pajamas, skinny and wild-eyed, alone on a metal bed.

"In here," she said, towing him toward the telegraph office. "Just be quiet for a minute." She knew the message she had to write, and she wrote it quickly, confirmed it, and paid with a clatter of pfennigs. She nearly forgot to take her change, until the clerk cleared his throat. She spun away, flooded with nerve. There. She had done it.

"Mutti? What's wrong?" Ani asked as they reentered the street.

"Just keep walking," she said. "We'll talk about this when we get home."

"What's wrong with me?" he whispered. His face tilted up at her, his expression lost and spinning.

She stopped then, and lifted him all the way up into her arms. He was too old to be hugged that way and he sagged as his legs clumsily found their way to either side of her waist. She pressed him close anyway, tucking his head into her shoulder. People turned to stare. She didn't look at them, but from the corner of her eye, they took on familiar shapes—an elderly neighbor from Hubertstrasse, Marta the housekeeper, Herr Geiss. They were all watching her, judging, tensing, ready to report.

A feeling like a laugh spread through her chest.

"Nothing's wrong," she whispered, but Ani was letting go. He fell to the street until his toes touched and then he pushed away from her.

"I want to go home," he said, pointing toward the streetcar tracks. "Can I ride on the outside today?"

"No," Liesl said, alarmed. She smoothed her rumpled skirt. What had just possessed her? She looked up to Dr. Becker's window and saw him watching her.

"Please?" said Ani. "I'll be careful. Please. Please. Please." He started to flick his head to the right.

She lowered her voice to a whisper and cupped his cheeks. His head jerked against her palms. "Not today. It's not safe."

He jerked again. "Another day. Please?"

"All right. Another day," she agreed, wanting to hold him again.

"Mutti, let go," he said.

On the way home, they stopped to pick up Jürgen, who had made a repeat visit to the Hefter household after Frau Hefter's numerous requests. A silent housekeeper ushered them into a parlor where Frau Hefter leaned on a fat, rolled armrest, blond and elegant, holding the baby. Liesl's distaste for the woman increased at the sight of her now, in her cozy home, with all her perfectly healthy Aryan children. No one was threatening to send them away.

"My daughters just fawned over him the whole morning," Frau Hefter said, handing Jürgen to Liesl. "They want more babies. All in due time, I say." She cupped her hands over her belly and smiled at Ani. "Why don't you go find the other boys and girls?"

Ani looked at Liesl and she nodded vigorously, not wanting to appear hesitant. He licked his lip and dashed into the other room, where the gabble of children's voices rose and fell.

"So what did the doctor say?" Frau Hefter asked when he was out of earshot.

"He's fine," Liesl told Frau Hefter in a steady voice. "Just a nervous condition. Losing his mother, and now his father so far away."

"We all have nervous conditions these days," said Frau Hefter, but it didn't seem possible that the war had invaded this house. In the other room the Hefter children with their nanny were engrossed in some arithmetic lesson: counting cups and spoons. Their voices were as cheerful as the Hefters' windows, each of them shined spotless. "How are your tenants?"

"They're settling in," Liesl said, wondering what the other woman had heard.

"Quite a lot of them, I hear."

"Eleven."

"Eleven? That's practically a whole village."

"Yes, well, I should be getting back," Liesl said, anxious to get Ani away from the others, to talk with Uta about the telegram. Had she really sent it? Had she really asked Frank to come home?

"Sit down, sit down," Frau Hefter said. "When was the last time you got off your feet? Have some tea." She poured a cup and held it out to Liesl. A bitter scent drifted up—it was real tea. Liesl inhaled deeply. She hadn't had real black tea since she'd lived at the spa six months ago. She put Jürgen down on the floor and accepted the cup.

"I shouldn't stay," she said, listening for Ani.

While Jürgen investigated the Oriental rug, Frau Hefter started talking about the problems her other friends were having with refugees— petty theft, terrible manners, unwelcome advances. She sounded so sympathetic Liesl found herself sharing Frau Winter's terrifying stories and the Winter boys' careless treatment of the shared kitchen—and the Dillmans, don't get her started on Frau Dillman and her manners. "It's like we're living in a tenement," she exclaimed. "Not one minute of quiet or privacy for any of us."

"You poor dears," said Frau Hefter.

"I know I shouldn't complain," Liesl said. "I know others have it worse, but they act like—like they can just take over."

Loud footsteps slapped down the hall. "Mother, Mother!" One of the gold-haired Hefter girls ran in, holding her slate high. "Fräulein Schultz gave me a perfect score!"

"Show me," said Frau Hefter.

"We had to add up the diamonds in Cinderella's crown and then subtract the lumps of coal in her stepmother's stove. Ten diamonds minus four lumps of coal. That leaves six."

"My goodness. Six what?" said Frau Hefter.

Her daughter turned to her, confused. She gripped her slate with both hands, offering the numerals to her mother. "Just six," she said.

"But they aren't the same thing, diamonds and coal." Frau Hefter brushed Mathilde's hair from her forehead, and glanced at Liesl. "You can't pretend they are."

Mathilde cocked her head. "No. I guess not."

"So it's not a good lesson."

Liesl's cheeks began to burn. She couldn't tell if the woman was implicating her or not, but the meaning was clear: You don't mix with those who are different than you. You send them away. You send them to Hadamar.

"Keep the coal," she said hoarsely, rising. "It's worth more these days."

As Mathilde rushed from the room, Liesl tottered across the carpet toward the baby. Her legs felt as thin as sticks. "I'm sorry, I need to get out of here," Liesl said, but a plane passed low overhead, drowning her words.

"Pardon," Frau Hefter said when the roaring died. "I missed what you said."

"I hate the sound of them," Liesl said, picking up Jürgen and wrapping him in her shawl. "The planes."

Frau Hefter blinked, and for a moment Liesl saw a different expression steal over her face. It was almost sympathy. And then, just as quickly, it vanished.

"I'll never forget one question I got wrong in school," Frau Hefter said. "'What's after the Third Reich?'" She paused. "I said the Fourth. Can you imagine?"

"So, let me get this straight," said Uta. "You sent Frank an emergency message to come home. Today of all days." While Liesl was gone, the broadcasts had come from Berlin. The city was under heavy attack. "But you didn't explain why."

"I'm going to follow up with a letter," Liesl said, biting her lip. Regret was quickly overtaking the bravado she'd felt earlier in the street. Coming home, touching the familiar doorknob and banister, hearing the news of the smashed capital, she had been acutely struck by everything she had to lose.

She hadn't spoken to the boys yet. She'd wanted Uta's advice first, and they were downstairs in the wash kitchen, stealing a quick conference while they took down a row of Uta's stiff dried underthings. Jürgen was napping, and Ani was upstairs playing alone, waiting for his brother to come home from the ration lines.

"A letter? How long will that take?" Uta said. "Your telegram urges him not to wait. You don't want him to wait, do you?"

"No, but I don't want him to put himself in danger." Liesl ran her fingers over the ribbons of a salmon-colored corset.

"To desert, you mean."

The word made Liesl flinch, but she nodded.

"He won't get a furlough. Not now," said Uta. "So you are asking him to run."

"I could send another telegram."

"That would make his superiors suspicious." Uta sighed and looked off in the distance. "Bastards bombed the railroad stations. There isn't anyone at the stations but civilians trying to flee."

Liesl folded her arms. "I can't let them take Ani," she said.

"How hard would it have been to persuade that doctor to change his mind?" Uta said. "Or to get a second opinion?"

"Not hard for you," Liesl said sourly. She ripped the last corset from the line and tossed it unfolded into Uta's basket.

"You can have that one if you want it," Uta said, more gently. "It doesn't fit me anymore."

"I don't want it," Liesl said.

"Maybe Ani does need help," Uta said. "That twitching business is new since I came."

Maybe Ani did. Liesl was sure some parents would be grateful to get a problem child off their hands, to let Germany's exemplary physicians help their son recover from lead poisoning. She might have listened to such advice if Dr. Becker hadn't mentioned Hadamar.

Liesl had seen a doctor from Hadamar once at the spa. She could still hear the cool, pitying way he'd said *minderwertiger Kinder. Inferior children.* She vividly remembered the short film he'd shown of his patients. A boy with two clubfeet swimming toward each other like pale fish. A girl with a drooping, toothy mouth and vacant eyes. A teenager with a mashed-in forehead whose pants still puffed over a diaper.

No, maybe she had been reckless for writing Frank, but she couldn't let Ani go to such a place. She was going to search the house again. She was going to walk Ani's route to school and scour every block with her eyes. She would get a second opinion. Hans would help her. Breath flooded her mouth, tasting of dried soap and mildew and kerosene.

The door slammed upstairs. Maybe Hans was already home. The thought of actually telling him about the lead poisoning made her falter. She could see his stern, boyish face filling with pain.

"He blamed me," she said to Uta.

"Who?"

"The doctor. He made it seem like—" She swallowed. "Like I was a neglectful mother."

"You?" Uta said scornfully. In the milky light of the wash kitchen, her movements looked slow as she bent down and lifted the laundry basket to the next line of clothes. Liesl waited for Uta to say more, but she didn't. She just started in on the shirts, pulling them free of their pins and folding them. Then she sniffed and wiped her eyes with the back of her bare wrist. She wasn't wearing her bracelet.

"You can stay here," Liesl said. "You don't have to go back there."

Uta cleared her throat. She straightened. "I wouldn't spare the rod. Ani ate something. Make him tell you what it was."

"You want me to beat the truth out of my son?"

"Always worked for my brothers."

Across Liesl's mind flashed an image of the Müller boys with their perpetually snotty noses and stained shirts. There wasn't a particle of them that was as sensitive as Ani. She knew children—hadn't she run the *Kinderhaus* for seven years?—and the thought of striking a boy like Ani made her ill. A retort rose to her lips, but she suppressed it. Uta was upset.

"I'm going upstairs," Liesl said. "And I'm going to talk to them both. About the lead." She turned away, then paused. "And I don't want anyone to know about me contacting Frank. Not even the boys. I told Ani I was writing to my aunt. To ask if we can visit."

"Go visit. Get far away from Frankfurt. Get away from any city," said Uta. "And take the corset, for Frank's sake. It'll lift your breasts up into sweet little loaves."

Liesl made a grimace, but she grabbed the lingerie. As she turned away, she thought she heard a creak somewhere in the cellar.

"Who's there?" she asked, her eyes adjusting to the gloom of the coal cellar, the family's shelter, the hole to the Geiss house. She couldn't see anything but the shadows of shelves, and when she reached the stairs, they were empty.

Neither of the boys seemed to understand the news at first. Hans seemed angry for some reason, and Ani looked at her with a puzzled face, as if she were explaining some complex mathematical equation. But when she announced that if Ani didn't improve in the next two weeks, the doctor wanted to send him away, Ani's face crumpled and he wailed like a baby. Hans shot up from the sofa and started flinging wood into the stove.

"That's not fair," he said. "You can't do that."

"It's not me," said Liesl.

"You want him to be sent away," Hans said, his lower lip extending. "And me, too. You want to be alone with my little brother."

"Hans. Watch your mouth," Liesl snapped, but she felt tears blistering in the corners of her eyes.

"I don't want to gooooo." Ani's wailing woke Jürgen, who began his own complaint from the other room, and then Frau Dillman knocked on her floor to protest the noise, which made the baby cry louder.

"I don't want to g-g-o," Ani said as Liesl rushed to the study to scoop up Jürgen.

"Would you please and forever stop being a baby," Hans said.

"I don't want to g-g-go," Ani sobbed.

"Then tell us what you ate, so we can tell the doctor, and all of this can be over," Liesl said when she came back into the room, patting and shushing.

For a moment, Ani's face opened, but then he glanced at Hans, and his expression shut again. "I didn't eat anything," he said with lowered brows. "I didn't."

"Ani," Hans said. "Just tell, or they're going to send you away."

Jürgen squirmed to get down and began to crawl across the floor toward his oldest brother's feet.

"Tell us now, Ani," Liesl insisted. Uta's advice flashed in her mind, and she reached for Ani's shoulders. What kind of mother couldn't get the truth from her own child? If Ani just told, the doctor would trust her. Her fingers tightened over his bony arms.

Ani cowered, blocking his head with his hands. "I didn't eat anything," he whimpered. "You're hurting me."

"Don't hurt him," shouted Hans.

Out of the corner of her eye she saw the baby watching her uncertainly. Jürgen's lower lip began to tremble. Her resolve died. She couldn't do it.

"Then I want us to search this apartment together. Every inch," she declared with hollow conviction. "And then I'm finding another doctor."

"I don't want to go to another doctor," said Ani.

"Our father is a doctor," Hans said. "He'd never send Ani away."

"No, he wouldn't," said Liesl. "I'm writing to ask him to—to contact Dr. Becker." She wiped the wet corners of her eyes.

Hans seemed surprised by her tears and averted his gaze. When Jürgen reached him, Hans lifted him up, looking so much like his father in the motion of his body, the tenderness of his hands.

We need you. Liesl thought. *All of us.*

Jürgen smiled at Hans, but then he looked around anxiously for her.

"You're my brother," Hans said, jostling the frowning baby. "Why can't I hold you?"

Two days passed. Berlin was on fire. Ordinarily Liesl could shove the air raids on other cities to one painful corner of her mind, but with Uta in the house, glued to the radio, moaning and shaking her head, the destruction punctuated every hour. The Reich Chancellery was burning. St. Michael's Church had been bombed to a broken shell. The street of linden trees in Uta's old neighborhood was a sea of bricks and branches.

And through all this, no word from Frank. Liesl was sure that his silence meant that he hadn't gotten a furlough. He must be intending to desert. Or perhaps the telegram had never reached him?

She opened an atlas and looked up Kiedrich and Hadamar, the towns that Dr. Becker had mentioned. Less than fifty kilometers away. Too close. Her dread increased.

The doctor from Hadamar had visited the Hartwald Spa in early 1940—she remembered because it was the winter that Uta had started singing at the spa after lunch, and while she was waiting for Uta to begin, Liesl had overhead the conference next door through the thin walls.

So often the meetings in the spa's private room were military in nature—this or that campaign, the giant oak table overflowing with maps and atlases, the names of Ukrainian mountains, Balkan towns. Liesl was so accustomed to tuning out these conversations that she heard the name "Hadamar" several times before she realized the man was talking about the city near Limburg. And he was talking about children. The hope that he might be some bigwig in education made her drift closer, peeking through a crack in the wall to get a good look at him. She harbored dreams of getting her teacher certificate and running her own kindergarten one day. Powerful men came to the spa. Perhaps this one could help her get a scholarship.

The man at the front of the room was tall and almost bald, with an unsmiling mouth and dark eyebrows that arched sharply downward. With expressionless eyes, he rattled off a set of figures about the cost of long-term mental patient care in the current German system. Two words stuck out to her. He said them often, and each time with a kind of detached pity, the way one might talk about a hopelessly broken machine.

Minderwertiger Kinder. Inferior children.

Liesl watched, transfixed, as he turned on a projector and showed his film of the boy with the fish feet and the toothy blank-eyed girl. The twisted human visages made the viewers grunt and look away. Matches flared as the officers lit cigarettes. The movie went to a black screen with the word "Hadamar," and then a camera revealed a long ward filled with beds, a tall brick building with arching windows.

Hadamar was not a school. The man was not an education official.

Herr Doktor? someone said, and queried about the likelihood of parents releasing their children to the state asylum for treatment.

The doctor smoothed his tie. *A questionnaire is being prepared that will soon go out to all public health officials and mental institutions. A qualified team will evaluate the answers and determine which patients must be admitted and which terminated.*

But what about the parents? the questioner persisted. *Surely some will protest.*

Irritation flashed across the doctor's face. *Procedures will be implemented to ensure parental compliance.*

Liesl pulled back from the crack and strode away. She found a table close to the stage and listened with fierce concentration to Uta's songs, hearing her friend's sensuous phrasing, every flat and sharp note. Liesl stuffed herself on *Sachertorte.* Everyone understood that the Reich's future depended on a strong and able population. These decisions about human potential were best left to Germany's superior doctors. Yet Liesl couldn't help feeling as if someone or something were following her all day. Whenever she looked back, she saw blank sunlight.

Hadamar. She vaguely remembered the bishop of Limburg later protesting the euthanizing of patients at the institution, and that the deaths had been officially stopped by Hitler's own orders. But what had they done to those poor children in the film? She would never hand Ani over.

Unable to sit still, even at night, Liesl wandered dry-eyed and cold through the apartment after the boys and Uta were asleep. She plucked up pillows. She looked behind curtains. She searched the cellar, staring into the sauerkraut vat, wishing it could tell her what secrets it had heard. She told herself that she was still looking for whatever lead Ani had eaten, but she also peeked in high places where he could not reach, and cleaned dust off the curving moldings with her finger. She stood on the black velvet cushions of Susi's Biedermeier chairs to reach even higher. She shook out all the fabrics, the rugs, the curtains, speckling the moonlit snow with dirt. She washed the walls one night, all the way to the ceiling, watching the clear water run over the back of her hand.

Her nocturnal activities made her tired and cross with everyone: the baby for tearing apart a bookshelf and scattering the volumes all over the floor; Hans for abandoning his brothers to play with the Dillman and Winter children; Uta for telling Liesl again that she allowed the boys to run all over her, why didn't she just lay down the law? Only Ani escaped Liesl's ire. He'd become almost heartwrenchingly obedient, his blond head appearing at her elbow every morning, asking how he could help her that day, and she'd think, *There is nothing wrong with this child*. Yet later she would find him in the kitchen, begging some invisible person not to lock him up, or at the stove, trying to melt an iron pan to make shackles for his ankles, and she just wanted to fold him into her arms and fix him with all the love she had.

The second opinion confirmed Ani's lab results. Although the other doctor was kind to Liesl and Ani, he seemed unwilling to contradict Dr. Becker.

"Dr. Becker has the best psychiatry expertise in Hannesburg," he said nervously. "I'm sorry," he added, and rubbed his bald head.

"What do you know about this Kiedrich asylum?"

The doctor leaned forward, lowering his voice. "My advice—Keep the boy out of the state system altogether. All the institutions around here are funnels to Hadamar."

"What happens at Hadamar?"

The doctor opened the drawer to his desk and shut it again. "I'm sorry. I have too many other patients waiting." He called to his receptionist.

"But what am I supposed to do?" Liesl said.

He sighed. "Hide him. Take him to the country."

The country. Just the thought of seeing a farm again made Liesl's heart lift a little. Although Hannesburg had no strategic importance, it could become a target anyway. And yet she couldn't send Ani alone, and how would she get any news to or from Frank if they all left home? How could she decide without him?

Surely the asylum wouldn't admit Ani if he improved. The boy was eating well now, and his color was coming back. If his numbers went down, Dr. Becker would have to rip up his form and let them go home. Wouldn't he?

If, then. These bargains she played with herself. She'd been playing them for years. As if she were the one who held the power, and not him, and not them—the state she'd once worshipped because it had paved over the ache of her homesickness and orphanhood, because it had justified her running away from home, from a conventional life, to be an independent woman.

Motherless, fatherless, Liesl had woken every morning in that first year at the spa, lifted her eyes to the Führer's portrait hanging at the *Kinderhaus*, and pledged him her service. In return, his kind brown eyes offered her protection and a kind of benevolent severity. *I trust you to be a good girl,* he seemed to say. *To keep your virtue.* And she had, knitting socks for his soldiers, nurturing his officers' children, watching and nodding at anti-Bolshevist films in the evening.

She couldn't name the day it started to change—maybe the afternoon she'd met Frank, or maybe eavesdropping on the Hadamar doctor, or maybe when the quiet, gentle piano player disappeared because he was rumored to have Jewish blood. Maybe it was the first air raid siren, or the tenth. Her pride started to leak away and in its place grew fear. She wasn't afraid of getting caught—no, her papers were good, her reputation spotless. Her days passed in the same old way, with the same three meals: a common breakfast and *Mittagessen* with the spa staff, a lonely evening supper in her room. At night, a book, or rarely, when Uta prevailed, dancing with the officers. The Führer still watched over her, but his mouth looked downcast, then cruel.

Then, at some point after 1940, after Paris fell and London was burning, a new kind of etiquette swept through them all like a chilly wind. Suddenly trust and good faith were out of fashion, and it was more seemly to be careful about what you said and to whom you said it. Imperceptibly, Liesl's anxiety deepened, worsened as the Wehrmacht began to lose instead of win, as more citizens were drafted to military projects in the east, and gaunt, dull-eyed gangs of political prisoners fixed the streets. By 1944, everyone was sure the spa would close, the staff deployed elsewhere, back to Berlin, off to factories. A wrong word might get you a bad assignment. Liesl found her eyes shifting from side to side as she spoke, checking to see who was listening. Her spine stiffened and it hurt sometimes to bend to pull on her stockings. Uta planned to go to the capital, to get a job in an officers' club. *Come with me,* she'd begged. *You can get work as a typist.* And Liesl had agreed, until the evening Frank, widowed two months, had walked through the door of the *Kinderhaus* with his wilting bouquet of violets.

If, then. If Frank never came home, then what would she do now?

That night Liesl dreamed of standing alone under a night sky, facing a black hillside. The whole world was behind her, silent, deserted, destroyed. Only the hill was alive. Tall, stalk-like flowers bloomed all over it. They had been burned to a crisp.

You must speak for us, they rattled at her.

She held her hands over her ears, thinking, *Leave me alone.*

She woke the next morning relieved to let the day's routines take over. First stop, a tiptoe downstairs to fetch Jürgen's milk, without alerting Frau Winter and inviting a new barrage of advice. She opened the icebox door, noting that the Dillmans had somewhere procured eggs and butter and had not shared the information. She noted that the Winters had left their dirty pots in the sink again. She poured Jürgen's bottle, set it in a pan on the stove to warm, then added some sticks to the fire.

A board squeaked and she spun to see Hans creeping out of the cellar. His cheeks were pink and he didn't look sleepy at all.

"It's early to be up," she observed.

He grunted and grabbed a heel of rye from the bread box, wolfing it down.

"What were you doing down there anyway?" she demanded. "Are the Winters down there, too?"

"No."

"The Dillman girls?"

"I was sleeping," he said, his voice high and defensive. "Sometimes I sleep down there."

"You'll catch your death. It's freezing." She reached over and touched his hands. They were hot. He looked away.

"Hans, was someone else in the cellar?" Those Dillman girls. It had to be.

Hans didn't answer. One of his cheeks was brighter than the other, flushed all the way across the bone. He bit and chewed, staring into the space between her waist and his body.

"I'm going to ask you one more time," said Liesl. "Who was in the cellar?"

He finished the crust and wiped his hands on his trousers. "I told you," he said. "No one."

"All right," said Liesl. "I'll ask Herr Geiss if he's heard anything."

Hans's head shot up. His eyes burned into her now.

Not the Dillmans. The realization spread. Was it possible? Berte Geiss was eighteen. Hans wasn't even ten yet.

"Hans," she said gently. "Are you—"

Just then Frau Winter entered the kitchen, humming one of her tuneless songs. "Your milk is boiling over," she said.

Liesl lifted the pan and whacked it down on an unlit burner.

"Can I go?" Hans snarled.

She felt Frau Winter's eyes on her, judging the mutinous tone of her son. "No," said Liesl. "You're going to stay within my sight for the rest of this week. No trips upstairs or downstairs, and Fräulein Müller will run the errands."

"That's not fair!" shouted Hans.

Frau Winter regarded them with keen interest as Hans ran for the door. Liesl grabbed his arm but he twisted away and bolted up the stairs.

"You know what I do?" said Frau Winter as Liesl poured the milk, wincing as the glass burned her fingertips. It was too hot.

From the rooms above she heard Jürgen begin to cry.

"No," Liesl snapped. She topped off the bottle with cold milk from the icebox. Was it still too hot? She couldn't tell.

"I think they are running around and around because they are looking for their father," said Frau Winter. "And they can't find him anywhere."

Their father. She tested the milk with her finger. She couldn't tell. The baby's cry shook her skull.

"And so I tell them that Führer is their father. The Führer is watching them," Frau Winter said from behind her. "Because maybe they aren't scared of me. But they are always scared of him."

Liesl ran up the steps, cupping the bottle's rim, wishing she'd brought the nipple to seal it. The white liquid sloshed. Jürgen wanted milk exactly the heat of a body. He recognized that heat though he had never fed from his mother's breast. She heard Hans's voice inside, then Uta's.

What would Frank do about Hans's lying and sneaking around with that girl?

Not girl. Woman. Hans was ten years old.

The stove door slammed, the latch rattling into place. Jürgen cried louder.

"Those peasants and their *hamstern*," Frau Winter called after her, holding up old, soft rutabagas in both fists. "They're hoarding everything. Eating their bacon while we starve in the cities."

Liesl tripped on the top step, her hand slipping on the milk. The bottle clonked on the steps, sloshing half its contents before she caught it.

She heard Frau Winter sigh, a little half-caught breath. Liesl's aunt used to make the same noise when Liesl accidentally dropped an egg or tore her skirt.

Cursing herself, she used her apron to mop the milk. She could feel Frau Winter watching her. The cloth soaked the liquid, already smelling faintly sour. Her eyes watered and she blinked the tears away. "It's not broken," she said aloud. She rose again.

She was just about to enter the apartment when she heard a soft, retreating knock on the house's front door, as if the knocker's hand was reluctant to actually touch the wood. She turned to see the silhouette of a small man standing beyond the window, his shoulders muscular, his neck bulging with a scarf. She hesitated, wondering if he had news about Frank.

"You go to your baby. I will get it," said Frau Winter. She bustled earthward, her old-fashioned black skirt rustling.

Liesl ran up the steps.

"Someone is here," she shouted to Uta, bursting through the door, grabbing Jürgen from his cradle. "Where did Hans go? Did you see him?"

"He went to his room," Uta said. She had abruptly stopped listening to the radio. Her panicked look was gone, replaced by dull incomprehension. She deflated into the sofa each morning until she was nothing more than a hump of wool afghan. "Who's here?"

"I don't know. It looks like a tiny man," said Liesl, and then she heard her neighbor's voice rising from downstairs: "Fräulein who?" and then, "Fräulein Müller!"

Uta's face contracted. With sudden energy, she threw off the blanket and leapt up.

"Hide me," she said, pressing her rounding belly. She had taken to wearing Liesl's apron all the time, like a *Putzfrau*, and her pale thumb traveled over a stain from yesterday's chicken soup. "Tell him I've gone."

"Don't be ridiculous. It's probably just a telegram for you," said Liesl, hoisting Jürgen so he balanced on her hip. He reached for the milk. She held the bottle higher. "Hans!" She yelled in the direction of the closet he shared with Ani. "Where did he go?"

Uta grabbed the afghan and padded across the room to the balcony door, flinging the blanket over her shoulders. "I'm not here," she said in an urgent voice, tugging at the lock, the hasp. "Don't let him find me."

Liesl set the milk down on a table, almost dropping it again.

"It's too cold. You'll catch your death," she hissed. She could hear Frau Winter talking loudly to the man below.

"Help me get this door open," Uta pleaded. "Please."

Jürgen bawled.

"Please," Uta repeated, yanking on the handle.

Liesl set the baby down in his cradle again, letting him wail as she helped her friend slide the door open and tiptoe in her stocking feet to the part of the ledge that was hidden by wall. "Here," Liesl said, and kicked off her boots, throwing them at Uta. Uta shoved her small feet into them. Her mouth had crimped at the edges and her blue eyes stared out from a stiff mask. Even her blond hair looked suddenly darker, as if someone had soaked it in oil.

She stood against the wall, looming over the back garden, the view of the brewery, the roundness in her figure shrouded by the blanket. Her breath gusted and vanished.

Jürgen squalled. Liesl shut the balcony door, cold air blasting over her. She scooped the baby again in her arms. "Shh," she said, and grabbed a nipple, ramming it on the bottle, her hands fumbling, then succeeding, popping it in the baby's mouth. "Hans," she said.

Knuckles rapped on the door. "A visitor for you," Frau Winter sang out.

"Hans," Liesl said again. "Can you get the door?"

"A visitor for Fräulein Müller," Frau Winter said.

"She's not home," Liesl sang back. Signs of Uta were strewn all over the room: her cigarettes, her handwriting scrawled on a shopping list, a ghost of her lipstick on a teacup.

There was a silence outside, and then a knock, harder.

"Hans," Liesl said. The boy did not appear. Jürgen guzzled, milk leaking from the corner of his mouth. The knock.

"Frau Kappus," said a man's voice. It was silky and officious. "Open up, please."

"Just a moment," Liesl said, smoothing her hair, licking and biting her lips to bring blood into them.

Still she waited. The boy must be hiding in his room. No time to bother with him now. She carried Jürgen to the door, his mouth still working the nipple.

"*Guten Tag,*" Frau Winter's voice said again. "Frau Kaaaapp-usss. This is her door. She is wife and stepmother to three—"

"*Herein, herein,*" Liesl said, her hand trembling on the handle.

The man's eyes were exactly at the height of hers and she saw them first. They were darker than black coffee and set deep and close together, and they absorbed her in a glance. His mouth was sensual and full. His lips quirked when she touched her bare neck, as if he had anticipated the effect he would have on her.

"May I help you?" she said.

"He comes to see Fräulein Müller," said Frau Winter.

Jürgen sucked at the last of the bottle, making squeaky, slurping sounds. He'd drunk it too fast. She raised him to her shoulder and thumped his back.

The man cleared his throat.

She gave him an apologetic smile. "Oh," she said. "You must be Herr Heinz," she said, inventing a surname. The man didn't blink. He was staring past her, into the apartment.

"No," he said, and introduced himself. His voice was deep and pleasant. "She wasn't expecting me."

"Well, I don't recall that name, but Uta knows so many people," Liesl said.

The man stepped across the threshold and shut the door on Frau Winter's jutting chin. His lightless eyes soaked in every centimeter of the room. His silence and the way he searched unnerved her. She couldn't quite put her finger on it. It wasn't just looking that he was doing, but hunting. Her spine hurt from standing stiffly. The baby felt like lead in her arms. What was she supposed to say to this man? Uta hadn't told her what to say.

"Maybe she mentioned you and I forgot," she said. "My sons have been ill and I can't remember anything these days. She left yesterday."

He eyed the impression in the sofa pillows. "Where did she go?"

"I don't know," said Liesl. The words were tumbling out now. "She wouldn't say. But she was terribly worried about her friends in Berlin. Did you come from there?" She took the empty bottle from Jürgen.

The man didn't answer. Liesl could feel the presence of Uta on the balcony, freezing around her unborn child, as the man's eyes traveled over the cuckoo clock, the painted Madonna, their little black radio, the rocking horse with the nearly hairless mane. A chill went through her. Through his gaze, she saw how easily each of these everyday artifacts could be unstitched, undone: the radio wires ripped like guts, the horse's glass eyes picked out.

To fill the quiet she chattered about Frank's deployment to the capital.

The man barely nodded at her prattle. Instead, his eyes moved to Jürgen, fastened to her side. The baby looked up, solemn, with Frank's blue eyes. The man smiled, and his face brightened until it was boyish and charming again.

"Fräulein Müller—she was well?" he said.

"She didn't catch anything from us, thank goodness," said Liesl.

Jürgen chuckled, and the man smiled again. And then, as if it belonged to a separate body from the smile, his hand reached out toward the baby.

"He's not yours, is he?" he said. His palm covered Jürgen's entire skull, the baby's ear, his golden hair, then his eyes.

Liesl wrenched Jürgen away, holding him so tight he cried out.

"She was only here a few days," she whispered.

"A few days?" He sounded bored. She followed his eyes out the window. The winter light made a distance of the town—the shuttered houses, the park with its withered gardens. And the imaginary ripping began again: the roofs unthreaded, neighbors unraveled from their clothes and left naked, corpses. He wasn't looking at her, but she had never in her life felt so exposed.

"I told you, my children have been sick," she heard herself whine. Her knees buckled and she had to grip the sofa to stand.

"Tell her I'll be back for her a week from Sunday." He opened the door.

"Don't take the book of Mother," Ani said.

Hans looked up from shoving his spare shirt into a rucksack. His brother lay on the narrow bunk across the small closet where they slept. Hans wished Ani would get up. He wished Ani would make sense when he talked. But the frail-looking boy on the bed no longer responded to his will. Ani suddenly seemed impervious to all outside influences: Hans's exhortations to play, their stepmother's constant questioning, even the threat of the doctor taking him away. Instead, Ani staggered and flopped around, muttering replies to invisible people around him, mixing up words. The worst thing was, he didn't trust Hans enough to tell him what he'd eaten. The worst thing was, Hans couldn't trust him to stop.

Ani's sickness was like having a troll in the house, a great hulking, hairy thing that couldn't be overlooked or drowned out. It followed Hans: into the bathroom, which smelled funny after Ani's use, in the closet bedroom, where he woke to Ani slapping his head against the wall. The troll said nothing, but the look it gave was troubled and greedy. It cast its giant shadow everywhere, except down below with Berte. There in the cramped dark next to the girl, the troll did not come. It could not pass into the circle of air that seemed to vibrate around Berte like a kind of wordless singing. Hans had never looked at a girl so much, or been so entranced by another body: the smooth way she rose and sat, her awkward little laughs, the feathery touch of her hair on his arm. Sitting beside Berte, Hans felt his mind sharpen with purpose. She wanted to escape. He would help her. He did not think past that moment, that resistance, or how he would feel if Berte was gone. He pictured only his defiance. He would help her, and hurt them.

"I mean Mother's picture," said Ani now. "You're running away, aren't you?"

"I'm not running," Hans muttered, and put his palm to his brother's brow. "Do you have a fever again?"

Ani's forehead was cool. "I never had a fever," he said. His eyes clouded in some indefinable way. "I'm glad you're staying."

"I'm not staying."

"But you said you were."

"I'm *going* away. Not running away."

"Why?"

Hans couldn't explain. He didn't understand it himself, but he could still feel the pressure of Berte's arms around him in the cold cellar air.

"I don't have to be a prisoner here," he mumbled.

Ani poked his finger through the gap in the blanket. "Hide," he said urgently to the air in front of him and ducked his head. "There isn't much time."

There was a commotion in the hall outside, like a flock of birds descending, the voices of his stepmother and neighbor separate at first and then all chirping at once.

"It's almost too late," Ani whispered, his eyes hollow.

Hans threw his rucksack over his shoulder. "You hide. I'll be back soon," he said. He crept from the closet room and into the study, where a second door led out on the staircase. He listened until he heard his stepmother and the stranger enter the apartment through the front.

Then he slipped out, passing a railing he'd cracked with a flying ball a few days before his father left for Weimar. Vati had been furious. *You don't know who's down there,* he'd shouted. *You don't know who you might hit!*

He'd grabbed Hans by the shoulders. *I was six years old when my father left for war, and I had to become the man of the house, understand?*

Hans reached the door.

Outside the air would be gray, and the open lawns of the Kurpark would seem like targets for enemy planes, and the streetcars would be running late, if at all. He would go farther than he had ever walked alone, past the hospital where his father had worked, and to another train station, where he would meet a man coming from Berlin and give Berte's letter to him.

You're the only one who understands me, Berte had said.

His stepmother called his name upstairs. The house began to close around him like a coat.

The man who opened the door to their apartment was so short his elbows bent to hold the stair railing. Yet his eyes made Hans think of tar.

"I'm sure she went back to Berlin," he heard his stepmother say from inside. "She was so bored here." Then her frightened face appeared by the man's shoulder. "Hans," she cried.

He turned and ran.

A long minute after Liesl's knock, Berte Geiss came to the door. She was wearing the same outfit she always wore, a gray cropped jacket and tight skirt, her hair fluffed around her young face. She wore an orange and red scarf in her pocket and traces of lipstick, like an American actress. She looked neither pleased nor worried to see Liesl.

Liesl held a parcel in one arm and Jürgen in another, a heavy wool shawl draped around them both. She'd never felt old in this neighborhood of plumping wives and haggard refugees, but Berte Geiss's sleek combination of glamour and insouciance unsettled her. The girl was playing a part in a movie, not living real life.

"*Guten Tag*," Berte said, opening the door. "My father-in-law is out."

"I came to speak to you," said Liesl. Her body still felt wobbly and tense after Uta's lover's visit, her friend's pale weeping, but her head was clear. She would find Hans. She would keep her sons close.

Berte eyed her coolly. "Your baby is getting fat," she said. "That's good, isn't it?"

She didn't invite them in, so Liesl walked up the stairs, until their bodies flanked each other and Berte had to step back or push them over. Berte gave way, letting them into the warm, dim vestibule. "Excuse me," she squeaked. And she pulled out a handkerchief and dabbed her nose.

"Excuse *me*," said Liesl. "I won't stay long. My eldest son has run away. I thought you might know where he is."

"Try the market? He's obsessed with running errands for you," Berte said, coming to a stop beside a buffet table. A heavy china candelabra drooped over it, filigreed with cobwebs. Liesl had feathered it clean last time she was here. The drapes were closed, but she could see the thick soft layers of dust on all the furniture, as if it were ever so slowly growing a beard. She briefly felt ashamed for Herr Geiss—had he expected his daughter-in-law to become his maid, too?

"You really don't know where he is?" said Liesl.

"No." Berte shrugged. "If I did, I'd tell you."

Liesl examined her. She was fairly sure the girl was lying, and embarrassed, too, but Berte did not blush.

"You can't keep track of boys," Berte added. "They do what they want." She stepped forward and made a comic mouth at Jürgen. He grabbed the air in front of her.

Liesl set her newsprint parcel down on the buffet. "Hans is too young to be your friend," she said.

"I don't know what *that* means," said Berte.

"I think you do."

Berte touched her hair. Her eyes met Liesl's and held them.

Liesl looked away first, gesturing to the parcel she'd carefully wrapped with newsprint. "Herr Geiss told me you have a fondness for horseradish. I found this jar when I was cleaning our house. I thought you might want it," she said, and turned toward the door.

She heard the girl clear her throat. "Everything you say is being overheard, you know," Berte said from behind her. "She tells my father-in-law all kinds of things about you."

Liesl stopped in her tracks. "Who?"

"Your tenant. The upstairs one. I don't know how you can stand her."

The baby began to squirm. "Do you mind if I set him down a moment?" Liesl said.

Berte made an accommodating gesture with her hand. Liesl set the shawl on the floor and placed Jürgen on top of it. He headed toward the hollow of space under the buffet table. "He likes caves," Liesl said.

"Primitive instinct," said Berte. "The love of caves. Self-protection, I guess."

"What does she say about me exactly?" Liesl fought to sound calm.

"Oh, she's worried you're going to be harboring a deserter, for one," Berte said airily. "And that your crazy little boy will set fire to the house one day. She honestly doesn't know how she can bear it all." She cleared her throat again, a tiny sound. "Not without a strong man around."

"Set fire to the *house?*" Liesl said. "Ani has never harmed anyone in his life."

"That's what my father-in-law told her," said Berte. "He's quite fond of your sons. And anyway, he just went away on a business trip, so he's preoccupied."

Liesl tried to sort through the pieces of information Berte had just related. Of course their house was crawling with Dillmans—the girls strewed themselves everywhere—so it was possible one of them had overheard a private conversation between herself and Uta. *Feind hört mit.* The enemy was listening, all right.

"Just thought you should know," said Berte.

The baby peeked out at them and grinned, batting the table legs with his hands. A funny expression crossed Berte's face. "He looks a lot like Hans," she said.

"Yes, well," Liesl said. "I should be going. Thank you. For letting us come in." She plucked Jürgen from his cave and wrapped the shawl around them both again. The whole process took a couple of cumbersome minutes during which Berte watched her in silence. "It's so cold out there today," Liesl added, and hitched her skirt with her free hand to take the steps down to the walk.

"He really ran away?" Berte called after her.

Liesl nodded without turning around.

"I know he likes to go to the old brewery," Berte said. "He found some cigarettes there once. He's convinced he'll get lucky again."

Uta stumbled after the younger Kappus kid, loping and hopping ahead, his disintegrating shoes barely touching down on the snowy cobblestone before he lifted them again. "Hans," Ani called to the shuttered houses, the woolly gray smoke. "Hans, Hans, Hans."

Every time Uta's boots slipped, she felt the nausea at her center slide, too. If she fell, it would fall with her. If she halted, it would halt, slosh, spread. Even when she slept, it sank through her dreams, a sea creature squirming through soft seaweeds. She gripped the bracelet on her wrist and soldiered on.

She'd insisted on leading the search, partly to escape the apartment where he had found her, to flee the furniture and walls his eyes had touched, and partly to escape Liesl's worry and pity. Her friend's woeful gaze followed her everywhere, and Uta couldn't stand it. She couldn't stand Liesl crying over her. If anyone heaped any more worries on Liesl, the poor girl would crack.

Yes, she would have to go back to Berlin, and once she went back, she would be back forever, living in the rubble. Germany would lose the war. Men like him would be destroyed, and their women dragged through the mud. Emmy Göring and all the ladies with their stolen furs and jewels would be paraded in front of the world as bloodthirsty crows who'd fed on the corpses of the murdered. It didn't matter that Uta hardly knew Emmy Göring, that she herself had refused to accept such gifts. Uta had never lusted for property, only company, only room after room full of elegant people. And she'd been to the right parties. She'd flattered and laughed in public. She would be standing in the edges of photographs, a pale, glowing face.

The Kappus boy led her past the wall where the party posted its slogans: ALLE RÄDER MÜSSEN ROLLEN FÜR DEN SIEG. ALL WHEELS MUST ROLL FOR VICTORY. He was humming a breathless little song to himself and didn't look up.

Hans would have looked up. He was that kind of boy, always looking at the skies, always reading the signs. Which one was he following now? She didn't think he was at the brewery, but it was the only clue they had.

Ani led her down the road toward the last open pasture in Hannesburg, now an expanse of lumpy snow and yellow grass. The brewery property divided Liesl's neighborhood of pleasant modern villas from the Alt Stadt, densely packed apartments where people still lived without cellars or indoor plumbing. The brewery lot was vast for the middle of town: on one side of it stood the rectangular ruins of what must have been a stable once. On the other rose a fence, its black iron gates tipped with white, around an ancient brick edifice with two towers. Whoever owned the building did not maintain it. The windows were cracked or missing; the locks on the gate had rusted. Nevertheless, improvements encroached. Beyond the far side of the building, the town had built a public shelter for families from the Alt Stadt. Uta had seen it on another walk. The shelter's sign had been bright and new, its door swept clean.

The cobblestone ended at grass, and Uta stumbled.

"Slow down," Uta said crossly, her stomach lurching. She put her hand in her coat pocket and touched the curve. She shouldn't be sick this late. Women were sick early and then they got over it, and then they started to show. She had gone through four months without sickness. In the first three, she pretended that nothing had changed inside her body because the long expanse below her ribs remained flat as ever. Then one day, her bracelet felt tight on her wrist. Her stockings kept snapping off her thighs. Her legs and hips had gotten fat, and the fat was different, plush and creamy as goose liver. Her body had begun plumping itself.

"Hans," the boy called. They crossed the pasture on a bumpy, trampled trail and into the shadow cast by the brewery, drawing closer to each other. She could tell the boy wanted to take her hand, but she did not hold it out. Her own fingers were cold and they preferred to remain in her coat.

Ani's head bobbed around at the height of her growing waist. The tips of his ears and nose were rosy, accentuating the hollows in his cheeks and temples. He didn't look like a proper child, but some creature made out of sticks and snow and blue dye that would collapse and melt away by summer.

What terrible thoughts she had.

"Hans," she bellowed through the iron fence. Snow slid from the tips of the posts and tumbled down in little crumbs. On the gate hung a sign for the public shelter, pointing toward the other side of the building. Someone had scrawled KEIN JUDEN—NO JEWS—beneath it. Beyond, the brewery wall was blank, scored only by the narrow windows, and archways for three rotting doors.

"Why on earth would he come here?" Uta said to Ani.

"He finds things," Ani said.

Uta's stomach churned again and she pressed her fingertips against her bracelet. Her lucky shackle. She'd always been so careful, and superstitious, too, that one mistake would protect her from another. But it hadn't, and this baby was coming. It might be all right if she'd felt something—hope or tenderness—when she'd held Jürgen, but instead she'd felt nothing. She'd cupped his round, warm bottom; she'd stared into his pretty blue eyes. She'd sniffed the fresh scent of his skin, and felt nothing but a mild revulsion at the crumbs of undigested milk in the corner of his mouth.

She staggered away from Ani. The boy remained, staring through the black rungs, his breath ghosting the air.

"You'll catch your death," she snapped. "I'm going home."

"There's a green bird in there," said Ani.

"*Ach*, Ani," she said, stopping but not turning around. She faced the new expensive villas, their snakes of chimney smoke, their balconies with the winter-vacant window boxes. Some people here still had three pairs of shoes and all their children living. Some people here rose and washed their faces and spread marmalade on their bread and expected to go on this way forever. The protected heartland, an illusion that Goebbels had spoon-fed them for years. They didn't know the doom that was coming. It amazed her.

"We need to go home now, or they'll start worrying about us," Uta said.

"I think it has a hurt wing," said Ani, folding his arms. "I'm not going."

"Well, I am," Uta said. Liesl humored him too much. She liked a touched child, a little golden boy. Liesl had always been fond of the old fairy tales; Uta remembered her rattling on about them at the Badensee when they watched the younger children splash in the water. She remembered the sand trailing through her fingers while Liesl spoke of the dirty little scullery maid dancing with the prince. It had all seemed possible once. "You better come, too, if you know what's good for you."

The boy didn't answer. Uta crunched out of the shadow of the building. As soon as she crossed into the gray sunlight, the uneasiness in her gut spread, her lunch squirting up her throat. She spat it on the snow. Yellow-gold, slickened lumps. Rutabaga stew. It had been almost as loathsome going down. She heard the boy come running. She peeked at him through her curtain of fallen blond hair. Beyond it, beyond him, she saw green. It was a tiny flash against the dull red wall of the brewery. When she straightened, wiping her mouth, it was gone.

What bird would live here, in this desolate place?

"You're sick, too," said Ani. His hands fluttered against her, as if he were trying to find a way into her coat. He elongated the last word, *Sie sind kraaank*, with a sigh for a fellow sufferer.

"You're not sick," she said. "Neither am I."

She pushed him away and stared through the iron fence, combing the brewery wall with her eyes. Nothing moved.

"You saw it." Ani's sudden grin made his face look thinner, skull-like. She thought she saw one of his twitching spells coming on, but instead he burst into speech. "You saw it, too. Wasn't it green? I think it's a parrot. Maybe someone lost a parrot. Can we go back? They live an old time. Long time."

Uta took out a handkerchief and dabbed her lips, smearing the cloth with yellow bile and red wax, her last good lipstick. Her last good anything from Berlin, the cigarettes and liquor gone. It was past time to go—to get out of the country, get a fake passport, get to Paris.

She tucked the handkerchief back in her pocket and swallowed the sour taste of her bile.

"You saw it," Ani repeated.

She knelt down before him, smoothing his limp blond locks back from his eyes. He could be her biological child. He resembled her more than he did Liesl or Frank, but her own son would never wear such a sweet, pathetic expression. "I didn't see anything," she said.

A tremor went through Ani. "I can still hear it," he said. "It's inside now." And then he made a whooshing noise. "I can hear. I can hear itIcanhearitIcanhearit."

"Shh," she said. "Let me listen."

She took a breath and cocked her head, pretending. The rising queasiness made it impossible for her to perceive anything beyond a meter's radius. Here was this boy and the crusty circle of snow around him. Here he was, too skinny for his age, a head on a pole. A tiny king reigning over a shrinking white plain. Beyond him unraveled the rest of the world: buildings, wings, blood, shadows.

"There's nothing there," Uta said in a low voice, hardening her grip on his hands. "And you know it."

The boy's eyelids flickered as if she'd struck him. Wordlessly, she pulled him to her new fat chest, his wren-like shoulder blades poking into her forearms as she squeezed him. She hadn't hugged a child since her brothers had been babies and the sensation of his cheekbones against her breasts startled her. Her nausea lessened. In its place she felt a fluttering in the tower of her throat. It felt like a word was trying to form there, and couldn't.

She pushed Ani gently away, and stood too fast. Spots burst before her eyes. As she stumbled, he watched her, his face dazed and pink.

"You be good for your mother," she said in a harsh voice. "You stop worrying her and get better, you hear?"

The boy took a few steps back, his eyes on the ground.

"She'd do anything for you," Uta said.

Clouds gathered in the west. It was snowing everywhere on the retreating German army, and soon the storm would be here. A cold wind touched her temples. She thought of the little collection of gold teeth that her lover kept, like wrinkled jewels, in a drawer.

"We could bring it birdseed," Ani said softly.

She walked ahead of him back across the pasture, past the broken mud puddles and the slogans, past the train tracks with their small cornices of rust.

Dusk drew long shadows around the rails, filling in between each wooden tie, one by one, until the second-to-last train looked as if it were rising out of a black lake. Hans rubbed his eyes as it shrieked to a halt.

No one had come from Berlin all afternoon. No man that Berte had described, with a long chin and a quick gait that made him trip over his own feet. Instead, mostly women and children departed the trains, always fumbling to hold on to one thing too many: baskets of carrots, bags of potatoes, and once or twice a live chicken. The women and children were coming from two stops away, where the town faded to open fields and farms. Hans knew they had bartered their curios and jewelry for limp, old vegetables and stringy meat, but he liked to imagine that the pink-cheeked mother hurrying by him had gotten lucky, that her closed basket hid *Lebkuchen* and sour cherry jam, fresh hot rolls, a smoked ham. She was taking it home to her seven beautiful daughters, and they would eat until their bellies strained their dresses. If he caught the woman's eye at the right moment, she would nod and invite him along, and he would become the girls' friend and protector, and take their giant German shepherd for walks. When their house got bombed, he would dig them all out with his bare hands.

The woman saw his stare and scowled at him. "*Strassenkind,*" she muttered. *S'troos kunt.*

"Where you headed, son?" said a voice.

Hans looked up into a face that was slack as an old wineskin. "Nowhere," he said. Then he noticed the uniform. "I don't need a ticket, sir."

"You've been here three hours."

"I'm waiting for a friend, sir," Hans said. "A soldier on furlough."

In the purple light, the stationmaster's blond mustache had a greenish glow. It moved even when the man's mouth wasn't speaking, as if the hairs were consuming themselves.

"He didn't tell me which train," Hans added.

"Where's he coming from?"

Suddenly he couldn't say the name—it was too big for his mouth. It was also a lie. Nobody was coming. He shrugged.

"Last train is in half an hour," said the stationmaster.

Hans fixed his face with an obedient look. "I have a letter to deliver," he said, and showed him the envelope, the name written in Berte's hand. "Then I'm going home."

The stationmaster drove his hands into the pockets of his coat. "You get too cold, you come inside my office," he said. "I got a little stove in there."

Hans thanked him and moved down to the far end of the station. He hunched his shoulders and leaned back against a column, trying to look as old as possible. He spied a cigarette someone had tossed to the snow. It was only half smoked and still burning. After glancing around, he picked it up and thrust it between his lips. He had smoked once or twice with his school friends but never developed a taste for it. Today the ash woke his mouth and he sucked deep, filling his lungs until they stung. He staggered a step, his legs suddenly exhausted from the long walk to the station and standing all day in the cold. His right hand clung to the cigarette and as soon as his breathing slowed, he sucked again, a bright cloud blooming in his skull. Another toke, and the bright cloud spun. Purple spread across the low hills. He smoked until the embers singed his fingers and he dropped the cigarette on the snow.

They would be worried now, the dark coming on and no sign of him.

He took out Berte's letter and examined it. Her handwriting was gappy and incomplete, but she'd underlined the name with a single, sure stroke. The name meant nothing to Hans. It floated in his mind with her description of the man's face, refusing to settle.

He was waiting for nobody from Berlin. He was waiting for her rescuer, who was no one. He was waiting for his father, the new surgeon at the new hospital there. His stepmother said she had written to his father a letter about Ani, but he hadn't written back. Vati would write back. She was lying about something.

The stationmaster reappeared at his elbow. "How will you get home? If your friend doesn't come."

"I don't live far away," said Hans.

The stationmaster asked where. Hans told him.

"Your mother's at home?"

"Yes." His mouth tasted terrible. He was starting to feel sick.

"Your father?"

"He's a Wehrmacht doctor."

"In France?"

"Weimar."

A train whistled and surged into the station. The engine's shadow passed across the stationmaster's face and he swiveled away, retreating quickly as if someone in the distance had called his name. From the sky snow began to fall. The frozen lace landed on Hans's cheek, melting as the steam gasped from the pistons and men began thumping down the steps and into the station. All of them had shoes, good or bad. All were dark or blond, tall or short, mustached or clean-shaven, fur-hatted or hunch-shouldered. Hans held out the letter, peering at chin after chin. He stood alone as the crowd eddied around him. A few people glanced at the white envelope. Nobody stopped. A flake of snow slid into his right eye, making it sting. Hans blinked. The arm holding the letter felt heavy. He switched arms, but the other ached immediately. He dropped both as the train materialized again before him, the passengers having all pushed past him.

A conductor appeared in the doorway between cars and looked down at Hans. He was a young man, someone who ought to be a soldier, and he retreated back into the compartment without asking Hans why he was still waiting when everyone was gone. The snow fell over tossed cigarette butts, expired tickets. It made a soft white sugar of the ground beyond the station. It fell heavier as the stationmaster and two men surrounded him, talking to him with their remote voices, clamping his elbow, towing him away from the train to a waiting car, a back seat.

"I haven't done anything, sir," Hans protested, alarmed. "I'm going home."

"Yes, you are." The stationmaster slammed the door.

The men drove fast, occasionally looking up at the sky, their headlights drawing yellow stripes on the shuttered walls of houses. Hans began to talk about the V-1 rockets that had destroyed London in the late summer. He loved the V-1s, even after they'd been superseded by the V-2s. The V-1s had the flavor of plums and the silence in the house after his mother's death, and the sweet softness of a baby's skull tucked under his chin as he carried Jürgen to his bath in the kitchen. The V-1s had given him purpose during those long hours when his father barely looked at him. He could still remember the radio broadcasts with their thrilling claims of "unchecked terror and destruction" in the streets of their enemies. The men driving the car did not respond to his commentary, except to glance back and grunt. He said he'd heard that the Führer was soon going to unveil a rocket powerful enough to reach New York. He had never said the words "New York" out loud before.

"New York," repeated the man driving, and his breath steamed the windshield.

The tires lost their grip twice, but they didn't skid until they reached Hans's street, the vehicle sliding until it came to rest before Herr Geiss's gate. The tops of the iron bars rose like bishop hats, dusted with white.

"You get inside now," said one of the men, cranking his head so that both eyes met Hans's. "Stop worrying your mother."

Hans trudged back to his own gate, letting himself in, making it only three steps before his stepmother hurtled out and gathered him in her arms. Her light hands touched the back of his neck, his ears. "You're so cold," she said over and over. Her face looked red from weeping.

Her tenderness shamed him. He shoved past her, up the stairs, ignoring Frau Winter and Frau Dillman peering from their own doorways, mothers upon mothers filling his motherless house. He couldn't get over the feeling that he wasn't there at all, even when he stepped across the threshold and Fräulein Müller moved for him so he could have the place closest to the stove.

"I'll fetch you some soup," his stepmother said.

Hans sank down to the sofa without comment. Jürgen slept in the cradle nearby, but he roused briefly to stare at his older brother with blue unseeing eyes before dozing off again. He was too big for it; his belly pressed its wooden sides and his legs had to curl to fit. His bedclothes were also old; his stepmother had stitched an extra ring of cloth to the cuffs to make them longer, and the cloth didn't match. At the sight, Hans began to blubber, his sobs threshing his ribs, while Fräulein Müller looked on. He hated crying in front of her, and he tried to stop, but it just made the sobbing worse.

"You had no right to worry her like that," she said with surprising gentleness, and rose. "She's got enough with your brothers."

He wiped his eyes and nose with the back of his hand. She walked to the corner of the room and took her hairbrush from a cabinet. Then she sat down in a chair and began to stroke her blond hair. When she was done, she would clean out the brush and throw the snarl into the stove, smelling up the room. She did it every night, and he hated it. He hated the stink and her lousy cooking, and how she wasted water and firewood, and sat forever on the toilet while everyone else crossed their legs. Stroke, stroke, stroke. Her hair crackled and shone.

"Whore," he said. Her right eyelid batted down fast, as if to stop an insect from flying into it.

His stepmother rattled into the room with a tray of soup. "Is it warm enough in here? Are you warming up?"

"I'm not cold," said Hans. He leaned over the soup. It shimmered far below him. If he let himself fall toward it, it would take a long time to hit.

"I'm not hungry, either," he said.

His stepmother sighed and perched on the last remaining chair. Her hands fluttered in her lap. The brush continued to move through Fräulein Müller's hair. Her eyes were set on something far away. The ceiling thumped as the Dillmans moved around.

"I suppose they informed you about the air raid on Weimar," his stepmother said in a trembling voice.

Hans didn't answer.

"We'll hear from Vati soon, I'm sure," she said. "He's due to leave for Berlin—" She shook her head. "Hans, I have something to tell you."

Hans could feel a soaked chill at the back of his collar where snow had fallen and melted. The warmth in the room stabbed his toes and fingertips. He rubbed his palms on his knees.

"The day we met with Dr. Becker, I wrote an urgent telegram to your father and asked him to come home. No matter what," she said. "You know what that means?"

He nodded.

"I haven't heard anything back. I don't know where he is." She spoke to the floor, her head in her hands, revealing her reddish crown of hair, its part uneven in the middle. "I was so scared for us," she said in a muffled voice. "But I'm more scared now. I'm afraid the neighbors overheard a conversation I had with you," she said to Fräulein Müller.

Fräulein Müller shrugged. "What can they do? He's not here."

So his stepmother had told her horrid friend about Vati, and not him. Hans wanted to make her sorry, but even more he wanted her to raise her head. He couldn't stand the sight of the uneven part, the hair falling over her face. "Vati will come," he said hoarsely. "My father will come home."

She pressed her fingers to her eyes.

"You could have told me," he said.

She took a deep breath, but she didn't say anything else.

Her soup looked good—a glisten of fat clung to its surface and the potatoes were cut in his stepmother's precise, thick pieces. He lifted his spoon, then set it down. He couldn't. He was so tired. He was so sick of grown-up lies.

"How was Ani today?" he said gruffly.

"He was . . . he was worried about you," said his stepmother. "He doesn't know yet. Any of it."

"He can't know about the telegram," Hans said.

"No." She met his eyes. They understood the same dark thing: If Ani knew he was the reason they summoned Vati home, and Vati never made it, Ani would blame himself forever.

"I want to tell him about the air raid."

"All right."

He set the soup bowl on the table beside him, letting it slosh. "Good night, then," he said, and rose.

"Hans, if you want to spend time with Frau Geiss," he heard his stepmother say rapidly, "I'd like it to be here, upstairs, with us."

"I don't want to spend time with Frau Geiss," Hans said.

His stepmother's lips twisted. She glanced at Fräulein Müller.

"I just want to go to sleep," Hans said, and he left the room, trailing melted snow.

He didn't go down into the cellar that night or the next morning. He was shoveling the walk when the girl appeared. He had never seen her outside, in the open air, and at first he didn't recognize her angular features or the lightness of her eyes. She looked older and faded, as if she had washed her skin too hard.

He was sure she would know by now that his errand had been in vain, but her voice sounded jokey and amused.

"I suppose he didn't show," she said.

He pushed the shovel under the snow. It snagged and scraped on the hard substrata, and when he lifted it, bits of earth and grass clung to the whiteness. Below, a scar of mud. He tossed the snow aside and dug again. He didn't know what to say to her. He couldn't stand the hopelessness in her eyes.

"He did show," he said.

"He did?"

Hans nodded.

"Did you give him my letter?"

He dug better this time and threw the clean snow aside. There had been no word from Weimar yet. In the morning, Ani had taken the news of the bombing silently and crawled back in bed, throwing the covers over his head. *Hide*, he'd said in a muffled voice. *Hide, hide.*

"Did you go?" The girl's voice cracked. "You didn't even go, did you?"

He saw something flash by the windows in her house.

"I gave it to him," he said quickly. "But he has to go to Poland. He's being sent to Poland today."

"How did he look?"

"I don't know," he said.

She bit her lip, rolled her eyes. "You boys," she said. "He didn't give you anything for me?" Her mouse ears looked pinker than ever.

He rubbed his mouth. A bit of snow clung to his mitten and stung his lip.

She took a step closer. He smelled her hair. He remembered its temperature, cool as well water, against his cheek, when she leaned against his chest, when they'd sat in the dark together, whispering all the things they hated in the houses above them, and promising each other if one got free, he or she would rescue the other.

"A p-poem," he stuttered.

"Aw, that's sweet." She pushed him lightly in the chest. Her arm sloped downward to do it. She was taller than he. "Well, where is it?"

"He made me learn it by heart, so it wouldn't get lost," said Hans, and he kept shoveling as he told her "The Plum Tree," the words electrifying his mouth, making his tongue aware of how it licked the back of his teeth, the roof of his gums. The image of the plum tree filled his mind, its branches lush with fruit that ripened and fell to the ground without being picked, that rotted, shrouded by a blanket of drunken bees. When he looked up, he was surprised to see her covering her face with her hands.

He had seen her weeping this way before. In the cellar's darkness he would have stepped forward to comfort her, but now they stood out in the open air and there was nothing he could do but let the sound of his words die.

A plane hummed overhead. Hans squinted up and saw it high up, a Focke-Wulf Condor, a transport plane, heading somewhere east.

Ani curled on his bed and listened to Fräulein Müller go into the bathroom and shut the door. He grimaced as he heard the rustle of her clothes, the sigh she always gave when she sat down. He wished she were gone. She kept telling his stepmother the parrot wasn't real, even though she'd seen it. She rolled her eyes whenever he tried to bring it up. She brought a sick smell into the house that unsettled him. It clung to her clothes and her cooking and the hair she threw in the stove every night after picking it from her brush. It was worst when he woke up at night from one of his nightmares. Sometimes he was falling on top of mothers and children; sometimes they were falling on him, into a ditch. The river running through the ditch was red. There was a drain at its bottom, drinking and drinking. Ani wakened with his mouth gaping, his nostrils thick with Fräulein Müller's stink.

Vati would get rid of her when he came home. Vati would find the parrot, too, coax it down from the rafters of the brewery. He would know how to raise a bird. Ani fell asleep every night wishing for Vati, trying to dream of him striding through the door, but by morning all he remembered was the bloody drain.

He dislodged the fifth and last tube from the hole in his mattress and pinched the bottom, moving the soft substance inside. Its consistency was softer than clay but thicker than liquid. He loved the feel of it between his thumb and forefinger, the way it gave into itself and separated and squished together again. He pressed it a few times, methodically, and then shoved it deeper into the crack of his mattress. He wouldn't drink the white softness inside, not this week, not until after his next doctor visit. But one day he would drink again. It wasn't like eating at all. It wasn't like eating at all; it was like breathing in. It *was* breathing, and Mother would fill him and make him brave. Mother would be him, the image of her that was almost all he remembered now, her white dress warm with sun, her white arms around him.

His fingers trembled as he pushed the tube down. Later. A grown-up would never find that crack. It was too small. The tube curled there like a seed, and he lowered his exhausted body over it, sheltering the secret.

Weimar

February 1945

The patient's brother reminded Frank painfully of Hans. The way he slouched, the way he stuffed his hands in his pockets. The pleasure of a good scheme written all over his face. The boy hooted as he watched the dachshund squirm over his older brother's lap, licking and sniffing.

"Robbi, Robbi." The bedridden patient shouted. "I can't believe you brought him all this way."

The dog stopped conversation all around. Doctors and nurses alike stared with dazed eyes at the full-snouted, wiggling joy. The dog didn't seem to know what part of its owner's body it wanted to touch first—it leapt and licked and clawed ears, then nose, then armpit, then wrist, then melted over the patient's lap like a giant pile of caramel. It scratched its floppy ear with a battering toe and leapt up again, as if to say, *Why are we still here? Let's go! Let's go!*

A handful of visitors had come and gone that day, but nothing compared to the arrival of the dog.

"This is Robbi," the patient said to his onlookers. "My brother brought him all the way from Schwarzburg."

Watching them, Frank felt a pang. He wanted Hans and Ani and Jürgen to be close brothers like this, willing to make sacrifices for each other. Mostly he wanted Hans to be gentler and not press his advantage on the younger, more malleable Ani. He hadn't been able to sleep last night thinking about them, with all the refugees in the house, learning bad habits from a bunch of roughneck kids.

A hand tugged his sleeve, and he looked down into a gaunt, unfamiliar face. Not his patient. "Someone's trading these," the fellow whispered, shoving a hard little object in Frank's palm. "Don't look at it now. I just want you to know."

Frank nodded and put the thing in his pocket. He went to pet the dachshund, finished with his morning routine, except for Hartmann, who as of yesterday was healing well, his apposing sutures already removed. Frank felt eager for the challenge of Berlin. For the first time, he nurtured a private, shameful hope that the war would continue. Another six months, that was all. Enough to learn, to earn a modest name for himself.

Frank was just heading for the ward's far doors when one of Schnell's soldiers came in, shouting for him, holding a telegram. Frank took it and kept walking, into the hall with the supply room. He ripped it open.

He had a hard time reading the words. The letters snagged and bounced.

ANI ILL STOP SEND MEDICINE STOP

Frank's fingers opened and closed on the paper, crumpling it to a tiny ball.

"Medicine" was the family's emergency code word for Frank himself.

She was summoning him home.

Someone appeared at his elbow. Her dark head came up to his bicep. Frank stuffed the telegram in his pocket.

"Is it bad news?" Frau Reiner said.

Frank fought for speech. "Maybe," he said. "One of my sons—" he breathed in sharply. "My middle son appears to be ill."

"I'm sorry. He's Anselm, right?" said Frau Reiner.

He nodded. Anselm. The name had never stuck, however, only the boy's feminine-sounding nickname. Ani had soft features. His nose rounded at the tip. His eyes were lake-green and wide. Even his milk teeth curved where most children's were straight. When Ani smiled, all Frank could see were circles and parts of circles, breaking and reforming like water around a flung stone. Ani was the healthiest kid from the day of his birth, never fussy like Hans, growing fat and dimpled at his mother's breast. When Susi died, Ani kept asking when she would come back. Each time, Frank had explained gently that she was gone forever, but the information was like oil on water: It never fully sank in.

"Your wife must be very worried." Frau Reiner looked over her shoulder. "Is she the kind who gets worried?"

"She's never sent me a telegram before." He wiped his mouth with the back of his wrist.

"You should sit down," said Frau Reiner.

"My Jürgen will be walking any day now," he announced. "The baby. All my boys start walking at nine months, just like clockwork." He felt his body lurch into step.

Frau Reiner took his arm and guided him to the supply room door. She opened it, sat Frank down on a box, and took a seat opposite him. The light was dim and the room smelled like wood and ether. His knees bounced.

"It happens quick, too," said Frank. "One day they're sitting. The next, they're balancing with a chair, and by the end of the week they're toddling around. *Hoppe, hoppe*." He made a little figure with his fingers and walked it across the top of the box. She regarded him steadily.

"So what are you going to do?"

"Ask for a furlough." He rubbed his face. No one had been granted a furlough since before Christmas. He wanted to read the telegram again, to make sure he'd gotten it right, but he didn't want Frau Reiner to see it. He touched his pocket. Then he remembered the thing the patient had given him, and he pulled it out.

It was a hard brass-colored capsule, the size of a bean, and it had a small inscription it. Frank read it and frowned, then showed it to Frau Reiner.

"They're trading these now," he said hoarsely.

She plucked the capsule and rolled it between her fingertips. "Cyanide," she said in a wondering voice. "I've never seen it. I mean, I guess you can't see it." She smiled a tiny smile.

"We can't allow it."

"Can't we?" she said thoughtfully. Her heart-shaped face tilted down. "Say I'm a good, loyal soldier. What if I fall into Russian hands?"

"Then you survive it," said Frank.

"What if I get starved and beaten and die of malnutrition anyway?"

"You don't know that will happen."

"The odds are great." She cocked her head. "Why not save me the suffering?"

"It's not for us to choose how we die," Frank said.

"You really believe that, don't you?" She held the capsule up to the light the way jewelers hold precious stones. It was bigger than a bead, but smaller than a child's eye.

Frank grabbed her wrist, pulling the capsule down, taking it back. The supply room door opened and Linden's face appeared. The light in the hall shadowed his eyes. They looked at Frank's hand cupping Frau Reiner's, then at Frank, and then the door slammed.

"Linden!" Frank shouted.

"Let him go." Frau Reiner gently retracted her fingers. "He's too jealous of me anyway."

Frank stared at her, absorbing the new fondness in her voice.

"You didn't know?" She winked at him. "I thought he would have told you. It started the night before Hartmann's surgery."

"I don't know what took you so long," said Frank, but he couldn't muster the old joking tone they used with each other. He was clutching the capsule in his fist and his head kept swimming back to the message from Liesl, its urgency and lack of information. Why wouldn't she say more? Why couldn't she say more? He sorted through worst-case scenarios: Ani had caught something from those filthy refugees. Ani had fallen and injured himself. Ani had leukemia or cancer.

The only thing clear about the telegram was its request: *Come home.* It did not say, *Write back.* There was no time for discussion.

"Are you going to be all right?" said Frau Reiner.

"If you were a woman," Frank said to the nurse, and then stopped. "I'm sorry."

She rose and went to the door. "Just ask the question, you idiot," she said, her hand on the knob.

"My wife asked me to come home now. In the telegram," said Frank. "How serious do you think she is?"

Frau Reiner opened the door.

"I don't know if she understands what she's asking," said Frank.

Frau Reiner made a noise in her throat. "If I were a woman," she said over her shoulder, "I would only be serious about two things: the life of my children and the life of my husband. In that order."

He asked Schnell for the furlough. Then he showed him the capsule. He held his palm out, expecting the captain to take it, but Schnell simply glanced at it and looked away. A red flag with the swastika hung on the wall behind his desk. The color drained everything else in the room: the chairs, a skat deck, a copy of a Karl May novel, and stacks of notebooks.

"Well," said Schnell. "I'm sorry you had some unhappy news."

Frank could feel the taut cords holding his head up. "My wife is young and inexperienced." That wasn't true. She was experienced with children. He'd seen her work with them for years. It was part of the reason he'd married her.

"Do you think our patients want to kill themselves?" said Schnell.

"No. Not now."

"Do they seem unhappy to you?"

"Unstable," said Frank, pocketing the capsule. "Every one of them is suffering from dystrophy."

"Dysh-trophy?" The captain pronounced it with a slur on the *s*.

Frank heard himself explaining the condition of the patients: They had been starved, frozen, and forced into sleeplessness. They had faced lice and fever and death.

"The Russians proved in the last war that too many pressures can create a dystrophic condition in the body," he said. When a man's cells were dystrophic, they were no longer capable of a normal reaction. If cells malfunctioned, everything went awry. A man could not respond to disease properly. He couldn't even sleep or digest nutritious food.

Was Schnell nodding? His hairy nostrils fanned with breath.

As Frank talked, his mind spiraled away again, thinking about three boys who'd lost their mother to death, and then lost their father to distance. And to top it off, he'd brought a stranger into the house and said, *Here she is! Your brand-new mother!* He'd regarded his marriage to Liesl as his own heartbreaking but valorous decision to move on because life demanded it, but what if he'd mired them all, most of all *her*, in a swamp of unending grief?

Frank continued, "They don't make good decisions as soldiers and they don't heal, at least not until the dystrophic condition has time to correct itself." His eyes fell on the capsule. "Sometimes that takes weeks. Sometimes months of quiet and routine. Given the easy chance to end their lives, I fear they might make the wrong decision."

Schnell pulled over one of his notebooks, scrawling something on a new page. Frank stood there, waiting for a response.

"Think of their mothers," he said in a hoarse voice.

More silence, the pen drifting through its sentences.

"About the furlough, sir? I'm leaving in a few days anyway, so perhaps my new position could be postponed—"

Schnell snapped his book shut. "You know, if we lose this war, it's because we took too much time," he said. "Don't waste any more of mine."

Frank had always found it easy to talk to Liesl, even in their ridiculous first meeting with that half-drowned kid. There had been something about Liesl's shy composure that had drawn him out, and for weeks after that encounter he'd avoided her, embarrassed. Liesl Nye wasn't hard to avoid. She either worked with children or hid in her room or sometimes took walks by herself around the grounds. Rumor had it that she had turned down several admirers, that she and her friend Uta were secretly lovers. Single young women who stayed single made others gossip, but Frank assumed she just didn't like the Nazi boors who leered at her.

Then one day, in the harrowing month after Susi's death, he'd walked by the *Kinderhaus* and heard the babble of children and Liesl's strong, sure voice above it. He peeked in the cabin window to see her flushed, animated face as she chased them and then crashed into a wooden chair squarely in her path. She laughed, but it was her look of complete surprise that got him. She hadn't expected the chair to be there. *So young,* he thought wistfully.

At home, his newborn was passed around the neighborhood day and night, cared for by other mothers with infants. His elder sons cried themselves to sleep. He jerked awake in the dark, listening for their tears. He was so tired that his hands fumbled to tie his shoes. When six weeks passed, Herr Geiss suggested a marriage service. Frank sat in interviews with the agent and two young, plump, pretty women who looked like vague replicas of Susi. He listened to them talk about their health and daily habits, their love of the movies and the Führer. They seemed swollen with innocence. It flooded their cheeks and spilled out of their mouths like milk. He asked for a different sort of candidate, someone hardworking and quiet, and was presented with a pear-shaped widow from Bavaria who took no sugar in her tea and assured him that he would never hear his sons whine again.

At first he found himself making excuses to pass by the *Kinderhaus*, to exchange a few words of greeting. He liked watching Liesl with the children—the happiness she seemed to cultivate around her in the small cabin. It reminded him of peacetime. The evening of the day he received his summons to Weimar, he picked a handful of violets from under a tree near the cabin. His clumsy hands ripped half of them out by the roots. He stood, stripping the dirt from the stems, wondering what he was doing. The violets were already wilting by the time he willed his feet to thump across the threshold.

Liesl was hanging hats back on a row of big nails. A bowler, a chef's hat, a straw hat, a nurse's cap. One of the nails was loose in the wall and as she turned it tumbled, pinging the floor.

"I'm sorry," he said, holding the flowers behind his back. "I scared you."

She didn't retrieve the nail. She stared at him, rigid, as if he'd come to mug her.

"They must like that game. Playing grown-ups," he said.

"Yes." She touched her cheek. "What can I do for you, Dr. Kappus?"

He cleared his throat. "I brought these," he said, and held out the flowers. She took them, but the damp stems stuck to his hand, and he almost had to wipe the violets into her palm. It wasn't a thrilling touch, but a clammy exchange of wilt. "Sorry," he said, forcing a laugh.

"I'll find some water." She carried the violets to the end of the room, where there was a small porcelain sink. He kept from turning his head but he was conscious of her red hair swept up and falling in the back, her hips, and that jaunty, clumsy walk that once again sent her knocking into her desk as she passed. Her hands slipped on the faucet before it turned.

"What happened to those Steitz boys—do you know?" Frank said, thinking of the day he'd first seen her, the sunlight on the water, Liesl rubbing cream from her finger. Ani hadn't been born yet, and Liesl had just been a pretty young girl shivering with cold.

He heard a clunk and saw Liesl setting the violets down on a desk. They sagged over an eggcup. "They were training to be officers last I heard." She shook her head. "I remember thinking they'd never grow up."

Frank cleared his throat and shoved the nail back in the wall, restoring the bowler to its spot. "You have an extra nail," he said to the wall. "I could give you a surgeon's cap."

"That would be lovely," said Liesl. "Anything that's not military."

"I studied to be a surgeon," said Frank, and blurted to her about his summons, wondering why his mouth kept talking. Middle-aged widower. Father of three. About to be drafted. How much more desperate could a man appear? He started backing away, toward the door.

"I wish you much courage," Liesl said, following him.

"Why not a soldier's cap?" Frank asked when he reached the threshold. "Surely that's all they want to play anyway."

She hesitated. "The boys—and girls—they get carried away. I stopped putting out war toys."

Their eyes met, and he saw a new emotion in them. She had fought for this tiny shred of control, perhaps paid for it. "I just can't watch it anymore." Her voice deepened. "All that dying."

Their faces were close. Liesl looked startled and ducked her head.

"Yes. Well, good night, then." He turned.

"I'm sorry I didn't have a vase," she said from behind him.

"Next time, I'll bring one," Frank said.

"I like sunflowers," he heard her say before he bolted into the night.

The dachshund was still in the ward when Frank hurried through at dinnertime, restless and sweating, unable to eat or face his friends, the happy new lovers.

The patients were playing a game with the dog, trying to get it to run between them for scraps of meat. In the early dark the dog's happiness seemed suddenly desperate. Its black smile sagged as it loped from bed to bed.

"All right, all right," said the owner. "He's getting tired."

But others egged the dog on. The dog's nails scraped the floor.

Frank arrived at Hartmann's bed and was surprised to find the poet neither reading nor writing. Hartmann was sitting up, head bowed. His hair hung over his cheeks in lank strips. At first Frank thought he was asleep, but he saw Hartmann's fingers clasping and unclasping.

Down the hall, the dog began to bark, excited and angry.

"Shut him up!" a patient shouted.

"You shut up!" someone shouted back.

Hartmann's posture wasn't good for a healing face. Frank gently touched his forehead and began to tilt him up. He paused when the light fell on the left side of the patient's mouth. The swelling was soft but definite, bulging the skin graft. The transposed skin had a yellowish cast. Beneath, the sutures were already straining in the rotting tissue.

The dog barked, and a scuffle broke out. Nurses hurried from opposite ends of the ward.

Frank let go of Hartmann's forehead, searching his own memory for any sign of edema in his brief visit the day before. He could recall only the roughened pink texture of healthy healing. Hartmann hadn't complained of discomfort. He met Hartmann's eyes. They were strangely blank.

"A setback," Frank said. "We'll treat it."

The shadows on the wall climbed and sank. Frank called a nurse and gave her instructions for treating the swelling, but he could already tell that it wouldn't work. The graft would die, and someone would have to peel it away, cut out the scar tissue, and try again. It could take months.

Frank pulled out a pad. *We'll treat this right away*, he wrote. He smelled the delicate, almost soapy odor of dying skin and pus.

Hartmann took the paper. *There's an investigator coming tomorrow.*

Frank read the message twice. He nodded, as if he understood the words.

Hartmann took the paper back. *They'll find what they want to find*, he wrote. *It's likely I'll be taken away.* He pulled in his knees and hugged them like a boy. It was hard to read his expression, with the shadows of the room and the puckering scars, but he didn't seem unhappy or worried. In fact, his whole being exuded an eagerness, as if he no longer had to wait for his fate.

I'll speak on your behalf, Frank wrote. The pen slid in his damp fingers. *You need time to heal.*

Don't risk anything on my account.

When Frank tried to touch his shoulder, Hartmann waved him away. Walking back up the ward, Frank felt for the capsule riding in his pocket. He could have crushed it or tossed it away by now, but he hadn't.

He didn't know how to say to Hartmann that he should want to live. You had to want to live. You had to respect life. But he knew his words would sound simple, and if he and Hartmann argued, Hartmann would win.

Frank didn't sleep that night. He looked outside at the guard station, the incinerator, the concrete wall of the cistern, and the pines beyond. There had been some warm days and the snow had hardened on the ground. The sky was deep with stars. He mentally started and scrapped several letters to Liesl, expressing his concern, requesting more information, explaining about his denied furlough. When the night sky began to lighten, he washed his torso in cold water and stood there, feeling his skin freeze. His nipples and belly tensed first, and then everywhere prickled with goose bumps. The sensation did not make him feel any more wakeful. He shoved his arms into a shirt and buttoned it. He lay back down on his bed and tried to read Hartmann's poems again, but the words buzzed and fluttered. He tucked them in his pocket. Down the hall, he heard others rising, and he emerged for his morning rounds, avoiding Hartmann. The operating room was empty, so he walked in and inhaled the smell of carbolic acid, remembering the soft, pulsing feel of the tissues he'd repaired and the drag of sutures through flesh.

He made his way to the cafeteria and drank coffee made from dandelion roots. There was not even chicory left in their kitchens. "Better brew in Berlin, I hope," Frank told the cook. "I'm leaving in two days."

The cook said he was sorry to see him go, but he didn't look sorry, just sweaty and weary. Frank sat down and stared out the window at the pine woods beyond the cistern, formulating his plan of escape.

To avoid Linden and Frau Reiner, he went straight to the ward. He did not want to tell them about Hartmann. He did not want to talk to Hartmann, either, watching him from a distance, a sleeping lump on his bed. He wanted to take the clocks down from the walls, every single one, and advance the hours, through afternoon and nightfall, and dawn again. To have the telegram miss him, to have Hartmann's infection fail to begin, because he was already in Berlin. To simultaneously be already on his way home.

The patients were eating their midday meal, a hard black gnarl of *Kommissbrot* and hot millet soup, when the first whistle came. Frank was holding a patient's chart. Then the earth shook and the bowls spilled on their unprotected laps. Men roared with pain. The chart ripped in his hands. It happened fast and slow. The rumble. The flash. Hot soup. The roar. Rip. Splashed everywhere. It was a joke. A ridiculous act of God.

Home. The back of Frank's neck went cold. He dropped the chart and ducked. Another whistle, another boom. He staggered forward. *Home.* It took a long time to pull himself straight. The sky broke over the roof, smoke smell pouring through the cracks in the walls.

He grabbed a cart of soiled linen and pushed it toward the far door, lurching with each explosion. Around him, men scrambled to get under their beds. Their legs snared in their blankets. They lost their hats and grabbed for them, jamming the cloth back on their waxy skulls.

Hartmann was four meters away. Sirens wailed. Then three. Soldiers poured into the ward behind Frank, shouting, "Everyone, down!" Then two.

"Everyone, DOWN!" Then one.

Frank pulled the capsule from his pocket, lurched right, and rolled it under Hartmann's bunk, seeing the brass glint and a hand close around it.

The cart jammed on a cot leg. Frank wrenched it free, lurched forward again. His boot slid on spilled millet soup and he almost lost his balance. Another boom, closer this time. Outside, flames rose beside the guard tower. If he could get to the cistern, he could hide on the ledge, make a break for the woods when no one was looking.

I'm tired, screamed a man behind him. Or maybe he screamed something else, something Frank could not make out.

I'm tired is what he heard. He burst through the doors.

Three steps onto the snow and he fell to his knees.

Propeller, nose, window, cockpit. A whir like a thousand bees. A blurred face.

Sprays of bullets pocked the snow beside Frank, but his body was whole, untouched. The plane passed over. He rose, the cold slapping his skin. The guard station was burning. Soldiers were lying in the snowdrifts, guns aimed at the sky. He put his head down and pushed toward the incinerator, the cistern beside it. The chest of his coat flattened against him.

As Frank shoved the cart up against the edge of the cistern, another bomb fell close by, smashing two houses at the edge of town. Their roofs caved in toward each other. He saw the soldiers swivel toward the fire; he saw the perfect moment: It opened for him the way a bow opens when you tug a ribbon just so and a woman's hair falls loose from it, onto her bare shoulders. No one was looking directly at him. He stepped to the edge of the cistern and hovered there, his right foot stepping out over the empty space.

The left refused to follow, at least not in the way it should—a clean jump to the ledge that once held the boards to the latrine. Instead it hitched, like a cripple's leg, and he lost his balance and tumbled into the concrete pit, falling past the stained walls to the thick frozen lake at the bottom.

He landed on his tailbone, then fell on his side, like a sleeper, his cheek smashing into an empty cylinder of Zyklon. The edge of the metal pierced the skin just below his ear. The ashy waste groaned and cracked, cold grit grinding into his hair.

Frank scrambled up immediately and lost his balance on the slippery sludge, smacking into the cistern wall, muck smearing his coat. He touched the cut with his cleaner hand. It was wide but not deep. His tailbone ached, but his legs and vertebrae worked. Inside his coat pocket, he found a handkerchief and pressed it to the wound. One breath, two breaths. He pushed himself upright more slowly, stepping around the Zyklon cylinders. Zyklon was used routinely for delousing, but the canisters' hollowed shapes, their warning labels (GIFTGAS! POISON GAS!) seemed ominous now. The other waste in the cistern was harder to identify: gray and black ash, freckles of white that could have been bone. He moved carefully across to a spot under the ledge. Best to hide for now, then figure a way out.

As the shock wore off, the smell set in. Then the shrieking and smashing of the air raid. Then the cold. He covered his nose with the clean part of his handkerchief and waited. No one had seen him fall, but the cart was up there. It could give him away. He edged closer to the wall but did not touch it.

The frozen sewage creaked. He looked down. He was standing on a charred femur.

Smoke drifted over the sky in gauzy veils. Frank could no longer hear the propellers screaming in the engines of the planes, just a dull insect drone. If Hartmann had taken the pill, he would be dead by now, his body found. The other patients would have emerged from under their bunks.

At first, Frank was sure Hartmann would use it, would take the sudden release, but the more he thought about it, the more he wondered. He remembered the boy Hartmann had been, so different from the rest of them, not just for his brains but his essential stubbornness. Hartmann on that wild day in the wine cellar, his face quiet, alert, refusing to take sips from the contraband bottle one boy grabbed off a shelf. Hartmann at the Kurpark with Astrid, steering her with a light hand at her waist to the sulfur fountains, fishing a glass goblet from his coat so she could drink from crystal. The other boys had ridiculed him for being swoony over a girl, but Hartmann had ignored them. He loved propriety, courtliness. The rough conditions of wartime must have festered his formerly gallant soul, but would such a man choose a coward's death? No, Hartmann would be obstinate enough to live to the end. To be convicted. To take his unjust punishment and force his murderers to stare into his destroyed face before they shot him.

A few bombs rattled the distance, and then, a light bouncing patter, as if the walker did not like letting his feet sink in the grainy snow. The iron door of the incinerator squeaked and yawned. Although Frank couldn't see the visitor, he was sure it was Bundt. Who else would walk like that? He hid under the ledge, pressing his bleeding cheek.

The iron door slammed shut. The latch rattled into place. There was a cough. Then a stream of gray dust tumbled down through the air, smacked the ice, and gusted up. Frank shut his eyes too late. They stung with grit. He held his breath until he could no longer stand it, and then he gulped the thick air, his stomach revolting before his lungs. He gagged and bit his fist to keep from retching.

Another shovelful of ash, freckled with bones and metal.

A roar tickled at the base of Frank's lungs and he had to swallow hard to keep it down. He screwed shut his eyes and pinched his nose like a swimmer diving into deep water. Three, four, five more waterfalls of filth.

The cart squeaked as it rolled away. Frank loosened his grip from his face. The ledge had done little to protect him. The fine dust covered his clothes and hat and hair. He could feel the grit when he blinked his eyes, and in the place where his collar rubbed his neck. He touched his ears, and his fingertip came away gray.

He heard soldiers shouting and retreated back under the ledge, crouching. He curled his toes back into his feet and hugged his own torso, tucking his hands under his ribs. He sang in his head. Not songs for the Fatherland, but the little lullabies he'd listened to Susi and Liesl hum to his babies. Funny half melodies with nonsense words and endearments, they had always seemed a private language to him, something meant to be hidden from the lives of men. Now he could hear their little notes spread through his slowly chilling body as the sky opened and it began to snow, white falling on the black ash.

He opened his mouth and caught some flakes, but they didn't relieve the caked dryness of his throat.

Someone shouted his name above. For an absurd moment, Frank thought it was Hartmann. He stood up a moment, gazing into the protecting clouds. Footsteps neared. Frank flattened himself against the crusted wall under the ledge, pressing every cell of his body back into the stones. He tried not to see his shadow, lying faintly over the heap of Zyklon cans.

Boots crunched to the edge of the hole. Chunks of ice fell and slid with the faint metallic sound of a penknife opening. Frank blinked. The warmth of his skull was melting the stone behind him. He could feel something slick leaking into his hair.

The voice called his name again. It was Linden. He was calling into the distance, but something broke his call, the way a line of trees would break it—as if the pine forest had moved closer to the cistern. Water trickled down Frank's skull. He listened hard and heard a faint but incessant drumming, like a herd plodding together. It wasn't trees but the war that approached. More soldiers or more patients? How many more? What had his father said about his own retreat? *One day I looked up and even the mud was crawling south and east.*

Linden called his name a third time. *Sorry, friend,* Frank thought. *We'll see each other again someday.*

"What is Schnell doing?" Linden said. "Turning them all back?"

The companion didn't answer.

Linden whistled. "There must be a hundred of them. Two hundred. Buchenwald must have been hit worse than here."

The prison camp. Frank's mind returned to the typhus rumor, Schnell's veiled threat. Would they leave the infected men behind? His lungs tickled. He wanted to cough but held it in.

"Look at him. He's sending them away," said Frau Reiner's voice. "Look at the rags they're wearing."

"They're prisoners," said Linden. "We serve soldiers. We have seven empty beds."

"Eight now," said Frau Reiner.

"Right," Linden growled. "Eight."

Frank strained to listen.

"Who wants to be the one who tells him?" Linden added.

"Not me," said Frau Reiner. "He'll find out soon enough."

So Hartmann had done it. A raw chill swept through Frank and he shuddered, choking on bile. His mind spun strangely to Hans and Ani: the two boys jumping off the stairs at home, first one step up, then two, then three, then five. With each step higher, they lost more control of their landings, until their bodies smacked the floor, sprawling on hands and knees. Frank wondered why he always let them get to that point of almost smashing themselves before he called to them to stop. Ani never wanted to stop.

"Go back!" someone yelled, followed by a gunshot. "Go back!"

"They ought to evacuate us all," Frau Reiner said. "Or we'll look like them by summer. Or him."

"Do you think he had it all along?" asked Linden.

"Who knows," said Frau Reiner after a moment. "Come on. Frank's probably on the ward by now. He wouldn't leave his patients."

Frank stared at his hands, suddenly aware of the intensity of the cold creeping into his fingertips, the wet sludge on the back of his head. He wouldn't survive out here overnight.

Shouts came from the direction of the hospital. Linden yelled back, "No sign of him!"

Their footsteps ground in the snow.

At dusk, Frank saw the first stars appear. He could see no pattern to them. His toes had to be frostbitten. How bad, he wasn't sure. They'd been numb for some time. His mind was blurring, too. It kept returning to his last sight of Hartmann, the hand beneath the bed grabbing the metallic pellet. He couldn't be sure that he had seen the hand. He couldn't be sure that he'd heard his friends correctly. He forgot exactly what they'd said, except Frau Reiner's last words: *He wouldn't leave his patients.* Twice he took in a deep breath to cry out for help, and twice he let it go, afraid.

Footsteps approached the hole again, and this time, the voices were quick, the words few before a shot rang out and something heavy crashed to the snow above. Frank heard the door to the incinerator groan open, then slam shut again.

"Fire's out."

"Take his shoes and throw him in the hole, then."

The other man grunted, and there was a silence followed by two soft thuds.

"What an idiot. Schnell had his eye on him for months."

Hartmann.

No. Not months.

Something scraped over the ground and tumbled, headfirst, onto the ice. Falling, it looked like a sack, and landing, a body again. The skull was already cracked. Its blood spattered everywhere. The man's eyes were invisible, his head a matted gob of hair and brain matter, but Frank would have recognized his small, delicate feet anywhere.

The footsteps crunched away. Winter wind rushed above the hole. The body was still. Bundt wore a thin shirt, and the small dark curls of hair over his shoulder blades and kidneys were visible through the linen. It matched the hair on his feet. Frank crept forward on the ice.

"Can you hear me?" he whispered. He lifted Bundt's wrist and felt for the pulse. None. The skull wound was tattered—not a bullet's torn entry, but the mark of a bludgeoning. He touched the edge and felt it give way like cartilage. He sat back on his heels and hovered there for a long time. Soldiers called from above. Frank staggered back under the ledge and sat down. The wetness in the corners of his eyes froze to beads. He patted his pants pocket and found a cigarette, tore through the paper, took out the small curl of tobacco, and thrust it in his mouth.

The chewing roused him. His teeth ground and ground. The spit gathering in the back of his mouth was thick and tasted like bark. His throat revolted and he spat the tobacco on the ash.

After waiting and listening, he scaled the one crack in the concrete that jagged up the western side and ended near the ledge. He couldn't feel his fingers or his feet, so he didn't know if they had a good grip. His body felt too heavy and unbalanced against the smallness of his footholds. He got almost two meters up and lost the right foot to the open air. Cautiously he kicked at the wall, finding the same crumbling gap. It would not bear his weight, so he held on tight with his fingers and scooted up the left foot, hoping for a lucky break, a crack he couldn't see. But his boot slid down the wall until it reached its old spot.

He hung in the dark and cold, unable to move.

He fell. He got up. He climbed. He fell. He got up. Climbed, fell. He threw himself against the wall so hard that his breath knocked loose from his body, and in his first few scrambling steps upward he was all flesh and no air—his body drew nothing into it—and then he gasped and tumbled again, without even reaching the height of the first attempt.

He searched Bundt's clothes and found nothing. Nothing to help him climb out. Also nothing else—no photograph or papers, no clues to his identity.

He sat back down, bruised and out of breath. As his body stiffened in the cold, his mind kept working in its slow, muddy way. Bundt. Hartmann. The same man. Not the same. The opposite. Bundt had longed to live. Hartmann had longed to die, had always loved death. Like the rest of them, Hartmann had raised himself into a man, a soldier—but not out of hunger. Out of despair. Because if you yearn to die, every gesture matters. Every speech could be the last. Every act could be the final act. The king the miller the judge the question. The crystal goblet bulging from the jacket pocket.

The end defines the hero, but is always deferred.

One day it abruptly comes: The doctor slides death across the floor. The patient's hand reaches out to grab it.

Fingers close.

The sky falls.

Frank didn't know what time it was when he propped Bundt's stiff body against the wall under the ledge and set a foot in the dead man's waistband, and a hand on his shoulder, and scrabbled and kicked his way up until he reached the ledge and looped one leg over. He lay on the ledge for a long time, breathing and listening. Below him, Bundt slumped like a man leaning back to watch a woman pass. He looked peaceful except for the icy tread marks on his face from Frank's boots. It would be obvious that someone else had been in the cistern.

Frank lowered a leg and gently nudged Bundt until he fell face-down again.

The hospital was mostly dark but not silent. Kerosene light flickered behind glass and oilcloth. Inside, men were moaning, and nurses were still calling out names. Frank climbed over the wall and ran for the pines.

Hannesburg

March 1945

"I saw the parrot up there," Ani whispered in the dark. "She saw it, too. I know she did."

Hans pretended to sleep, but his breath was coming too fast and the blanket itched. He rolled over and stared toward the ceiling. Two days ago an official army notice had come, announcing that Vati had disappeared. Fräulein Müller had read it aloud to them, and his stepmother had almost burned herself, reaching toward the tile stove for balance. *Der Vermisste. Missing in action.* Ani dropped his dinner plate for no good reason and stared at the wreckage, surprised, and then Jürgen bumped his head on the corner of a table, and no one could stop him crying for half an hour.

Only Hans did not feel scared. He trusted his father. His father would come home and straighten it all out. He just wished Vati would hurry. A week had already passed since the raid on Weimar.

Dr. Becker had been called away to Frankfurt, so his replacement, an overwhelmed medical resident, examined Ani's lab results while Liesl and Hans sat side by side on a narrow couch.

The lead concentration in his blood is lower, he said finally, setting the paper in Ani's file.

He's better, then. Their stepmother snapped her purse shut. *Can you tear up the psychiatric evaluation form?*

The resident rubbed his bloodshot eyes. *I'm not qualified to do that, Frau Kappus. You'll have to see Dr. Becker again.*

But Ani can stay home?

Ani can stay home.

His stepmother had spent all the next day on a loud and joyful cleaning bout that sent even Fräulein Müller out to the market and the lending library. Yet Ani wasn't really better. Just two days ago he had twisted his ankle falling down the stairs. Ani claimed it was an accident, but one of the Winter boys said he'd seen Ani spread his arms and leap.

"Why doesn't your brother ever play with us?" Grete Dillman had asked him. She was the ugliest and sauciest of the neighbor girls, the kind of person who spat her words instead of speaking them.

"Ani's too young."

"I heard they want to lock him away in a loony bin."

"No one wants to lock him away," Hans had retorted. "And you have so many freckles you could be put in a zoo."

That shut Grete up. He hadn't liked being mean to her, but she talked too much.

"I saw the parrot," Ani whispered again, bringing Hans back to the dark closet he shared with his brother.

"I'm sleeping."

"Will you go with me to look for it?" Ani asked.

"Sure," Hans muttered.

"But we don't have any food for birds."

"I'll get some seeds."

"Where?"

Hans threw off his covers and sat up, staring across the short, dim space to his brother's bed. "Trust me," he said. "Don't you trust me?"

His brother didn't answer. Upstairs, someone started walking around, creaking the boards. The naked feet of the Dillman girls.

"Vati would want you to trust me," Hans said.

Ani did not reply. Ani never wanted to talk about Vati anymore, not since the report that he'd gone missing.

"Or don't you remember Vati?" Hans said.

"What kind of seeds are in the jungle?" Ani's voice was small and remote.

"Do you know how far away the jungle is?" said Hans. "Someone's been feeding it birdseed."

"Maybe it's trying to get back."

"Maybe," said Hans. "Maybe it was born in a cage."

His brother fell silent again. Hans flopped back. Above him, he heard a high sound, the sag of springs. The Dillman girls were going to sleep. They slept four to a bed; he'd seen it when he'd been upstairs. Two girls slept one way and two the other way, their feet tangled in one another's hair. The oldest one was thirteen; the youngest, four. Frieda was the prettiest, but she was shy.

"We should go to sleep," Hans said.

"I was trying to sleep," said Ani. "You just woke me up again."

"I'll get the seeds, all right?" Hans said.

But he didn't.

Instead he went as often as he could to the brewery pasture, where a loose federation of older children gathered. It wasn't just his old schoolmates anymore—it was the Dillmans and the Winters and other refugee children now billeted in town. The refugee kids were bolder and coarser, and they weren't afraid of bombings or their mothers, and they were so many! The sheer numbers of kids enthralled them all. They could have formed their own army.

For days they'd been playing a game called Kidnap in a crumbling rectangle of brick and stone that was the foundation of the brewery's former stable. The rules were simple: The girls and smaller children were always imprisoned in a low stone stall, and one gang of boys defended them, while the other gang tried to engineer their escape. As soon as the captives escaped, the roles reversed. The girls and younger children were always the prize and the burden. There was never a victor for long.

One other rule kept the game in check: You couldn't touch a girl. You could order her around if she was your bounty. She had to do what you asked, such as make you mud cakes or fetch you a cup of water, but touching was off-limits, unless it was for assistance. Hans never asked the girls to do anything. He didn't dare, but he fought for them valiantly. For his efforts, the Dillman girls insisted that Hans be the one who lifted them over the wall when they escaped. Sometimes when his hands gripped their ribs, he felt a warm ache inside.

Under the guise of doing errands on overcast days, Hans joined the game. Daring the Lancasters and Wellingtons that cruised high over the clouds, he was almost happy. To run across the packed snow and mud took his mind off his brother, and worrying about when Dr. Becker was coming back, and his missing-in-action father. Whenever Hans came upon the game, it was already started, and whenever he left, the other children played on. He wouldn't have been surprised if he showed up at midnight and their dark bodies were there, fighting and fleeing each other.

Hans kept to himself about the game at the stable, and his stepmother didn't ask. She seemed afraid of him since he'd run away. He didn't tell Ani, either. His brother would ruin things by acting strange. Hans was relieved that Ani appeared to prefer staying home, orbiting the baby and their stepmother and the awful Fräulein Müller. Hans wanted his own time to daydream about the Dillman girls, and about Berte slipping back down to the cellar to beg him to be her friend again. Most of all, he wanted to imagine Vati coming home and fixing Ani. Vati would have to stay hidden until the war ended, but he could have Hans's bed and Hans would sleep on the floor.

Hans couldn't picture the war ending, although that was all that the adults talked about. He didn't believe the Amis would make it past the Rhine and across the cities and farmlands to Hannesburg. He couldn't fathom enemies on his own streets, walking past the, slogans like, our hearts beat for our country and the red flags on the roof of the *Rathaus*. The Americans and Russians might conquer other parts of Germany. The country might grow smaller. They might become like castle dwellers who retreat to their stone keep, but the German army would hold its ground, and his father would return to the front when Ani was well again.

At the end of that first week of Vati's disappearance, Hans arrived at the edge of the pasture to hear a familiar, nervous giggle. His stomach contracted and his pants slid toward his hips. He grabbed his waistband, hunting the rubble with his eyes.

One of the refugee boys was screaming toward the prison stall, where Ani stood alone, separated from the clump of girls and small children. Ani stood very still and straight, his arms welded to his sides. It looked as if someone had hammered him into the ground. There was a rope around his neck.

"I said, 'Move!'" shouted the refugee kid.

"I said move!" Ani squawked back.

Frieda Dillman grabbed Ani's rope and tugged gently. He squawked again and lifted his arms and coasted away along the broken wall.

"Stop it, Ani," pleaded Frieda. "Just play the game with us."

Ani squawked again. A clod of dirt hit him in the face. He fell over, his arms still straight.

"*Irre*," Hans heard the other kids say. *Loony*. He watched in horror as the advancing team threw more clods on Ani, and the younger boy bounced and twitched, and then the girls pulled him to his feet. Ani struggled for balance, his arms still outstretched. "I said move! I said move!" he repeated in an awkward falsetto.

"Loony, loony, loony!" shrieked Grete Dillman.

"Stop!" Hans shouted, and broke through the children to reach his brother. Up close he could see the bruises already swelling on Ani's cheeks and where the rope had bitten into his neck. His brother glanced at him, showing no sign of recognition.

"Stop!" Ani squawked back.

"Ani!" said Hans. "Go home."

"Ani go home," mimicked his brother. His eyes sickled up as if something was funny, but no laugh came out of his mouth.

"Who did this to him?" Hans shouted at Frieda Dillman. She was the second oldest, already with a bosom that pushed out her shirt. Her forehead crinkled. She stared at him as if he were speaking another language.

"Who put the rope around his neck?" Hans demanded.

"He wanted to play with us," scoffed Grete Dillman, tossing her braids. "Everyone knows he's crazy."

"He's not crazy," Frieda said faintly.

"Crazy," Ani echoed.

"Why are you talking like this?" Hans said to him.

His brother just stared at him with his sickled eyes and then let out a squawk.

"Shut up!" Hans grabbed for his brother, but Ani flapped free and began to run headfirst into the wall. Hans groped for the rope, his fingers closing around it. His brother choked and fell into the slush.

"Ani," Hans cried and tumbled to the ground beside him, hugging his brother's thin shoulders. "I'm sorry," he whispered, as Ani curled his knees in, still coughing.

"Shut up," Ani imitated in a whisper, but the parrot voice was fading. "Shut up. Ani. I'm sorry."

"Let's go home," Hans said, and he ignored the others as he helped his brother to his feet and loosened the rope from his neck. He threw it to the ground and put an arm around Ani's shoulder, guiding him away.

As soon as they passed a few blocks and started crossing the Kurpark, Ani's color returned. "Are you all right?" said Hans.

Ani touched his mouth with his fingers.

"Why did you go there?"

"I saw the kids playing. They're scaring it away," Ani said.

The parrot again. "Just stay at home," said Hans. "All right?"

"You don't stay at home."

"I'm older."

Ani scratched his neck. It was mostly dirt on his face, not bruises. It would wash off.

"It's not that fun anyway. The game," said Hans.

"Then why does everybody go?"

"I don't know," said Hans.

He couldn't explain why the game of Kidnap kept drawing him back, nor could he remember what his days were like before he started playing it. The game hadn't existed and now it did. His body wore the marks of it, the bruises on his shins and hips, but it had made a deeper impression on his mind. All day, at night, he catalogued his opponents: what fellows were good runners, what fellows could push him down, and who got tired first. The teams always shifted; that's what made it so hard to win and so hard to quit.

As he and Ani reached their street and passed under the branches of a familiar chestnut tree, Hans worried about who was winning. The sides would be uneven without him. He wouldn't be the one to lift the Dillmans over the wall anymore, not if he stayed away. He stopped still and let his brother walk on. Ani turned, his expression puzzled.

"You're safe now. I'm going back," Hans told him.

Ani's face fell. "Don't go."

"I have to go," said Hans. "One of them is going to trade me some sunflower seeds. For the parrot. If I don't go, I won't get them, and then we can't lure it out."

Ani continued to regard him sorrowfully.

"Don't tell Mutti," Hans said, backing away, passing the chestnut. "You know you weren't supposed to be there."

His brother's face grew smaller and less distinct. Hans couldn't see the bruises or dirt at all anymore. A few more steps, and Ani was just a small figure in a canyon of leafless trees.

As soon as Hans slipped into the apartment that night, his stepmother was there, wearing one of Marta's aprons and smelling of turnips. Her red hair sprang from a bun at the back of her head, and her cheeks were pink from hovering over steaming pots.

Ugly, Hans thought, though he knew it wasn't true. She never looked ugly. She just looked different, sharper and more angular than his mother. She'd never hit him, but her presence was always a blow. He tried to hurry past her.

"What happened to your brother?" she demanded. "Where have you been?"

"Nowhere," he said, squeezing by her into the living room.

Fräulein Müller was sitting on the sofa. She promised she was leaving that Sunday, and it wouldn't be soon enough. "Fetch those for me, will you, Hans?" she said, pointing to the blocks his brother had swept to the floor.

As he bent, he heard his stepmother storm in after him. "Your brother was hurt out there," she said. "He's been hiding in your room since he came home."

"He's fine," said Hans.

"He's not fine. And I assumed you had nothing to do with it, surely not his own brother, so I went and knocked on the Dillmans' door and gave them a piece of my mind." She paused, catching her breath. His stepmother had been giving the Dillmans a piece of her mind a lot lately: about the noise, about the messes in the wash kitchen. "Then Grete Dillman told me *you* were there."

"I didn't know Ani would show up," said Hans. "I brought him home as soon as I saw him. Why did you let him out?" He threw the blocks on the couch next to Fräulein Müller, narrowly missing his baby brother's fist as he grabbed for more.

His stepmother stepped closer to him, her shadow lengthening in the gaslight. "What happened outside?" she said.

He couldn't tell her. The memory of the rope and Ani falling to the slush made him too unsettled to talk. "We were just playing a game," he mumbled. "Ani got carried away."

"Hans," his stepmother said. He saw her glance at Fräulein Müller. "Hans, I want you to stay home and play with your brother and do your studies in the afternoons. If you disobey me, you'll be . . . locked up. In your room."

A short laugh escaped his lips. He gaped at her in disbelief. *Locked up?*

"You're the one who let him out," he said.

His stepmother looked over to her friend again. Fräulein Müller made a tower and Jürgen knocked it down.

"Strong boy," Fräulein Müller said approvingly. "A boy can wreck the tower, but a man learns how to build it." She took the baby's pudgy hand and closed it around a block. It was clear Fräulein Müller had put his stepmother up to this, with all her muttering about not "spoiling" them. Well, she might set rules, but he refused to listen.

"I'll go lock myself up right now," he said, knowing he didn't sound like himself. He didn't sound like any German son talking to his elders. Both women recoiled. He marveled at his insolence, but it continued to spill out. "If that's all right with you. Is that all right?" he asked, and left the room before they could answer.

Ani curled on the bed, quiet but not sleeping.

"Did you get my sunflower seeds?" he asked when Hans came in.

"Not yet."

Ani sighed.

"I want to tell you something." Hans took the atlas from under his pillow and spread it on the floor. "Vati is on his way," he said. He ran his finger over the bird's-eye distance between Weimar and Hannesburg, coasting over hills, rivers, the finished and unfinished Autobahn.

"How do you know?"

"I just do. I see it in my head. Like a dream, only I know it's true." He waited for his brother to protest, but Ani nodded. "He's walking. That's why it's taking so long. He's trying to stay in the trees."

Ani watched him silently from his bed. There were still red marks on his neck.

"He has to be good at hiding and sleeping in the cold," said Hans. "And sometimes he has to take eggs from people's henhouses so he can eat something."

Hans traced a different route, following the roads. "He has a gun, but he doesn't use it. He promised his father that he would never kill anything, unless it was a mercy."

"Is that true?" Ani said.

Hans looked up. His father had told him that once, but he couldn't remember when or where. He nodded. "Grossvati made him promise. Anyway, he's coming, and I don't want you to be scared. He's coming home."

"Why didn't you get my sunflower seeds?" said Ani.

Hans's cheeks burned. "He didn't have them," he said. "One of the other kids is going out to a farm again soon."

Ani began to blink rapidly. "But it's winter now."

"They cut off the sunflowers' heads in summer and dry them," said Hans.

"Is it a mercy to kill sunflowers?" asked Ani. Blink, blink. Blink, blink.

"*Ach*, Ani. Grossvati wasn't talking about flowers," Hans said. His brother still looked upset. He tried to change the subject. "Remember when we went to Onkel Bernd's?" he said. It had been just last spring, but it seemed like ages ago now. Their mother had been big with Jürgen and she'd taken them for a week at their father's friend's dairy farm. "We made a castle in the hayloft and hid from Mother, and she got so mad at us. Remember?"

He choked on the last words. Mother hadn't been able to climb the ladder and find them, so she'd called and called, while they'd hid, giggling. Ani had seemed closer in age to him then, shoulder-to-shoulder beside Hans in the scratchy pile of bales.

Ani shrugged.

Hans cleared his throat. "If you sniff a sunflower seed, you can still smell the July sun inside it. Mother told us that."

"I don't want to smell it," said Ani.

The baby pulled himself up and swayed, beaming between Liesl's and Uta's knees. In the afternoon light, he looked as jolly as a cherub painted on a cathedral ceiling. Liesl and Uta were supposed to be letting out the seams of Uta's dresses, but Jürgen's elation at learning to walk was infectious, and the two of them had been sitting there, needles and thread cast aside, for the better part of an hour, watching him stand and tumble. The two older boys were outside shoveling the front walk.

It was the second Friday since Uta's lover's visit. Liesl had two days left with Uta, and two dresses to restitch at the waist. She could not believe it was true. Her needle kept pricking her finger when she sewed. *Don't go.* Yet the closer it got to Sunday, the more Uta whisked about with a giddy air, as if she were listening to some upbeat polka the rest of them couldn't hear. No sign of fear, no concern for herself or the child inside her. "Don't worry about me," she'd said whenever Liesl asked. "I'll go back with him and I'll be fine. I'm always fine."

Always fine. Even though Uta was too pregnant now for an abortion. Even though the Red Army had crossed the Oder and would soon advance on Berlin.

Liesl slipped her fingers into Jürgen's fists and directed him slowly toward Uta. "Walk to Tante Uta now," she encouraged. The baby took a step and buckled, landing on his rump. He looked up at them, astonished.

"It's like he forgets he can fall," Uta marveled. "Until whump! He falls again."

"Try again, fall again," Liesl said, and then spoke what had been on her mind all day. "I did write to my aunt, to see if we all could go to Franconia. Us and the boys." The words had flown from her pen, explaining Ani's predicament, her wish to see her cousins again. "You could go first and we'd meet you."

Uta didn't reply for a moment. "That's kind of you." She looked at Liesl. "But you know the black sheep never goes back to her flock."

Liesl flushed. She knew it wouldn't be the same for Uta. Everyone in the village still remembered the broken elopement between the tavern keeper's daughter and the burgher's son. The Josts still owned half the town, although Hans-Paul was elsewhere, overseeing his father's eight canning factories, married to an heiress with thick lips and no children as yet.

"You'll be safer there," she said uncertainly.

"Don't worry about me. What about Frank?"

Liesl felt the child's weight tugging on her hand. She propped him with her knee. "He can come for us or send for us," she said.

"Really," said Uta. "He's just going to waltz into the nearest station and buy a train ticket?"

"That's not the point," Liesl said, wishing she could articulate the series of bargains she'd made with herself. If she waited for Frank, the worst would happen: A telegram announcing his death or arrest would come in his place. But if she didn't wait, the telegram could never reach them. The inevitable would be lost somewhere. She stared into his photograph every night and tried to remember the way he said her name. She relived their conversations and recalled the weight of his arms around her shoulders. But as each day passed, it was getting harder to feel his presence. Where was Frank? What would Frank want? When she closed her eyes and tried to picture him, all she saw was Ani, his boyish face uplifted, waiting. Ani needed to go.

"I'm doing it for his sons," she said. "When Dr. Becker comes back—"

"Do you think Dr. Becker is really worrying his head about one sick child?" Uta said.

Liesl kept her face neutral and forced herself to shrug. Uta didn't know about the note that had come last week from Dr. Becker, requesting another visit with Ani. Liesl had torn it to shreds and tossed them in the stove.

"But I want to get Ani somewhere quiet. I want you somewhere safe. I wrote to Frank's friend Bernd. He has a farm. But he never wrote back."

Uta's reply was interrupted by the apartment door opening, and Hans and Ani marching in, Ani bearing a bundle of small sticks, Hans holding a basket and an envelope.

"It's from Frau Hefter," he said.

Liesl took the card and read it with growing surprise. "She says she's very sorry to hear that Frank has gone missing, and she hopes the children like blood sausage. She says she wants us to come to a Frauenschaft meeting tomorrow." The next words made her stumble: "She says there are neighbors upon neighbors lined up to help us with meals. We just have to say the word."

Frau Hefter. Liesl couldn't get over it. She hadn't seen the woman since the day of Ani's bad news, except for brief greetings in the market.

"I like blood sausage," said Hans.

"Is there any cake?" said Ani.

"There, see?" said Uta. Her expression was hard to read.

"See what?" Hans's head snapped up.

"But this is too much," said Liesl. "Why are they being so kind to us?"

"Maybe they've wanted to be kind all along," said Uta. "Maybe you don't have to go."

"Go where?" said Hans.

"Let's see what she packed." Liesl set the basket on the floor and the boys swarmed it, even baby Jürgen, twining his soft fingers over the wicker side and shaking the paper. The exploration of the basket gave all three boys glorious expressions—they hadn't had something good to open in so long. They were gentle with one another: Hans handed Ani the parcel to open, and Ani gave Jürgen the string to dangle in his fist. Ani yelped when he saw the marzipan tube, somehow saved since Christmas. He looked so pleased it was painful. Hans turned a tin of sardines over and over in his hands. There was even a small sachet of black tea for Uta and Liesl.

"No cigarettes," commented Uta, but she sounded impressed.

When the basket was empty, Hans lifted up his baby brother and balanced the wicker bowl on Jürgen's head like a helmet. "*Sieg Heil!*" he said, saluting.

The baby dimpled and swatted at his brother.

Ani laughed with delight. "Jürgen is our general," he said, patting his younger brother's back.

"Careful with him," said Liesl, but she grinned at the boys and they grinned back.

The baby punched skyward. The basket tumbled and spun across the floor. They all cheered.

"Hurry up in there," Liesl said, pounding on the bathroom door. "I'm going to be late for the meeting."

"Why is it so important to be on time?" came Uta's muffled voice.

"So I can make an appearance and come straight home," said Liesl. It was Uta's last day in Hannesburg. Liesl didn't want to leave her side for an instant, but she had to go to the meeting or she would look ungrateful for Frau Hefter's kindness. Uta volunteered to stay with Ani and Jürgen while Hans went off to help a neighbor chop firewood. Ani wasn't fit for company yet. He'd taken to flapping from room to room, pretending he was a bird.

"Please hurry," Liesl said to Uta.

Uta opened the door. She'd spent all morning plucking her eyebrows, and her penciled hairs darted up her forehead.

"If there's cake, I want some," she said. "I've been dying for some cake." Then she walked over to the couch, pulled a blanket up, and closed her eyes.

"You don't have to go back with him," Liesl said.

"Present me with another option," Uta said in a muffled voice.

"All right, I will." Liesl bent down and patted Jürgen, dozing in his cradle like a loaf that has outrisen its pan. He would have to move to a real crib soon. Frank had promised to build him one when he returned. She blinked hard.

She clomped down the hall. In the past few days, Hans and Ani had made another fort of their closet room, blankets drooping from the hooks that had once hung coats, casting cavernous shadows over both their beds.

"Ani!" she said, and the boy hatched out, his fair hair feathery with static. Overall, he looked better—not well, but better. He hadn't gone outside since the day the children had hurt him, and the bruises were gone. He wasn't complaining of stomach pain anymore. If she could get him to the country, away from the rough kids and constant air raid alarms, he could continue to improve. Last night, she'd written a polite note to Dr. Becker explaining that she had found a new doctor and declining any more of his services. She'd post it on the way to Frau Hefter's.

"Fräulein Müller is going to stay with you and Jürgen while I go to the meeting."

"Why can't I go?" said Ani, holding his green blanket aloft.

"I need you to help Fräulein Müller with the baby," she said.

The boy made a face, but he didn't protest.

"Can birds be born in bars?" he said, then corrected himself when he saw her puzzled expression. "In a cage?"

"You and your questions," said Liesl. "I suppose so. Why?"

"Parrots live really old," said Ani. "I could live really old if I were a parrot."

"I like you as a boy." She kissed him and hurried from the room.

Uta was sitting up again, next to the cradle, puffing on a cigarette. "You can't show up in those boots."

"They're all I have," said Liesl, plucking Jürgen from the cradle and hugging him to her.

"You take my word for it: The others will be wearing their finest at *her* house," said Uta. She stared into the clouded air in front of her.

"No one owns anything fine," Liesl protested.

"Oh, yes they do," said Uta. "They may live fifteen brats to a bedroom but they've got a silk blouse and lace hanky stashed away to impress the Empress Hefter. Trust me."

"Oh, for God's sake," said Liesl, but she slid out of her warm sturdy boots and put on the evening slippers that she had worn to the dances at the spa. "I won't be gone long." She handed the baby to Uta, ignoring his protests, and ran out the door.

Uta was wrong. Of all the people in the room, only the infants were well-dressed—swaddled in thick blankets and suits that predated the war. An infant did not run and fall in the mud or stain his pants with gooseberry jam. An infant didn't wear out the elbows of her dresses or have holes in her heels. Hovering by the table with its few proffered *Kuchen*, the older children all wore mismatched sizes and patterns. The women's stockings and footwear were in the worst shape. It was clear who had darned a hole more than once, or who had run out of polish. Even Frau Hefter's skirt seams were slightly faded, and the buckle on her right shoe had been obviously repaired.

Liesl took an empty chair, trying to think of something to say. The women's conversations, all hushed, seemed coded by long acquaintance, only first names mentioned, and fragments of news. Most of it was bad news. She gathered that one woman's son had lost an arm in France and was home now, but never left the house. Another mother was worried about her daughter, who'd stopped hearing from her fiancé. Another kept complaining about someone named Heinrich, and what he had stolen from her. Uta would know how to interject, how to turn attention on herself long enough to be included, but Liesl sat there stiffly, biting her lip. Cups clattered against saucers. The air smelled of bitter ersatz tea and the dregs of cologne the women dabbed against their necks.

She was surprised when Berte Geiss sat down beside her, holding an issue of *Frauen Warte*, the national magazine for women. "Good reading?" Liesl said.

"It's all right." Berte looked prewar, her legs smooth as tusks, her prim blue skirt topped by a white silk blouse with puffy sleeves.

The magazine had changed since Liesl had last read it, in her first days at the spa, trying to accustom herself to the idle talk of the mistresses and female staff. Back then, the articles had focused on motherhood and fashion, and the supporting roles women could play to their beloved soldiers, workers, and farmers. But the articles Berte flipped through were about making temporary furniture after an air raid, and profiles of the women who served the war as anti-aircraft gunners. In the illustrations and photographs, the female faces seemed thinner and more determined, as if the war had sharpened them.

Liesl debated about saying something to Berte about the transformation. She didn't approve of Berte, but the girl had kept her distance and left Hans alone. And they were neighbors, after all.

"The women of 1945. We all look so grim in the pictures," she said finally. "You'd think we're made of iron."

"This issue is actually a year old," Berte said, flipping the page. "They didn't have any newer ones."

A plane roared low overhead and the room fell quiet. It was a curious kind of quiet. No one stopped talking, exactly, but they stopped knitting and sewing and gesturing in response to each other, and the words just cluttered in the air, unlistened to, until the whine of the engines lessened and the plane rose out of earshot. When the chatter resumed, every conversation in the room revolved around someone missing or dead: a brother, a father, a son, even a few daughters and sisters. And worse, nothing really distinguished missing and dead. People used the same past tense to talk about them.

"Has Hans come to talk to you about his father?" she said.

Berte's eyes were fastened on an ad for Nivea cream. "No. Hans has not come to talk to me," she said, enunciating each word. "I believe that was prohibited."

Liesl threw up her hands. So much for trying to be friendly.

Two of the Hefter boys came in, hauling a hay bale.

"What is this?" several of the women cried.

"Friends," said Frau Hefter, clapping her hands. "I give you the latest example of peasant *hamstern*. I had to trade some lovely hand-painted porcelain for this bale of straw." She pulled out a few booklets from her skirt pocket and held them up. "Today we're making slippers for our soldiers in the hospital. Their boots are in awful disrepair." She paused, her eyes falling on Liesl and Berte. "Let's do this together. There should be enough here that everyone can work in partners, doing one slipper each."

The boys cut the twine on the bale and began doling out handfuls. The smell of the dried straw pervaded the room. The scent was like an autumn field after a long hot dusk, like the days when her whole family pitched in at haying time, raking the straw cut by the mower. Her aunt and uncle sang folk songs. They all wore long sleeves to keep from scratches and bugs, and hung the sweat-soaked clothes outside to dry overnight, donning the stiff cotton again at dawn. Liesl could still remember the salty taste of her own dress sliding over her head and mouth.

She tried again with Berte. "I've been thinking of moving the children to the country."

"Which country?" Berte took the straw and pamphlet the Hefter boys delivered to them.

"I mean a farm. For Ani's sake," said Liesl. "I think the quiet would help him."

Berte snorted. "There isn't a quiet spot in all of Europe right now."

"Porcelain for this stuff!" exclaimed a neighbor, the straw sliding through her hands. The other partners were bending together, giggling over their clumsiness as they tried to understand the pattern. One person had to hold four blades at either end and make a loom, while the other person wove single blades through. You were supposed to make a tight flat mat for the sole, and then use felted gray wool for the shoe. Three things were clear: The hay was from last summer. The footwear would be brittle, uncomfortable, and mostly useless. And the women would make it anyway.

"Who's going to wear this crap?" whispered Berte.

Frau Hefter's eyes swung toward them.

"Never mind," Liesl snapped. "I'll do it. Read your magazine."

But the girl took the straw and started to sort it, too, hissing through her teeth. All around Liesl and Berte, the room fell into the hum and buzz of separate conversations, but the two of them remained silent. The sound of the other women talking made Liesl feel intensely alone. She wished Uta had come.

Berte suddenly spoke. "Your upstairs neighbor is going to work for us."

"Who?"

"Frau Dillman. The old man hired her as his new *Putzfrau*," said Berte.

"She can hardly keep her own house straight," Liesl grumbled.

Berte rolled her eyes. "I don't think she's coming to dust and mop."

"Oh." Liesl blushed.

Berte smirked. "At least she'll be too busy to eavesdrop on you now." Her voice sounded friendlier. "Look. I'm sorry about what happened with Hans. I just wanted to get out of here, and Hans said that he would help me get a message to someone." She looked Liesl in the eyes, pressing her painted lips together. "I knew I could trust him. He's that kind of kid. I hope I didn't hurt his feelings."

Liesl fumbled with another piece of straw. It broke as she tried to weave it. "Where will you go?"

Berte didn't answer for a minute. "Nowhere," she said in a small voice. "I'm stuck."

Liesl didn't know how to reply. Uta was stuck, too, and Liesl couldn't help her, either. She turned the slipper over and tried working the straw through backward. The stalk slit her knuckle, making it bleed. She let the slipper fall and sucked on the cut. The blood tasted rich and strange.

"I'm no good at this," she said.

"No one is. You want to go? I'll go with you," said Berte.

Liesl shook her head. With Uta leaving, she needed friends.

"You go," she said. "I'll finish both."

A door slammed. "Dresden is totally destroyed!" shouted a voice.

The room fell quiet as a boy ran in, declaring the city was burning; two or more separate attacks had flattened the central core and were sending fires raging through the rest. From somewhere the tinny sound of the radio began to seep through the questions and replies, and people shushed to listen. Liesl saw Berte slump forward.

"I'm going to be sick," said Berte, cupping her mouth.

"I'll take you to the bathroom," Liesl said.

Berte shook her head. "Outside," she said through her fingers.

Liesl rose and grabbed Berte by the shoulders, steering her through the falling straw, the unfinished shapes of men's feet. The wives crowded closer to the radio.

"But there are such big factories there," protested a woman. "The Americans invested a lot of money in them."

"Firestorm in the city center . . ." said the voice on the radio. "Walls of flame . . ."

Liesl shoved through them, towing Berte. "Excuse me," she said. "Excuse me." They passed Frau Hefter, her pretty face condensed by fear, then a threshold, and then the cold air. The windows of the houses flashed with the orange light of late afternoon. Liesl stopped, uncertain. The girl's hand fell from her mouth and she gulped for breath.

"Do you want to go back in?" Liesl asked after a moment.

"No."

"Home?"

Berte nodded.

Liesl checked the skies. Clear, empty. She knew she ought to say a proper good-bye to their host, but she towed the girl away from the house. Berte was still breathing hard.

"Did you know someone there?" Liesl asked gently.

"No," said Berte. "Everyone I know is in Berlin. Or dead." She made a little noise, almost a laugh. "I thought it would be easier to live among strangers. That way I wouldn't care if—" She glanced sideways at Liesl. "I know I'm supposed to be stoic like the rest of you. Your husband's missing. But no weeping, right? They had a sign up in the public shelter near our apartment: NO WEEPING."

"I'm not stoic," said Liesl, but she didn't know what else to say to the girl's outburst. She couldn't tell Berte about Frank. She was suddenly anxious to get home to Uta, to convince her once and for all to hide somewhere instead of going back to Berlin. She squeezed the girl's arm and they hurried along in silence, heads down, as if they were afraid of being seen.

When they reached Liesl's gate, Herr Geiss emerged from his front door. He had something hanging from his fist. It was Ani, bent in half, stumbling.

"Trying to steal from me!" Herr Geiss shouted, lurching down his front steps. Ani clattered after him. Old paintbrushes fell to the snow. The boy crawled among them, whimpering.

"Careful," Liesl shrieked. "Please—"

Herr Geiss scowled. "I caught him sneaking down my stairs."

Liesl turned to Ani. "But where is Fräulein Müller?"

"She left," said Ani, talking woodenly to the snow, the scattered brushes. "The man said he could give her a ride in his car, but not me; I didn't have to go."

"Where's your baby brother?" Liesl cried, and tore away from them. Herr Geiss called her back, but she barely heard. Her feet floundered in the snow—oh why had she been so vain to wear these useless slippers! The glass-plated door seemed to get farther and farther away.

"Frau Winter," Ani said. "Frau Winter has him. I didn't have to go. You said I had to go, but I don't. He said I don't."

Liesl stopped, her coat falling against her damp neck. She groped for her pockets, for a handkerchief. She pulled out the wool scarf, pressed it to her chapped lips. "Was it the man who came before for Fräulein Müller?"

"No," said Ani. "She took her suitcase. And your boots. I didn't have to go." He was still on his hands and knees, staring at the brushes in the snow, and his head began to twitch. Liesl grabbed his hand and towed him to his feet.

"Frau Kappus. If we could discuss the matter at hand," Herr Geiss said, his chest puffing.

"Leave her alone," Berte said.

Herr Geiss cleared his throat. "Go inside, Berte." His face was still furious.

"I think you should leave her alone," Berte's voice rang out.

"Go inside," he repeated, louder.

Berte turned slowly and walked up the steps. She looked back once at Liesl and gave a sad shrug, as if to say, *What else do you expect?*

"Now, about the boy," Herr Geiss said again.

Ani trembled under his gaze. Liesl cupped the boy's shoulders and propelled him toward their door. "Go ahead in. I'll be along in a moment."

To her relief, Herr Geiss said nothing. She bent and picked up the paintbrushes from the snow. They felt lighter than sticks. Their handles were rough with spattered paint. The bristles had been poorly washed and she could see the colors they'd been dipped in, green and white mostly, and one ochre. She made a quiver with her fist and held out the five brushes. Between them, the tips had hardly any hair at all.

"Ani took these?" she said, forcing herself to put one word after another. "I don't think he meant any harm."

The old man accepted them slowly. "They belonged to my wife," he said.

"I saw the picture she painted of Ani and his mother," Liesl said.

His heavy eyebrows rose.

"When you asked me to clean your house." She coughed. "It was a good likeness," she said.

"It was a good likeness," Herr Geiss mumbled, tucking the brushes in the pocket of his shirt.

"I don't think he meant any harm," Liesl repeated.

"I hear that he's been ill," he said.

"He misses his mother," she retorted, surprised by the umbrage in her voice. "I don't know why no one accepts what grief does to people."

One brush slipped loose from the others, and Herr Geiss caught it.

The temperature of the air was dropping. Liesl could feel it in the squares of wrist skin between her gloves and coat. She couldn't imagine the homeless in Dresden surviving a night this cold. And Frank—

"I should go in now," she said.

Herr Geiss raised his eyes to the front balcony, where Frau Winter had hung several pairs of boys' underwear and a woman's lacy girdle.

"This used to be a nice street," he said, turning away. "A very nice street."

In the study, propped on the dresser Uta had used, a note on thin white stationery:

Dear Frau Kappus:

An associate from Hadamar was in town for the day, and I am sending him with this letter to your address to examine your son. Our last meeting left me concerned about Anselm's welfare and the safety of your household. After hearing that your husband has been declared missing and your own repeated attempts to avoid another visit, I consider it best to involve an expert opinion. Dr. Pfeizer will be able to personally escort your son to Hadamar if he determines that this is the proper course of action. I trust that you understand that resistance in this matter will be considered a criminal offense.

Sincerely,
Dr. Paul Becker

There was a P.S. in Uta's hasty scrawl: *Dr. Pfeizer determined that he won't be back again. Help yourself to my things. I left what didn't fit me anymore. Love, Uta.*

"Ani, I want to talk to you," Liesl called out, but she stayed where she was, reading the note again, slipping it back in the envelope, opening the dresser drawer. It was empty except for Uta's gold bracelet.

Liesl stared down at the bracelet, trying to move. Recognition had frozen her: Uta had been preparing for a day like today—for a grand gesture and an exit. She could have left the country altogether. To buy a fake passport, to start a singing career elsewhere. Instead, she had come to Liesl, and then given everything to her—her money as a bribe to Dr. Pfeizer, and the bracelet in the drawer. Liesl could picture it clearly, having seen Uta operate so many times before: Uta's giddy laugh, her sidelong looks, her hand on the doctor's arm gently guiding him out the door.

And if Uta hadn't done it, Ani might be gone by now. Taken to Hadamar. Liesl knew she would have screwed it up somehow, she who didn't "understand" men—she would have been too truthful or fearful, and she would have lost him.

She lifted the bracelet. In all her years of friendship with Uta, she had never slipped it on. The metal felt cold and heavy, and Liesl had a hard time fixing the small amethyst clasp. The bracelet was too big for her, made her thin wrist look stickish, as if she were a girl playing dress-up with her mother's jewelry.

"Ani," she mumbled. "I need to talk to you."

She raised her arm, and the bracelet slid up to her elbow. She lowered her arm; it tumbled down to her hand, almost slipping off on its own. Raised, slid. Lowered, tumbled. Raised, lowered.

She needed to retrieve the baby, quiz Ani, refill the stove, heat some milk, cobble together some supper, fill a washpan, scrub the dishes, let down the blackout blinds, turn on the radio, sort the laundry for tomorrow, give the baby a bath—but she couldn't. She just kept moving her arm, like someone slicing the air to make a point, or signaling another person a long way off. The gold band moved with her, up and down, trapped on its axis.

The next morning, Liesl combed her hair back and fixed it with a tortoiseshell pin. She found a smidge of Uta's lipstick in the bathroom cabinet and rubbed it on her lips. A fleck of soot smoothed her eyebrows. Her best blouse and skirt were ironed and crisp. She took the photograph of Emmy Göring that Uta had cut out from some magazine, spoke to it silently, practicing her responses to the man who might come looking for her friend. *I don't know where she is.* At this, Emmy's lovely aging face appeared downcast, almost forgiving. *She disappeared one afternoon.* Emmy's thin lips pursed. There was a butterfly on her dress, just below her right shoulder. *I was at a Frauenschaft meeting.*

Liesl sat by the stove with the baby, jumping up at every noise. Hans had gone out. Ani was sitting with his *Setzkasten* open, waiting for her to call a word so he could spell it. She named simple words, like "rain" or "cold" or "egg," and sometimes she had to say them again because he forgot what he was spelling. For three minutes he sat there, holding an *A*, as if it contained some peculiar mystery, and then set it down, saying, "What's the word again?" She tried not to think about how he would fare in school. All the children were behind now, she told herself. And besides, Ani was a good boy. He tried to listen. That's all teachers really cared about. And he was safe—she'd woken up that morning without fearing for his life for the first time in more than a month. He was safe. Hadamar had passed them over.

She turned on the radio to hear reports from Dresden, the announcers listing the numbers of bodies in the streets and interviewing politicians who decried the attack on civilian Germany. It was still impossible to know who was alive and who was dead. *Tens of thousands still missing*, said the announcer. He made it sound as if "missing" were a consolation, better news than "dead." But missing didn't console. Missing meant you couldn't put bread on the table without thinking, *When has he last eaten?* You couldn't hear a dog bark without wondering if he was being chased. The passage of hours—light to the dark to the light to the dark—none of it felt real. The sun and the moon were the same, because you lived in stalled time. Your days gaped like a ripped pocket: Everything that you put into them fell out again.

And yet she still hoped. Frank was almost home. And if Uta's lover came today, it meant Uta was also free.

Liesl licked her lips so much the color wore off them, and her armpits grew damp and wrinkled by sweat. Jürgen rubbed his nose on her collar. She looked at the windows. The glass panes had a cold gray hue. She could see them blasting inward as shards. She wished she could pull the blackout blinds now, seal herself and the boys away.

Finally she left Ani and stripped off the ironed skirt and blouse, laying them out flat on the couch where Uta used to sleep. She put on an old housedress, fumbling with every button. Her temples hurt from trying not to cry. Her hands found the portrait of Emmy Göring on her dresser and crumpled it. The actress's chin smashed into her blond curls, her calm eyes disappearing last. Liesl worked the paper until it was a tiny ball and shoved it in her pocket.

She told Ani to come down to the kitchen, to keep at his spelling and watch his brother while she prepared their midday supper. Ani set up his tiles again and waited. But suddenly Liesl couldn't think of anything to spell. The words that came to her mind were too big, too vague, like "friendship" and "homesick." He would never manage them.

She tried to think what Ani would know. He knew grief. He had lost his mother and yearned for her. He must yearn for concrete things. She missed Uta's laugh and Frank's warm strong arms and the way her aunt used to run a comb through her hair. Ani must miss Susi's touch and Susi's voice. He'd told her that he had taken the paintbrushes from Herr Geiss because he loved his mother and wanted "to make her." To paint her? Yes, to paint her.

"I need a new word," Ani said.

Liesl searched the kitchen. "Bread," she said.

B-R. He stopped. His head flicked to the right.

Ani was lost, too. He lived in the world of the windowpane, caught between outside and inside.

"What's the word again?" he said after a whole minute passed. He frowned at her expression. "Mutti, what's wrong?"

She pressed her handkerchief to her mouth, trying to swallow the sob. "It's all right," she choked out. "You finished spelling it already."

The boy watched her, puzzled. "Why did you change clothes?"

"I was cold," Liesl said. She fisted the handkerchief and tried to smile at him. "You need a new word. How about 'bird'?"

A mysterious parcel arrived the following week. Liesl unwrapped it slowly, knowing what was inside by the familiar weight and hollowness, the smell of leather and sweat.

He's taken me back. He's quite pleased and proprietary about the child, and spoiling me far too much. Only three months left, and then I'll come visit you, and you can show me everything I'm supposed to do. I'm not a natural mother like you, and I will need lots of training! And don't worry your head about Dr. Becker—he was eager to pass on the case to his Dr. Pfeizer, and Dr. Pfeizer was happy to drop it. I hope you find my castoffs comfortable.

The paper was tucked in the heel of Liesl's boot. Another paper, tucked in the left boot, said simply, *Forgive me.*

Liesl read the first letter again. It didn't sound like Uta at all. Liesl's mouth filled with a sour taste. She wound the paper around her finger until it curled, and then pulled it free, and wound it again.

Forgive me.

Never, Liesl thought. *Not for endangering your own life.*

Not an hour went by when she wasn't telling something to Uta—Uta, her conscience, skeptical and loving. *I think Berte may become a friend, after all . . . It's silly, but I think whatever Ani ate might have been in Herr Geiss's house . . . I looked at the map and counted the kilometers—even if he was walking, Frank would almost be home.*

Liesl threw the curls of paper in the stove. She couldn't forgive Uta, but she couldn't stop talking to her. She would never stop talking to her.

Motherland

Hans rubbed the crusty sleep from his eyes and turned down the street to the brewery pasture. Another air raid last night, close enough to sound the sirens, to hear the thunder of bombs, but not to feel them shake the earth. *Not you*, they seemed to drum. *Not yet.* For hours, he'd huddled next to Ani and his stepmother in the cellar, now crowded and smelly with bodies, and waited for the attack to come. He'd waited with the candles lit, then blown out. Waited with silence, with Frau Winter whispering a story to her restless sons about a girl who ran outside during a raid and dragged herself back with an iron pole through her belly. *It was broken from a street lamp*, she said in a wondering voice. Hans had waited with the stink of sweat and the explosion of someone's fart, and the humiliating awareness that Berte was on the other side of the hole, probably thinking the fart was his. The lack of sleep made him feel raw and old now. He had the feeling that all his morning dreams had been bad dreams, but he couldn't remember them, only their sticky, shadowed residue.

Hans was done with his errands, but he didn't want to go home. He didn't want his stepmother to give him another job to do. He could see from the commotion of bodies in the old stable that a game of Kidnap was on. He dropped his parcels at the edge: winter-soft tubers and sunflower seeds—finally Ani's sunflower seeds! He jogged to join the team that was down a man.

The snow had given way to mud. Even the girls were filthy. The streaks on their cheeks and hair made them seem desperate. More of a plunder and less of a treasure. When they shrieked, their voices sounded harsh, crow-like. When they ran, they kicked up spatter.

"Kiss my boots!" the oldest Winter brother commanded the girls after he'd rescued them. He climbed into the stone stall and gestured for them to kneel in the mud. "I freed you. Kiss my boots." He was tall and hawk-like, with hair on his upper lip. He smoked in the bathroom at home and used up all their newspaper. Hans hated and admired him.

The five girls stared at him, fingering a braid, chewing a lip. The other boys shifted from foot to foot.

"That's against the rules—" Hans started to say.

But Frieda Dillman was already sinking down and kissing the shoe. She bolted up again, swabbing her lips. The others quickly followed. The game resumed. The girls were locked in Hans's team's prison, then escorted to safety, and then someone else shouted, "Kiss our shoes," and the girls lined up again. Hans saw the backs of their necks below their wool hats, and that one girl had a strawberry birthmark at her nape. His lips and fingers were numb with cold. He didn't understand what was happening, only he was fighting with the other team again— not just throwing mud and running, but grappling body to body—and as he was flung to the earth he saw the girls shoved up against the wall and heard their shrieks, some of them frightened and others pleased, and he rose and tackled and threw a boy down, and pushed his own hips into the scratchy wool coat of a girl, and her eyes widened as she crashed into the stone wall, and then an elbow snaked around his neck and he backed off, choking, and heard the first tear of cloth and the first real scream, and then he was hitting the ground, his cheek mashing into slick mud.

He rose, his feet sliding, his arms swinging. His back wasn't even straight when he saw the torn fabric and the bare breast beneath, a little pillow of flesh puckered by a single dark red button. Frieda Dillman pulled her jacket closed and staggered away.

Above them, three planes droned.

Hans turned and ran for the edge of the lot, shoving the rutabagas in his coat, the sunflower seeds in an inner pocket. He heard the footfalls of others beside him, but he didn't turn his head. He didn't look left or right but kept his eyes on his shoes, skimming from the wet mud to wet cobblestone to the sandy path of the Kurpark and back to his own street.

His stepmother and brothers were still at the lending library, where they went once a week. Hans put the vegetables in the pantry. He washed himself fast with lukewarm water from the top of the stove. He ran upstairs. He put the sunflower seeds on Ani's bed. But his heart kept thumping and he didn't know how to calm it. He pulled out the atlas and traced a different route for his father, going south to Rudolstadt, and then east to Bad Vilbel, through the Black Forest. Then maybe a short leg by train, and then what? What was taking Vati so long?

He heard the thuds of the Dillmans returning, heading upstairs to their apartment. He curled in his knees and held them tight. His eyes traced cities and roads, but in his mind, he saw Frieda Dillman's bare breast. He laid his head down on the atlas, as if listening to it. After what seemed like hours of waiting, he dozed, waking only when he heard the lock to the closet door click. He bolted up.

"Ani," he said. "I'm in here."

"I heard what happened to Frieda Dillman," said his stepmother's voice. "I heard you were part of it."

There was a coldness in her tone that he'd never heard before. He faced the white-painted door, words of apology and explanation stuck in his throat.

"You'll stay there and think about what you've done," she said

His eyes fell on the sunflower seeds. "Can Ani come in?" he said, his throat rusty. "I have something for him."

"Ani will sleep in the study with me and your brother," she said. "God help us, there won't be an air raid tonight." He heard his baby brother gabble to himself as she carried him away. The vocalizations sounded almost intelligible. Hans strained to hear them. He thought he heard *good boy, good boy*, but then it sounded like nonsense afterward.

Liesl carried the key to the living room and set it down on a shelf, beyond Jürgen's reach. She let him pull himself up on her, his head banging into her knees as he balanced on the floor. So she'd finally put her foot down. Liesl wished she could tell Uta. She wished she had the energy to be proud or relieved, but she didn't.

Locking Hans up merely produced another thing to wait for: the moment when she let Hans out. She would add it to her expanding list: for Frank to return, for the raids to end, for Ani's health to be restored. It saddened her to realize that she'd seen enough of Ani's behaviors— the twitching, the stumbling, the conversations with the invisible—to know what triggered them, and if she kept Ani away from loud noises and crowds, she could minimize his outbursts. What else could she do but lock him up, too? Her aunt's reply had been kind, but Liesl could read between the lines: There simply wasn't room for them all in Franconia. And wouldn't it be safer to stay put in a small spa town?

Was it safer? Liesl's constant dread of raids, of the American invasion, made it hard to focus. She found herself stunned by the simplest tasks, changing Jürgen's diaper or lighting the stove, her mind blanking on the steps it took to finish. According to the radio, the Americans were less than a day's train ride away now, and within weeks, they would be here. The Americans. She had first formulated an impression of them from seeing *Gone with the Wind* when it had played at the spa. In *Gone with the Wind*, the Americans had worn blue and gray uniforms and ridden horses. The Yankees seemed seedy in comparison to the Confederates, who'd fought nobly for a bad cause. Afterward Liesl and Uta had argued whether or not Scarlett O'Hara deserved what she got: a handful of earth, a red sky.

I don't think she'll ever be happy, Liesl remembered saying.

I don't think she wants to be, Uta had replied.

The Americans weren't fighting on their own land now, against their own people. They had no faces. They hid inside their tanks and planes and shot their bombs. They were marching on the Rhine. The banks of the big slow river were crawling with men from both sides, and reports from the north and west were full of death. Dams broken, a flood in the Ruhr, trapping whole German divisions against the onslaught. Boys and old men from nearby villages taking their places behind the Wehrmacht with their pheasant rifles and rusty revolvers. How long could they hold out? The clocks ticked faster every day. The squeaky bicycles outside sounded as if they were crying.

And now this. Liesl had come back from the lending library to a sobbing Frau Dillman, standing in the threshold of the Winters' apartment.

"There you are," Frau Dillman said, turning. Her face was blotchy with rage.

"Go get us some firewood from the coal cellar," Liesl told Ani.

He looked at her as if he didn't understand.

"Go," she said.

She waited the endless moments it took Ani to enter the kitchen and clomp down the basement steps before she ascended with the baby to meet the other women. She was certain she'd done something wrong in the house (left the water running somewhere?), but when she saw Frau Winter's cool expression, she faltered. She gripped Jürgen tighter.

The story emerged in shrill tones and gasps: The neighbor boys, including the Winters, including Hans, had attacked her daughters.

Attacked where? Frau Winter wanted to know.

And how?

And who?

"Surely not my sons," said Frau Winter. With each question her face looked narrower.

"Frieda said it was all of them," said Frau Dillman. "But by name, she mentioned 'Hans Kappus.'" She held out the cloth she'd wadded in her hands. A flimsy coat, with a jagged tear in the cotton.

Just then Ani returned with the load of firewood. "Bring it upstairs, and get some more for tonight," Liesl choked out. The women didn't say anything as the boy shuffled up the stairs, clinging to the rail with his one free hand, but Liesl could feel their judgment. "That's a good boy," she called after Ani. He did not turn or quicken his steps. Finally he went into the apartment, clicking the door behind him.

Frau Winter fingered the loose threads briefly and then dropped her head. "Your daughter," she said quietly. "She is . . . untouched?"

"I think so. My other girls say so," Frau Dillman said, wiping her eyes.

"That is good. Then I won't kill my boys. Just beat them senseless," said Frau Winter, turning away. "I'm very sorry to your Frieda," she said with her spine to them. Her narrow shoulders slumped. She went into her apartment and shut the door.

Frau Dillman was still trembling. Liesl put her hand on her shoulders but the other woman brushed it away.

"I wanted my girls to be safe," Frau Dillman said in an accusing tone.

"She is safe here," said Liesl, hearing Ani open the door. She didn't want him to know about this. "She must be mistaken about Hans."

Frau Dillman shook the ripped cloth. "You've seen how he looks at them! Like he owns them," she shouted. "And you and your airs from the day we came! 'Could you please not hang your laundry outside?

Could you please *refrain* from *clomping around*?' Like we are some kind of cows!"

Ani descended slowly, his hand on the rail. Frau Dillman's face pulsed with fury. "And *that* one," she said.

"My sons have never hurt anybody," Liesl retorted before Frau Dillman could say any more. "You don't have to be afraid for your girls. Not in my house."

Frau Dillman reared back. "I am always afraid for them," she said, and thrust the cloth under her arm. She huffed up the stairs past Ani. "Always," she said to him.

Now the key was on the shelf, and Liesl had to explain to Ani why his brother was locked in his room. She'd sent Ani downstairs for one last load of wood. He was taking a long time, as if he also dreaded their conversation.

She set Jürgen down with his blocks and began to feed the stove. The orange heat of the fire baked her face. She blinked and kept her eyes averted as Ani stumbled back in. His ankles extended from his pants. He needed bigger clothes. It surprised her that he was growing.

Ani dumped the firewood in the box beside the stove, rattling the logs so they collapsed in a mostly even pile.

"Your brother is locked in his room," Liesl said. "And you're not to go in there."

"Why?" Ani's eyes were wide.

She still didn't know how to say it. "He and some other boys ripped Frieda Dillman's coat."

Ani looked toward the hall to their closet room. "For how long?"

"What?"

"How long does he have to stay in there?"

The crime hadn't even registered, only the punishment.

Behind them, Jürgen reached out and scattered his blocks across the floor. Liesl shut the stove door. "Until I say he can come out," she said, because she didn't know how long to lock up a boy . . . a day? Two days? It was Uta's idea; it had been Uta's solution to Hans's increasing disobedience. Uta had seemed to think that Hans would emerge a different boy, chastened by the discipline he needed. At least he was being quiet now.

"Can I talk to him through the door?" asked Ani.

"No."

"How about Morse code?"

She reached out and took his hand, pulling him toward her. His steps were stumbling, reluctant. He kept his head down.

"Ani, look at me," she said, and lifted his chin. "It's not a game. Your brother hurt a girl."

His eyes met hers, and his lips began to shake. "But I want to miss him. To see him."

"I miss him, too," Liesl said. She put her arms around him and hugged him, then checked the hem of his pants. There wasn't any fabric left to let out. He would need new trousers from somewhere.

She gave him an extra squeeze and let go. His eyes were still troubled. "Am I a loony?" he asked.

The word knifed her.

"You ate something that was bad for you," she said. "But it doesn't mean you'll be sick forever."

He ducked his chin.

"What did you eat, Ani?" she asked gently, for the hundredth time. "If you'd show me, we could get rid of it together."

His body went rigid. "I can't," he said. "I can't."

She reached for him again, but he hopped back, squawking. His arms rose into wings and he flapped to the other side of the room. Jürgen looked up from his blocks and watched him. Then the baby began to gabble his brother's name, *Anh, Anh.* She plucked him up and sat back on the sofa, holding his damp, warm weight. "That's right. That's Ani. That's your brother."

The older boy climbed on a chair and drew his legs under him.

"You're growing, Ani," she said. "You're going to be big soon, like Hans. Did you know that?" She couldn't look at Ani, perching like a bird, so she talked to Jürgen's soft head. "You'll have to tell your baby brother all about your mother, so he doesn't forget her." Her voice was hoarse.

Ani didn't answer. He stared straight ahead. Then he lifted an outstretched arm to his cheek and rubbed his nose and mouth against it, as if he were preening feathers.

Hans couldn't sleep, so he kept plotting his father's journey home, penciling different routes on the map. Vati curving east by accident, almost meeting the Russian army. Vati hiding in a castle ruin and staying there until the coast was clear. Vati on foot, on bicycle, on a train. Hans started to feel his own thighs aching from the long walk, his own toes freezing and hardening with frostbite. He imagined a farm wife rescuing Vati, half dead in her barn, and hiding him in her hayloft. Soon Vati would be here and he would listen to Hans. He would understand that Hans never meant to hurt Frieda Dillman, and he would make his new wife sorry for locking Hans up. *Stay out of the affairs of men,* he would tell her.

Hans found the badge of the RLB and traced the star on the map, then wrote his own name inside it. He liked how the shape confined the letters and made sense of them. *Hans Friedrich Kappus.* He swore his own oath: to love and defend his brothers forever. Especially Ani. He wasn't going to ditch him for the other kids anymore. He mentally added a promise about the parrot: *If it's in my power, I'll find it, Brother, and bring it home.*

He grew hungry. He plucked up the little bag of sunflower seeds and stared at it. Then he ate one, only one, and watched the door.

It wasn't yet light out when his eyes opened. He woke thinking he'd heard a click, but he didn't believe it. No noise came from the hall. He pushed himself from his bed and walked barefoot across the cold, stinging floor to the doorknob. He bent down and peered through the keyhole. Blankness and a still wall beyond. If he could shrink to half a centimeter tall, he could crawl out and lower himself on a thread to the floor. He was still entertaining the thought when his hand reached up and tried the knob. It snagged—locked!—no, it wasn't locked; it was rolling all the way to the right and the door was swinging loose in his hand. He held it halfway and peered into the dim hall, seeing no one. He listened for noises, but the apartment was still. It was as if an invisible snow had fallen through the rooms and coated everything. His breath sounded loud in his ears.

"Ani," he whispered. The silence was complete.

He shut the door carefully and dressed, tucking the sunflower seeds in his pocket. He looked around for a peg to jam in the lock, to make it look as though he'd let himself free.

Before leaving, he pulled the seeds out again, and plucked a single black one from his palm. He left it on Ani's pillow. A clue only Ani would understand.

As Hans crossed the pasture, he glanced over at the stable ruin, seeing it for a moment as it once must have been: a long brick building, with doors for the horses, their broad noses poking out. A romantic place, full of golden straw and the chance to ride away on the back of a stallion. Now it was empty, laid bare by decades, the rubble glistening with frost. Hans wondered if anyone would show up today, or if the game was over for good. Remembering what happened to Frieda made him heartsick and angry. It was all the Winters' faults for changing the rules. They could have played forever if they had followed their own rules.

Hans looked around again to make sure he was alone, then flattened against the ground and shoved under the gate that guarded the building from trespassers. He walked up to the building, suddenly awed by the sheer walls, their age, the gaping oak door he stepped through. The instant reek of mildew made him blink and wrinkle his nose. It was hard to imagine busy workers here, or the giant brew kegs that had once held beer. The building had been empty as long as he'd been alive, a vaulting cavern, its second floor burned away by a long-ago fire. Char streaked the inside walls and the rafters above. Cobwebs and dust hung like wigs from iron hooks.

Hans reached into his coat pocket, fisting his hand carefully around the hard shells inside. He drew his fingers out, still balled, and slowly opened his palm. A few sunflower seeds stuck to his fingers and he combed them down with his other hand, making a tidy black pile. Then he extended his arm out, waiting for the parrot.

He hoped the parrot would understand him as animals understand each other. That a silent communion would pass between them, and the bird would fly down and eat from his hand. That it would come home. It would sleep in their room at night, and ride on Ani's shoulders by day, as though his brother were a seafarer returned from a long, strange voyage.

Sirens groaned on the daylight outside. The groan divided against itself, and divided again. Voices called in the distance. Metal clanged.

On the far side of the building, people were entering the public shelter. It had a giant iron door fastened to bolts. On one of his scavenging missions, Hans had studied the door before, entranced by its size. It latched from the inside and could hold back fire.

He hesitated, forcing his palm to stay steady. The daytime raids were usually factories and railroads, not the center of town. He stared into the black seeds, willing the bird down from the apse.

The seeds popped into the air and he staggered forward. He was almost to his knees before his ears registered the crash. The blast was so loud, it made his teeth rattle. The black seeds tumbled to the earth. He dropped to gather them and the building shook again. He crashed to his elbow, bruising it. With quick fingers he scraped up most of the seeds, shoving them in his pocket. Another blast. He bit his tongue. Tasted blood.

Damp dirt tumbled from overhead, pattering his hair, the back of his neck. He struggled to rise. Another blast. The walls seemed to be throwing themselves higher, away from the earth. A brick thudded the floor a few meters away. Hans bent like a sprinter and launched himself forward toward the brewery door, the gate beyond.

Another crash slammed his temple into the doorjamb. He fell, holding his brow, feeling first the impact and then the pain. He rolled to his side, half in the shadow and half in the light. His eyes blinked through a heavy rush of tears. He rubbed them away with his arm, his buttons scraping at his skin.

Outside, planes ripped over the center of town. The prim lines of the castle, the red roofs, and the plaster city looked tiny under the onslaught. Oblongs plummeted from the aircrafts. Ash and mud rose a few delayed instants later, as if the earth had swallowed the artillery and was vomiting it back up.

Hans dove under the fence, shimmying through the mud, lurching to his knees, rising into a run. Just before he passed out of sight of the brewery entrance, he looked back for the parrot.

He saw no movement, but he felt a cold intelligence inside the building, watching him.

The sky thundered again and his legs collapsed. He smashed the wet grass, then ran alongside the worn brick wall, taking the corner. In the distance, he spied the big iron door, the wall above it marked with a white-and-black sign. The shelter was for the Alt Stadt, for the poor people with no basements of their own. A few meters and he would be there. His mind flashed to the people inside—haggard, toothless mothers who shrilled at their snot-nosed kids, elderly men who didn't remember to wipe themselves. His stepmother and brothers would be at home in their own cellar, frantic for him.

The siren wailed. A plane tore through the air overhead, low enough to glimpse its blister of machine guns, pivoting left and right. Hans sprinted the last ten meters.

The plane passed, bullets tattering the ground, making the wet soil pop like grease in a pan. Hans slammed the damp door. "Let me in!" he screamed, beating the metal.

Another plane circled. Hans hugged the door. "Let me in!" he called again.

A small object tumbled from the plane's belly and into the pasture behind the brewery. Hans braced himself for an explosion. It did not come.

"Let me in!" his voice was still calling, rising on the "in," so that the word became a scream.

A shadow coasted over Hans's face. He glanced up. The underbelly of the plane was right over him—the rivets, the silver blur of the engines—but its noise was so loud, so total, that the sensation of its passing was like a sudden blindness. Hans clawed at his eyes.

The plane surged skyward. Hans pummeled the door. He punched it so hard his knuckles split, and then he punched it harder.

The siren wailed, a long drawn-out sound that broke the roar of the planes. A peculiar quiet followed—not a silence but a lower, whining drone as the planes took the sky. Hans pressed his ear to the door. He could hear the people murmuring inside. Why couldn't they hear him?

He screamed out his name, his address, his father's and mother's names. Why couldn't they hear him?

"Just let me in!" he pleaded. The whine was getting louder.

"Let me in!" His bloody knuckles hammered the door. The planes were circling. They would bomb again. Hans scrambled back, waiting for the lock to unclick, but the door did not budge.

He pushed himself to standing. He would run. He had to run. A plane descended, shrieking over him. He fell back on the door, his hands folding themselves over the back of his head, so tight they mashed his shaking face into the metal and he tasted the flat, cold flavor of his father's stethoscope, and helmets, and knives. He shut his eyes.

The baby balanced on one foot, wobbled on his axis, then let the second foot down on a lump of carpet and toppled with a whump. He pushed his behind in the air and rose again, holding the sofa. One foot, then the next. One foot, then the next. His soft woolen socks crushing under his weight. One foot. He was treading beyond the sofa now, to the open space between furniture and stove. He was walking toward the green tile with his arms outstretched.

"He's really walking! He's walking! My baby brother's walking!" Ani shouted from his perch on the sofa.

"Right into the stove," Liesl said, scooping up the taut spring that Jürgen had become. He squirmed to be let down and started his march again, this time toward the table where Uta used to pile her ashtray and stale candies. Now it held a map traced with Hans's hand, and a star at the edge of it that bore Hans's handwritten name. Hans was going to find his father, or to join the fighting, but either way it was clear that he had intended to go far.

She'd checked the lock, found the little peg he'd jammed into it.

She'd bribed the Winter boys to ask at the train stations. "Why don't you wait for nightfall?" Frau Winter had said when she'd seen Liesl's panicked face. "He'll come home when he's hungry."

"It will be too late by then," Liesl insisted.

She'd hugged Ani while he cried, and then praised him when he'd raised his head and said, hiccupping, that he had to be brave for Jürgen.

"Now I can teach you to fly," Ani said to his brother, grabbing him under the arms and straining up. As Liesl cried out, he hefted the baby into the air and then lost his own balance. They both tumbled to the ground. Jürgen looked stunned but he didn't wail.

"He doesn't need to fly," she said, reaching out a hand. But Ani was already trying to lift his brother again, shoving him forward. "Stop it," she cried.

A door slammed downstairs and sirens began to blare. Liesl grabbed Jürgen in midtotter and told Ani to get the extra blankets. Her orders were cut off by another siren. She staggered, grabbed for the door handle. There was a heavy cracking sound toward the Louisenstrasse, and then the sky began to beat and thunder. The windows ground in their casings. She glanced out, hoping to see Hans running, but the street was empty, and shimmered strangely, like a street in a mirror's reflection.

Ani appeared, shrouded in green wool, a stricken look on his face. Another boom, and plaster broke from the walls. She yelled to him to hold the railing, but he simply launched down the first set of steps, a green hump tumbling earthward. The doors to the Winters' and Dillmans' apartments opened and slammed. Frau Dillman, the Dillman girls, Frau Winter, her cluster of boys. The staircase was a river of bodies. They were pushing each other toward the dark narrow steps. Liesl took one last look for Hans and then plunged after them, clutching Jürgen, who started to squall at the top of his lungs.

Another boom, and plaster fell from a nail hole, dribbling down the wall. Frau Dillman screamed and shoved her daughters with her fat arms, but Frau Winter was not to be beaten to the cellar, and she scrambled ahead of them all. Her body tipped like a tall bottle. The siren groaned. The Dillman girls bobbed and shrieked, their heads full of pin curls that glinted in the last of the sunlight. Another boom. They leapt and plunged en masse into the cellar, their hands clawing at the stone wall. Liesl heard a shrill scream and saw Ani disappear under the wave of bodies.

"You're crushing him!" she cried.

The booms and sirens stopped for a moment, and a sudden silence struck. Jürgen wailed and then looked around, as if surprised by the sound of his own voice. She heard Ani whimpering.

"Don't crush him!" Liesl shouted, but the explosions began again.

By the time Liesl made it into the cellar with Jürgen, their supplies were all over the floor and Ani was curled up beside the shelf, cupping his face while the others eddied around him. Liesl ran to him. She couldn't hear her own voice trying to reassure him.

Nearby, Frau Winter was collapsed over a long gash in her arm. She moaned while her gaunt sons tried to bandage it with a shirt.

Frau Dillman, face stony, herded her girls through the hole in the wall, where Herr Geiss and Berte waited for them. A lantern was already burning there. Another boom, muffled now. The arching cellar bricks trembled and spilled grains of mortar. Liesl adjusted Jürgen on her hip and pulled Ani with her to a pinch of room beside Herr Geiss's hole.

The explosions lessened, and Liesl tried to pry Ani's fingers free. "Ani, look at me," she shouted. "We're safe now. We're in the shelter you and your brother built." Internally, she willed Hans to make it home. Ani shook her off and covered his eyes again, flicking his head.

The last Dillman girl trailed through the hole. She was holding a moth-eaten doll by the neck. "Hurry now. Don't stay in there," her mother shrilled from the other side. Liesl's eyes met Frau Winter's and a question flashed between them: Which one of their sons had initiated the attack on Frieda?

Not mine, Liesl thought, and in Frau Winter's gaze she saw the same stubborn doubt.

The explosions came in waves. A boom. The house shook. Liesl ducked, covering Jürgen's head. Then rattle and rain, quaking, stillness. She raised her head, and just when her dry tongue passed across the dirt on her lips, just when she'd stopped clutching Jürgen so hard, another boom. Cans clattered on the shelves. Ani rocked and twitched, his hands cupping his eyes.

The suitcases against the near wall leapt. One sprang open, blossoming shirts and underwear. There was a scream from the other side of the hole and someone ran through, grabbing for the luggage.

It was Frieda. Her cheeks were red. Her new breasts strained against her sweater as she tried to shove the suitcase closed. It seemed like hours, her struggle. No one helped her. The Winter boys sat with their toes practically touching Frieda's, their mouths slightly parted, their hands over their ears. If Hans had been there, Liesl would have made him offer a hand, but Hans was outside—in that hell—because of Frieda. Liesl couldn't set the baby down. Frau Winter's head was buried in her bloodied arm, her voice braying the Lord's Prayer. The candles flickered and sputtered.

Finally Liesl scooted forward on her knees, still holding Jürgen, to assist Frieda. When another explosion shook the cellar, she reached out for a wall but misjudged the distance. Her hand fell through the hole between the cellars. She toppled. Jürgen gripped her neck.

"Mutti!" she heard Ani scream as her head banged on dirt. She tried to push herself up, clinging to the baby, but another explosion came and she tumbled. Jürgen began to wail. She could see into Herr Geiss's side, the folded legs of the Dillman girls, and the dark hulk of the older man. His face was in shadow. She shifted Jürgen to her left arm and pushed up with the right, shoving back into the light, into Ani, who clung to her.

As soon as Liesl cleared the hole, the Dillman girl rushed through, clutching the closed suitcase. Another explosion, and Jürgen's wails grew urgent. Frau Winter's praying sang somewhere underneath it, gnawing Liesl's ears.

She shushed the baby, though she couldn't hear herself, though soon another wailing joined his, the voice older and rawer, but the pitch and rhythm exactly the same. She saw the cellar's eyes swivel to Ani. He squatted birdlike, his arms clamped to his sides, and screamed. His throat pulsed. His trousers climbed up his legs, exposing his bare shins and making his feet look like claws.

Liesl eased over to him, holding Jürgen against her ribs, and tried to put an arm around him. "Ani," she called.

He raised his arms wing-like, clobbering her hard across the chin. She fell back. Another explosion and Ani launched up. For an instant he flew on the shaking air and then fell headfirst into one of the shelves. Cans tumbled off, rolling everywhere. Ani flapped again, throwing himself toward the ceiling.

Liesl saw the Winter boys look at each other, then their mother. En masse they scrambled toward the hole to Herr Geiss's side. Their bodies moved in slow motion, gaining footholds, losing them as the explosions rained down. Dirt pocked their faces. As Ani screamed and flapped, smashing into walls, the boys disappeared, one by one. Finally only Frau Winter was left. She gave Liesl a pitying glance and shoved through, her black skirt trailing.

With the others gone, Hans's green curtains suddenly came into view, hanging mildewed on the walls. Ani clawed at them, dragging the cloth down. The curtains snagged on his arms. They fluttered. He shrieked and tugged them high, his white face shining. His feet barely touched the ground. He seemed to be dancing on the broken, shifting air. He toppled, slamming the empty sauerkraut vat. Liesl tried to reach him, but she tripped on a can and lost her balance, almost dropping the baby. She sank to her knees, sobbing, cradling Jürgen.

Another boom. She was crouched across the cellar when one of Ani's green wings dragged across a candle. Fire burst over the tatters of cloth. The flame cast its sudden brightness. Ani's screams changed. She bent and dropped the baby on a trampled blanket, then ran for the burning boy with her arms outstretched.

The plane surged over Hans and past the castle before it dropped its bombs. They fell like mulberries from a bowl and then the sky split into clouds of flame and dust. Hans peeled himself from the shelter door and ran back toward the brewery. His pants hung on him, wet with piss, and made his legs snag with every step. He retraced his footprints back to the brewery fence and shoved himself under, lying on his back. The metal snagged on the soaked bulge of his crotch. He kept pushing. The pants groaned and tore. His penis shriveled against the touch of the cold wind. He whimpered but he kept shoving—*there*, he was through—then he tugged the torn flap free from the wires.

The planes were circling back. He held his pants closed with his hand and sprinted inside the brewery. He didn't know he was sobbing until he got inside, and his loud, harsh hiccups broke against the ancient walls.

"Shut up," he shouted at himself. He pounded his fists into his quaking gut. "Shut up! Shut up!"

The rafters gaped above him, revealing nothing. He sobbed until he retched, falling to his hands and knees. Drool dripped from his mouth. He stared at the dirt. He stared at the scattered black seeds. The wet flap of his pants hung open.

A loud explosion made the building shake. Dust fell gently. He listened for wings and heard in the distance, far beyond the brewery, the feathering roar and crackle of fire.

He crawled under an old ledge in the wall and tried to make himself smaller, squeezing his knees into his face, one arm tightening over his ears, the other over his eyes.

After the air raid ended, he sat very still, unable to bring himself to move. He stared at the rafters until nightfall, and after nightfall he stared into the darkness, still cupping his knees. He played a game of closing his eyes, then opening them suddenly, and searching the blackness for the walls he knew were there.

Sometimes the walls moved. They were five, ten meters away, and sometimes they were centimeters from his nose. They had a reddish-black hue. They were the texture of felt, then of fur. Once he thought he saw feather patterns, a series of long straight stripes with spokes radiating from their lengths, but the moment he pushed his nose forward, the wall disappeared.

He was aware of things happening outside the brewery. He heard the giant iron door swing open and people stampede out, crying and howling at the fires and destroyed buildings in the center of town. He heard a man call that the power was out. He heard fire trucks racing, and the lower, rumbling growl of an army convoy. He heard a house fall in. He was pretty sure anyway. There was a long groan, and then a crumbling crash that sounded like boards and rocks being eaten by a giant mouth.

He made two bargains with himself.

If I go home, they will still be alive.

If I don't go home, they will still be alive.

He remained frozen between the choices.

Sometimes he heard his own desperate voice begging to be let in, and he tried to lock the memory away.

The walls came closer. The walls drifted a kilometer off. They were the color of a night river. He could dive into them.

If I go home, they will still be alive.

If I don't go home, they will still be alive.

He couldn't get up now and walk home. His body hurt too much, and he was afraid of the dark outside the building. He was afraid his voice was still shrieking out there somewhere.

So when he heard someone calling his name, he squirmed his spine deeper into the dirt and clung to his knees. He stayed there when he heard the fence shake. He was so perfectly still an ant could crawl over him and think he was a stone. But he heard a grunt, and then a scraping sound, and then the voice was closer and it spoke his name urgently.

There was a hiss, and light flooded over him, making the ceiling's cobwebs glow like an old woman's hair.

His stepmother's face appeared, covered with soot and mud.

He shrank deeper. His spine scraped the wall. It made the softest rustle. She turned and saw him. She ran closer, the oil lamp bobbing in her hand. He felt his face crumple and he pushed his fists against it. He ground his dirty knuckles into his eyes as she set the lamp down and pulled him into the nest of her lap, kissing his head. "They wouldn't let me in," he said in a choked voice.

She rocked him gently, gathering him up with her thin arms, holding him against the cold. He wept so hard he shook.

"Shh, now," he heard her say. "You're here." And she kept saying it every few moments, but softer and softer, until he had to stop sobbing to hear it.

Before they set out for the walk back, she told Hans quickly about Ani, about the burn on Ani's right arm, and how she'd wrapped it in salve and a torn sheet. She said that Ani had calmed after the explosions stopped. "Right away," she said, because she saw Hans's worried face. (It wasn't exactly true: First Ani stopped flapping, then he stopped screaming, and finally he just lay there and breathed, like a rabbit exhausted by a trap.)

"When we came upstairs, he saw the sunflower seed you left him. He said I would find you at the brewery," she finished.

She did not say that she didn't believe Ani at first, that she was afraid to venture out. All the unexploded ordnance everywhere. The chance of another raid. Being mistaken for a looter by the RLB.

She did not say that it was Berte Geiss who made her go, who volunteered to stay with Ani and Jürgen on their side of the cellar. The young woman had suddenly emerged from the hole. "Go," she said, her face pale but her voice strong and sure. "I heard what Ani said. I'll watch them. Go."

Liesl would never tell Hans how harrowing it was to step out alone, on the black, broken streets, and fumble her way to the brewery with no light, every tiptoe a step that could end her life. Their street had not been bombed, but the farther she'd ranged from their villa, beyond the neighbors of neighbors, the more destruction she'd seen: a roof punched in and smoldering; shattered window glass and drifting pieces of paper; the pit where a house had been; a pile of rubble where three men dug furiously, all wearing the stars of the RLB. Stones and ash spun under their shovels. One of the men smoked furiously while he dug, the embers of his cigarette dropping tiny sparks. It took Liesl a moment to recognize that it was Herr Unter, the old man who sold her rabbit meat. The dimness accentuated the lines of his face, making him look ancient.

Liesl heard boots clack on the cobblestone and hid in a threshold while a soldier in uniform passed, peering left and right.

She listened to the men dig, wondering whose house it was.

"I heard her," said one of the men hoarsely. "The little girl. She called out. I'm sure of it."

The others did not respond. Their blades clanged the stone.

When Liesl was certain it was safe, she crept out over a path of broken glass and did not look back.

Farther along, a water main had broken and she had to cross a frothy, filthy river, soaking her boots.

Then the black plum of an unexploded bomb had appeared right in the middle of her path. She'd stopped altogether, staring at it.

Frank is dead, the bomb whispered. Its sinister message paralyzed her. *Frank is dead.*

She had not allowed herself to imagine it until that moment, her nostrils clogged with smoke, her eardrums still ringing with the sound of explosions. Something had fallen on Frank. Something had lifted up under him and hurled him into the air like an animal shaking off a rider. Something had buried him. Her mouth opened, and it felt as if she was breathing in something solid; walls would fill her instead of air, and she would harden.

A shrill whistle a block away broke her reverie and she stumbled sideways, around the bomb, into deeper shadows. She'd had to feel her way then, wincing at every crunch of glass or gravel.

The entire journey—less than a kilometer—had taken her two hours.

The way back with Hans seemed easier, but it went no faster. They picked their way lightly through the rubble, hardly stepping down. The boy understood to be quiet and motioned when he needed to point out a shard of twisted pipe in their path, a sudden hole. They hid together when they heard someone shout, "RLB! Who's there?" and Hans's breath made a damp patch on her waist.

When they reached their street, Hans paused. Liesl watched him gaze on the downed sticks and leaves, the rash of black soot on all the walls and the blinded windows, but every one of the houses whole and entire. Then he spoke. "I didn't mean to hurt Frieda," he said in a small tight voice, and then he burst into tears again.

Liesl did not put her arms around him this time, although she wanted to. She watched him weep, watched until his shoulders stopped shaking and he wiped his eyes. "Then apologize to her and her mother," she said in a calm voice.

The boy held back.

"Come on," she said.

"Is Vati dead?" he said.

How had he guessed her fear? She staggered and caught herself. A stone rolled away from her feet. "I don't know," she said.

They walked forward in silence. When they were just a few houses away, she tripped again. This time a muscle wrenched in her ankle. She cried out.

The boy grabbed her arm, steadying her. A ray of moonlight illuminated his face, and in that moment he looked so much like Frank she almost gasped. She leaned into Hans, suddenly exhausted, and felt him lean back at her. They held each other all the way to the gate.

Jürgen was asleep in Berte's arms when they returned. In fact, both boys appeared to have been dozing, Jürgen on Berte's lap and Ani lying against her side.

"You made it," Berte said weakly.

Two of the Winter boys had also returned to claim some free space, their lanky limbs stretched on the bare earth. But the others still crowded in the Geiss cellar. Light and whispers trickled through the hole.

Liesl spoke into it. "He's been found," she said. "Our Hans. He's safe."

There was a silence and then Herr Geiss spoke. "Glad news," he said.

She felt Hans step forward beside her, saw the contrite expression on his face. She saw his mouth working on the apology he had to utter to Frieda and Fran Dillman.

"Where's my parrot?" Ani's voice rose. "Did you give it the seeds?"

Beyond the hole, Frau Dillman whispered something and her daughters giggled.

Liesl gripped Hans's arm and pulled him back. He could apologize to the girl later if he wanted, but she wasn't going to give that woman—or any of them—the satisfaction of hearing him now. Not when they'd left her alone with a baby and a burning child.

Hans seemed confused, but then he shrugged and slumped down beside his brother.

"Where is it?" Ani said again.

"I gave it the seeds and it flew away before the raid," Hans said after a moment. "You were right. It wanted to go back to the jungle." He looked at his brother's arm, bandaged in strips of one of Frank's old shirts. "Does it hurt?"

Ani turned his hollow gaze on Liesl. "It's going to die," he whispered.

"You don't know that," said Liesl.

"It's too far to the jungle," said Ani.

Liesl looked to Hans for help, but he sank down on the cellar floor and pulled a blanket up into a hood, cloaking his face. "I'm tired," he muttered.

"In the morning we can find everything," Berte said in a strained voice. "We just all need to sleep."

"Sleep would be nice," said Herr Geiss from the other side of the cellar, and Liesl heard Frau Dillman titter again. A wave of loathing swept through her. She hated them all: the ones who'd ignored her son's fists on the shelter door, the ones who'd left her alone with Ani burning. The one who'd let her best friend go, the one who'd let Ani sicken.

She took Jürgen from Berte and settled against the wall.

Berte leaned forward on her arms and began to cry softly into her knees. Liesl touched her hair but the girl shook her off.

"I'm all right," she said, sniffing. "I'm all right. Get some sleep."

But Liesl couldn't sleep. She just kept checking her sons—Hans, Jürgen, then Ani. Hans and the baby slept. Ani stared into the darkness, holding his burned arm. He hardly blinked or moved his head. His wet eyeballs caught the light. Sometimes he reached up a hand and ran it over his own face, his fingers probing his nose, his lips, as if he had never felt them before.

Late in the night, more explosions.

After it ended, there was no answering rat-tat of anti-aircraft fire, Liesl realized with a fresh dread. The flak towers were down, the Luftwaffe gone. There was no one to protect them now.

The morning drew a halo at the top of the stairs. It pulsed and beckoned. *New world, new world,* it seemed to say, as if they had all voyaged somewhere strange and dangerous.

The hole flooded with traffic. The Winter boys darted from the Geiss cellar into Liesl's and ran upstairs, followed by the Dillman girls. Hans sprinted after them. Herr Geiss barged through to look at Ani's burn. He pronounced it minor, but he looked at the boy thoughtfully for a long time, and his heavy chin fell to his chest.

Liesl wanted to talk with him, but the mothers were needed in the kitchen to mete out food. Liesl avoided Frau Dillman's eyes as they made a hasty congress to discuss their collective stores: a few loaves of bread, some potatoes, a smidge of lard, horseradish, rutabagas, cabbage, a tiny chunk of salted ham. Gas and water were off. Firewood and coal were low. They could smell the burning from the city's center. The stench was greasy and sharp, as if someone had roasted rubber. Frau Winter hailed a boy passing in the street, who told them the post office had received a direct hit. Probably fifty dead there alone.

Fifty dead in one place. Such a small number, after all the tallies from the battlefields. Yet the boy's words nailed Liesl's feet into the floor.

"Where will all our letters go?" asked Ani.

"They'll find them," said Hans, standing by the stairs. "They'll deliver them."

Frieda Dillman came bounding up the steps behind him. At the sight of Hans, a shadow crossed the girl's pretty features, and she tried to turn around.

"Frieda," said Hans.

"Don't you dare go near her!" Frau Dillman called out as her daughter descended underground again. The look on Hans's face was that of a beaten dog.

Liesl was about to retort when she felt Berte Geiss's hand on her shoulder.

"We'll cook it in shifts and take it downstairs," Berte said. "Liesl and I will take the first shift. There's no telling if there'll be another raid today."

But there wasn't. Instead the skies cleared, and a light rain fell overnight, soaking the debris and making it all the heavier. The next morning, the families returned to their upstairs rooms, but the house remained at war. Hans did not apologize to Frieda, and no one apologized to Liesl. Doors slammed. Voices rang.

Later Liesl was fetching vinegar from the cellar when Herr Geiss emerged through the cleft. He had been out all day with the air raid committee, tallying damages. Instead of exhausting him, the burden energized him. He seemed younger, and handsome in a sea-captainish way.

He cleared his throat and watched Liesl move the earthenware lid.

"The boy," Herr Geiss said. "He belongs in a safe place. Where people can care for him."

"I care for him," said Liesl.

"Your husband requested that I watch over his house," Herr Geiss said. "I'd like to take Anselm to a doctor."

Liesl straightened carefully. "He's been to a doctor," she said, looking Herr Geiss in the eye. "The doctor thinks the air raids unnerve him. He recommended I send Ani to the country."

She waited for Herr Geiss to inform her that he would arrange it, that he would gladly carry out his longtime threat now that Ani was behaving like a bird and Hans was attacking the Dillman girls. Instead her neighbor looked down at his feet.

"I walked around Hannesburg today and I don't know how you managed it," he said. "I couldn't walk a safe path by daylight and you did it in the dark. Both ways." He cleared his throat. "Only a mother could do that."

Liesl was so stunned she almost dropped her jar of vinegar. She didn't know what to say. Footsteps thumped overhead.

Herr Geiss reached into his pocket and pulled out a sealed and dirty envelope. "Twenty-three," he continued. "Twenty-three bodies we dug up yesterday, half of them holding letters in their hands. I can't make out the address on this one, can you?"

He extended the envelope. Soot had streaked the ink past recognition. Only the first name of the addressee was readable.

"Heinrich," she said aloud, still in shock.

"Yes, but Heinrich who and Heinrich where?" Herr Geiss shook his head, and slid the letter back in his pocket.

Later that day, ashamed by her own unneighborliness, Liesl resolved to sort things out with Frau Dillman. Yet when she encountered the other woman on the landing, Frau Dillman drew back with a haughty goose-like expression and hurried away. So Liesl started plotting instead for a moment alone with Frieda, but Frieda's mother had somehow elevated the childish incident at the vacant lot into a premeditated onslaught on the virtues of her daughters. All night she kept her girls under strict surveillance, inside her apartment, except for quick, messy forays to the common upstairs bathroom.

After Jürgen went to sleep, Liesl decided to try one last time. She was pulling on her housecoat to go upstairs when she heard a voice coming through the vent in the wall.

"*Irre, Irre, wo bist Du?*" the voice whispered. *Loony, loony, where are you?*

Liesl stormed upstairs and hammered on the door. "Stop it," she shouted through the wood. "Stop that right now." She heard the girls giggling behind the door.

"I'd like to talk to your mother."

"She's not here." The girls whispered, and Liesl heard Frau Dillman shushing them.

After that, it was too late. The moment was over.

She couldn't think about it anymore. She didn't have the space in her mind, which grew more and more preoccupied with her fear of Frank's death. She'd denied it so long it had grown large and shadowed. She could be wiping her face dry with a towel, and the drag of the cloth against her cheeks would remind her of a sheet passing over the face of a dead man. She could be lighting a match and the flare would make her think of a gun firing, a bullet entering Frank's body.

And then there was Ani. He had hardly talked after the night of the bombing, and for days all he did was ask for water. All day. Twitching and jerking.

"May I have some water?"

"May I have some water?"

Water had been hard to find, carried by buckets from a working well near the Louisenstrasse. The entire house depended on one full vat of it in the wash kitchen. The vat ran out fast and the Winter boys and Hans took forever to replenish it.

Yet Hans made life bearable. He ran all the errands and sat with Ani and tried to draw his brother out. Watching them together made Liesl realize how much the boys had splintered apart since January, since the arrivals of Uta and Berte. As Hans and Ani built vast block castles and invaded each other's kingdoms, she could remember the old days—when Ani had been able to get through a conversation without stumbling or looking vague, when he'd moved about like an ordinary little boy, restless and bouncy. The old days. Only three months ago.

She was dusting and straightening the fallen books in Frank's father's study when she heard a knock downstairs. She took the steps slowly, aware of the Dillmans' 'door opening and closing above her. *Let them spy,* she thought. *We have nothing to hide.*

At the bottom, she peeked through the glass beside the entry, catching the outline of a tall male figure. No doubt someone with bad news. She steeled herself and opened the door.

The man was white-bearded, his shirt half tucked. His pants had stains at the knees. His eyes twinkled. He reminded her of woodsmen she'd known as a child.

Without saying a word, he winked and handed her a note.

Dear heart:

*Onkel Bernd is an old friend, and he's taking good care of your "medicine."
Send him back with Ani, if Ani's well enough to travel.*

Kisses,
F

Liesl read the note three times, unable to keep a huge hiccupping sob inside her chest. She closed her eyes against the weak March sun. She closed out the cherry tree, the branches already nubbly with dark red buds. She closed out the iron gate, the cracks in the neighbor's roofs, the soot smell on the wind. A stillness spread like water from her center. Frank was safe.

"Perhaps you'd like to invite me inside," said the man.

"Onkel Bernd," Liesl exclaimed. "I'm so glad you got my letter. Come upstairs." She herded him inside, his heavy boots announcing their passage across the foyer. "We live on the second floor now," she said loudly. "I think last time you visited the Kappus family had the whole house."

She saw the other apartment doors open a crack as the Dillmans and Winters investigated the new visitor. The cracks were not wide enough to see who was looking—mother, or daughter, or sons. Liesl tried to make her face look pleased but unsurprised.

Onkel Bernd ducked to enter the apartment and stood, spraddle-legged, while she called the boys. Hans emerged from the study looking puzzled.

"Go get your brother, too," Liesl said. She wanted to ask him everything about how Frank arrived, how he'd escaped Weimar—but she was afraid their voices would carry.

After a moment, Ani appeared, holding his bandaged arm. The long red burn was healing but his color was still poor and his eyes hollowed by exhaustion.

"Boys," said Onkel Bernd, nodding at them, but looking curiously at Ani.

Liesl ran forward and showed them the note. Hans read it first and faster, his face lighting up. Ani puzzled over the words, frowning. "It's Vati," Hans whispered. "He's back."

"Shh," said Liesl, looking at the door.

"He wants you to come, Ani," Hans whispered to his brother. "Why not me?"

Why not me? Liesl thought.

"I'm scared," said Ani.

Frank was asking the impossible. She couldn't send Ani alone. She wouldn't divide their family. She ushered their visitor deeper into the room, setting him down on the sofa in Uta's old spot. She turned on their radio, blasting a replay of one of Goebbels's speeches, hoping it wouldn't wake the baby from his nap.

Two thousand years of Western civilization are in danger. One cannot overestimate the danger.

"I got your letter," said Onkel Bernd. "But I'd already heard from Frank. He planned to use the farm all along. He's been working for me and sleeping in the hayloft."

"He's well, then," Liesl said, trying to keep her voice low. "He's really all right."

Onkel Bernd nodded. "He had a narrow miss with officials in Bad Vilbel." He rubbed his chin with the back of his palm. "He's lost some weight," he added.

Total war is the demand of the hour. We must put an end to the bourgeois attitude that we have also seen in this war: Wash my back, but don't get me wet!

She waited for him to say more, her hands straying to the boys' soft heads. Onkel Bernd gave an uneasy glance at the radio.

"I don't know what else," he said.

The nasal voice of Goebbels pulsed over them, his shouts punctuated by rising cheers. Liesl recognized the speech. It had first aired the winter around the fall of Stalingrad. They had played it at the spa, and the S.S. officers talked about it while they were eating boar and pheasant off white tablecloths, and hundreds of thousands of men were dying in the east. It made her sick to hear it now, but its volume would drown anything out.

She lifted her chin. "This farm—is it secure?" she asked. "Couldn't we all go?"

The man shook his head. "I wouldn't leave this house if I were you," he said. "Americans roll in, and you're not here? You may never get it back."

He had to take them all. How could she make him understand that she had to escape this house, too?

"But surely—" she said.

"There are still sympathizers in my neighborhood," interrupted Onkel Bernd. "You all come, and they start asking questions. A boy could be anyone's kid—nephew, cousin."

"I don't want to go," Ani said, grabbing hold of her skirt.

"We're a family," she protested.

"Now, young man. Your father's waiting for you." Onkel Bernd reached out and put a hand on Ani's shoulder.

"No!" Ani shouted, twisting away. "No!" He danced off, flapping.

"Ani, quiet," Liesl said, putting her hands over her ears. If the neighbors heard him—

"What if I go, too?" said Hans. "Ani, what if I go?" The yearning filled his face.

Goebbels yelled over rising cheers: *Everyone knows that if we lose, all will be destroyed.*

Onkel Bernd nodded reluctantly. "That could be managed," he said.

Hans flipped the radio dial. "I'm ready," he said into the sudden quiet. Ani looked confused, but he'd stopped dancing.

"Go kiss your baby brother good-bye, but don't wake him," Liesl said, and went downstairs to the kitchen to pack a rucksack for the boys. She didn't have much besides bread and cheese but her hands kept dropping things, so it took forever, and when she tried to write a note to Frank on the back of his, her fingers shook too hard. There was too much to say, and then Frau Winter walked in carrying two buckets of water, so she crumpled the paper and stuffed it in her apron pocket, then pulled the drawstring of the rucksack closed.

Frau Winter poured the water into pots. "You have a guest?" she said.

"The boys' uncle," said Liesl. "He's taking them to the country. So Ani can have a little peace." Her voice quavered on the last words. Let them hear it. Let them all hear it. She was sending the boy away. "Only the older ones," she added. Her smile felt like a grimace. "The baby and I will stay here."

"Oh," said Frau Winter, setting down her buckets. "I'm sorry you can't go, too."

Liesl burst into sobs. She reached for her handkerchief and the crumpled paper fell on the floor, Frank's words just visible, *Dear heart.* She saw Frau Winter scan them before Liesl grabbed them and shoved them back again. She hurried from the room.

Wiping her eyes with her sleeve, Liesl cradled the rucksack like a baby all the way up the steps. Then she sat down and wrote a real letter to Frank, explaining as best she could about Ani's lead poisoning, about the doctor's advice, her fear that Ani would be taken away, her telegram, the second doctor from Hadamar, Uta's bribe, and his departure. Her description of events sounded like a series of complicated excuses and mistakes, but she couldn't let Frank see Ani now and not know how hard she'd tried to keep the boy well. She handed the letter and rucksack to Hans, who was already dressed and standing by the door. He wore his grandfather's heavy, threadbare coat. Ani wore Hans's. Liesl kissed Hans on the forehead, ignoring his blush. She turned to Ani and held his cheeks gently in her palms.

"One thing about growing up in the country," she whispered, "I used to see all the stars at night. Will you look at them for me?" she said. "Will you look at all the stars I can't see anymore?"

"How will I know which ones they are?" said Ani.

She kissed him, tears spilling. "You'll just know."

She straightened and faced Onkel Bernd, looking into his crinkled brown eyes. "Tell him," she said, "tell him I miss him."

With the older children gone, the upstairs neighbors not speaking to her, and the Winter children sick with a flu, Liesl submerged herself in the baby's routine—eating, drinking, diapering, naps—grateful for its dullness and warmth. She watched the weather outside the window, and listened to the radio, knowing most of it was lies. The March wind had brought warmer air, but the nights still frosted the garden, making black icicles where cinders had fallen on the roses. Downstairs the Winter children sneezed and coughed. She could hear their illness through the vents and shrank from it. Sickness crawled over the earth. Hundreds more refugees had been arriving in Hannesburg each day, pushing their wet carts and wheelbarrows, the children hungry-faced and solemn, the mothers chattering in their sloppy Eastern dialects. They clogged up the air raid shelters until locals drove them away, and then they settled at the abandoned paint factory at the edge of town. Wet laundry and shabby little fires sprouted around the once-tidy building. If the Amis bombed Hannesburg again, the factory would likely be a target.

One day Liesl's friend, the cook from the Hartwald Spa, stopped by to tell her that the once-glorious operation had shut down completely. "The whole place is looted," the cook moaned, wiping her eyes. "People started stealing as soon as the last officer left. They even tore down the chandelier." The cook shook her head when Liesl offered her a place to stay. She was heading home to her family on the western outskirts of Berlin. "Some may have no pride left, but I do."

Liesl had known the spa's demise was inevitable, but she couldn't help feeling that her own past had been looted and ruined, stripped of its meaning. Who was that lonely red-haired girl who once huddled by her radio, taking comfort from Hitler's speeches, who had knitted dozens of wool socks one winter to warm the cold feet of soldiers?

"I was innocent," she said to Jürgen one day. He grabbed her face and explored it with two wondering hands. "I think I was innocent." The words choked her.

Liesl emerged once to visit Herr Geiss and tell him that the boys were safe. He greeted her news with curious neutrality. He seemed preoccupied with something else. His eyes kept moving to the windows while she spoke. The dust was no longer thick in his main room, but the walls were still bare and it smelled stale.

"Well," she said, rising. "Now Ani will get some peace, and Hans will be away from bad influences."

"Bad influences!" Herr Geiss grunted. "With the Americans driving tanks through Cologne?" He crowded after her until she was out the door. Within minutes, a lorry pulled up and men began unloading tall crates into the Geiss house. They moved cautiously, as if the contents were fragile.

Liesl decided not to wonder what was inside, but the news about Cologne compounded her sadness about the spa's closure. This was a different kind of blow—not to her own past, but to the country's. The city's name had always struck her as one of the most beautiful in Germany: Köln—the sound was shiny and rich, the gold of a bishop's chalice. The Roman settlement had grown up through medieval times to a grand city with a Gothic cathedral that towered above it all. Throughout the war, constant bombing raids had killed thousands of its citizens and sent the rest fleeing to the countryside, but the shell of the old Cologne had still belonged to them, to Germany. And now it was just gravel beneath the tanks of the Amis.

She pressed her face into the baby's neck, grateful for his comfort. Jürgen would be ten months old on Easter. He hadn't been sick again since that one fever, and his limbs were strong, his eyes alert. He was making distinct sounds now, too. Not words yet, but hard consonants like *g-g-g* and ohs and ahs.

Sometimes he peered past her suspiciously, as if he thought she might be hiding Hans or Ani behind her back. "They'll be home again soon," she said. A note in Hans's hand divulged little except that they'd made it to the farm and Ani was improving in the fresh air.

I just want to find one quiet piece of the world, and stay there and live a humble life, Liesl wrote back. Uta would laugh. She wanted to be a daisy of the fields again. Uta had not written. Uta was probably living underground. Berlin was under daily assault now.

Several days after Palm Sunday, Liesl buried jars holding the records of Frank's army draft and their years of working at the spa alongside a parcel with the house's best silver. She did it in the dark, after Jürgen was sleeping, sinking a spade in the cold wet earth of the garden. She made sure no one was watching, ran upstairs, and brought down Uta's bracelet, shoving it deep in the ground under the jars, and piling the dirt over them all. The fragrance of the thaw made her knees weak. It reminded her of planting time in the fields of her early childhood, holding her mother's hand, jumping in the rows left by her uncle's plow. She cried herself to sleep that night.

The next day, Frau Hefter came to the door to enlist Liesl in a cleanup crew for the rubble in the city center.

"My daughters can watch your little one," she said. "We need strong arms and backs." She recounted all the women who had joined the effort, this widow and that widow and that orphaned girl. She asked how Hans and Ani were faring in the country, and then without really listening to Liesl's answer, she announced that her husband was missing.

"Still doing his duty, no doubt," said Frau Hefter. The last she'd heard from him, the Red Army was marching on the POW camp where he was based. "They were breaking down the camp and moving the prisoners west."

"I'm sorry," Liesl said. "It's hard . . . waiting for news."

Frau Hefter didn't even blink. Her blue eyes shone. "And my Georg has joined the Volkssturm."

Georg Hefter was just a few years older than Hans, a skinny teenager who rode his bike too fast around town.

"Oh," was all Liesl could say. She reached out and squeezed Frau Hefter's arm.

Frau Hefter clicked her tongue against her teeth. Then she thrust her chart at Liesl, showing her what time slots were open. "We won't win the war by giving up now!" she shouted as she departed.

The next morning Liesl left Jürgen with the Hefter brood and their nanny and headed to the town center to join a small horde of women who were clearing it with wheelbarrows. A dense cluster of buildings there had been burned to walls and empty arches. Taken together they appeared not to rise from the earth, but hung from the sky like cages. A single wall jutted, holding nothing at all. Its innards puffed out: yellowed mortar, mold, ancient newspaper. Drifts of rubble rose around it, clogging thoroughfares with broken concrete, brick, roof tile, cinders, and worst, fragments of cloth and black spots that could have been spilled oil or blood. People had started to pack down trails over and through the drifts, but their web of paths made the landscape look permanently altered, as if it might never be level again.

Now that it was daylight, Liesl saw that such ruins scattered like oases throughout the town, near strategic targets. The Americans had not destroyed Hannesburg, merely jabbed wounds in it everywhere. This wound was the biggest. Three lines of women worked the rubble. One searched for whole bricks; one stacked the bricks neatly in piles; one shoveled useless debris into carts. Scarves shrouded their hair and faces. They wore heavy aprons and housedresses, and dust streaked their stockings and skirts. They had the preoccupied air of ants after their mound has been disturbed. Liesl searched for Frau Hefter, for any familiar face, but if any of these women had been at the Frauenschaft meeting, she didn't recognize them now. She had the desolate sense that all those hopeful, panicked wives were gone now, vanished, burned up in the night of the raid. These women knew the war was over. The Americans were coming. There were no men left to fight, no weapons left to aim but pride. They were cleaning up.

The closer Liesl got, the more the air stank of rotting flesh, and she paused to knot her handkerchief around her mouth like the others. It was hard to breathe through the cloth, but the fabric dulled the sharpness of the scent. Bend, lift, straighten—her back remembered the old aches of the harvest. Her hands remembered the scratches and scrapes of plucking and digging. When she finally found a perfect brick she carried it down to the women making stacks.

It was then that she spotted Frau Hefter. Her back was to Liesl, her blond hair bound up in two thick braids and pinned behind her head. Frau Hefter was muttering to herself as she stacked the bricks, her hands deft, the picture of effort.

"I finally found one that wasn't broken," Liesl said, holding out her brick.

Frau Hefter made a startled noise and turned. As soon as Liesl saw her face, she realized her mistake. It wasn't Frau Hefter; but another woman with similar coloring but with uglier, fleshier features, masked by a scarf. Her eyes were red, as if she'd been crying. They settled on Liesl without recognition.

"Just set it on down, with the others," the woman said. She had a coarse accent. "Right there." She pointed at a pile.

Liesl didn't move, still confused by her error.

With a grunt of impatience, the woman grabbed the brick and set it on her stack.

"Liesl, over here."

Liesl saw someone waving from half a block away. It took her a few moments to identify the slender figure, the doll-like face. Berte Geiss. Thank heavens there was someone she recognized. Liesl walked over the loose rubble with her hands held out, to stop herself if she fell.

"It's better here," said Berte. "The RLB already cleared the worst of it."

Liesl sucked lightly through the scarf. She could still taste the rotten gases and she shook her head. "I'm not much help," she said.

"Chin up," said Berte, and handed her a shovel. "Help me fill this cart. It's just dust left here now."

They worked together in silence, falling into an alternating rhythm.

"You seem so much older than when I first met you," said Liesl.

"Do I?" Berte shrugged. Her eyebrows rose behind her scarf, as if she were smiling. "Have I gotten all wrinkled already?"

"No, I didn't mean that," Liesl said seriously. "I mean that you seem so capable."

"I thrive in a crisis," Berte said. "I've been through this total war before, remember? It's old hat. Besides, I gotta get out of the house. The lovebirds are driving me batty."

Liesl breathed again. The handkerchief tasted of her own sour spit. "Is it that bad?"

"She even makes eyes at him when she dusts," Berte said, and imitated Frau Dillman's jiggling chest.

Liesl laughed aloud at the imitation, but then was struck by a sudden sadness. She had never reconciled with Frau Dillman. She threw herself into shoveling. *You can marry that old man*, she thought, spiking her spade into the ground. *But you'll always be his Putzfrau.*

They filled five wheelbarrows and dumped them, then moved on to a new location, on the rim of the *Rathaus*, and began shoveling ash. The cinders made a higher, softer sound against the shovels, almost a music.

"How are the boys?" Berte asked.

"They like the farm life," Liesl said truthfully. "I knew they would." After a moment's hesitation, she queried Berte about the crates that her father-in-law had moved into the house.

"Oh, those," Berte said. "He's been storing some of my mother-in-law's paintings somewhere and he thought he better bring them home."

Frau Geiss must have done a lot of paintings, Liesl thought. "Did you know her?" she asked. She had been curious about the elder Frau Geiss since she'd cleaned her house. She remembered the artist's tenderness in her portrait of Ani and Susi.

"Uli's mother? Met her twice before she died," said Berte. "She didn't approve of our marriage. Said I shouldn't get married so young." She thunked a heavy shovelful of earth into the wheelbarrow. "I guess she did, and she regretted it."

Liesl and Berte were washing their faces and hands at the city pump when they heard the shelling begin. It had come, distant as thunder, several times in the past week, but this shelling was loud and near. Full of whistles and shrieks. A boy climbed up on a roof and looked east. He shouted that he could see a dark line moving on the roads. His mother begged him to come down.

By the time the boy scrambled to the ground, the women had emptied their last loads and were piling the shovels. They spoke in whispers, as if the approaching Americans could already hear them. The metal dropped with loud clatters. The wooden handles clanked together, a drumbeat of common purpose. *Get home. Get home now.* Liesl felt the displaced sensation again, as if she were some other mother hearing the news. She glanced up at the pale dome above. What if more planes came tonight? What if the American soldiers took their revenge on women and children?

Beside her Berte looked strangely serene.

"You seem happy," Liesl said, an edge in her voice.

"It's almost over."

But Berte plodded on the walk home, and Liesl had to keep slowing her pace to let her catch up. "Please," she said, breathless. "I need to get Jürgen."

"They won't reach here until tomorrow," Berte said. "I think we can make it home before tomorrow."

"I just want to get him," said Liesl, her mind flashing with terrible images of Frank, Hans, and Ani hiding in a hayloft while tanks rolled through the fields below. What if Jürgen was the only one she had left?

"And I just want to see these streets as German for one last time," said Berte. "Don't you? Tomorrow it'll all belong to someone else." She waved a hand at a house's brown-painted shutters and the cracked glass window of the bakery, at the white tower that rose over the town. "And we'll belong to someone else, too."

Liesl burst into the apartment with Jürgen, already mentally sorting and packing what else to bury in the yard. The china. Anything with a swastika on it. She wondered what could be burned.

She heard something thump across the floor and stood still, heart pounding.

She was reaching to turn on a lamp when a male voice said from across the room, "Don't be angry about the rabbits. Hans and I will build them a hutch for the balcony tonight."

Liesl switched the lamp on, and Frank's body sprang out of the darkness. He looked too thin and had grown a beard, and he was wearing a ridiculous hodgepodge of clothes—pants too short in the legs and a shirt too short in the sleeves and a giant, poorly knitted shawl thrown over it all. His eyes fastened on her, then Jürgen. She stared back, unable to believe it was him. She didn't recognize the expression on his face. He looked so hungry, but his mouth curled as if he had tasted something bitter.

The silence extended. And then she ran to him, baby and all, lurching into an embrace.

"Careful, careful," Frank murmured as he folded them both in his arms.

"Where are the boys?" she said into his shirt, and at almost the same time, he said, "Where have you been?" then answered, "They're down with the chickens. Is this my baby?" He smiled at Jürgen.

"I was clearing rubble," said Liesl, and then she burst into tears. "They were going to take Ani away—" she said, sobbing. "I wouldn't have sent that telegram, but I was so afraid—"

"He's going to be all right." Frank said, but he moved away from her. "Is this my boy?" he said to the child.

Jürgen gurgled back and Frank gently shook the baby's fist.

"Ani's getting better every day," he said.

She gulped and shook, her face wet. "He's better?"

"You should have seen him with the animals," said Frank, and described Ani spending hours in the barn, currying anything with fur until the cows' and ponies' coats crackled. "They would have won all the prizes at the fair." Ani ate well, too. Especially after he was allowed to sample from Bernd's secret store of cheeses, Frank said, adding a chuckle that sounded forced. His stories sounded wrong, like the off-color jokes she used to overhear her uncle telling. She had never been able to fully comprehend their details, and their endings mystified her.

"And he slept well?" she interrupted.

Frank was across the room again. "Most nights," he said.

"Did he tell you anything?"

"No." Frank sighed. "Let's not talk about this right now. I just want to see my son. And you."

But she couldn't stop. Frank had to know how hard she'd tried. "I looked! I looked every day. I asked him every day," Liesl said. She felt her lips drawing back, baring her teeth, and she covered them with her free hand and turned away.

A silence fell between them. Frank walked back and took Jürgen from her. The baby squirmed and stretched his arms for Liesl. "Muh-muh," he said.

"That's your father, now," Liesl said softly.

The baby whined. A rabbit whumped into view. It was small and black with one white spot on its back. Frank carried Jürgen to the window.

The rabbit hopped to her shoe and sniffed. It sniffed the toe, then the side, the heel, one long ear flopping. Then it loped slowly away. Liesl wiped her eyes. "They're lovely."

"I'm trying to keep Ani from naming them all," Frank said. "He wants them all to be pets."

"It's not safe for you here, Frank," Liesl whispered.

"Muh-muhhhh," Jürgen wailed. Frank handed him back.

"I had to be sure you were provided for," said Frank. "Things are going to get worse after we surrender. There won't be enough food. I want you and the children to have your own meat and eggs and the seeds for a garden. It won't be an easy year."

She pressed her cheek into Jürgen's head, trying not to cry again. She didn't like the way he said "you and the children." The baby frowned and grabbed her hair.

"How did you manage to get into Hannesburg?" she asked.

Frank picked up the bunny with one swift hand and petted its head.

"We had quite a ride," he murmured. "Four rabbits, three chickens, and two sons on top of the lorry, and a father riding under the crates."

The bunny twisted and he let it down. It bounded behind the couch.

"I want Ani to be safe," Liesl whispered. "All of us to be safe."

"Ani will improve," said Frank, his eyebrows contracting. "He's a strong fellow, and he's pulling through. You'll see when he comes upstairs." He took a step nearer to her again, his beard still startling her every time she looked at him. "And I'm here now. Isn't that what you wanted?"

"Someone will denounce you," said Liesl.

"You have to understand something. This is my house," Frank's voice rose. "This is my father's house. I'm not abandoning it."

She started to shake again. How could he be so loyal to this simple brick and plaster, that staircase and that balcony, when it all could be blown up tomorrow? Better to flee where bombs would not follow them. To keep flesh and bone whole. "We have to think about what's best for—"

He cut her off with a look, and a bitter salt filled her mouth. He wasn't the same Frank. First that beard, and then the angles of his face and body, his scrawny hips—he wasn't the same man anymore.

"We should turn on the radio," Liesl mumbled, fumbling with the knob. A march was playing. "We shouldn't shout."

The door opened behind them and Hans and Ani stormed in. After three weeks they both looked ruddier and fatter, and Ani wore a pair of new baggy trousers cinched at the waist with twine. Liesl knelt down and opened the arm that wasn't holding Jürgen and they jostled in to hug her with silly grins on their faces. She didn't know what she'd expected of their reunion, but it felt just right and too brief at once. The boys extracted themselves and began patrolling the room. Jürgen demanded to get down, too, and pulled up on the legs of his brothers.

"The chickens are thirsty," Hans said loudly to his father. "We need a lot of water for them. And a water trough."

"Where are my bunnies?" Ani said.

She studied him as he rooted among the furniture. He seemed older, his face ruddy, his movements smooth and confident. If he was getting better in the country, Frank ought to have stayed. They all ought to go back together.

"We'll have eggs for Easter," said Frank. "And a beet for dye. Susi always liked that tradition. The boys, too."

Did he think she was Susi now? Would Susi let them talk about holiday decorating when the Americans were coming, and Ani needed quiet, and Frank could become a prisoner of war?

The radio changed songs. A familiar stink rose from Jürgen's vicinity—he'd soiled his diaper.

"Their mother used to write their names in wax so when they dipped the eggs their names would show," Frank said.

"I can write my own name now," said Ani.

"I'm sorry," Liesl said. She could feel herself starting to tear up again, and she turned so they would not see. "The baby needs to be changed." She ran with Jürgen to the study and shut the door.

God knows, he'd had time to think, to prepare. The whole endless march through the snow, the days in the basement in Bad Vilbel, he'd felt his own skin tighten around his ribs; he'd felt his head swim with daydreams of roasts and strudel, felt his teeth going loose in his mouth, and calculated what he would need to save his family from hunger. The animals. The seeds. The wood and nails and chicken wire. A saw and sandpaper. Two hammers, one for him and one for his eldest son. The latch and hook for the gate. He'd even thought about the noise it would take to build the hutch by dark, and he'd hung blankets over the living room door to muffle the sound.

Frank didn't care if the neighbors noticed his presence. Even if they could find some authority left in Hannesburg willing to arrest him that night, it would take hours and hours. He just wanted to finish the hutch. He'd showed Hans the plan, sketched out on a scrap of envelope, and they'd each built a side while Ani watched, stroking the rabbits and telling them not to be afraid. Ani was part of the blueprint, too. Frank wanted him to see them making a safe, secure home. Shaping something in the wreckage.

"You're a natural," he told Hans, and saw his face burn with pride.

By the time the first candle burned low, they had finished the walls and floor. It was time to fit the door. Frank had thought of the smaller nails he would need to hold the wire to the door, and the tiny taps it would take to send them into the wood. He had saved those blows for Ani. He sent Hans to get another candle and beckoned to his middle son. "Here," he said, taking a nail from his mouth and holding it against the wood. With his other hand, he gave Ani the hammer. "Just the slightest tap now."

He waited, ready for the hard smack that would inevitably come, bruising his thumb. He felt Ani's eyes on him.

"Why is Mutti hiding?" the boy said.

"She's not hiding. She's changing the baby."

"She's taking a long time."

Frank flushed. "She'll come out when she's ready."

The boy continued to regard him. He set the hammer on the floor.

"Go on," Frank said.

Ani rose and ran toward the study. He threw back the blanket and disappeared behind it, then shut the door.

On his long journey home, Frank had not thought about Liesl, or rather he had thought about Liesl often, but as an agent in his plans. He'd thought she would understand him, as she'd always understood him before. In her quiet way, she would be grateful for the animals, the hutch, the seeds he'd brought for a garden. She would see these gifts as he saw them: promises of survival.

He would tell her about his desertion after the boys had gone to bed, starting with his escape from the cistern and his hungry, exhausted days in the forest. He would describe his relief at finding a gamekeeper's cabin, at resting there and eating someone's old dusty provisions until his frostbite healed. He would skip the long days walking, getting lost, retracing his steps, and turn to getting arrested, rotting anonymously in a cellar converted to a jail cell while a local official asked around for the reward he would get for handing the deserter over. *The man's greed saved me*, he would say. *He thought I might be worth something.* One night, the man's daughter inexplicably let him free. After that, it was surprisingly easy getting to the farm, easy to find Bernd and ask him to get a message to his wife. He would not be ashamed of the desertion. After all, he'd done it in the name of his family. And he'd worked hard, mucking stalls and butchering hogs for the sake of a few chickens and rabbits, the supplies for a hutch, also in the name of his family. And risked his life to get those things here, all in the name of his family.

But what he hadn't expected was that his family would change. That Hans would act gruff as a little man, that Ani would be . . . whatever he had become. Frank had a hard time finding a word for it. As a doctor, he might spin a diagnosis around the symptoms of lead poisoning: impaired cognition and motor control, confusion, fatigue. Yet as a father, the best term he could come up with was "maimed." Ani had been maimed. In mind as well as body.

He would never forget Ani stumbling toward him with his burned arm and hissing with pain as he'd wrapped both tight around his father. Or watching Ani struggle to tie his shoelaces. Or waking to see Ani stumbling after a cat around the dark farmhouse, whispering to himself, *If we don't cry out, they'll think we're dead. They won't hurt us if they think we're dead.* For two weeks, Frank couldn't hold more than a two-sentence conversation with his second son, because Ani's mind wandered so easily and because he mixed up words—"farm" for "barn" and "shell" for "coat."

All Ani wanted to do was see the animals in the barn, but his desire had a compulsion to it, as if he couldn't stop being with them. He'd come back from his endless grooming sessions, eat with a silent, distracted air, go obediently to sleep, and wake screaming from terrible nightmares. Day after day, night after night.

And then one night, Ani had slept the whole way through. And then two, then three nights in a row. He ran without tripping over his feet, and the clouds in his eyes began to clear. When a new pony was born, he'd begged to name it White Wing, and ran around all day grinning when Bernd said yes. Whole paragraphs erupted from his lips when he described the splendors of the horse. He'd stopped twitching and flicking his head.

Ani's turn toward wellness in a few short weeks astonished Frank. He'd never anticipated his own son would be living proof of his thoughts on dystrophy, how the constant pressures on Germany's soldiers had made it impossible for them to heal. But Ani hadn't been a soldier sleeping out in snowy, lice-ridden trenches, waiting for a Russian attack. Ani had been a six-year-old in a sturdy house, with a mother and brothers, and food on the table. Ani had fallen ill after Frank had gone, but long before the terrors of the air raid. He had succumbed under Liesl's care.

Frank had read and reread Liesl's letter, but her order of events confused him. He asked Hans to tell him the story of Ani's illness from the beginning. He could tell that the older boy hadn't paid much attention. Or hadn't been privy to much. There had been doctor visits, yes—not with the doctor Frank recommended, but someone else, Dr. Becker, who had found a high concentration of lead in Ani's blood. And then things got murky. Though no one seemed to know what caused the lead poisoning, the doctor had wanted to send Ani away to an asylum.

Why?

I don't know. Maybe he didn't trust Mutti.

And then?

Hans shrugged. *Then another doctor changed the first doctor's mind.*

It sounded contrived. Why had Liesl sent the telegram?

Because she was afraid Ani would be taken away. Before the second doctor came.

So if she knew the second doctor was coming, why did she summon me?

She didn't know the second doctor was coming.

She didn't summon him?

No. The first doctor sent him. The second doctor was going to take Ani to the asylum, but he changed his mind.

Why? Why did the doctor leave without Ani?

He thought Ani was well, I guess.

But Ani isn't well.

He belongs with us, Vati.

Yes, he does . . . Hans, did your stepmother ever hurt Ani?

No. No. She saved him during the air raid. Me, too.

Then the boy had told him the story of Ani catching fire, himself getting stuck at the brewery, and Liesl's rescue of them both.

Frank had ridden the whole way to Hannesburg curled in a ball under the soiled crates, and deliberating about how to greet Liesl. How could he be anything but grateful for what she'd done? And yet she had let his sweet, trusting son grow frail and twisted inside—so how could he not feel anger, too?

Yet the moment he'd lit the lamp in his besieged house and seen his wife and son standing there, holding each other, neither anger nor gratitude filled him. *I am a failure*, he'd thought, looking at Liesl's wide, trusting eyes. He'd wanted to fall down in front of Liesl. To bury his head in her apron and cling until her hand gently raised him. But she seemed so afraid of him, so afraid of letting him touch her. Did that mean she was hiding something about Ani? They needed to talk, but every moment was speeding toward the next, today crashing into tomorrow like a ship into another ship. He didn't have enough time.

Hans came back with the new candle and sat down, watching. Frank nailed the wire into the door with tiny precise knocks. His hands still worked. The frostbite hadn't ruined them.

He heard a noise and looked up to see Ani leading Liesl into the room. Her face was puffy from crying.

"Look, Mutti," Ani said in his old, clear voice. "This will be the rabbits' house. We're making it together."

He pulled her by the hand and smoothly sat her down beside Frank. Liesl swept her legs beneath her, folded them up, swan-like. Frank pressed the wire down and pinched another nail, motioning to Hans. "Give your mother the hammer," he said.

He waited, hardly breathing, as she hefted the handle, staring at its round metal tip. She didn't seem to know how to hit with it. He wrapped his arm around her, holding her wrist. She flinched but did not pull away. They raised the hammer together and brought it down lightly.

"Where's the baby's cradle?" Frank asked her later, looking around the lamp-lit study. Jürgen was drinking his nightly bottle, watching his father with huge eyes.

"It's too small," Liesl said. *He's been waiting for you to build him a crib,* she added silently.

"So where does he sleep?"

She pointed to a little carpet she rolled out every night for herself and the baby.

"On the floor?"

"I sleep with him. It's not so bad," she said defensively. "I was afraid he'd fall off the couch."

Frank shook his shaggy head. He pulled one of his father's books out, then shoved it back. He seemed to be formulating some response, but it did not come.

"We can all stay in here. You can have the couch," she offered. "It's perfectly comfortable."

"What happened to *our* beds?"

"There wasn't room for them. I loaned them to the Winters." She paused. "I could have moved all the books and the desk instead, but I thought they were more precious. To you."

Frank blew out through his lips. She wondered if he'd wanted to make love to her that night. She wished she knew how to ask about such things. *You don't have to ask*, she heard Uta's voice say.

Frank turned away from Liesl and sat down lightly on the couch, as if testing it out for purchase.

Jürgen tossed down his bottle. "Muh-muh," he said, reaching for her.

"He sleeps soundly," she said. "Once I put him to sleep, we can . . . we can talk, if you like."

She wasn't sure which one she dreaded most, the talking or the lovemaking—the complicated ways they could hurt each other. She just wanted time to stretch instead of collapse.

This is your last night in a German house, she heard Uta's voice again.

As Liesl dressed the baby in his nightshirt, an awkward silence fell. She felt Frank watching her and it made her hurry too much. When she pulled off his sweater the baby squalled. She fumbled with the buttons, the diaper pin. Finally the baby was dressed, his thin hair erect with static. She smoothed it down. He shook her hand off and tried to pull up on the bookshelf.

Liesl watched Jürgen balance, uncertain what to do next. "He's a good walker," she said.

"He is," Frank said.

"I'll take him to say good night to his brothers," Liesl said.

"Good," said Frank.

When she came back a few minutes later, Frank was examining his hands. "When I got frostbite out there, I was worried I'd lose sensation in my fingers," he said. "That I would touch things, but I wouldn't be able to feel them anymore." He flexed his fingers.

Liesl carried the baby over and squeezed Frank on the shoulder. "Once you start thinking like that, you can't stop," she said.

He looked up at her. "I never would have told Susi that. She wouldn't have understood," he said. "But you do."

Liesl set Jürgen in Frank's arms. "Hold him while I make our bed," she said, and she felt them both watching her as she spread out the little carpet and then a folded blanket next to it, then dug into the couch beside him and found three pillows, one for each of their heads. The simple task calmed her. She was making a bed; that's all she was doing. In her German house. On the last night and the first. With her husband, who was home.

"Go out and say good night to the boys," she told Frank. "When you come back, he'll be asleep."

To her surprise, Frank looked grateful for the instruction, kissed his son, and rose.

She set the baby down on the far side of the carpet and lowered her body next to him, already singing her nightly lullaby. The baby's eyes followed his father out the door and he rolled to his feet and started to totter after him.

"Stay here, now," Liesl said, laughing.

Frank scooped him up and carried him back, chuckling. It was the first time they'd laughed together in how long?

Four months. And when will we laugh again? Liesl thought, and then saw Frank's smile fading as he recognized it, too.

When Frank came back, sinking down beside her, the baby was asleep, as promised. At least she could accomplish that. She curved her body to Frank, hoping that he would hold her, but he lay stiffly, staring up at the ceiling. She watched the outline of his nose and chin.

"Did you have enough food for them?" he said after a moment.

It took Liesl a moment to understand he was talking about Ani. "Of course."

"And did he eat it?"

"I thought he did," she said. "The boys always eat well." *Except when Uta cooked,* she added mentally, *but that was only a week or two.*

"Did you notice his loss of motor control or his cognitive impairment first?"

"I'm sorry. I don't understand." The floor suddenly felt hard and uncomfortable.

"Was he stumbling or was he acting bonkers first?"

"I don't know," she said, trying to keep the edge from her voice. "He grew more . . . upset after you went missing. He started talking to himself."

"What about the twitching?"

And on the questions went, Frank spitting the next one out before she had time to finish responding to the last—the queries similar but not exactly the same, probing to get at some truth she did not know how to reveal. How could Frank grasp it anyway? He hadn't had to live through the nightmare of Jürgen's first illness, the insanity of clearing out the house for the refugees, Hans's constant disobedience. He'd never contacted her the whole time he was fleeing home. He'd never had to live with her fear of his death.

She shrank away from Frank, pressing back into the baby's soft warmth. She just wanted to get to the part where they trusted each other again.

"You're not falling asleep on me, are you?" he said.

"No," Liesl whispered. "I'm sorry. I'm just tired."

Frank shifted. She felt his eyes searching for her across the dark air. "Liesl," he said softly. "We have to know everything so we won't let it happen again. We have to learn."

She lay there, silent, thinking, *What if you can't stop things from happening again?*

"My boys love you. As a mother," Frank said. "I can see it in each of them."

She was all stillness now.

She felt Frank reach for her, clumsily brushing her breast before he took her hand, stroking the palm, the fingers. "They talked about you all the time. Hans told me how you rescued him. Ani made me stay up one night and watch the stars because he said you asked him to."

"He's doing better, isn't he." Liesl said, a catch in her voice. She didn't want him to let go of her hand. "When he came to get me today, he seemed like the old Ani." How tender the boy had been, asking her to join the family again, showing her where to sit.

Frank squeezed her hand. The clock in the living room chimed ten times. In another twelve hours, the Americans would be in Hannesburg, and then what would happen to Frank—

"I can't wait any longer for this," Frank muttered, and kissed her. His lips pushed against hers so hard, his tongue in her mouth, her tongue in his. In one motion, he slid his arm under her body and hauled her to the couch across the room. She bit off a moan as he set her beneath him, pressing his thighs into hers. He had always been so gentle and slow with her, but now his movements were quick and decisive, unbuttoning her, pulling her breast to his mouth with one hand, his other traveling up under the hem of her nightgown, touching between her thighs. She reached for his hips. He batted her hands away, kissing her breathless again before lowering his head down her body, tasting her.

Afterward, they stayed on the couch, lying intertwined so they both could fit on its narrow shelf. She propped her head on Frank's chest, and he told her about his journey home, getting lost in the woods, climbing a tree—it all sounded like a boyhood adventure, until the night he was following a road through a darkened village and a dog began barking.

"There wasn't anywhere for me to run. The snow was too deep in the fields," he said.

Within moments, the barking dog became a woman screaming, then a man shouting, then a gunshot fired over his head.

Frank had been caught. They threw him in a cellar. A girl brought him water and bread. "Her father tried to interrogate me. I didn't tell him my name, but he found some poems on me that belonged to Hartmann, so that's who I said I was. The fellow told me I was under arrest for desertion, but he didn't seem to have any authority but his gun." Frank lost track of time in the cellar because it was always dark, but he was sure he'd been there for several days. "Luckily for me there was a big snow during that time, and the roads were slow going."

"And then the daughter came down one night and let me go. I don't know why. Maybe she read Hartmann's poems. Maybe she thought I was a poet. Couldn't make heads or tails of his stuff myself. But maybe it saved my life."

"What happened to Hartmann?"

Frank didn't answer for a long time. She heard him swallowing.

"He didn't make it."

She moved to her side and pulled him around her. The clock chimed again. It was two in the morning now.

They didn't have any more time to talk if they wanted to sleep before the Americans came, and Frank's hand was gliding up her hip again, circling her waist, and she was turning to meet him.

Liesl watched Frank and Herr Geiss from her kitchen window. The men were sitting on the second floor in the Geiss house, in the room with the long pane that overlooked the Kappus villa. They sat with their legs crossed, on either side of a green bottle of liquor, talking and sipping as if neither of them were in the slightest danger. Frank had dismissed her fears that Herr Geiss would betray him for desertion, and clearly he was right. The old man looked as delighted as a father welcoming home a prodigal son. He leaned toward Frank, and Frank was lapping up the attention, helping himself to pour after pour and roaring with laughter at Herr Geiss's jokes.

She had a thousand household chores to do but she couldn't tear her eyes from the window. The existence of Frank—across the yard, the dinner table, in her bed—still astonished her. Her insides swirled with so many new or bygone emotions that she didn't think she would be able to eat for days. She would simply feast on relief (he was home), shame (he still blamed her for Ani's illness), lust (she wanted him), fear (he would let himself be arrested), and hope (he would hide).

Stay with us, she'd whispered when they'd first woken up that morning. Frank had put his finger to her lips, then kissed her hard.

She heard footsteps behind her and saw Ani balancing a handful of brown speckled eggs against his chest, advancing to the counter beside her. "Be careful!" she sang out, rushing forward.

"I can do it," he insisted, twisting away. "Let me do it."

To Liesl's surprise, he tiptoed all the way to the counter and set the first egg down.

"One," he said proudly. "Two. Three. Four." The fourth egg rolled, but he stopped it ably with the heel of his palm. The brown orbs balanced, fragile and unbroken, on the hard surface. Ani's recovered dexterity thrilled her, and how long had it been since they'd tasted fresh eggs? Here they were, smallish but miraculous, Frank's gift to the house. She glanced gratefully, fearfully across the yard, up to the window where her husband still paced. She wished he would come back to her. She was envious of any happy moment he spent with someone else.

"One from each hen," Ani said. "Can I go see if the Americans are coming?"

His nonchalance shocked her—as if he were watching a game of marbles! "No one is leaving this house," Liesl said.

"Upstairs," Ani said impatiently. "They can see the western road from upstairs."

"Did the Dillmans invite you?" They hadn't reconciled with the Dillmans. They hadn't said anything to the Dillmans or the Winters about Frank's arrival. Both would have to be done, but she didn't know how.

"Grete did. She said I could come. Just me."

Liesl wondered if the Dillman girls were up to some sort of trick. She still hadn't forgiven them for the loony business, and she didn't understand how Ani could, either. She was about to refuse Ani's request when footsteps thundered down the stairs. She followed the boy to the threshold to see Frau Dillman descending rapidly, wearing her house robe and slippers.

"He needs to hide," she said, nodding, when she saw them. "They're here. I saw the tanks with my own eyes. They're at the city border now."

Without waiting for an answer, Frau Dillman flung open the door and ran down the walk, her slippers floundering in the spring mud.

It took Liesl a moment to realize that Frau Dillman was talking about Herr Geiss and not Frank.

They all need to hide, said Uta's voice. *But you can't ask a man to do that. Ask him to fight, to die—anything but hide.*

Exhaustion spread through Liesl's limbs, sore from a night with Frank and from hefting a shovel yesterday. She had the sudden urge to run upstairs and crawl under the eiderdown and pull it tight over her head. Instead she watched the woman's progress, and the men at the window above, noting Frau Dillman's advance.

Frau Dillman stopped and waved at them, a taut, anxious gesture, like someone trying to hail a departing ship.

Herr Geiss did not return the wave. Instead he scowled and bolted from his chair, pulling Frank away from the window. Frau Dillman paused, gave a cloudy huff of breath, and kept walking straight up to the front door. Her robe flapped, revealing her bare ankles. The cold spring wind didn't make her wince at all. She appeared to have entirely forgotten herself.

"Mutti, can I go see? Please?" Ani asked.

Liesl watched, spellbound.

"Pleeaaase?" Ani shouted.

"All right!" she said, exasperated. "But you are to stay inside this house, do you hear me?"

She held her own elbows as Frau Dillman pounded on Herr Geiss's door, as the voices of the men echoed up from the cellar, Frank pointing out his hens, the rabbits. They sounded as if they were two vacationers touring a farm, not an army doctor and a Party man on the day their city was surrendering to the Americans. Liesl marveled at their arrogance, their bravado, as her upstairs neighbor kept up her knocking.

Finally the Geiss door opened, and Berte peeked out, blinking. She said something to Frau Dillman, and the other woman pushed her aside and went in.

Liesl heard Herr Geiss down below, urging Frank to take something he'd offered.

"No," said Frank. "No. I'm staying."

The words chilled Liesl. The men wouldn't let the war go. Her hands balled to fists. *What about us?* she wanted to scream.

Frau Dillman's voice broke shrilly through the men's conversation. "You need to hide!" she shouted. "You told me you were leaving."

Herr Geiss spoke in a voice too low for Liesl to hear. Liesl stared into the white, blossoming branches of the cherry tree, hardening her resolve. She wasn't going to let him get arrested for the sake of honor or duty. Frau Dillman might be helpless, but Liesl had a claim. She was Frank's wife.

In all his life, Hans had never heard a silence like this. It reminded him of a candle just after it has blown out and the darkness closes in.

Yet the silence was on only one side, the German side, on the side of his brothers and stepmother, and the neighbors' wives and the neighbors' children, the ones who just four weeks ago had been playing the game of Kidnap. He still couldn't look at Frieda Dillman, though she always seemed to be crowding the edge of his vision with her tightly clothed body and sad eyes.

From the Americans emerged three distinct noises: the gravelly grind of the tank wheels pressing the road, the slippery whisper of a soldier reaching into a bag and tossing, and the flap-flap of sticks of gum hitting the pavement in front of the children. Occasionally the Amis would talk to each other from the sides of their mouths, and their voices sounded like radio voices, tinny and distant.

The column was long and slow; it seemed to stretch through Hannesburg all the way to some other city, maybe across the ocean, maybe even to some other century. The Americans rode in armored trucks. Some men stared out; others looked down at the guns on their laps. Helmets crushed their hair onto their foreheads. A lot of them were moving their mouths, though they didn't seem to have any food, and Hans realized they must have been chewing the same candy they'd thrown.

He stepped away from his brothers and stepmother so he wasn't touching anything at all, and slowly slid his shoe over two foil-wrapped pieces of gum. He stood on top of the gums, crushing them, until the whole column passed and the people started turning away. The whole time he thought about the gums, sweet and thin, waiting for him and Ani.

It was midafternoon when he bent and pretended to tie his shoe and slid the silver sticks in, feeling a stab of betrayal as he did so. He saw other mothers kicking the gum away from their children.

"Poison," he heard one mother say. He also noticed that many of the pieces had mysteriously vanished, though no one was chewing.

"Hurry, Hans," his stepmother said. She looked different this morning, as if she'd finally stepped in out of a storm, and he realized with a start that she was happy that his father was home, that she was *in love with* his father. It had never occurred to him before. His country had lost. The air raids were over. His town was full of Americans now. His father had filled the cellar with little bags of seeds. Things would start growing soon. She was in love with Vati. Hans followed her, trying to float on the slim pieces of gum instead of step on them. His mouth watered. He couldn't wait to get home.

"The rabbits need more greens," Ani announced, tugging at their stepmother's hand when they reached the corner to their street. "I told Vati—"

"Shh," she said.

"I told him I would stop and get them," he whispered. "At the Kurpark."

"Absolutely not!" She grabbed Ani by the wrist.

"Just to the park? Vati said I could go," said Ani, pulling loose. "The Amis are gonna stay forever anyway."

Their stepmother seemed startled by this comment and took a long time to respond. Jürgen yawned and fell against her neck. She ran her hands over her front, ribs to waist, a gesture Hans remembered his own mother doing before she entered a crowded room.

"Not forever," she said, but her voice lacked conviction. "Come on. Everyone home."

Liesl stared at the rabbit hutch on the balcony. Frank had finished it. The rabbits hid in the corner, out of sight, as if all along they'd been waiting to disappear. The living room was empty except for the coop, and it smelled like sawdust and fur. The walls of the coop were also done, but it still needed a roof and ledges for nests. Jürgen reached for an edge of the wall, gripping it with his fat fingers.

Frank appeared from the Icebox, drying his hands.

"Where are the boys?" he said.

"They're picking grass in the yard," said Liesl. "They're in love with those rabbits."

"So are those little Dillmans," said Frank, and told her about introducing himself to both families upstairs and downstairs, giving them fresh eggs.

"You shouldn't trust them," Liesl said.

"We don't have a choice. Besides, they seem relieved to have a man here." Frank picked up his son and kissed him. Jürgen squirmed and cried. "What's the matter?" he said.

"He's just getting tired," she said.

Frank continued to hold the baby, and the baby's cries escalated.

"Ready for his nap," Liesl said, holding out her arms. Yet as soon as Frank handed the baby over, Jürgen quieted and grabbed at her hair.

Frank began to pace.

"Susi never had your gift for infants," he said. "She liked the boys better when they were walking and talking." He looked at her, a searching gaze that made her uncomfortable. She walked to the couch and sat down.

"They're all good boys," she said to the top of Jürgen's head.

"Sometimes I still don't get it," Frank said. "I didn't have anything to offer you but three grief-stricken kids and my own absence, and you took it." He cleared his throat. "You took it like it was a gift and you raised my sons when I couldn't." He walked back toward her and then crouched by her feet. "The whole time I was running home, I thought, why would she, except that she wanted a family, and this war took all the other men away."

In his nearness, he looked younger, earnest, endearing. Liesl's gaze fell to her wedding ring, the one that had been Susi's before her. She wished the boys would come back, would light up the room with their bickering and laughter. She wished Frank would just accept the simple fact: We are together now. She didn't want to think about the past or the future.

"And I thought, how can I be the man she deserves?" Frank's voice cracked. He touched her knees. "I can get home. I can save my son. I can feed my family, and I can hide like the others, and when it's safe—maybe months, maybe years—I can work again. It doesn't have to be medicine. I'll do anything."

Liesl twisted the ring, feeling the gold pull away from her skin.

Frank kept holding her knees and talking, describing how everything changed the moment he stepped across his own threshold. He saw the walls that had protected his mother and father, his wives and children, and now new families. He saw the shelter his sons had fixed in case the rest of their home was destroyed, and the hole his neighbor had made to make it possible for one house to escape into another. Everything was porous now, nothing closed, nothing fixed. A man could create himself anew.

He sounded giddy as a boy.

"You should rest," she said. "You haven't rested since you've been home."

Frank rose and towered over her. "I'm not leaving again," he said. "I'm not hiding. When the Americans come to this house, I'm going to be with you."

What was he saying? He touched her shoulder. His hand weighed like a sack of meat. She shook it off.

"Liesl," he said.

She shook her head, her legs clenched, her neck stiff, while Frank waited, shifting from foot to foot. There was a noise on the balcony as a black rabbit crossed the hutch and sniffed the mesh. Its ears swiveled back and forth.

"You'll break their hearts," she whispered.

The rabbit hopped back to the shadows. Frank touched her shoulder again, and this time she let him. She let him draw her up from the couch and close his arms around her and Jürgen. She breathed into the linen of his shirt, her legs weak and shaky.

What will you do if Frank never comes home? she heard Uta's voice again.

The door swung open. Hans stood there, frowning. "Ani's gone," he said.

Ani rounded the corner and then took off for the brewery pasture. He knew where the soft sprigs poked up through the soil. He knew because his mother had once showed him where to gather sorrel for *Sauerbraten*. He remembered walking beside her, tugging the tender shoots.

No one watched that field. No one would chase him away. He sprinted, and the women on their way to the ruined market stared, their hands tightening on their empty bags. He ran harder, even when one shouted at him, "Slow down! I thought there was a Yank behind you."

Not a Yank, but surely Hans, once they figured out he was gone. Vati would send Hans right away, and Hans was fast. Faster. Ani could feel the old weakness in his bones and muscles, but he was getting strong again. His head was clearing, too. In the country, under the stars, he'd stopped having bad dreams and started to have good ones. He wanted to own his own yellow barn and fields one day. He'd announced it to his stepmother last night. She asked him why, and he said, because he liked growing things. Then she told him about sowing her own garden when she was a child—potatoes, peas, and cucumbers in a ring of daisies and asters. She told him about wandering barefoot in the rows of new barley with Fräulein Müller, and imagining they were queens of barley and all the green plants were their loyal subjects. Then she'd fallen silent.

Is that the end? he'd asked.

The end of what?

The story.

No. But I forget the rest. She'd sounded sad.

Can I see your farm sometime, Mutti?

She'd pinched the bridge of her nose and covered her eyes with her thumbs. *Yes, yes, of course you can,* she'd said and smiled.

He knew she was not lying and she was not leaving. She would never leave them. He knew because of the way she looked at his father, and his father looked at her. It was as if a thin gold chain attached them. He remembered the same gold unspooling between himself and his mother, and how her love for him tugged him back whenever he ventured too far from the house. His recognition of this new love filled him with purpose. He would be a good boy. He would not cry or fall down. He would take care of Jürgen and show him how, in turn, to care for the bunnies. He felt bad for sneaking away, but he didn't want the animals to go hungry.

He reached the edge of the pasture. It was thick and brown, with a few patches of melted snow. But here and there he could see the green shooting up beneath, and he began to bend, to grab and tear. His nose filled with the sweet aroma of ripped grass. He stuffed his pockets. He saw the small flat leaves of clover and picked it, too. There would be more. It didn't matter if he stripped these few tender things out from the roots. More would grow. More and more. This was just the beginning.

He was almost ready to head home when he saw it.

Under a big hummock of dead grass, it hid, about the length of a grown man's shoe. A flash of bright green. Beneath it, red. The arch of a wing. A claw.

He paused, his heart beating in his throat. He sneaked closer. He was reaching when his foot bumped something hard.

White light.

Fly up.

While Liesl was putting Jürgen down to sleep, she heard a knock on the door. Not Hans and Ani. Hans and Ani wouldn't knock. They would just pile in, full of noise and purpose, Hans collaring his brother to show him off, safely returned.

Instead, it was Frau Winter announcing that a few streets over, the American officers were moving three whole families out of their villas.

"Their new headquarters," she said.

Liesl listened to Frank thank her for the information and deftly herd her out, far quicker than she ever managed to do. The door thudded shut. After a few moments, the baby's eyelids fluttered, and Liesl tiptoed out of the room.

"What did she say about the Americans?" she asked Frank when she rejoined him in the main room. He was sanding a few patches of rough wood on the hutch.

"They're moving people out," he said, his hands moving up and down, fine dust falling to the floor.

Liesl watched it fall, resisting the impulse to fetch a pan and broom. Instead she swept up Hans's small handful of grass and put it in a clean ashtray.

She wanted Frank to understand that she wasn't changing her mind about his plans. A father should do whatever he needed to stay alive for his family. There wasn't anything more honorable than that.

A squall rose from the other room.

"I'll get him," Frank said, throwing down the sandpaper.

"He might go back to sleep," Liesl said, but Frank was already down the hall. She picked up his coat, noting the missing button, and went to her sewing box to search for a match. The baby cried louder and then miraculously fell silent as Frank began to sing.

She heard the creak of feet outside the door, a rustling. "Come in. Quietly," she said, irritated at the boys. "Your brother is trying to sleep."

There was another creak.

"Come in," she said, rising. "Hurry it up now."

Then she heard an adult male cough.

"Who is it?" She froze. Her mind went to Uta's lover. But he had no reason to come back here.

"RLB," said a gravelly male voice.

She twisted the knob and saw Herr Geiss standing there, holding a large bundle inside a blanket. The old man was wearing the silver star of the air raid committee, only it appeared as if someone had picked out some of the stitches and left others. A hand could reach up and rip it right off his coat.

"Herr Kappus, please," the old man said hoarsely. The lines of his face looked carved by knives.

"He's with the baby," she said. She heard Frank abruptly stop singing.

Herr Geiss adjusted his hold on the bundle, hitching it higher up his chest. She smelled something scorched.

"Get him, please," said Herr Geiss.

The shadows of the living room shifted and she felt Frank appear behind her.

"We in the Reichsluftschutzbund extend our deepest regrets," Herr Geiss said, his stoic expression collapsing. "There was a piece of unexploded ordnance on the brewery grounds . . ." He trailed off. A tiny blade of green drifted from beneath the blanket and fell to the floor.

Frank shoved past Liesl and took the bundle from Herr Geiss's arms. He made a wordless sound, clutching the blanket tight to him, revealing the shape of a small head and shoulders.

Their old neighbor stepped back and bowed his head. Above and below, doors in the house clicked shut.

"The field was marked for clearing," said Herr Geiss, touching his star.

Liesl heard a slam. Hans bounded up the stairs, his face open and expectant.

Don't come back now, she wanted to say, but she couldn't breathe. She groped for air with her lips, her tongue, but nothing entered.

She tried to see the closet room with the eyes of an American soldier. She viewed the two boys' beds, jammed up against opposite walls, neatly made, and a painting of boys in sailboats above. She saw the light flooding from a small high window. No sign of a grown man anywhere. The room was as tidy as the rest of the apartment. The room had been scrubbed like the rest of the rooms. The sheets had been laundered and the blankets had been shaken over the balcony and the floors washed (not waxed—there was no wax). She breathed in. The smell was still there. Charred flesh. It permeated everything. The cemeteries were full—they'd had to bury Ani in the backyard. Frank had insisted they bury him—he dug the grave at night, all night—and then Frank had simply vanished, his body still present, but his spirit elsewhere. He was a man walking alone across the deep snow.

She covered her mouth, smelling the sourness of her hand. One day, all day, she had walked around the house like this, with her mouth and nose cupped in her fingers, and Frank had pulled her palm down and told her to stop. *Stop doing that. Stop covering your mouth.*

But she couldn't stop, and Frank didn't ask again. Instead, he began to obey her in everything. Every day he obeyed her more and more. She told him he couldn't leave her. He stayed. She told him to hide. He hid. He squeezed his too-big body under his eldest son's bed and pretended he was a mouse. Her orders; his compliance—it was the only thing that tethered them to their hours. Frank barely spoke above a whisper; his leaden eyes saw only what she pointed out. When he moved, his old grace was gone, replaced by a rickety gait and arms that flopped uselessly. He could not eat. He never once uttered the boy's name. No one did.

She dropped her hand to her side.

She walked to the window and looked out. Three weeks in Hannesburg and the Americans had finally reached Hubertstrasse. They were two doors down—an officer and three enlisted men. She recognized their ranks now.

News had come from the farm. Onkel Bernd arrested for God knows what. Half the animals slaughtered to feed a hungry battalion. No refuge there.

News from the neighborhood was worse.

Herr Geiss and his crates had been taken away, the old man locked in prison. As his last act, Herr Geiss had left a long letter explaining his daughter-in-law's innocence, said Berte, who reappeared, hair matted and eyes dark with shadows, after two days of interrogations. She would not say what Herr Geiss was guilty of.

"Better you don't know anything," she said.

Because they would ask. The Americans were rounding up the men first, but the women would be next.

Frau Winter. Frau Kappus. Frau Dillman. They would all be next.

Sure that God had abandoned them all, Liesl put her faith in bribes. She bribed Frau Dillman and Frau Winter with all the hens' eggs and rabbit meat besides. It was a simple bargain: They protected her husband; their children would eat. The butcher had nothing but offal to sell. The green grocer, some moldy barley. Trucks could not run because there was no fuel. Train tracks had been blown to twists of steel.

People in Hamburg are eating ash pancakes, came the rumors.

People in Cologne are eating grass soup.

Berlin had not yet surrendered, but nobody said *Heil Hitler* in greeting anymore. They said *Bleib übrig. Survive.*

Liesl said nothing to anyone in greeting or good-bye. She couldn't bear talking. It made her taste the rot and burning in the air. She confined herself to the simple commands of the household, leaning on Hans for errands and firewood and water. Get this. Find that. After two weeks the gas was back on and they had light, but they kept the house dark, and Frank in shadow. Hans was likewise quiet, almost machine-like in his actions. He spoke in a dazed tone. He had not yet cried. Frank had not yet cried. Liesl's eyes leaked all the time, but the action didn't feel like crying. She touched the wet on her own cheeks and marveled at its strangeness and salt. The tears seemed alive, while every other part of her had withered and dried.

Only the baby moved without caution. He seemed baffled by the walking ghosts around him, and when he wailed, his voice was shrill with anger. He smacked books down from the shelves and bit Hans when his brother pulled him away. The teeth made four red marks on Hans's arm, one of them deep enough to bleed. Hans sucked at it. Liesl wondered dully if he was also trying not to smell death.

Now Jürgen was sleeping and Hans was out scrounging for greens and seeds for the animals. The chickens were getting stringy and had laid half as many eggs this week. The bribes would not last. In desperation, she had crept downstairs at night and dug in the garden for Uta's bracelet, but without success. She'd found the jars, but the familiar gold band simply wasn't there. As if it had never existed.

Frau Winter. Frau Kappus. Frau Dillman. The Americans would come, floor by floor. Both Frau Winter and Frau Dillman had promised Liesl again at Ani's burial that they wouldn't reveal Frank's presence to the Americans. Frau Dillman had dispensed her forgiveness with dignity, adding, *We need a man here*, and made all her daughters pledge, too, their freckled faces solemn. But the bribes would not last.

There was a scrambling noise under the bed.

"I have to piss," said Frank.

"Shh. There's a jar next to you." She had thought of that. She went to the window. There was the officer, tall and black-haired, smoking a cigarette by their front gate. He called to Frieda and Grete Dillman, who were on their knees, weeding the garden, and they stood up together, their heads demurely down. Liesl saw the officer say something to Frieda, and Grete respond. Frieda smiled shyly. Grete pushed her sister forward and Frieda stood closer to the officer. She did not lift her head as he spoke to her, but she reached up slowly and tucked a strand of hair behind her ear. *So young*, Liesl thought. Even younger than she and Uta had been when the war started.

Liesl heard the sound of liquid filling the glass. The stench of urine filtered into the room. She reached under the bed. She saw the helpless curl of Frank's hand. She took the warm jar to the Icebox and dumped it down the sink drain, avoiding her own reflection in the mirror. The toilet did not work because the water mains had not yet been fixed.

There was a knock downstairs. *You won't find anything here*, Liesl thought. Her face had been expressionless so long it hurt to frown. She set the jar on the floor. Her hands felt dirty from the urine, and she turned the faucets, hot and cold, before remembering that no water would come. She stood there, frozen, her fingers out, the taps running nothing all over them, as Frau Winter opened the door and the sounds of the Americans entered her house: the clamor of boots on the floor, English and German words mixing.

Liesl finally examined her reflection—her shocked eyes, the clumsy part in her hair, the deepened wrinkles around her mouth—unable to recognize any of it. Was this the face that others saw when they looked at her? Had she ever been young? Had she ever been as sweet and ripe as Frieda Dillman?

Stay free, she willed Frieda Dillman, and it struck her.

A daughter didn't want her mother's life. A daughter would trade anything—why not a piece of information?—for a new future.

And then it was too late.

Just as Liesl rushed back to beg Frank to get out from under the bed, to face his fate as he'd wanted, the soldiers were already climbing the stairs to the second floor, saying his name, announcing his arrest.

Liesl's interrogation took place in a villa that had belonged to a Frankfurt banker and his wife, now converted to an American headquarters. When Liesl arrived, Frau Hefter was already waiting among the other women in the former parlor. She smiled graciously, as if she'd invited Liesl for tea, and patted the empty seat beside her.

"They've already called your name twice," said Frau Hefter, her eyebrows raised.

The room stank of sweat and cigars, and the rain-soaked coats of the other wives. Liesl felt several of them turn to look at her.

"I can't see why," she said. *They killed my son. They locked my husband away. What else do I have left?*

"No, I can't, either." Frau Hefter tipped her head and then smiled again. She had become a widow with four children (Georg had died defending Berlin; his elder brother in Poland), evicted from her house and living in an apartment in the Alt Stadt next to Marta, the old housekeeper, but she talked about none of this. Instead, she gave Liesl instructions on growing parsnips in window boxes. Two of her fingers had been crushed removing rubble, so she gestured with blackened nails, shaping wooden boxes and plants in the air. Her breath smelled terrible.

The interrogations were running behind. The room grew steamier and Liesl's hair stuck to her face. Each passing moment made her more restless. "How much longer, do you think?" she said.

"The rest of our lives," said Frau Hefter, and this time she did not smile.

When Frau Hefter's name was called, she did not greet the wiry and pale American captain who was doing the interrogations, although he spoke polite German. She wove through the woolly knees of the other women with her head high.

They could all hear the questioning. The captain's words were muffled by the gold-striped walls, but inside the room, his politeness was gone. His tone reminded Liesl of the sound of a knife being sharpened.

Our husbands told us nothing, not even what you did to them. For weeks, news from Frank had been scarce—the Americans wouldn't deliver mail to the POW camp—and then he'd suddenly appeared home, released to work on a labor crew closer to Hannesburg. His body had shriveled from hunger, his ribs like accordion keys, and he had lost several teeth and much of his hair. Frank's spirits and body were so broken that Hans was afraid of him and spent all his time out of the house, trading film and cigarettes with the Americans to get food for the house. Liesl found herself treating Frank like a frail old man, and he hadn't objected, sucking down soup, letting her wash his hair and shave his beard. He was even quieter than before, and smiled at no one but the baby. At night, he did not hold her, lowering himself down next to Jürgen instead. After a week, a truck came to take Frank away again. *He never did anything but heal the wounded. He never did anything but love his family.*

When Frau Hefter came out, she bent down to whisper to Liesl, her face still coldly beautiful. "Don't listen to his lies, dear." Her foul breath gusted.

Liesl was next. She took her seat on a bench that was still warm from the women before her. She answered questions about her date of birth, her marriage, her address. The captain's face was pleasant enough, but she could feel his loathing. There were posters around town showing photographs of Jews starved to skeletons, and above, in English, REMEMBER THIS: NO FRATERNIZATION! The Americans had cut off their food relief. They wanted Germans to starve and they wanted them to starve in silence, unspoken to, unheard.

The captain leaned forward on his elbows.

"Frau Kappus," he said in a flat, nasal German. "Who dug the hole in your cellar?"

She shifted in her chair. "Our neighbor," she said. "Herr Geiss."

"For what purpose?" The captain's right eyelid must have been damaged somehow. It hung a little lower than the left. The left eye was the kind one. The right eye was the eye of contempt. It hung, slant-lidded, over the desk of some erstwhile German bureaucrat. The bureaucrat's papers had been cleared away, but not his precious collection of steins on the shelf nearby. The Americans were careless like this; they did not come to live, only to occupy.

"For what purpose?" he repeated.

"If one of our houses was crushed, then we could escape through the other."

"And you say Herr Geiss did not come into your house."

"Not often." Her gaze landed on a stein in the shape of Bismarck's head. The top of the stein was Bismarck's helmet. To drink from it, you had to open the prime minister's skull.

"And he stored nothing in your house."

"Not that I know of."

A shuffle of papers, then a picture of Uta in an evening gown next to her lover, his white collar unbuttoned, his mouth twisted as if he had just heard a joke.

"I also have a report that this lady, Uta Müller, stayed in your home for almost a month and was visited by this gentleman."

"Uta stayed with us, yes. The gentleman only came once." Her lips suddenly felt too thick to talk. "Do you know what happened to her?"

"Quite a lot of connections you have in Berlin," said the captain. "You tell me."

She fell silent. She would have heard from Uta by now, if Uta was still Uta Müller. She had poked around in the garden again for the bracelet, and found nothing.

"Tell me what happened to the stolen art that your neighbor was trafficking," the captain said.

"The stolen art?"

"You must have seen the crates going in and out."

"I saw some crates, but I didn't know what was in them. His wife's paintings." She swallowed. "But Uta didn't have anything to do with that."

He knew where she was. He wouldn't look at her with that closed, cunning face.

"She didn't have the energy to leave the house," Liesl added. "She . . . she was carrying a child."

For the first time, she saw surprise register in the captain. His right eyelid quivered and his mouth curled at one corner. No, not surprise. Disgust.

Somewhere in the room a light bulb was flickering. She could see only one lamp before her, and it burned bright and steady. It had a bronze base in the shape of an eagle. The eagle had a fish in its talons.

"You know where my friend is," Liesl said in a hollow voice.

The captain slid the picture back into a file.

"I didn't have anything to do with Herr Geiss's business. And Uta, we were old friends," she said. "We didn't talk about the—the war."

"You worked at the Hartwald Spa together, serving elite S.S. officers for over a year, and you never talked about their crimes."

She wished she could do something with her clammy hands. "We worked there, yes," she said. "We had conversations about the men, but not about what they did."

He blew out through his teeth.

Indignation surged in her. "I kept to myself," she said. "I didn't stay down at night."

"Stay down where?"

Stay down at the banquets, the dances, in the arms of men. Stay for the music, the laughter, the gladness of being on top of the world. Suddenly she saw the officers in her mind: the blackness of their uniforms, their slick heads, their wolfish, flashing teeth.

"I could have married one of them," she said. "But they frightened me."

The captain leaned back, folding his arms. "You could have married one of them," he repeated, his brow furrowing.

"I had offers," she said, her face burning.

He shook his head, as if her statement amazed him. The flicker was getting worse, pulsing every other second.

"I see," he said again. "So instead you married Dr. Frank Kappus, who was arrested and sent to a POW camp for his service at Buchenwald."

"He didn't work at Buchenwald," she retorted. "He didn't even know the name of that place." The accusation had arisen after Frank's arrest, after someone had requested his official records from Weimar, and they registered his treatment of a patient at the camp. It wasn't true, and Frank had already disproven it with statements from his hospital. Yet the stain had remained on his record.

"Or perhaps he didn't tell you about it? Like everyone else in your life—your neighbor, your old friend—they didn't tell you anything at all?"

She shrugged.

"What did you talk about, then?"

"The children," she said.

"What else?"

"Food. Coal," she said. She couldn't help it. She had to look around, find the lamp. She cranked her head to the back of the room. Where was it? There, on the wall. A torch socket with a little glass holder, the smallest light in the room.

"It needs a new bulb," she said, pointing.

His voice rose. "You never had conversations about your country and what it was doing to the Jews?"

She turned back. The flicker was driving her crazy. She felt her eyes beginning to blink in time with it.

"Frau Kappus."

"No."

The captain's face contorted again. Flick, flick, went the lamp.

"Our middle son . . . was ill," she said. "They wanted to send him to Hadamar."

The captain regarded her, chewing his lip. So he knew about that, too, and he didn't care. The American flag hung behind him, dripping its red and white stripes. She blinked with the flicker, her eyes sore and dry. Her throat convulsed. *What do you want me to say? You know everything. You must have it in your reports. My baby is hungry. His brother wants to die. My husband came home from your prisoner-of-war camp looking almost as thin as the Jews. Maybe we believed the lies about them. Maybe we didn't look when they were taken away. We didn't know where they were going. Now we can't look at all. I can't look at him and he can't look at me, and no one can understand us but the dead.*

The captain said Uta's lover's name. "They were found together in his apartment," he said, looking at his desk. "It appears he shot her, then shot himself. Suicide." He sat back, hitched at his green pants. "I'm sorry."

He didn't sound sorry. He didn't sound human at all. His voice was a buzzing noise between his language and hers.

"He was a bigwig at Plötzensee. A real saint," the captain said sarcastically. "Used to treat his whole unit to champagne every hundred executions. But you had no idea."

But you. The flicker. *Had no idea.* The flicker.

It was an effort to speak. "I said we didn't talk about him."

"I see," the captain said again.

She shut her eyes, and for a moment she couldn't see it. Then it began again, a tiny white pulse through her lids.

"She was an old friend," Liesl said. "We talked about our dreams."

The captain rubbed his eyes. "All right, Frau Kappus," he said slowly. "You're dismissed. Your house will be searched tomorrow."

"For what?" she asked hoarsely. "We have nothing hidden."

He looked at her blankly and then called to his assistant in English. The knife-like tone was gone. His voice was soggy with exasperation. She didn't understand all the words he said, but he spoke the word "wife" over and over. *All these wives*, it sounded like he was saying. *All these know-nothing wives.*

She bowed her head as she walked out of the room, down the stairs, into the bright sunlight. Her reflection flared on the glass window of a shop across the street. There she was: a woman slumped in a dark coat, fading handkerchief tied over her head, shoes falling apart. Her eyes looked farther away, too, even though that was not possible. Eyes couldn't move backward inside a head, but that's what hers looked like and felt like, as if the space between her and the rest of the world had widened, and she had a harder time seeing across it.

You look like a crone, she heard Uta's sharp words. *Show them you have some spine.*

Liesl didn't straighten. She kept her eyes on her feet, sidestepping cracked cobblestone or rubble, anything that could explode. She had been walking that way since the air raids and it made her dizzy to look up, to peer down the avenues, where scorch marks still scarred the walls.

Better to play a game with the ground, to find the safest, easiest path. Better to clutch her empty purse, as if someone might rip it from her. From every other block she heard the pounding of hammers.

July 1945

Dear Frau Kappus—

Thank you for your letter in June, and for your interest in our efforts to find homes for the juvenile survivors of Hadamar and other institutions. Please also thank Father Georg for carrying these messages between us.

I am sorry to hear of the loss of your son. It must have taken great strength and resolve to contact me. I deliberated for some time before I replied because I have no desire to compound your grief.

Let me tell you first about the history of our enterprise. In January and February of 1945, we built a small ward in our convent with the hopes of smuggling out juveniles from Hadamar and its feeder facilities. Although the state-organized euthanasia program was officially curtailed, we knew enough from insiders to be aware that doctors were still prescribing hundreds of lethal injections to patients deemed "unfit to live."

By March, our ward was ready. We arranged with our contact on the inside to smuggle twelve patients to our facility. They came to us in a medical delivery truck: four bundles of three children, each in thick blankets. I could have lifted each of those bundles with my own arms. The children were so emaciated it was clear that all our resources, including the services of a Limburg doctor, would not save them. Moreover, the escape had terrified the children. Five died that night, others in the ensuing weeks.

Of the twelve, one survives. Rudy was the eldest. We estimate that he is sixteen. Now that he has gained weight and recovered his muscle strength, he is an affable fellow with mild mental retardation and a tendency to seizures. He has "terror nights" every few weeks, where he wakes screaming and thrashing and sometimes tries to hurt himself. We are all quite fond of him here, and it pains us to see him remember his agony. He rarely leaves our building out of fear of being abducted, and I expect we will become his permanent guardians.

You asked if we needed resources, and hinted at the possibility of adoption. Although little remains of the population of Hadamar, the surrounding feeder institutions still have patients. Many of those patients are also severely malnourished and otherwise damaged by their living conditions. We are working with the institutions to provide adequate nutrition and nursing to the survivors, but our volunteer doctors do not recommend the relocation of those patients now, unless their immediate families claim them. Quite simply, in most cases, it is too late.

I am sorry not to provide you with more hopeful information. We would gratefully use any more gifts you wish to make in the name of your son Anselm, and you are most welcome to visit us any time. In the meantime, thank you for the wooden toys you mailed us—your husband is quite an ingenious craftsman—and Rudy takes great joy in spinning the tops.

My sincerest thanks and prayers,

Sister Johann
Limburg

It was late August 1945. Hannesburg had cleared its rubble. The smell of fresh wood pervaded the Alt Stadt, but underneath a bitter, smoky odor still lingered.

Frank had gained back ten kilos of the twenty he had lost in the spring, and his ribs no longer felt as if they were trying to escape through his skin. He could sleep four hours at a stretch and eat without panicked gulping. He had been fitted for dentures to replace the five teeth missing from his top jaw, three from his lower. When Frank talked, he felt the plates moving and pinching his words, and heard the soft lisp of Hartmann's mouth when it had sighed. The noise made him cringe but feel strangely less alone.

He didn't know where he fit anymore.

Not in his country. The citizens of Buchenwald's neighboring towns had been paraded past the stacks of naked, starved bodies piled outside the liberated prison camp. International papers showed photos of the citizens' horrified, averted faces as they walked the white rows. *Write again to your friends in Weimar*, Liesl had urged him. *You were never there. Get them to fix your record.*

I wasn't there, Frank thought. *But I was close enough.*

He didn't belong in his town, either, overrun by American GIs from its rubbled Alt Stadt to the moss-covered Roman settlement at its outskirts.

Nor on his street. Herr Geiss had hung himself in prison. His daughter-in-law was secretly "engaged" to a buck-toothed kid from Selma, Alabama, USA, and seemed to enjoy inviting his comrades over to loot the old man's house for souvenirs.

Nor did he belong in his home, with its ever-changing tableau of refugees upstairs and downstairs. The Dillmans were gone, but the housing office had replaced them with a noisy brood of Schneiders. The Winters had taken in their own boarders, an elderly aunt and uncle who somehow made it west, and filled their apartment to splitting.

Not even in his own rooms. His eldest son had little use for him, and Jürgen was so attached to Liesl he rarely looked around for his *Vati*. Sometimes when Frank felt especially self-punishing, he tried to remember Ani's face, but it hurt so much that his mind went black.

Logging had torn tendons in his knees, muscles in his back, and he didn't like standing straight anymore. He could hardly keep his teeth in when he talked. The man in the mirror wore a sullen, hangdog expression. He had lost. He was lost. Some days it seemed as though the two states amounted to the same thing.

All the Allies had won, but the Americans most of all. Young GIs in green undershirts loitered on blankets in the Kurpark, smoking, waiting to be sent home. Their indolence was the hardest thing to take. Victory was theirs, and they accepted it as easily as the sunlight.

Frank knew his eldest son secretly admired them, knew that the extra food and cigarettes that Hans brought home weren't just found, but traded for, soldier by friendly soldier. Hans had a secret life in English, muttered in the bathroom and with his schoolmates, but Frank forbade it in the house. He could not hear the nasal sounds without feeling his stomach cramp, without remembering a giant, muddy field of men, surrounded by barbed wire, and how he'd asked for penicillin for his neighbor with pneumonia. "Penicillin"—it was the same in any language, but the American guards had pretended not to understand. When Frank had persisted, one had jabbed him with his rifle butt, saying, *Nix, nix, you stupid Kraut!*

His son couldn't see it, couldn't see how the American soldiers' gifts to children were motivated by pity. He couldn't see how their careless generosity mocked and demeaned the children's parents, who could not provide for them.

All Hans saw was this:

His father, the surgeon, was now a lowly laborer on a logging crew north of town. His father, the proud driver of a Mercedes, was now sunburned and stooped from soreness, and hobbled on foot everywhere he went.

His stepmother refused his baby brother milk because there was none, and let Jürgen go barefoot, because she had no shoes for him.

His other brother was a mound in the yard.

And then Hans saw the happy Americans, swimming and shouting in the Kurpark pond, their well-fed bodies flashing as they cleaved the water.

Frank was fixing a loose latch on the rabbit hutch door when he heard his eldest son's feet whispering on the wood behind him. He didn't turn. He was nursing a thought that had occurred to him the week before: As much as he hated logging, he liked working with wood. If he couldn't practice medicine, perhaps he could build things: furniture, cabinets. The principles of construction were not so different with flesh and wood, and wood lasted longer. It made something dead alive again. He worried that Liesl and his sons might not understand the decision. He thought Hartmann would have.

"Vati." Something in Hans's voice sounded strange. "I found these. In Ani's mattress."

Frank turned. On his son's open palm, seven silver tubes twisted like worms. Frank lifted them, one by one, surprised by their lightness. He read the contents, his heart pounding. Not enough to kill a child, but enough to cause harm.

"They were stuck in there really deep," said Hans.

"Lead white," said Frank. It felt as if his skull were squeezing inward, closing off his sight. "Where would he get these?"

There was a pause. "From Frau Geiss's studio."

"How would he get in there?" Frank's voice rose.

His son hung his blond head. His ears were pink. "Followed me through the hole in the cellar," he mumbled. "He liked to look at the painting of Mother."

The painting of Susi and Ani. Herr Geiss had given it to them at Ani's funeral. Frank had framed it and the whole family had hung it together in his father's study—still Frank's and Liesl's de facto bedroom. In all the harshness of those days after Ani's death, the effort had been a single moment of communion—Hans holding the picture while Frank hammered the nail; Liesl holding Jürgen, whispering through her tears, *That's your mother and your brother.*

So many shades of white in that picture—Susi's dress, Ani's face, the wall, the sky. The paint was as thick as butter, tufting at the edges. Frank's head throbbed. He took a breath. "He must have been trying to paint something with them."

"I didn't find any paintings," said Hans. "He never made any paintings."

Frank avoided the boy's gaze. He squeezed one of the tubes, feeling the last wetness shifting inside. "Did you ever catch him eating this?"

"No." His son's voice was breathless. He was waiting to be blamed. Or for someone else to be blamed.

A silence fell between them. Frank's head hurt so badly he couldn't look at his son. It hurt whenever he heard the name "Anselm," whenever he saw a blond boy Ani's age, and each and every Sunday afternoon when they ate their meal together. The absence at the table ate with them, a giant soundless mouth that gobbled their attempts at conversation. He blinked into the darkness of the hutch.

Flashes from the past months broke through: Ani hugging a lamb at the farm; the boy's dismembered body in the blanket, its entire right leg lost except for a jutting femur. Liesl hadn't been able to look—she'd begged Frank to cover it, to hide it—she was always trying to hide things, to pretend they didn't exist: Hide! Hide! Hide from the doctors; hide from the Americans. Her hysteria to conceal, wasn't that at the heart of this—

Every night Liesl slept near Frank in the room of their dead, under his father's books, his wife's and son's picture. Every day she dressed his baby boy and fed them all that could be found. She scoured their pots. She wiped their floors. She patched their threadbare clothes. She did not blame him. They could not blame each other, but in their grief, she had begged Frank to hide and he had. He had retreated like a rat until the Americans flushed him from his hole. Liesl's once-red hair was growing strands of gray, and her ribs and hipbones jutted from hunger. She looked older than twenty-five. She would go on this way, feeding and tending, never blaming, and his sons would scorn her because their father scorned her, not openly, but secretly, under his breath, as he sawed through trees in the dusty woods.

And his sons would hate themselves because their father hated himself. Because every time he walked home past the new wire fence around the brewery pasture, he thought, *I let him die.*

The brewery pasture was green now, thick with grasses that no animals grazed. In a few months it would yellow and sink under snow, and unless the Americans lifted the bans on international food relief, his sons would have nothing to eat but the rabbits in this hutch and the chickens downstairs, and the few jars of potatoes and cabbage Liesl was right now canning with Frau Winter in the kitchen. Thank God she had made some friends among the women—Frau Winter, Berte Geiss, Marta, and even that prissy peacock, Frau Hefter. They held each other up. They had cleared most of the streets themselves. They bartered— one woman's handful of eggs for another's supply of yarn—so that every family had almost enough. There was something between them that the men could not touch.

Yet soon the families would have nothing to burn but the few scraps the Winter boys stole and Frank carried home in his pockets, and Frank would lose even his small salary from his lumber work. And then the winter illnesses would strike. And whom would they blame but themselves if Jürgen or Hans fell sick, and their skinny bodies had no reserves to fight? Frank could bear giving up on surgery, on the entire medical profession. He didn't long for riches or respect. He just wanted the assurance that his other two sons would live.

And he wanted his family again, as whole as it could be.

Frank closed his fist around the paint tubes. His palms and fingers were scored with calluses and cuts. It stung his hand to close it.

"Even if he ate them, they'd give him a stomachache for sure," he said finally. "But that's all."

"But it says 'lead' on there," Hans said. "Dr. Becker said—"

"You'd have to eat a hundred of these tubes to get Dr. Becker's numbers," Frank lied. "It was something else."

"But there isn't anything else," Hans said in an anguished tone.

"I'm going to throw these out," said Frank, pocketing the tubes. "I don't want your mother to see these."

"But—"

"I don't want you to mention this again," Frank said, louder and clearer. He could feel the sharp ends of the tubes pricking his thigh. "I don't want you to trouble her." He looked his son in his own blue eyes, his own face, younger and irrevocably hardened.

Hans turned away and stuck his finger in the wire mesh of the hutch. A white rabbit hopped into view, whiskers trembling. They were always hungry, too.

"She has enough trouble keeping all of us fed and well." Frank's voice broke on the last word.

The rabbit sniffed at Hans's finger and hopped away again.

"All right," Hans said. "I won't tell anyone."

They stood in silence for a moment. A plane flew overhead and they both flinched.

The rabbit loped slowly back into the shadows of the hutch, hanging its head.

"Give it something," Frank said gruffly to Hans, fishing in his other pocket for the carrot he'd pulled from the garden that morning. "It came to you," he said. "So give it something."

He handed his son the limp vegetable, warm from his body heat. Hans shoved it through the mesh and the bunny thumped back, eager, trembling, biting into the flesh with its sharp white teeth. At the sight of the boy feeding the mute, trusting animal, Frank was flooded with a new feeling, so rich and tender it was like a swallow of fresh cream.

It was relief. The feeling was relief.

Sometimes during that first starving winter after the war, Liesl remembered things that she wasn't sure had happened. The memories seemed tethered to her hunger, to the state in between living and dying, when sleeping did not rest her body and breathing felt like gasping. They'd run out of food so fast: With the country divided and broken, the supplies Frank intended to supplement their family all winter were soon all they had to eat. In November, he killed the last rabbit and the rooster. By January, the once-robust Jürgen grew nervous and thin, and Liesl secretly went out begging American soldiers for their finished cans of meat and beans, hiding in an alley, cleaning the remains with her finger and feeding them to the baby. In February, with the aid ban lifted, Red Cross packages finally began to trickle in, but Hannesburg ran out of coal. Liesl and Frank took the children into their beds at night to keep them warm. Hans and his father arranged themselves head to toe, complaining loudly about each other's feet, then fell fast asleep.

Liesl held Jürgen in the dark and monitored each shallow breath. As she drifted, willing his fragile life to endure, the memories came.

In one, it was an autumn morning in the villa, in the bedroom she shared with the baby. Frank had already left for his deployment in Weimar. Gas masks, a gift from Herr Geiss, lumped on her dresser.

The warped, empty faces lined up next to her wedding photo like ghoulish spectators.

She was staring at the masks, pondering the best place to store them, when Ani pushed open her door. He padded in and hovered over the baby dozing in the cradle. His blond hair stuck out in all directions, and his eyes were gluey and unfocused.

"Where do the people in my dreams go when my dreams are over?" he asked, picking up one of the masks, poking his fingers through the eyeholes. The scent of the black rubber rose.

Liesl put her arm around Ani and drew him toward her. She gently took the mask from his hands and set it out of reach.

"Whom did you dream of?" she said.

"Mother," he said, then frowned. "And . . . people. We were lined up in the Kurpark. To drink from the fountain."

A good dream, then, Liesl thought, relieved. "That's easy," she said. "They'll come back tonight, only with new faces and places."

Ani had been pleased by the rhyme. "New faces and places," he had repeated, leaning into her. "So I'll see them again?" His chin lifted, his expression anxious and buoyant at once.

"Yes, you'll see them again."

When they were girls in Franconia, Uta liked to dive down in the small cold lake where teenage girls and young children spent the hot days, while their parents and brothers worked in the fields. Uta would buckle her back, feet flashing, and disappear for what seemed like forever, then come up with a closed fist, grinning.

"Look," she shouted at Liesl, wiping the streams from her eyes. With her hair slicked by water, her face looked more rugged, almost boyish.

She opened her fist to show a handful of glittering pebbles and silt. "That's the bottom."

"No, it's not," Liesl said, because she wasn't brave and she didn't like to dive. "It's only the bottom if you leave it there."

Before they could fight, some younger child called to them, and Uta let the water wash her hand clean.

There was never enough time to argue. She and Liesl were needed elsewhere. They charged side by side toward shore, toward rescue.

That was the moment Liesl remembered most of all: the noisy togetherness of it, and the drag of the lake against her shins, and how they'd had to step high, so high, to run.

ACKNOWLEDGMENTS

In the spring of 1942, my father's mother died in childbirth, leaving his father alone to care for three boys under the age of six. They lived in a villa in a small city in the heart of Nazi Germany.

When I started writing this book, I knew these facts: the death, the widower, the orphans, the era. I also knew that my grandfather remarried within months and was drafted in 1944 to work at a hospital in Weimar. In early 1945, with the Russian army advancing, he deserted his post as a radiologist and made his way back to his family on bicycle. En route, he stayed in an attic in Thüringen, where he stowed a packet of letters from his new wife in the wall. He buried his gun in the ground outside. He was soon to cross into the American zone.

In the 1980s, a Thüringen couple renovating their home found the letters in the wall and contacted my uncle, who still lives at the villa where my father grew up. In this way, these urgent wartime missives from a new wife and stepmother to her new husband made their way back to our family, and, ultimately, to me.

While I translated these letters with my father, I began reading other accounts by women and children in the Nazi era, among them Winfried

Weiss's *A Nazi Childhood,* Irmgard A. Hunt's *On Hitler's Mountain: Overcoming the Legacy of a Nazi Childhood,* the anonymously penned *A Woman in Berlin: Eight Weeks in the Conquered City,* Dagmar Barnouw's *Germany 1945: Views of War and Violence,* and Alison Owings's landmark oral history, *Frauen: German Women Recall the Third Reich.* Like many children and grandchildren of Nazi-era Germans, I was obsessed with two questions: *What did they know about the Holocaust, and when did they know it?* Like many, I felt it important to sort this out so I could know how to judge them and my own inheritance.

My father is a good man, who has always expressed clear love and devotion for his parents and his children. My grandparents died when I was young, but they also struck me as generous and kind, and my grandmother, rather courageous for single-handedly raising three small kids at such a harrowing time. When I started working on this book, I obsessed over the idea of complicity, how "good" people could nonetheless participate in one of the most brutal regimes in contemporary history. The questions *What did they know, and when did they know it?* were key to this investigation. How was it possible that my grandfather worked so close to Buchenwald and still insisted he had no knowledge of the crimes committed in that camp? How could my grandmother be such a loving mother to her stepchildren and not teach them what the Germans had done? My father claims he learned about the Holocaust only as a teenager, at an exhibition at the Paulskirche in Frankfurt, half a decade after the end of the war.

Hindsight is always a delicate issue in historical novels. The author and the reader often have a distilled set of facts about an era that the characters do not possess. Perhaps no era is more traveled and judged by readers than World War II, and so we collectively assume that all books about Germans in the 1940s will be books about complicity or resistance to their government's murderous practices. In fact, most books are. The narrative we get is the one we expect.

Yet the more I thought about my grandmother's letters, the more I realized they weren't about Naziism. Or rather, that Naziism shadowed her world, but it was illuminated by the antics and accidents of three small boys, by conveying through code that she was sending secret supplies to her husband for his imminent desertion. Yes, she was afraid—of denouncement, of the ever-increasing air raids, of enemy invasion. And yet her narrative was not about totalitarian law, the bloody battles, the Jews and the camps. It was about family, and, paradoxically, it was about protecting her new sons' innocence in a time when the sky was literally falling.

The more I wrote, the more I knew I had to change my fundamental questions. I could not use hindsight as a knife to slice through the past and find anything but what I expected to find. Instead of asking, *What did they know, and when did they know it?* I began to ask, *What did they love? What did they fear?* and in place of a prefabricated fable, a complicated human story began to emerge.

It was painful to write from this perspective. It was painful to keep the Holocaust offscreen, to mention Jews only a few times in the book, and then go to dinner with my Jewish friends and family. I used to sit across from them and think, *There is a lake of blood between us, but right now, in this chapter I am writing, I am pretending it doesn't exist.* Many times, I tried to change the story to allow my main characters to think or do something that showed their heroism in the face of the cruel Reich, and every time I had to cut the scenes to be faithful to their lives at the time. It is perhaps possible only for a perpetrator's descendant, far away in America, to rewind the psyche like this. One cannot simply undo the murders of one's grandparents.

As I was making these discoveries on the page, my infant son fell gravely and mysteriously ill. Thousands of ulcers appeared in his GI tract and failed to respond to dozens of medical treatments. He was full of bleeding holes. As I spent the next few years in and out of the hospital with him, I began to wonder about the chronically ill and disabled children I saw on the pediatric ward and how they would have fared in Nazi Germany. I wondered where such innocent frailty fit inside the Third Reich. The answer was, of course, another horror: Hadamar, an institution not far from my father's hometown that killed and burned thousands of the mentally ill and handicapped. *What did they love? What did they fear?* When these questions addressed Ani, the book spun against the dark void of Nazi pitilessness, even for their own children.

I could not have written this book without my father's willingness to share his family stories, in conversation and on the page. Thank you, Dad. I have always admired you with all my heart. I also want to thank my mother for her lifelong passion for history and truth-seeking. To my brothers Paul, Thomas, and Peter (my go-to Euro scholar), thank you for decades of encouragement, wisdom, and good-humored teasing. My uncles Ulrich and Gerwin also helped generously with reconstructing their childhood history—thank you.

Heartfelt thanks also go to the following invaluable readers: Rita Mae Reese, J. M. Tyree, Katharine Noel, Malena Watrous, Glori Simmons, Jeff O'Keefe, Melanie Abrams, Bruce Snider, and Sarah Frisch. Thank you also to the Community of Writers at Squaw Valley and my workshop cohorts there.

Thank you to the Stegner program at Stanford University for giving me the time to complete this, and special thanks to Eavan Boland for her inspiring translations, *After Every War: Twentieth-Century Women Poets,* in which I first began to hear how the voices of German women were shaped by war.

I'm ever grateful to my agent, Gail Hochman, for her bighearted support of this novel, to my editor, Dan Smetanka, for his brilliant eye on the final draft, and to Counterpoint Press for taking risks on so many books that need to exist.

Deepest thanks to Bowie and Bruce, for teaching me how to write like a mother. Thank you, Kyle, for showing me how to be a storyteller, for giving me the hours I needed, for your constant faith, mischief, and love.